Ragdolls Don't Lie

Sarah Flint

Grosvenor House
Publishing Limited

Ragdoll's don't lie

With a Metropolitan Police career spanning thirty-five years, Sarah has spent her adulthood surrounded by victims, criminals and police officers.

Now retired, she divides her time between her family, writing in the office of her cottage in Surrey and walking the fairways of her favourite golf course.

She has three grown up daughters of whom she is very proud.

Also by Sarah Flint

Mummy's Favourite
The Trophy Taker
Liar Liar
Broken Dolls
Daddy's Girls

This book is published by
Grosvenor House Publishing Ltd
Link House
140 The Broadway, Tolworth, Surrey, KT6 7HT.
www.grosvenorhousepublishing.co.uk

A CIP record for this book
is available from the British Library

Print ISBN 978-1-83615-183-8
eBook ISBN 978-1-83615-184-5

For Tina

We met in the last few days of her life across a hospital ward and chatted about reading and books. She was surprised and pleased to meet the author of some of her favourite books – and I was over the moon to randomly meet the first total stranger who'd read all my books. She made my day and I will always remember her.

Prologue

There was a baby screaming somewhere in the distance but the dull thudding in her head muffled its plaintive cry.

She opened her eyes, hoping that having sight of her location might somehow clear her ears. It didn't, and the noises grew louder. She raised her eyebrows and blinked several times at the sound of splintering wood, squinting through murky lenses as the room filled with huge bellowing men and women with clipped, unfriendly faces. One was leaning over her now calling out her name, shaking her by the shoulder. They all wore uniforms and the black serge filled her personal space, casting judgement on her ability as a mother.

She was unfit, useless, a disgrace.

The baby's cries had dropped in volume now. The little girl was being rocked in the arms of one of the uniformed figures, while another rifled through cupboards in the kitchen, boiling the kettle, pulling dirty bottles from the sink, searching for milk powder. There was none. In the back of her mind, she remembered that she was supposed to have got some more, last night, on her way home from getting her drugs at the 'front line' in Brixton, with Mia held tightly in her arms.

But the shops had been shut and, anyway, she had no money and Mia had eventually grown too tired to cry any more, falling asleep in her arms on the bed, until now, when the screaming had restarted. It was Mia's small, shrill voice she could hear.

Mia, that was it. Her baby. Her ex-partner's baby, but he wasn't here. He wasn't here because of her. He was in prison. She had seen to that too.

The noises were more muted now. A bottle had appeared as if by magic, clean and filled with milk and Mia was feeding. The uniforms were moving about, muttering, tutting, pulling the covers back on Mia's cot, poking at the remnants of powder and tin foil on the coffee table, scanning the chaos of her dirty kitchen, the disarray of her small flat.

'Disgusting.' She heard the word but didn't clearly know to what, or whom, it was directed. She'd heard the word many times before as a child in the unholy whisperings of neighbours, when her own mother had been drinking, when she'd been left to search for any scraps of food around the kitchen, in the bins, in the dog bowl. Now the word was being directed towards her.

'We'll be taking your baby into care,' a voice was saying now. 'Under section 46 of the Children Act 1989. Your baby is at significant risk of harm. She's clearly failing to thrive. Poor little scrap.' The voice was gruff and angry, but the sentence was final. They were taking Mia. But they couldn't take Mia. Could they? Not if the baby was fed. Not if it was she who fed the baby.

'You can't take my baby,' she roared, throwing her head back and pulling her clothing aside to expose an empty breast. 'I can feed her. I can.'

'Not with that, darlin',' the male voice laughed nastily. 'So I'd put it away if I was you.'

She pulled the grubby T-shirt back across her body and tried to stand, but felt hands holding her down, preventing her going to her child. She reared up again, a last-ditch stance to get to her baby but it was no use.

Crumbling against the headboard, she folded her legs up to her chest and reached one arm up under the pillow, her fingers finally locating the body of the doll she had owned since childhood. Goldilocks. The doll that she now shared with Mia. Her other hand she balled into a fist and raised to her lips, her mouth locating the shape of her thumb, sucking hard on its smooth skin and dirty nail.

The shapes were filing out of the door now. Mia was going and she was being given instructions. Who to speak to. Who might help. How she might get her child back, but it made no sense. Nothing made sense. The instructions were set down in a wad of paperwork, dumped on the coffee table.

'We'll be in touch.' She heard the words shouted by the last person in line, the last person leaving the flat. The door slammed shut and the voices dwindled away.

Then silence.

'You can't take Mia. You can't take my baby. She is all that I have,' she whimpered almost inaudibly into the clothing of her doll, her mind turning now to who had done this to her.

She knew who it was. It had to be that woman. There was no one else! No one who would have betrayed her like this. And yet she'd trusted her. She'd given up everything for her. Until now.

Now Mia was gone. Now she was on her own. Now, things had changed.

Chapter 1

One month later

It was dark in the woods, dark and frightening – and the boy was scared.

He was used to light. Light from the neon street lamps, light from the TV, laptop, phone screen. His sister always made sure their little flat was filled with light. Light and love. It was how it had been since his mum had passed away, suddenly and inexplicably from a disease that shouldn't have caused her to die. For a while, everything had become dark – thick, black grief which gradually turned to rage. It wasn't fair. His sister was all he had left now. She had done what she could, but in the end it wasn't enough.

He wanted a family, had always wanted a family and when the older boy had offered him one, he'd jumped at the chance.

Now, though, he wished that he hadn't.

Now he could never escape. He knew that for certain. Once initiated, the shedding of blood and the distinctive tattoo fettered him to the older boy, to the gang, for life. He could never pay the ransom and be free.

He was theirs to do with as they wished – and they wished him to sell drugs.

So that's why he was there, to sell weed. Even though he'd rather be tucked up at home with his sister. Even though he was scared.

A storm was brewing. He shivered as a gust of wind blew the limbs of the trees, making them bend and sway, bristle with anticipation. He too bristled, not with hope but with fear, even though he wasn't allowed to be weak or frightened. He had to be strong, fearless – and he had to ignore the hairs standing up on the back of his neck, and the slow seeping pool of sweat that had gathered at the base of his spine.

Wiping his brow, he pulled out his phone and checked on the time. Nearly one. His sister would be worried but she knew not to make a fuss. No phone calls. No frantic visits to the police. She didn't dare make him look foolish in front of his friends. The time flicked over to 1 a.m. Any time now he'd get the deal done, then he'd be on his way, jogging home, another task complete.

A twig cracked and he spun around, staring into the blackness of the glade, just off the main path, the light from the phone temporarily blinding him to the shadows.

'Who's there?' he called out, his voice sounding shaky, his reluctance to meet in this specific location coming to the fore. He cleared his throat and tried again, this time louder, more outwardly confident. 'Come out. I've got your weed.'

Another twig snapped as a small log flew through the darkness and hit the bushes in front of him. He stared at where it had landed, mesmerised for a few seconds by the movement, his brain realising in that moment why he'd been summoned to this spot. Through his confusion came the sound of footsteps crunching through the foliage behind him. He swung round but it was too late, far too late. The ambush had started.

As the moon moved out from behind a cloud, he saw the hard glint of a blade coming towards him, again and again, slashing, stabbing, slicing through his skin. He fell to the ground, red hot pain burning through every cell of his body. He couldn't run. He couldn't fight. He couldn't die. Please God, he couldn't die. Not here, not now.

The grass felt warm and sticky where he lay. He raised his arms up over his face and opened his eyes desperate to see his sister one last time – but all he could see was the flash of the knife as it was plunged deep into his chest.

'Take that, you bastard.'

The voice sounded through the gloom, coarse, jagged, brutal. But he wasn't a bastard. He wasn't. He was just a boy. A family boy. A lost boy.

As he blinked the veil of blood from his eyes, he started to sob.

'Maria,' he cried. 'I'm so sorry, Maria.'

Chapter 2

'All units. Wimbledon Common. Ambulance on way to one male stabbed in the chest. Believed serious. No description of suspects.'

There was a short pause before half a dozen units responded.

'Let's go,' shouted DS Charlie Stafford to her team, over the sea of monitors in their new office at Wimbledon Police Station.

She picked up her radio, sighing with frustration as she acknowledged the call. London was in the grip of an epidemic of knife crime and nobody could say when, or if, it would end.

The team were already on their feet. 'Yes, ma'am,' Paul called out, in the clipped tone of a soldier. 'Anything you say, ma'am.' Charlie caught his eye and gave a surreptitious shake of her head, but she couldn't help the smile that flickered onto her lips. None of them could get used to her new title, never mind she herself. She'd only recently passed the sergeant's written exam, so theoretically she wasn't even a fully-fledged sergeant, but with the number of police officers cut to a bare minimum, tonight she was the 'acting' inspector, in charge of the night duty CID team. It was a huge responsibility. One wrong decision and a suspect could walk free, a trial could be lost.

She pulled her rucksack out from under her desk and took a deep breath. Paul was already at the door; Naz and

Sabira scrambling to grab some cordon tape and a few extra crime scene logs. Bet remained at her desk, her eyes already glued to the fast-moving message thread, preparing to assist with any intelligence gathering required. Although officially restricted to 'light duties' while awaiting an operation on her spine, nothing would stop her from working in a proactive role, be it from an office, or out on the street.

Charlie smiled towards the older woman as she fell in behind her team. With her previous boss, Detective Inspector Geoffrey Hunter suspended from operational duty for 'poor decision making' on the back of their last murder case, Bet had become her counsel, her colleague's long experience and unerring knowledge of the law proving invaluable. As she ran to catch the door, she glanced across at the small subsidiary office Hunter should be occupying. The whole team had been outraged at his suspension. Hunter was admired and respected by every officer from the rank of inspector down – and it was a matter of the greatest consternation to them all that senior officers allowed themselves to be swayed by politics, rather than coming to the aid of their much-maligned foot soldiers. *'The Job's fucked'* had always been the favourite saying of the old sweats in the canteen, and this time, with Hunter gripping the rails, she had to agree.

The atmosphere was heavy and oppressive outside the building. Thunder growled from behind charcoal grey clouds and flickers of lightning bounced and sparked off the roofs and uppermost windows of nearby houses. With Paul at the wheel, the rest of them jumped into the CID unmarked car and Charlie swung the magnetic blue light up on to the roof, wishing that Hunter was there to take charge, instead of her.

The first units were just rolling up on scene, précising the details. The victim was male, aged about sixteen and apparently deceased. He had been found by an insomniac, out for a late-night walk. There were numerous slash wounds across the body and a large kitchen knife was sticking out from his chest. There was no description of suspects.

'Shit!' Charlie checked her watch. 'What the hell is a kid of sixteen doing on his own on the common at two o'clock in the morning?'

'Well, he sure as hell wasn't on his own. That's for sure,' murmured Paul, navigating through the quiet main street, past the Centre Court shopping centre. Everything in Wimbledon was a pointer to the tennis.

Charlie stared out through the window, mulling over what she knew of her new patch as the car shot up Wimbledon Hill, towards the affluent residential area of Wimbledon Village. Designer shops, beauty salons and boutique restaurants lined the route, each tasteful window display targeted at the pockets of their rich clientele. From what she'd so far gleaned, the gangs were a fairly new phenomena to SW19, some travelling from as far afield as Balham and Lambeth to do battle, each group drawn from local communities according to post codes or ethnicity; white, black, Hispanic, Southern European, Eastern European, Chinese. And Wimbledon Common seemed to be the location of choice, seemingly because there was little in the way of CCTV to prevent them from coming and going as they pleased.

Paul dropped a gear and shot around the roundabout at the top of the hill.

'I just wish we knew all their faces,' she said, verbalising her continuing thought process. 'Back in Lambeth we could have named every gang member and where they could be found skulking about, dealing their drugs, and organising their county lines.'

'Wimbledon must be more lucrative than many of their other target areas,' Paul offered. 'And takes far less organisation. They'd just have to exchange crack cocaine for pure coke.' He sniffed. 'The users in SW19 expect a far superior quality of cocaine to stick up their noses.'

'They also expect us to keep their kids safe on the streets.' Charlie's voice was stern. Her eyes fixed on a large house at the edge of the common as they drew to a halt. Its lights were on and the curtains drawn back. Caught in the frame was a middle-aged couple staring out at the police activity, the blue strobe lights casting an eerie tinge across their faces. Looking at them, she could well imagine their fear as they watched the burgeoning numbers of emergency services and equating it to the threat to their children.

Paul nosed the bonnet of their car into a gap between the trees opposite the house.

'Right, let's see if we can put their minds at ease and get someone in for this quickly.' Charlie opened her door and stepped out on to the grass, glancing across at the crime scene tape wound round the trunks of a circle of trees and a number of uniformed officers spread out along its perimeter.

Unbelievably for the time of night, the atmosphere here was electric, with small pockets of hooded-up youths eying each other, whilst intermittently filming police activity on their phones and screaming abuse. The hatred from one group to another was palpable. Each stood at a safe distance from the other, far enough away to gain a head start should their sworn enemies try to rush them, but close enough to throw out the odd threat across the no man's land in between.

'Did you see anything?' asked Charlie walking straight to a group of three teenagers leant against a nearby tree. Even in the mugginess of the night they wore thick black tracksuits with the hoods up covering their heads, leaving only a small round peephole through which to peer. 'I said. Did you see anything?' she repeated into the silence.

The oldest of the three stared her up and down and shook his head sullenly. He was tall and lanky; his shoulders curved inwards and his spine arched over as he slumped lazily against the trunk of the large oak. The edge of a tattoo poked out from behind the fabric of his hood, the sharp point of a knife etched in ink across his olive-coloured cheek. 'Didn't see nothin'. Just thought we'd come up and find out what's happenin'.'

'Do you know the victim then?'

The two shorter youths glanced across at the tall skinny one, clearly the leader, before he shook his head and stared into space. *Keep your fucking mouth shut* was clearly the order of the day.

'Is he one of yours?' persisted Charlie. It was clear from the various groups that they'd come to find out.

The leader reached up and pulled the cord of his sweatshirt even tighter, covering the tattoo and turning the gap, through which he squinted, into a thin slit of menace. 'He'd better not be,' he replied, speaking into the cloth of his hood, before rotating slowly on the spot and heading off.

She watched as he and his minions sauntered nonchalantly towards the road in an exaggerated swagger, then she turned towards another group.

'You wanna talk?' she asked, taking a step forward and staring hard at a stocky black youth with a mouthful of gold teeth and a scar down the length of his cheek. The youth fixed her with a stare, shook his head slowly and sucked on his teeth, before he too melted away with his followers.

'Or you?' she shouted to another group who were already on the move.

They were clearly the postcode gangs from around the area, but Charlie was used to dealing with their sort. She'd never been intimidated by large inner London gangs, so the false bravado of these straggly groups of young men was of no consequence. Front them out and they would back down. Show frailty and they would seize the initiative. If armed they'd be unlikely to risk arrest, and if not, they wouldn't want to show out as weak. So as hostile as they tried to look, the aggression was toothless. None wanted to put their heads over the parapet, so one by one they slunk away into the night.

'Funny that. No one wants to help,' she shouted across to Paul, splaying her hands in frustration. It was always the same. The wall of silence was erected at the drop of a body. No one dared speak up for fear of retribution, and the reluctance to assist in prosecutions meant the cycle was unremitting. One murder bred another, and another, and another. Each gang had a reputation to uphold.

'Well, that appears to be our motive.' She beckoned to Paul, and once in protective gear they started towards the inner crime scene. '*They* obviously believe it's a gang hit and once they know for certain who's down, it'll be time for revenge.'

The route they followed mirrored the path thought to have been used by the victim and his killer, a well-worn bridleway across the common from the road, which had now been isolated for forensic examination. It ran for a distance of approximately one hundred metres before branching off into a small glade. The deceased was still in situ, lying in a large patch of partially clotted blood and as Charlie looked at the body, her head filled with despair.

The youth was more child than adult, with smooth, skinny arms and gangly legs from a recent growth spurt. His limbs stuck out at random angles where he'd fallen and his head, made bare by the paramedics, was tilted to one side. He wore a dark grey, hooded tracksuit, with deep bloody slits criss-crossing its arms and legs, stained red. The front had been cut open by the paramedics to expose a thin, scrawny teenage chest and abdomen.

Her vision was drawn almost immediately to a large kitchen knife sticking out from the smooth skin of his adolescent body. The blade was inserted almost up to the hilt and the metal handgrip stuck out grotesquely in the light from a hastily erected crime scene lamp. In addition to the numerous slash marks, blood had seeped from the wound, down both sides of his chest, a solid dried-up stream of crimson that had congealed in large clots on the parched grass at either side of his body.

It was an effort to tear her gaze away from the awful sight, but as she approached, she forced her eyes away from the stark metal weapon and concentrated instead on the victim's olive-coloured face. The skin of his cheeks looked so soft, and he had absurdly long, curling eyelashes which were thick and luxuriant, in comparison to the smattering of facial hair along his jawline and neck.

In death, he looked like a child, young and innocent, oblivious to the evils of the world, sleeping peacefully on a soft green bed within the seclusion of a silent wooded copse. Casting her eyes over the youth's outstretched, untidy limbs however, Charlie knew that once in a gang, at the impressionable age of sixteen he would have been unable, or unwilling, to go against the orders of his elders.

'Found by a person who couldn't sleep and was out for a walk?' She aimed her query at the uniform duty officer standing to one side.

'Yes, sounds a bit strange, but there's no accounting for insomniacs. We've checked his name out and he seems genuine. Lives nearby and walked in along the route that we've now established, and saw the body. Says there was no one else around. One of my units is taking his statement.'

Charlie smiled gratefully. 'And the victim? Any idea yet who he is, or which gang he's affiliated to?' There was no doubt in her mind this wasn't a random encounter. The murder was in a known gang hotspot, in the middle of the night and it bore all the hallmarks of an arranged meet, almost certainly for a criminal purpose.

'Well, he's got no identification on him and, so far tonight, no one his age has been reported missing,' replied the duty officer. 'But then that's not uncommon. Most of the parents have no idea what their kids are doing, and even less power to stop them doing it. If they even care.'

'I wonder if there's any connection between the youth with the knife tattoo we spoke to just now, and this boy?' Charlie turned to Paul. 'Same sort of ethnicity as this lad. Southern European by the look of them both?'

'I'd say so.' Paul squatted down and pointed to the boy's left arm. Protruding from the sleeve of his tracksuit, along the back of his hand was the tattoo of an identical knife to the one on the cheek of the tall, lanky gang leader.

'The Dons.' The duty officer bent down next to Paul to better see the tattoo. 'From the area of the Roehampton Estate they call Little Italy. They all have a zombie knife tattoo. Where it is on the body depends on their ranking in the group. The higher and more visible the tattoo is, the more important they are in the social hierarchy. They're probably the worst gang around here. And when their boy doesn't make contact, they'll put two and two together...'

'And we'll have another death on our hands.' Raising her gaze from the dead boy, Charlie stared into the sky as a flash of lightning lit up the silhouettes of the nearby trees.

A storm was pending in every sense.

Chapter 3

By the time Charlie and the team had returned to the station, a name was being mooted for the victim and arrangements were in hand to contact his next-of-kin, an older sister, for confirmation.

The boy was indeed only sixteen, had never known his father and had been brought up by his sibling after the death of their mother from hepatitis. It was a tragic story, but similar to many they'd heard before.

As they scaled the stairs and walked into the new office, Bet rose from her seat and beckoned them to one side. She'd assembled a whole wall of photos in the time they'd been gone.

'Gather round, team,' Charlie took up the cue. 'By the time you're next on duty I want you to have memorised this lot. I've a feeling we'll be coming into contact with most of them in the next few weeks, and knowledge is power.'

Naz, Sabira, and Paul shuffled up next to each other, and stood gazing up at a who's who of the local postcode gangs. Staring back at them from under chillingly named groups were the vacant eyes of adolescents, most aged from twelve to twenty-five years, many with convictions for possessing offensive weapons, assaults, drug dealing, public order and the like. The majority were male, with just a small contingent of females, mostly caught carrying weapons for their partners.

Glancing around the photo boards it was clear that the younger members had the more recent convictions, in all probability press-ganged into doing the dirty work of the elders. Many of the young faces bore the marks of conflict; jagged scars, disfigurements, even mutilations. One had lost an eye, another had a partially severed ear, and yet another had the mottled scar tissue of an acid attack.

Looking at them, Charlie couldn't help thinking they were a lost generation, with little prospect of escape from their predetermined fate, and no motivation to try.

'These are the Dons.' Bet pointed to about a dozen faces stuck on a large sheet in the shape of a pyramid. 'At the top, we have the leader, nickname 3D, so called from his full name, Dante Dario Donati. He was born in Lombardy, but has lived in this country for most of his life. He's twenty-four and has risen up the ranks due to his love of torture. He'll literally write across his victim's skin with a knife to press home a message.'

'And I bet none of his victims will put *that* in writing.' Charlie moved closer and stared into the cold dark eyes of the olive-skinned leader she'd so recently met. 'He was on the common just now, with a couple of his mates. I'd recognise those eyes anywhere. Not to mention the knife tattoo across his cheek.'

'The zombie knife.' Bet winced as she pulled out a magnified photo of the tattoo on 3D's cheek. The blade was thick and serrated and the hilt was a grey embossed metal, with green strapping. 'They're all required to have the same tattoo as their initiation – and to be trained in their use. But only the leader is allowed to tattoo his face.'

'You'd think it would set him out as a target?' Paul commented.

'It probably does.' Bet pulled out a couple of pages with the word 'deceased' in bold red lettering across two other olive-skinned faces. 'But to them it's a game. Life is cheap. 3D is their third leader in two years. When he gets taken out, so the deputy steps up, and it's likely to be this guy, Franco Nannini, nicknamed The General.'

'I didn't see him there.' Charlie stared at his face, before casting her eyes to the bottom of the pyramid. 'But here's our victim. Rocco Fontana, nickname Boy Blue.' She concentrated on an image in the lowest row, clearly the expendable category. His baby face stared out at them; his eyes framed by the same strikingly long, curled eyelashes.

'Did you know that Rocco means *rest*?' Sabira chipped in. 'It's what Madonna called her son. I've always liked the name.'

'And Little Boy Blue fell asleep under a haystack,' Charlie pulled a red biro out from a stack of pens on the desk and lifted it to the photo. She drew two straight lines diagonally across the boy's face and wrote 'deceased' in capital letters between them. 'Rest in peace Rocco. I promise we'll do everything we can to bring your killer to justice. You might have been dispensable to the Dons, but I'll bet you were loved by your sister.'

⊠ ⊠ ⊠

'So who are the Dons' sworn enemies?' After a brief break they were back at Bet's wall, with Charlie posing the questions.

'The Soldiers are. They're a black gang from Roehampton, a few miles away.' Bet pointed to a second pyramid. 'In the last few weeks there've been several scuffles between them, a load of provocation on YouTube and two minor GBHs. Until now no one's died, but Boy Blue's murder is guaranteed to up the ante. They both want a piece of the drug market in Wimbledon Village.

'The Soldiers' leader is McKenzie Kamara, or Mak 10,' Bet continued, with a nod to the top of the pyramid. 'With eighteen-year-old Kelvin Olawi, nickname Boxer, as second in command.'

Charlie pointed to Mak 10, recognising him as the stocky male with the gold teeth and scar. 'He was on the common, but I didn't see Kelvin Olawi.'

Bet frowned. 'If Mak 10 was there it must be serious. It's rare you get two leaders together in case it all kicks off.'

'I don't know about you,' queried Paul, joining Charlie to study the board. 'But I thought it felt unusually tense up there. Boy Blue had only been dead for about an hour, but it was as if neither leader knew for sure what was going on.'

'Yes, I agree,' Charlie nodded, chewing on the end of a pen. 'They were all desperately trying to look chilled, but their body language gave them away; watching everything, listening in to conversations, like they were trying to work out who the dead boy might be. Normally they'd know everything. It's not as if one of them inadvertently wandered into the other's turf. The common's no-one's home turf.

'And... they left with barely a whimper. Didn't want to get caught up with us, in case they had to mount a rapid counter attack.' She threw her pen down on her desk. 'Word certainly travels fast around here, and unless we get going then a revenge attack will happen equally as fast.'

Chapter 4

It was late morning when Charlie drove home at the end of her night shift. Today she would be staying in her own rented flat in Clapham to get her head down rather than her usual, several-times-weekly, trip to her family home in Surrey. A murder investigation saps every officer's energy, and if they were to act swiftly, she'd need every minute's sleep she could get.

'Hi Mum.' Charlie spoke through her hands-free.

'Hi Charlie.' Her mother, Meg, sounded subdued. 'Are you on your way home?'

'I'm stopping at mine today,' she replied. 'I have to be back to work in a few hours' time. We had a murder last night.'

'Oh dear. That's awful.' Her mother barely paused a second before continuing breathlessly. 'When will you next be coming home?'

She sighed inwardly. 'Mum, don't worry. I'll still keep in touch and I'll be back as soon as I can. You know I'm always on the end of a phone if you need me, or if it's urgent dial 999.'

Charlie could read between the lines and the reality was upsetting. In the last few months her mother had changed from being a strong, independent woman to the shell of one, almost too nervous to leave the house – and now, seemingly, even to stay at home on her own.

Since being released on licence from a Scottish prison and turning up unannounced on Meg's doorstep, Iain Frazer had been intent on wheedling his way back into Meg's life, much to her consternation.

Being Charlie's biological father, Frazer was also trying to rekindle his relationship with his daughter, though she was far better at freezing him out. She had no wish to resume any kind of contact with a man who had not only terrorised her mother, but stabbed a man to death during a drunken pub brawl in Glasgow. As far as Charlie was concerned, police officers caught and imprisoned murderers, they didn't fraternise with them. Just because they shared the same DNA didn't mean that she should forgive and forget what he'd done.

For her mother though, every day was filled with anxiety. While Charlie's younger half-sisters, Lucy and Beth, were at uni, blissfully unaware of the ongoing problems, Meg now sought her reassurance, or presence, as often as possible. It was painful to watch her decline, but in a strange way it had drawn them closer together. They spoke regularly, saw more of each other, and this year had been the first time since his death they'd travelled together to the grave of her brother Jamie, on the anniversary of the date on which he'd drowned.

She could hear her mother's laboured breathing through the speaker. 'Are you okay, Mum? Has anything happened? You sound tired.'

'No, nothing's happened. It was all quiet last night, dear, but I'm not sleeping too well knowing he's out there somewhere.'

'Try and get a kip during the day then.' She was almost at her flat and, on past form, she knew that if it was quiet at her mother's, it'd be her turn to be in for a surprise. As she pulled up outside, she wasn't mistaken.

Two bags of dog's mess were hanging from the letterbox of the communal door. The tops of the bags had been pulled open and excrement smeared against the wood. There was no doubting that Iain Frazer was responsible. It was the type of sick harassment that seemed to bring him pleasure.

At first it had been flowers and notes, no doubt intending to somehow make himself appear repentant and solicitous – but these tokens had long since disappeared. In their place were now dead or dying blooms, and a whole array of filthy, stinking sundries left in obvious places. For now, Frazer was sticking with fairly juvenile, psychological warfare, but there was no doubt he was very capable of worse. Both she and Meg were under no illusion that his actions would escalate and then God knows what he would do. With a conviction for murder up his sleeve, the possibilities were endless.

'For fuck's sake,' Charlie swore under her breath. It was all she needed after a long and traumatic night shift. She climbed from her car and gathered her stuff, keeping alert for any signs of her father's presence, but all she could see and hear were the trappings of morning; the drone of cars, the footfall of commuters, the hum of life.

She pushed open the gate and stepped into the front garden, her eyes peeled for any sign of movement, the twitch of a bush, the rustling of leaves, the telltale evidence of stealth but there was nothing. If Iain Frazer was there, he had no intention of letting her know. Unbidden, a shiver ran down her spine, followed just as quickly by a shudder of irritation. She was used to dealing with the blatant. Common criminals, committing common crimes. Not devious, evil head-fucks slinking about in the shadows. Her father should show himself, then she could sling him back in prison for breaking his conditions of residence

– but he was far too clever for that. After his first few appearances he now rarely came out into the open, and if he did, he was dressed in bland dark clothes, his facial features covered for anonymity. If they called the local police they would arrive after he'd gone and even though both she and Meg could swear it was him, proving it would be impossible. For now, he held the upper hand.

Lifting the bags of excrement from the door she moved to the side of the block, tossing them into a wheelie bin. Her mother had always maintained he was devious, but even with the improved relationship between the two women, Charlie felt as if she didn't know the full story.

She returned to the front door, her mind mulling over this thought. Slipping the key in the lock she pushed open the door and stepped into the communal hallway. Inside was gloomy and the space smelt of musk, one of the other residents having left out a perforated gift bag of pot-pourri to chase away the smells of the city. She stood for a few seconds allowing her eyes to acclimatise to the shadows before climbing the stairs and opening her own first-floor front door.

A pile of letters lay on the mat – several of the other residents knowing her occupation, had slipped her post thoughtfully through her individual letterbox. It was a heartening gesture, particularly as these days it seemed as if she was rarely there at all. She brushed them to one side with a foot and closed the door, leaning back against it to ensure the locks clicked into place.

After taking a deep breath she launched herself along the hallway, stopping at the bedroom briefly. The curtains were open and the sun was shining directly on the window, making the room hot, stuffy and airless. The bed was still made and her childhood sailor-attired teddy bear lay where she always kept it, wedged in between the two pillows. Except that today it seemed skewed to one side. Or was it? Her tired brain was playing tricks on her. The door was secure, the windows were too. The post was undisturbed. Iain Frazer was getting to her.

'For fuck's sake,' she said out loud this time. It was her standard self-rebuke, designed to stiffen her resolve and dismiss her fears. She shrugged her unease away, opened the window, and leant forward to set the toy straight.

Then to the kitchen where she ran a bowlful of warm, soapy water, added some disinfectant and flicked out a new dishcloth.

She carried the bowl downstairs, towards the communal door, her body tense, knowing that if he was there, she was at an immediate disadvantage with both hands gripping the water container. It always amazed her that subliminally her brain thought like a police officer, and her body reacted like a police officer. As she stepped out on to the doorstep and started to scrub at the dried excrement, gagging at the stinking faeces, she lamented the fact that, even when off duty, she was constantly expected to *act* like a police officer too.

Chapter 5

The woman had always hated lawyers.

Solicitors and barristers for the prosecution were the worst. Arrogant bastards. They'd made a point of looking down at her all her life, squinting at her over outsized designer spectacles, or from underneath their ridiculous silver/grey wigs. She'd been judged by them, more so than any of the qualified Crown Court judges, the rails of whose docks she had occasionally gripped. No, the prosecution lawyers had found her guilty without a shred of evidence, then convicted and condemned her, not because of what she had done, but because of who she was.

She was scum as far as they were concerned.

The criminal defence lawyers were almost as bad, as were the probation officers, the prison staff, the shrinks; all wanting to get their two pennies' worth in, to kick her when she was down, shove her face into the dirt. She was the lowest of the low. A street sex worker. A whore. But she was far more than that. If only they knew.

For the moment though, she required their expertise. She had to set the record straight, right a wrong that she herself had instigated – and for that she needed their help.

Pulling her thin cotton T-shirt down over the bones of her ribs, she waited outside the police station. Even though it was a warm Spring day, she still shivered in the mild breeze, her arms twitching slightly as she hugged her body tight. The edge of one hand skimmed a half-full breast, a finger catching against the nipple, sending milk flooding to the surface. Much of her supply had dried up but the remainder leaked out, wetting the soft fabric, spreading out across her chest so that even total strangers could witness her shame. She had no baby to suckle. No child to give her gift of sustenance. Mia was gone.

A group of teenagers skulked by, their heads swivelling towards her as they passed.

'Look at the state of that,' she heard one sneer loudly. 'You dirty bitch,' the voice was directed at her.

'Fuck off,' she shouted in return, but the abuse smarted. It wasn't her fault that she was the way she was. It was her father's, her mother's, the system's. Every time she'd had love in her life it had been temporary; minuscule moments in her timeline that had been severed in anger from her story, or faded away into obscurity. Every person she'd ever trusted had let her down. Worse than that, some had intentionally betrayed her. Their actions had not been reckless – they'd been deliberate. Concentrated deeds designed to belittle, overpower, crush her completely.

'Good morning. Are you waiting for me?' Her mind was drawn from her misery to a grey-suited, grey faced woman, with brown framed rectangular glasses, hair pulled back in a bun and thick, dark red lipstick which matched the highly polished, maroon court shoes that she now tapped against the pavement impatiently.

She knew instantly it was the lawyer to whom she'd spoken on the phone. The woman was everything she despised in a solicitor.

'Patricia Goodfellow, from Clark and Co. Solicitors.' The solicitor held out her hand and she shook it briefly, watching how her face puckered up in disgust and how she wiped her hand surreptitiously against her leg when it became free.

'Are you ready to go?' Her manner was brusque.

'Yes, I'm ready.'

'And you haven't changed your mind?'

'No.' It wasn't worth the effort of expending any more energy on the question. They had spoken at length over the airwaves previously and she had explained again and again what had to be done, much to the chagrin of the solicitor. 'Are you sure you wish to do this?' the lawyer had asked on at least five occasions. 'You'll be opening yourself up to a charge of wasting police time, or possibly even perjury, if you now withdraw your previous statement.'

Or murder? The thought had bothered her only for a split second, because she didn't really care any more. She'd got away with it before and there was no reason why she shouldn't get away with it again. Besides, there would be time to explain the reasons for giving and then withdrawing the alibi for her partner, and for making her own allegation against him. She had been frightened, traumatised, in fear for her life. She knew all the explanations to give and she knew the system. God knows she'd experienced it in reality enough times.

No, whatever happened to her in the future was of no consequence. Her priority was to get Mia back, and the first step in that process would be getting her ex-partner released from prison. He may have hurt and abused her in the past, or chosen others over her. He may have betrayed her, or stood back and watched as she was almost throttled to death, but he was Mia's daddy after all, the father of her child.

'I'm ready,' she repeated, sniffing loudly and hugging her arms around her ribcage again. The knowledge that she was taking positive action, gave her an instant boost of courage.

'Okay, let's go then.'

Patricia Goodfellow pushed the revolving door to Lambeth HQ and they stepped inside. The lobby was cool, air-conditioned, quiet, in comparison to her more usual entry into a police station, through heavy security gates, into custody. Rather than the shouts and screams of handcuffed prisoners, the incessant chatter of other prostitutes and addicts and the inane protestations of recidivist criminals, here was relative peace. The occupants of the waiting room that morning looked, on the whole, to be victims. They sat in silent contemplation, their faces tight with worry, no doubt wishing they could be anywhere else than there.

'Take a seat,' Patricia Goodfellow indicated a set of metal chairs attached to the wall, and pressed her finger on the buzzer. 'I'll let them know we're here.'

She did what she was told, listening to the uncompromising way in which the solicitor trotted out her introduction and request. A message shrilled out over the Tannoy. The lawyer returned and smiled grimly.

'Hopefully they won't keep us waiting for long.' The underlying message was blunt. *They'd* better not keep me waiting for long – and nor had *you*.

Patricia Goodfellow pulled out her mobile and keyed in a number, but before there was time to speak, a plain wooden door with no outer handle was pulled open and a young, fresh-faced man, in casual clothing, popped his head round the door.

She had never seen the man before, a fact that irritated her.

'Ms Goodfellow.' He called out only her solicitor's name, then beckoned them over, standing on tiptoes and holding his arm at the top of the door so that Patricia had to duck to pass underneath. 'It's nice to see you, again.' He let his arm drop, as she was about to enter, allowing the door to swing back in her face. She thrust her foot forward preventing it from slamming into her head. Clearly, she was as invisible now as she had always been.

They were ushered into a bland grey interview room and they all took a seat; she and her solicitor on the far side against the wall, the policeman nearest the door, as if it was of no consequence that she had voluntarily attended the station. Maybe he feared she'd do a runner, but it was laughable.

Her solicitor pulled out a silver ballpoint pen and a notepad, flicking through a wad of handwritten notes until she reached an empty page.

The man unclipped a plastic file and pulled out a couple of statement forms.

'I'm PC Brownlow,' he said. 'I've recently joined the CID here. I'm sorry, but the officers who dealt with your case are not here any more. They've moved on to pastures new, if there's anywhere in London that can be called a pasture.' His lips curled up in a smile, but she didn't find him funny; in fact, she didn't find this new information even vaguely amusing. Yet again she'd been let down. Charlie Stafford, the one officer who'd dealt with her situation, who knew her, who had listened and believed her, was gone, and she was drowning in shit, with no one to throw her a lifeline.

'But how can I help.'

'I believe you know what this is about?' Patricia Goodfellow nudged her glasses to the end of her nose and stared sternly at the officer over the top of them, like a parent chastising their child.

She watched as a reddening stain crept up his neck and settled onto his cheeks at the solicitor's query. The man was evidently blushing, as if he'd been caught doing something naughty. She stared at the officer. He did actually look like an errant child, too young and naive to be a fully-fledged detective, but perhaps this wasn't a bad thing.

She put her hands out in front of her on the desk and focussed on the man. He could only be in his mid-twenties, not much older than she. Her eyes met his and she held his gaze, at the same time switching to thoughts of her baby girl, Mia. Where was she now? And who was she with? Genuine tears pricked at her eyes in an instant, gathering in pools at the corners. She allowed one to drip down her cheek, but made no move to brush it away. The policeman's eyes never left hers.

'I need to withdraw a statement,' she half sobbed. 'I've done something awful. I was frightened. My partner got sent to prison after I said he'd assaulted me but it wasn't him. It was someone else – and it's not right to leave him inside.'

She balled one hand into a fist and screwed it into her wet eye socket, brushing the tears away. 'Please,' she whimpered, keeping her eyes firmly connected to the young detective. 'You have to help me get him out.'

Chapter 6

Word on the street is that Rocco Fontana (nickname Boy Blue) was killed by the Soldiers. Charlie read the intelligence report and shook her head. There was no denying it was useful information, but was it enough?

'Let's go and speak to Maria Fontana, Boy Blue's sister. See what she's heard.' She yawned and stretched her limbs out, letting the printed report slip onto her desk. Only four hours sleep was already taking its toll, and that was without the additional worry of what her father had in mind to liven up her night. She beckoned to Paul and headed for the door. 'You can be my driver today. I'm knackered.'

'You okay?' Paul asked as they settled into the car. 'Is your dad causing problems again?'

'You could say that,' she wrinkled her nose at the memory. 'Just the usual crap... but I'll tell you later.'

The drive took them past the busy crime scene where forensic teams were still hard at work. In the sunshine the common presented as a light, bright, vibrant square of life. Elderly walkers, fluorescent joggers, parents with off-road buggies and exuberant children were dotted about inside its borders, making the most of its rural atmosphere. Passing it now, it was hard to imagine two, armed, gang members facing off against each other.

Boy Blue's home was on the Roehampton Estate, nestled in between the tennis courts of Wimbledon, the acres of parkland at Richmond and the Royal Gardens of

Kew. The difference between the haves and the have nots could not be starker.

Paul parked up and they set out on foot to the block where Maria lived, criss-crossing a small children's play area. It was sobering to realise that just a few years earlier Rocco had probably played innocently on the swings. They followed a path round the base of the block and up a set of stairs to the first floor. A small pile of floral tributes marked out the flat.

Charlie pulled out her warrant card, knocked on the door and stepped back to cast an eye over the messages. Most were handwritten on small rectangular note cards and spoke of Rocco as a much loved friend, taken too soon, now with the angels, among other words of condolence. At one end, however, was a single red rose, with a piece of notepaper attached to it with string.

She picked it up, reading the message out loud with a mixture of disbelief and disgust.

'RIP Boy Blue. Revenge will be ours.' It was signed, 'The Dons' and a simply drawn picture of two knives crossing each other in the shape of an 'X' concluded the message.

'They'd better not.' The door had been opened by a young woman dressed head-to-foot in black. There could be no doubt she was Maria Fontana, Rocco's older sister, as she had the same huge, baleful brown eyes and long, luxuriant eyelashes. 'But I know they will,' she added, staring down at Charlie's identification and beckoning them in. 'Unless you can stop them.'

'You must be Maria Fontana?' Charlie confirmed.

'Yes I am.'

'Can I keep this?' She was still holding the rose as she stepped onto the immaculately polished laminate flooring of the hallway.

'Please do. My brother was not called Boy Blue. His name was Rocco Fontana. Take it away. I don't want to see it again – and I don't want anything to do with what it threatens.' Maria ushered them into an exquisitely decorated and spotlessly clean lounge, before turning on her heel to face them. Her expression was set hard, but bottomless eyes gave away the depths of her pain. 'The boys who wrote this have ruined my life. They are as much to blame for my brother's death as the boy who held the knife.'

'I've read some of Rocco's history.' Charlie sat down heavily. She could well understand the young woman's words, having the same deep-seated grief after the death of her own brother. It still had the power to kick her legs from underneath her. 'I'm so sorry for your loss.'

'I'm sorry too.' Maria's voice was strong and unwavering. 'Rocco was all I had left. I have nothing else to lose.' She swept her arm around the room, indicating the numerous family photographs proudly displayed. 'Since our mother died, I've done everything in my power to keep Rocco safe. I've worked hard to keep our home nice. I even paid for him to have extra tuition so he could make something of himself. But then he met 3D.' She exhaled hard and her eyes became steely. 'That bastard changed everything. Rocco went from a sweet, home-loving boy to an angry teenager who argued with everything I asked of him.'

'Might that have happened anyway?' Paul asked quietly.

Maria Fontana swung round and glared at him. 'Not without that boy. I swear 3D had something on Rocco. My brother was frightened. You could see it in his eyes. I tried everything I could to get him away from 3D but in the end, it was no use. Rocco chose the Dons. He had the tattoo. He couldn't risk messing with 3D. And for what?' She picked up a silver frame containing a photograph of a classically dressed Italian woman and made the sign of the cross in front of it. 'Mama would turn in her grave if she knew what that boy had done to our Rocco. She always warned us to stay away from 3D's family, the Donatis. She said they were bad.'

'In what way?' Charlie was intrigued. '3D might have a reputation on the street, but he's nothing without his boys. None of them are.'

'No, you're wrong. 3D is more than that. This has been coming ever since he became leader. It's like he's been biding his time, secretly applauding what's been happening in the rest of London. The stabbings. The tit for tat murders. He craves violence. It excites him. Rocco said so himself one night. He came home petrified; ran up to his room in a terrible state and hid in a wardrobe. It took almost an hour before I could coax him out. He said that 3D had been mixing with some of the local club owners, you know, proper gangsters, the hard men of the drugs trade. 3D wanted them to use the Dons, sort of like middlemen. He was trying to stir things up, get his boys into the next league. Rocco said he was goading the Soldiers, sending out the young boys as cannon fodder to tempt them to bite. Once they'd started, he'd have the excuse to begin a proper turf war. In the end my brother became the fodder. He might not have known exactly when it would start – but Rocco knew it would.'

'So, if everything goes to 3D's plan, the Soldiers will get the blame, and he'll be expected to retaliate, upping the reputation of the Dons, and moving them into another drug dealing league? And we have no idea where it will end.'

'That's your problem now,' Maria Fontana said, tenderly kissing the photograph of their mother before putting the frame back in place. 'I've failed in my job. We all know where it's ended for Rocco.'

Charlie stood up to leave, thanking the young woman for her time.

She'd heard everything she needed to know. The word on the street was correct and it sounded as though the Soldiers had taken the bait.

Chapter 7

'Charlie, we have a suspect. Kelvin Olawi – nickname Boxer, second in command of the Soldiers. So, the rumours were right.'

As if to confirm Maria Fontana's words, Bet had jumped up as they entered the office. 'SOCO found a partial thumbprint on the handle of the kitchen knife that was used to kill Rocco Fontana. Although...' Bet grimaced and picked up a piece of paper on which she'd scribbled some figures.'

'Although... what?'

'The odds are one in sixty thousand that it's him – so they're good, but not decisive.'

'Hang on.' Paul pulled out his phone and clicked on the internet. 'Right, so there's just over nine point three million people in London, divided by sixty thousand.' He switched to the calculator. 'That means there are one hundred and fifty-five people walking about in London whose thumbprint will match.'

'But how many of those are signed up members of the Soldiers?' Bet was always positive.

'I would hasten to wager just the one, but I'd also hasten to add that the CPS will want a lot more before they'll run with it.' Charlie ran her teeth over her bottom lip. 'See if we can get any DNA fast-tracked Bet, and Sabira, go get a warrant for Kelvin Olawi's address before the court closes for the weekend. I don't necessarily want

Olawi arrested at this point, but we do need to stop him disposing of clothing and phones.'

She watched as they all sprang into action, then wandered into Hunter's empty office. The hot-seat had been offered to her as 'acting inspector', but it hadn't felt right. Now though it gave her the chance to speak privately to her old boss, as well as updating her new.

She sat down heavily, picking up the photo of his son in police uniform, following on in the family tradition. It had always made him glow with pride.

'Don't fuck it up like I did, by putting all your eggs into one basket,' Hunter's tone was flat when he finally answered the phone and had listened to her account of the situation.

'You didn't fuck it up, guv.' She raised her voice, trying to sound encouraging. 'And, it wasn't your fault.' A couple of suspects had slipped through the net in their last case and her boss was taking the flack. 'You can't be responsible for everything, and every one.'

'But *you* have to be.' Hunter's voice was serious. 'There are a lot of snakes out there and I want you climbing the ladder, not being dragged down by a snake like I have. Charlie, you've got to think outside the box. Treat everyone as a suspect until you are absolutely certain that they're not. You can't afford to be railroaded into the wrong course of action.'

'I won't.' She tailed off, regretting her last words in case she'd unintentionally given him the impression she believed this was what he'd done. He sounded so low, crushed by the very organisation he'd worked so hard for all his life. The thought prompted her to dial her new boss.

Superintendent Richie Woodall was one of the new breed of graduate-entry managers. They hadn't, as yet, been introduced but rumour had it his time in uniform had been a grand total of six months, before he'd retreated into an office, never to get his hands dirty again on the streets of the capital.

His voice, unlike Hunter's, was upbeat, polite and proper. He had clearly never been spat at, or faced the taunts of a hostile crowd of gang members – nor, in all probabilities had he delivered a death message to the parents of one of their victims. In her head she imagined a rather suave looking man, with dark gelled-back hair, and an immaculate three-piece pin-striped suit. More bank manager than crime manager.

'Thank you for updating me Detective Sergeant Stafford,' he said at the end of their conversation. 'It sounds like you have it all in hand. Let's see if we can't do the warrant in a, shall we say, consensual manner. The residents here don't look too kindly to the more forceful type of policing of which you're accustomed. I'd like to think they're more law-abiding and astute. Anyway, let me know if you need any more staff or funding and I'll get on to Human Resources.'

'Thank you, sir,' she replied, bristling at the overt politics of his comments. As far as she was concerned, a victim was a victim wherever they lived. 'I'll update you with the result of the warrant and with any arrests.'

'Excellent. Let's see if we can't nip this in the bud sergeant, shall we.'

'Yes sir.' She clicked the receiver to end the call, and swore under her breath. He could stay in his office as far as they were concerned. There was no 'we' in it. It was solely her and her team.

※ ※ ※

With the warrant for Kelvin Olawi signed, they gathered in front of a large screen for Bet's briefing. Charlie had been joined by Sergeant Ross McBride and his squad of uniformed battering rams from the Territorial Support Group, a couple of whom were competing against each other to recognise the faces of the gangs on the wall.

'These are the occupants you're likely to encounter when you go through the door,' directed Bet, as the room quietened. 'This is Wesley. He's thirteen, and he's itching to join his big brother Kelvin, who's deputy leader of the Soldiers. He's already been arrested in possession of cannabis a few times and is proving to be quite confrontational.

'Their mother is also shown at the premises. Her name is Constance Olawi.' Bet pulled out a raft of printouts and passed them around. 'Constance has form for assault and public order, amongst other things, so she's likely to be a handful.'

Charlie gave a nod to Ross McBride then turned to Naz. 'Naz, can you deal with her when Ross's team have secured the flat. She might be more compliant with you.'

'Is it because I is black,' Naz feigned a deep-south American accent and grinned broadly, to a ripple of laughter around the room. She always made Charlie chuckle with her brand of tongue-in-cheek humour, but it could only come from Naz. Naz was almost as close to her as her two half-sisters, and their shared history dictated that they would always remain this way. Charlie had literally saved both Naz and her son's life, and Naz would never allow that deed to be forgotten.

'I was thinking more of the fact you've both raised sons on your own.' Charlie lifted her hands in submission. 'I've been surrounded by women for most of my life, so don't ask me about young boys.'

'You've got a point.' Naz noted the details in her pocket book and winked in return. 'Show me down as the peacekeeper.'

Chapter 8

Charlie yanked subconsciously on her stab vest as she rapped on the front door. Executing warrants always involved an unknown risk and although this one gave them the legal power to use force to enter, her revised decision, in line with the comments from Supt Woodall was to knock – but it meant giving the occupants more time to prepare, a fact that made her uneasy. From within, came the noise of loud music.

'What do you want?' a woman had appeared at the kitchen window, and opened it.

'Can we come in and I'll explain.'

'Not without a warrant.'

Charlie held up the paperwork. 'We've got a warrant, so I suggest you open the door quickly.'

The woman swore out loud, before slamming the window shut and crossing towards the kitchen door. 'Boys, the feds are here. Get yourselves downstairs now.'

There was a pause, followed by the sound of footsteps clomping towards the door.

The door opened and the woman stood squarely on the mat in front of them, blocking their passage. 'So what do you want?' Her feet were a shoulder's width apart, her spine held upright and her expression severe. To one side of her, a young teenager leant against the wall, grinning lazily. This was clearly a regular occurrence.

'Mrs Constance Olawi, I presume?' No confirmation was forthcoming so Charlie ploughed on. 'We have a warrant to search your address, under section 8 of the Police and Criminal Evidence Act. Now, we can do that with your consent, or we can do so by force. Your choice.' Charlie's patience was ebbing away fast. The woman didn't move so she took a step forward, putting her foot against the door. 'Okay, I'm not waiting any longer,' she said, beckoning the uniformed officers to pass. 'In you go.'

The woman stood her ground.

With one swift movement the battering ram of bulky officers nudged Constance Olawi to one side and continued on down the hallway of the flat. 'You fucking bastards,' she screeched as the two officers at the end of the line took hold of her and the boy by the arms. 'Leave Wesley alone,' she continued, struggling against the hands that held her. 'You won't get away with this.'

'I have a job to do, and you are not going to stop me,' advised Charlie calmly, but firmly. 'So I suggest you calm down.' As she spoke, the youth from the second row of the Soldiers pyramid was marched down the stairs and into the lounge; a burly police officer on either side of him. 'So, this must be Kelvin, or should I say Boxer. Is that everyone?' she asked, turning to face the woman.

Constance Olawi nodded sullenly.

'Good. Well in that case let's get started.' She indicated for them all to be sat down in the lounge. 'We're here in connection with the gang murder of a young boy on Wimbledon Common last night. We believe that the Soldiers were involved, of which Kelvin here is a highly ranked member – but before we search the house, all of you are going to be searched individually, for everyone's safety.'

She indicated for Naz to take Constance into a separate room and followed them out, leaving the male officers to search the two boys. Constance was calmer now, in fact icily so, and it didn't sit right. Spitting, screaming hostility, in Charlie's experience was far easier to deal with than cool, composed, plotting.

Constance led them to a bedroom and they filed in together, Naz trying to make small talk along the way. It didn't work. In fact, her attempts seemed to antagonise the woman further.

'It's hard bringing up boys, isn't it?' Naz smiled amicably at Constance. 'I've got a couple of the little buggers myself.'

The woman sucked her teeth and said nothing. Her eyes narrowed and glazed over for what seemed like ages, before she opened them wide and stared Naz up and down.

'What do you know?' Her voice was calmly monotone. 'You're not like us, even though you try to talk like us. You might look the same but you're different. You're privileged.' She backed up against the wall and slid her hands into her trouser pockets, sending warning bells screaming around Charlie's head.

'Take your hands out of your pockets,' she shouted, lunging forward to grab Constance's arm, but it was too late. As Naz stood ready to start the search, the woman pulled a small metal vegetable knife from her pocket and swung it towards her.

'You're a coconut,' she shrieked. 'You should be ashamed of yourself. Get out of my house.'

Time slowed almost to a standstill. In horrified slow motion, Charlie's eyes fixed on the sharp, deadly blade as Constance aimed it towards Naz's chest. It skimmed the cover of her stab vest, slipping across the front of her body and piercing her upper arm, before clattering to the floor. Naz stood stock still, seemingly frozen, her eyes glued to the wound to her arm, from which a stream of bright red sticky blood spurted.

'Urgent assistance,' Charlie shouted as loud as she could, her body weight knocking Constance Olawi to the ground. She threw herself down on top of the struggling woman as several officers came hurtling through. Within seconds, Constance Olawi was restrained in handcuffs and searched, before being seated on a chair; two officers standing close to keep watch. Charlie was able to turn her attention back to her friend.

Naz was sitting on the edge of the bed, one hand pressed against the knife wound, her face ashen with shock. Her sleeve was a sea of red and blood dripped out from between her fingers and out from under the cuff at her wrist.

'I think it's hit an artery,' Naz gasped, as Charlie started to unzip her colleague's stab-vest and pull at her clothing to better see the wound.

'Has someone called an ambulance?' Charlie called out, trying to stay as calm as she could, while battling her own sense of panic. She heard a confirmation shouted from one of the officers in the hallway but the awful fear remained. Naz couldn't die. Naz was her friend. It had been she who had selected her and it was she who had made the decision to enter the flat in slow time – therefore, it was already in Charlie's head that she was entirely to blame. Her friend was now sitting horribly injured and she was responsible. Hunter had said as much.

Pulling a pillow case off the bed, she flipped it inside out and scrunched it up into a temporary dressing. She lifted Naz's arm and held the fabric hard against the wound to stem the bleeding, turning at the same time towards the officers in the room.

'Take Ms Olawi outside and call for a van,' she instructed. 'She's to be arrested for attempted murder.'

'And you...' she dropped her eyes to look directly at Constance, noting her lack of remorse in the thin smile playing on her lips. '...are the one who should be ashamed.'

Chapter 9

The bedsit was a fucking mess.

Looking down at the filthy bedding and unmade bed, the woman almost felt ashamed.

Almost.

For a short time in her sad fucking life, she'd been proud. Proud of how she'd dragged herself from the filthy crack houses of Lambeth. Proud of how she'd manipulated the situation to her advantage. Proud to have a new best friend.

But now, all that had changed. Everything had reverted to type. The type of home she had grown up in, the type of premises in which she felt comfortable, the type of lifestyle to which she belonged. But she had tried. Really tried. In fact, it had taken all her strength to get clean, and stay clean until after her daughter's birth.

But with Mia came excuses. The phone had rung, but the door remained shut tight. Her support structure had been gradually but unrelentingly dismantled. She had been abandoned by the one person on whom she had trusted, her legs effectively kicked out from underneath her.

'I'm so sorry,' her best friend had said. 'I'm so sorry... I've been so busy. I've been run off my feet. I'm so sorry... the kids are doing my head in. My husband's taken on more work so it's all down to me. I'm so sorry... I promise I'll come by and see you as soon as I can.'

But her friend hadn't come.

And while Mia had screamed with colic, even the phone had grown quiet.

So, she'd paced around her tiny bedsit trying to calm down, to rationalise why it always seemed to happen to her, but in the end she had snapped. Broken. It was just her. It was always her. It was her fucking luck. Her fucking life.

It was then that she herself had reverted to type. First one journey to the front line in Brixton, with Mia strapped to her chest, then a second. A chance to become reacquainted with old friends, new mothers, other whores; the family of prostitutes who did whatever was needed to put food on the plates of their children, or crack cocaine into their own veins. At first, she'd been glad of the company, the banter of her comrades, the unquestioning acceptance of her choices. At first, she'd resisted the draw of the drugs, determined to prove she could be trusted to look after a home – and her child.

However, in the end she was weak. She had always been weak. Her legs walked her unimpeded towards her previous hangouts while her willpower crumbled about her feet. Without the strength of support, she was lost.

It hadn't taken long. One hit and she was hooked again. The rest was history.

She threw herself down on her bed, closing her eyes to the sight of the cot, the grubby bedding, the stains, Dilly the dinosaur toy with its cute little head perched on the end of its incredibly long neck. Mia's fingers had been able to encircle that neck, to swing it about in the air, and pull it to her sweet little giggling mouth, with her perfect pink lips and smooth gums. Mia had loved it. Mia had lost it. Mia was gone.

She forced herself forward, reaching out to take hold of the little dinosaur, stroking it against her cheek. In a second, her nostrils were filled with the scent of her daughter; milky, slightly sweet overtures of her feed, but so emotionally evocative. She could almost feel her baby in her arms, hear her soft murmuring breaths as she slowed into sleep. Disconsolate, she placed the dinosaur back in the cot, smoothing out the bedding and hitching the covers up so only its head was visible. Tears ran unabated from the corners of her eyes as she laid back against her own pillow, but she wiped at them angrily. Tears could do nothing to bring Mia back. Ms Patricia Goodfellow, from Clark and Co. Solicitors could do nothing to bring Mia back. 'We're criminal defence lawyers, not family lawyers,' she'd explained pompously, propping her glasses on the end of her nose and peering over the top, much as she'd done to the young copper when they'd last met.

'Sanctimonious bitch,' the words had slipped out through gritted teeth as they'd parted. She'd seen the solicitor flinch and it had made her smile. The bitch had played her part and now, with any luck, she'd never have to set eyes on her smug, self-righteous face again. With her statements set down on paper and her ex-partner's lawyers informed, it was now down to them.

A *matter of days* is what she'd been told, but their promises had melded into a jumble of legal terminology and hope. Allegations withdrawn. Alibis reset. New information. New evidence. Grounds for appeal. A new court case. Miscarriages of justice must be rectified quickly. Innocent men must not stay imprisoned.

The assurances had come thick and fast. There would be questions needing answers. Old cases to be opened, reinvestigated, but for now she didn't care. In *a matter of days*, Mia's father would be released, pending an appeal. In a matter of days, they'd be reunited. She'd be waiting at the prison gates to bring him back to her bedsit. They would talk, fuck, score together; as they'd done for most of her life – and he would forgive the impetuosity of her previous evidence and allegations. He would love her in his own way again. She would share the photos of Mia, and he would be proud and help her to get Mia back, because he was strong, and because he didn't give a fuck about anyone or anything.

And when she'd let him think he was back in control, she would tell him all about the friend who'd abandoned her and who didn't care. The friend, who he already hated, and who must have sneaked back and forth when she was out, taking stock of the condition of the room, the whispers of her neighbours, and who had betrayed her to the authorities.

Picking up her old ragdoll, Goldilocks, she moulded her back into shape, straightened out her clothing and pulled two hairs from between the folds of the material; one short and dark, the other long and red. She let the hairs drop to the floor, watching as they were wafted away on a breath of air from the window, remembering to whom they'd belonged.

Yes, she would tell him everything, or almost everything.

She wandered across to the mirror, her pale green eyes taking in her lacklustre skin, her sunken eyes, the dirty blonde hair. It wouldn't take long to scrub away the veneer of drugs and return to her youthful looks. He liked her looking young and fresh-faced. She would bend to his wishes, give him the recognition and respect he craved, treat him like an alpha male, and in return, well, he would do everything she asked.

She turned her head and focussed on a painting on the wall. It was a picture of stepping stones spaced out across a small river meandering lazily under the shadow of the North Downs. Her best friend's daughter had painted it, and excitedly pointed out the shape of a horse in the foreground, cattle to one side. Box Hill she'd said it was. A favourite spot of the family.

She dragged her eyes from the scene, jealousy and hurt burning through every cell of her body.

The girl was lucky to still have a family – a mother, father, brother – while she had none.

But soon, very soon, in *a matter of days* she'd have one of her loved ones returned to her arms. And then there'd be two, at least, to fight for her own little family unit.

If that happened, she *might* just forgive her friend and possibly, with a bit of time, forget her betrayal. But if the authorities couldn't be persuaded to return their daughter, then what would they do? What should they do? That scenario couldn't be tolerated. Life without Mia was unthinkable. She had to have the chance to prove that she could be the mother she'd always dreamt of becoming; the kind of mother she'd read about in story books, and seen waiting at the gates of primary schools. The kind of mother who didn't stand back silently as their child was abused by their father – who didn't commit suicide in front of their child. The kind of mother that she had never had.

The more she mulled over the question, the more there seemed only one feasible resolution taking shape in her head, the consequence of desertion gradually crystallizing in all its grisly details. She sat down on her bed, staring again at the picture of the countryside, thinking the unthinkable, as the idea grew and grew and took over her mind. If Mia had been taken from her then she must do the same to her betrayer. An eye for an eye. A tooth for a tooth. A child for a child.

Chapter 10

The corridors and waiting rooms of the hospital were crammed full, with patients spewing in and out of the various departments; corralled in oversized beds into cramped lifts, while others clung tightly to chairs wheeled along too fast and too carelessly by over-worked porters. Charlie felt herself swept along with the crowd, all eager to locate the right ward.

Charlie hated hospitals. Somewhere in the chasms of her mind she equated them to death, rather than the return to life and good health. This time was no different, and a tight ball of anxiety was filling her chest. After finding the equally busy ward she was ushered to the calm of a private room where Naz now lay. A nurse bustled in behind her.

'How is she?' Charlie leant towards her sleeping friend and took her hand, staring at the white bandage covering the whole of her upper arm.

'Stable now, but she lost a lot of blood. It'll take a while for her to recover her strength.'

'But she will recover?'

'Yes, she will.' The nurse wrapped a cuff around Naz's other arm and pressed a button on a blood pressure monitor. She was an older, more matronly woman, as round and rosy as an apple, and with laughter lines that splayed out at angles from kindly brown eyes.

Charlie held her breath as air filled the strap, then deflated with a loud huff, making her subconsciously do the same. 'All good.' The nurse noted down the reading.

'That's a relief.' It was the biggest understatement of her life. For the first time since getting promotion she totally understood what it felt like to shoulder the full burden of responsibility. In the most brutal way, she'd learnt that every strategy had a consequence, and this particular consequence had almost proved fatal. She had allowed her judgement to be swayed – albeit reluctantly, while abiding by her superintendent's wishes – and the softly, softly approach had almost cost Naz her life. 'She's one of my best officers,' Charlie put words to her thoughts. 'And a great friend.'

'I can see that.' The nurse squeezed her arm gently, then checked Naz's pulse. 'That's good too. She'll be fine.'

For the first time since the attack, Charlie visibly relaxed. Her shoulders drooped and some of the tension drained from her neck. 'I've learned a valuable lesson,' she admitted, chewing on her bottom lip. 'Next time I conduct a search warrant on a known gang address I'll resist the temptation to put political sensitivity before common sense. It's easier to go in hard and then lighten up, even if it risks ruffling the feathers of a few law-abiding people.' The image of Maria Fontana came to mind; she'd been distraught but still supportive.

'I know exactly what you mean.' The older woman nodded her approval. 'Sometimes I help out in A & E...' She tailed off. Nothing further needed to be said.

'Anyway, I'll leave her to sleep,' Charlie took a step backwards. 'But please tell her when she wakes that I visited – and that we're all wishing her a speedy recovery.'

'Only 'cause she wants me back at work!' Naz's face broke into a grin and she opened her eyes. 'Do you really think I could sleep through all that? And it wasn't your fault, Charlie. I should have seen it coming.' She tried to sit up.

'Woah there, young lady.' The nurse straightened up and put her hands on her hips. 'Stay right where you are. You're going nowhere until I say you can.' The tone of her voice brooked no dissent and, in that instant, relief and laughter washed over them both. It was like a clip from Carry on Nursing.

'And that's my decision.' The nurse glanced from one to the other and shook her head. 'Now, off you go,' she shushed Charlie away with her hands, but at the same time winked towards her. 'And don't argue with me because, unlike you, I'm *always* right.'

❈ ❈ ❈

Constance Olawi and her youngest son were holding court in the custody office when Charlie returned to the station.

Ross McBride was standing nearby.

'What's Wesley in for?' Charlie asked.

'Obstructing police. While you were dealing with Naz, he kicked off big time. Refused to be searched, and then refused to calm down. In the end we had no choice. Personally, I think it was more for effect. There were quite a few of the Soldiers outside, shouting and causing a ruckus by the time he was whisked away.'

They watched, as Wesley, still screaming abuse, was marched off to a detention room, before Charlie turned to his mother. Constance Olawi, despite being unglamorously decked out in a grey prisoner's tracksuit was being equally vocal. Her blood splattered clothing had been added to the wealth of evidence already mounted up against her.

'You're lucky you're not facing a murder charge,' Charlie said bluntly. 'And we're lucky to still have our colleague.' She swung round and handed the hospital doctor's preliminary report to the custody officer. 'Thankfully my officer is now out of danger.'

'That's a shame.' Constance Olawi ran her tongue over her teeth. 'I must be losing my touch. She got what she deserved. It's time you lot learnt to leave us alone. Still, better luck next time.'

Charlie was appalled. With splashes of Naz's blood still staining the sleeves of her shirt, the urge to somehow make Olawi pay for her words, was compelling. Instead, she swallowed her rage, took a single step forward and looked her straight in the eye.

'There won't be a next time,' she said calmly. 'Because, even without the huge amount of evidence we already have – this place is fully cctv'd up – and you've very kindly admitted your intent to kill my officer.'

🏵 🏵 🏵

Half an hour later, Charlie had calmed sufficiently to phone Paul, who was still on scene at the Olawi home. As a result of the assault on Naz, the flat was now a crime scene, so Kelvin Olawi had been allowed to leave, pending anything significant being found to bolster the partial fingerprint.

'How's it going, Paul?'

'It's been all quiet since Kelvin left. I half expected him to play up too, but he just sat here, as quiet as a mouse.'

'Guilty conscience. I bet he couldn't believe it when Constance and Wesley kicked off. If nothing else, it created a nice diversion to take the heat off him.'

'Knowing how the gangs work, they probably planned it that way.'

The thought had crossed her mind but, with the imminent arrival of a specialised search team and the

SOCO at the flat, it appeared to have backfired in their suspect's face. 'So, have you found anything interesting?'

'Yep, we've seized a load of stuff, mainly from Kelvin's bedroom. Several phones, a couple of baseball bats, a knuckle duster, handwritten lyrics taunting other gangs, drugs paraphernalia, and a few items of clothing and trainers, though none with any obvious blood stains.'

'Sounds promising.' Charlie was encouraged, but not overwhelmed. None of the stuff mentioned was illegal within the privacy of Olawi's home, though his phone might prove useful in ascertaining his movements, and the lyrics and weapons would be invaluable in showing his gang affiliation.

'We've also got an iPad of his which can be sent off for a download of YouTube and other social media. Wouldn't it be nice to find some footage of the Soldiers making threats to the Dons?'

'Hm, yes it would. It'll also help with identification of all the Soldiers – and probably a few of the other gangs. With any luck there'll be some interesting footage of 3D and the Dons, seeing as they're sworn enemies to each other.'

'There was loads,' Paul agreed. 'Looks like things have been brewing in this neck of the woods for some time.'

'Talking about the woods,' Charlie sat down at the desk and fired up the computer in the privacy of Hunter's side office, having decided, for the time being, to make use of it. 'I had a text from SOCO while everything was kicking off, asking me to check out an email she'd sent. Hang on.' She navigated a seemingly endless list of unread emails until she found it. 'Ah, here we go. She wants me to take a look at the exhibits, especially the knife. Apparently, it has a swirly pattern engraved on its handle which is quite distinctive.'

Clicking on the list of exhibits, she scrolled down through a number of sundry items found nearby; cigarette ends, screwed up Rizlas, a couple of empty fast food cartons, all of which would assist in identifying possible suspects or witnesses. Towards the bottom of the list was the exhibit to which the SOCO referred. It was a photograph of the bloody kitchen knife used to kill Rocco Fontana, the knife on which Kelvin Olawi's partial fingerprint had been found.

'Oh my God!' She couldn't quite believe what she was seeing. Quickly she pulled out her mobile phone, took a photo of the image and sent it on to Paul. 'Take a look at the pic I've just sent you Paul. I'm willing to bet ten quid that you'll find others the same as that in Constance Olawi's kitchen.'

'Hang on, Charlie. I'll take a look.' She waited, listening to the sounds of muffled movement as her colleague made his way to the kitchen. She could hear his breathing, heavy and staccato as he moved about, pulling open cupboards and drawers, poking around amongst the cutlery.

There was a sudden scuffling as Paul wedged the phone to his ear. It was quiet for a second, then... 'Bloody hell. It's only one of a set!' he said, excitedly. 'We might only have had a 1 in 60,000 chance of the partial fingerprint belonging to Kelvin Olawi, but with the rest of the set in his kitchen...' He gave a low whistle. 'He's going to have some explaining to do. No wonder he was so quiet.' He stopped talking suddenly. 'So, what made you so sure?'

Charlie sighed heavily. It didn't give her any pleasure to admit how she knew, but at least it would assist the murder investigation.

'Because the knife has the same pattern on it as the one that Constance used when she tried to kill Naz.'

Chapter 11

There was a folded notelet lying on the doormat when Charlie finally pushed open her front door that night. It bore a picture of a nightingale singing on the branch of a tree. Closing the door with her elbow she bent down and picked it up, smiling at the name on the bottom of the beautifully scribed message. It had been penned by the elderly lady in the flat below hers and it read.

Dear Charlie, I hope you don't think I'm speaking out of turn, but I was waiting for a friend to visit at lunchtime today and saw you go out. A little bit later, I saw a man hanging about outside the block. He was there for a long time, looking up towards your flat and moving about in the garden. Somehow, he managed to get in through the communal door and went up to yours. I don't know what he was doing but he stayed there for about half an hour before I saw him leave again.

I've been very worried as I know you've been having a bit of trouble lately - so I thought I'd let you know.

All the best
Olive x

For a second, she froze. Even though there was no description given of the man, there was absolutely no doubt in her mind it would've been her father. Not that she called him her father. He had given up the right to that title with his violent behaviour towards her mother and the torment he still put her through. The fact that he'd also killed a man made him someone she wanted nothing more to do with. In her mind he was far worse than any one of the boys in the gangs because, while they were mainly young and illiterate, he'd been older, educated and if her mother was to be believed, pure evil.

She opened the front door and peered into the hallway. 'Iain Frazer,' she called out. 'If you're still here, you'd better come out now. Or else I'll call the police.'

As she spoke, the irony of her threat didn't fail to amuse her. Even though she knew she'd struggle to deal with Frazer single-handedly, she *was* the police, so what the hell had happened to her? On duty, she was strong, decisive and fearless. Right now, she was shaking like a leaf and barely able to string two words together.

Silence.

Olive had said in her letter that she'd seen him leave but could he have returned? Her mind spun back to the previous morning, to her sense that her sailor bear was slightly askew. There had been no other sign to make her think he had actually entered her flat, so she had to believe he hadn't, but the antisocial nature of his actions was ramping up a level. Even if he was not physically threatening her, his behaviour was making her more nervous.

She pulled out her phone, keyed in her security code, then shut it down again. She couldn't worry her mother, and the team were all knackered. As for calling the on-duty uniform troops, what did she have to show for her report? A worried old neighbour, a teddy bear that may or may not have moved? A feeling of unease?

For a moment an image of her ex-boyfriend Ben flickered into her mind. What wouldn't she give to have him here now? He was physically strong, an ex-soldier, with solid muscles and a steely determination to do what was right. He would see her father off – but she had no way of making contact, and no idea where he might be.

She pushed the door shut and leant against it, her mind churning over the things to be done. First thing in the morning, she'd check in with Naz, go after Kelvin Olawi, and look to charge Constance – but before anything else she needed to sleep.

Walking to her bedroom, she stripped off her bloodstained shirt and other clothes before sinking into bed. It had been one hell of a day – and one she had no wish to relive. But much as she tried to sleep, she couldn't relax. Her eyes, though stinging and gritty with fatigue, remained stubbornly open; visions of her father leaning over her coming to mind. He was getting too close for comfort. Far too close.

Chapter 12

Franco Nannini squatted behind a wall and watched as Kelvin Olawi jogged out of the recreation ground and passed him, before falling in behind.

Franco Nannini was The General. He was well over six feet tall and built like the proverbial brick shithouse. He worked out night and day in the local gym, occasionally adding an afternoon session to his fitness regime. His body was therefore eye-catchingly toned, and entirely deserving of the head-turning admiration he usually received. It was inked from head to toe in striking tattoos – his most recent zombie knife tat displayed with pride, running up the muscles of his neck to a spot just underneath his jaw. He was second only to 3D in the Dons hierarchy and he maintained his position simply by his sheer size and presence.

One day he would succeed 3D to the top of the pile, but for now that would have to wait.

Tonight, he'd been specially selected for a job. Tonight, it was his job to follow Boxer; to house him and to let his leader know the boy's whereabouts. The boy had wronged the Dons. He had wronged Boy Blue. Boxer had killed one of theirs.

So now, Boxer was his prey – and how sweet it was seeing him alone. In fact, Franco couldn't believe his luck – but he wasn't taking anything for granted. The recreation ground was the Soldiers' favourite hangout, deep in their territory, so without doubt there would be scouts around, checking for the enemy. He may be as strong as an ox, as fast as a big cat, as sly as a fox, but his skin was no match for a knife or a bullet.

No, Franco knew the score and he was therefore travelling suitably armed. He'd slipped in and out of front gardens to then lie in wait in one of the streets that led from the rec, hoping that when the Soldiers finished their meeting, they would leave by that route. It was beyond his wildest dreams to see his target, vulnerable and unguarded.

Franco broke into a trot, maintaining a safe distance, as he matched pace with Boxer, who was keeping a good speed and didn't seem overly worried about his presence. In fact, his prey didn't seem to be showing much attention to anyone else either; the young couple with arms draped around each other who stopped to watch his steady progress, the like-minded jogger with a Union flag cap, the pair of drunken friends, laughing and staggering home after a good night out. He was running as if he hadn't a care in the world.

But soon Boxer would care. The General and 3D would make sure of that. Soon the boy would feel the cold hard metal of a knife ripping through his flesh, and watch his own bright red blood spreading over his ebony skin. Soon Boxer would experience exactly what he had inflicted on Boy Blue.

He was turning left, then right, then right again into Chester Avenue, heading into a slightly more affluent part of SW18, with small terraced houses set along straight roads intersected by other streets in a grid. He smiled to himself as Boxer reduced his speed. With the periphery of the Soldiers' territory nearing, the number of possible defenders would decrease and any still present would become less able to so readily respond. He slowed too, stealing past a small cherry tree at the side of a driveway, his feet skidding slightly on some overripe windfall.

He squatted down behind the bonnet of a smart new Range Rover and watched as his target came to a halt outside a derelict property. The windows were boarded up and the side gate was hanging haphazardly. He saw the boy glancing up and down the street, apparently waiting for the last few weekend stragglers to move on past, before tiptoeing along the overgrown front pathway and vanishing into the rear.

He listened to the sound of a door scraping open – then shutting again, and he couldn't help grinning as he saw the tiny glint of torchlight moving around behind the splintered boarding of the front room windows. The house had been shrouded in darkness until Boxer had entered and appeared to be empty.

Scanning the nearby doors, he worked out the address of the house, then took his phone from his pocket.

'3D it's me. I know where Boxer is now.' He leant back against the tree, rubbing the zombie knife tattoo on his neck, his jaw moving up and down excitedly as he relayed the address and explained everything he'd seen.

'And...' he could barely contain his pleasure. '...it looks like he's all on his own.'

Chapter 13

'If you live by the sword, you die by the sword.'

The words broke into his dreams, or were they part of them? Kelvin Olawi didn't know. Opening his eyes wide didn't help. It was pitch black inside the derelict house, and the air was thick with danger. He blinked, trying to focus as an even darker shadow moved across his line of vision. The shadow morphed into the shape of a man. The man moved slightly. He heard a click. For a split second he thought it was the trigger of a gun being cocked, that any second his brains would be splattered against the dirty fabric of the sofa on which he laid. That he would die there, alone.

But there was no loud explosion, no crack of a bullet, no deadly thud as it entered his skull.

Instead, there was light – intense, blinding light – aimed directly at his face. His hands shot up automatically to guard his eyes, as his pupils recoiled into tiny pinpricks. Large blurry spots floated across his eyeline. He could see nothing now, not even the shape of the man.

'Who are you?' he croaked, but his throat was dry and he could barely move his lips. The man made no reply. Kelvin licked his lips and was about to ask again when he realised it didn't matter. This man, whoever he was, was going to kill him. What difference did it make knowing the identity of his assassin?

He pushed himself against the cushions of the sofa; in that instant marvelling at his own stupidity. How could he have persuaded his friends that he wouldn't be found? How could he have thought he could break the cycle or that he wouldn't be hunted down and killed? It was the way it was in their world.

He screwed his fists against his eyes, trying to erase the spots, to see with some clarity, but as soon as he cleared the haze, so his eyes filled instead with tears – for the father he never knew, for his mother so defiantly proud despite everything, and for his little brother Wesley who was so young, so impulsive, so determined to follow in his footsteps. He'd tried to be a good son, and a good brother, but it was so hard when you had nothing. He let out a sob, swallowed it back, choked on his tongue, opened his lips. He was fucking crying.

'Not such a big man now, are you Boxer?' the man taunted.

'Who are you,' he asked again.

The man shifted the torch, tilted it to one side, lifted an object into its beam. The object took his breath away. It was made of strong grey gunmetal, with a deadly sharp tip at the end of a long, serrated blade, and it glinted hideously in the spotlight.

'Who do you think I am?' the voice drawled.

The light swung away from the blade of the zombie knife, focussing instead on a spot on his chest. The man stepped forward, crowding in on him, filling his personal space. He wanted to scream for the shape to move back, get away from him, leave him be, but the seconds were compacting, the moments melting together.

He was a sitting target. He'd switched off his replacement phone to stop the feds tracking him after he'd left his mates at the rec, so he had no way to summon help quick. He tried to get to his own blade, kept ready in his pocket, to even up the battle – but it was too late, far too late. Time was draining away. It was almost gone.

He opened his mouth to scream at the sight of the man's arm, stretched up above him, the zombie knife grasped tightly in a black gloved hand, but his voice had shrunk to a whimper.

As the knife was plunged deep into his heart, Kelvin Olawi's eyes widened in pain, coming to rest for a final time on his executioner's masked face. He frowned in confusion, concentrating on the cold eyes returning his stare. The man's face blurred as his eyes filled with splashes of his own blood. He choked back a crimson tide, as images of his mother at the kitchen sink, and Wes screaming out in his defence sprung to mind – but the chance to fight was gone.

And as the man continued to slash at him with a separate blade, he recognised only too well the distinctively shaped handle of the zombie knife wedged inside his ribs. He could hear the blood gurgling in his throat as his breathing slowed to a halt and his mind became still.

He might not know for certain the identity of his killer but there was no mistaking his message.

Chapter 14

'Where the fuck can he be?' Charlie paced across the office floor angrily.

It was the beginning of a new week, and two days had elapsed since Kelvin Olawi had gone to ground – and they still had no idea where he might be. 'I just wish we'd brought him in when we had him at his home address.'

Everything about the warrant was coming back to haunt her.

'Don't let me ever be influenced by a senior officer again.' She aimed the comment at Paul but said it as much to herself as anyone else in the room. 'Except for Hunter, that is.' Her absent boss's warnings were still ringing in her ears, though thankfully Naz had been released from hospital the previous day and was well on her way to a full recovery.

No, the responsibility for her decision was ultimately down to her and, though well-intentioned, it had been proven flawed. She'd fucked up. The discovery that the murder weapon was part of a set in Constance Olawi's kitchen had come too late, and with no arrest or enforceable bail conditions, Kelvin had simply decided the address to which he'd been released wasn't for him.

So, now they were running around like headless chickens trying to track him down.

Their usual avenues were proving inadequate. Their informants were regaling them with rumours but nothing specific about his current location. The Dons were boasting that they'd taken him out in revenge for killing Boy Blue – but without proof, the Soldiers believed they were talking bullshit. But then the Soldiers were not producing him either.

'Have we got anything back on Kelvin Olawi's phone data yet, the one we seized on the house search?'

'We've identified numbers for Mak 10 and Wesley Olawi from it and they've both been making calls to a new number. It's a cheap, unregistered Nokia which Kelvin could have bought as an interim replacement. Especially if he knows we're after him.'

'And...' Charlie rotated her arm in impatience. 'For God's sake Paul. Don't leave us hanging. Where is it now?'

'If I knew that I'd have told you straight away.' Paul looked mildly put out. 'The last location we can find for it was on Southfields recreation ground at 00.18 early Saturday morning – then nothing.'

'Nothing? So, he switched it off?'

'Yep, looks like it. They all know it's the first thing we'll check these days to catch them out committing crime.'

'Or on the run from one.' Charlie looked up at the image of Kelvin Olawi on the board and frowned. 'I'll jack up a search team to scour the recreation ground in that case. It's one of the Soldiers' favourite meeting spots.' She turned back to Paul. 'And there's been nothing more to or from that number since Saturday morning?'

'Nope.' Paul shook his head. 'There have been dozens of calls made to it but none that have been answered. It's stayed switched off – and we haven't found any other possible numbers. The Soldiers have been filling the airwaves with calls though.'

'Trying to locate Boxer?'

'Maybe. It is strange he hasn't popped his head up – if for no other reason than to show 3D and the Dons up as liars.'

'Do you think that the Soldiers might actually not know where he is?' She was mulling over the possibility. 'He was pretty quiet the other day at his flat – but he didn't seem to particularly care that we were coming after him.'

'So why hide completely?'

'Because, now he's heard we seized the set of knives, he's worried we're getting closer?' Paul stretched out his arms and yawned.

'Could be the Dons have him?' Sabira sauntered across to Charlie. 'Remember in Lambeth when we had that spate of gang kidnappings?'

'Yes, I remember, Sab – but Kelvin Olawi is second in command of the Soldiers. You'd think if the Dons had him, they'd be bragging by now, or would have at least asked for a ransom.'

'True, but they didn't always, or at least not straight away. They kept their victims chained up until they were filthy dirty and starving, then recorded them being humiliated and posted the recordings all over the internet a few days later.'

They lapsed into silence while Charlie thought through the possible repercussions.

'Well, if Kelvin Olawi has been kidnapped, then we can assume that his life is under threat...' She paused and turned to stare at the wall of faces. 'And the most likely suspects will be the Dons. So, let's get the phone records of 3D and Franco Nannini, their top two, looked at. Let's see where they've been and what they've been up to in the last few days.'

Chapter 15

The woman stepped off of the bus and stared up at the high brick walls, topped with razor wire in front of her.

High Down prison was situated in a leafy part of Surrey, far away from the council estates of Lambeth. Here, there were trees, woods, open spaces, fresh air. It was like nothing she'd ever known before – apart from what she'd seen in pictures, or on the TV.

The colours seemed so vivid in real life. Unbelievably so.

For a full minute she stood taking in the scenery; the sound of birdsong replacing the dull rumble of traffic; the smell of diesel and decay substituted by the strange sweet scent of grass and wild flowers. The air even tasted more wholesome.

In the main, her life had been dirty and dank. With the exception of a few brighter interludes, all her recollections were of grey; grey walls, grey estates, grey skies, strained grey faces. And anger. She'd known so much anger – too much anger – and now it had infected her too. She was filled with the rage of a shattered life, a rage so all-consuming that nothing, and no one, could exorcise the wrath from her heart.

Except Mia.

Her little girl would have loved this. Her little girl would have grown big and strong and independent if only she'd been gifted the opportunity of a life lived here. If only she hadn't been taken away.

A pair of wood pigeons startled in the tree up in front, hoisting their chubby bodies upwards into the blue sky. Her mind flew to the picture on her wall. The scene painted within its wooden frame wasn't so different to this, nor was it too far away from where she now stood. She closed her eyes to the beauty of her surroundings, understanding with the snap of a twig underfoot that it was out of reach to the likes of her. It was only attainable to rich folks, like her friend. Not to her, or her child. And it wasn't fair.

It wasn't fair on her, and it wasn't fair on Mia, and she hated inequality. So, over the last few weeks, she'd initiated the first tentative steps in making it happen. She'd weaned herself off the worst of her gear, and she'd made her bedsit slightly more respectable. If the authorities still refused to listen, then she would make them – but she needed a bargaining tool. So, she'd scoped out the school her friend's child attended, her route home, her best buddy's house… and she'd dared to dream.

This first phase just had to go to plan.

Unwinding the band from her hair, she shook out her blonde locks in the gentle breeze, allowing each strand to loosen and become free. Properly free. Her hair was clean and citrusy fresh. She'd washed it this morning especially for the trip. In fact, she'd bathed her whole body, applied a mask of makeup and taken care in her choice of clothes. She knew exactly the type he liked, and today she was anxious to please.

At 2.30 p.m. precisely, the prison gate swung open. Not the huge heavy steel one, but the small door within it. She watched as it opened; the surrounding portal emphasising the pitifully small victory she'd achieved in getting him out. Justice might have been done – at least as far as he was concerned – but nobody would be rejoicing at his release. Two murders would remain unsolved. Two families would mourn the inequality of the justice system. One murderer would remain at large.

But that was life. That was her life.

Exactly two minutes later he appeared at the door. She heard the screw wishing him well, telling him not to return, that they didn't want to see him again. She'd heard the same sentiment on many occasions before. Empty words. He'd be back. He couldn't help himself. At some point in the future, he'd be driven back into the holding bay, marched through the numerous security gates and into prisoner reception. He'd be searched, showered and put in a cell. It was only a matter of time – so she had to make good use of the days, or perhaps weeks, that they had.

She stared at the man she had once, in her own way, loved. He hadn't changed much at all, except for bulking out in the gym. His skull remained closely shaved, the flesh of his face and head pockmarked and rough, with a thin layer of stubble peppering his chin and neck. The scar across his right cheek drew the skin into a thin jagged crevice, starting at his eye and slashing down to his mouth.

A thin plastic bag, looped loosely from one bulky shoulder, held his life's endeavours. It was almost empty, the mark of a wasted existence – but she didn't care. He might not have achieved much until now, but all that had changed. Mia was his achievement – their achievement. Their baby girl was the one good thing to have come from their relationship. Mia now had a father and a mother; a family who cared.

Unbidden, a frisson of fear shuddered down her spine.

She watched from beside a tree as he stood blinking in the light, his dark eyes ranging across the pavement. He hadn't spotted her yet and she had no idea of his mood. Would he forgive her, or would he want revenge? Had she, yet, forgiven him?

The next few hours would be fraught.

Stepping out from behind the tree she stood tall, sucking in her stomach and sticking out her breasts. Her clothing was sparse, thin and gaudy, a blatant attempt to take his mind off settling scores. She understood men – she understood him.

'Hi babe,' she called, strutting towards him and draping her arms around his neck. She felt him tense, the muscles of his shoulders and neck tightening against her embrace. It was a response she knew only too well, the eerie uncertain calm – before a fist explodes in your face. 'I thought I'd come and collect you. You know. Bring you back to mine, babe. I've got my own place now.' She was babbling. 'You look fit,' she tried again, relaxing into his body and pushing her chest into his. The seconds lengthened. It felt as if her whole life and that of her child hung in the balance. 'You know that I want you, babe.'

Nothing.

Desperately, she ground her hips into his, in a final, blatant attempt to win him over. He paused, the vein on his forehead bulging ominously, then she felt him respond. 'That's better,' she smiled. It was beginning to work. 'Let's go for a walk in the woods.'

She let the fingers of one hand slip down and skim against the hardening in his groin, before taking his arm with the other and easing him firmly away from the high grey gates of the prison. 'Come with me,' she stretched up, brushing his neck with her lips, sensing him shudder. Her strategy was taking effect, and suddenly she was grinning from ear to ear.

Perhaps she wouldn't have to rely on her backup plan after all.

Perhaps her dream might become a reality. She hadn't forgotten how to play him, and as his steps became ever more eager, she led him by the balls into a nearby glade, and greeted his homecoming against the trunk of a tree.

Chapter 16

Charlie stared down at the mutilated corpse of yet another teenager. It hadn't taken long to work out what had happened once the phone data had come in from Franco Nannini's mobile. Also, with only one derelict property in the whole of Chester Avenue, it hadn't taken too many guesses to figure out where Kelvin Olawi might be.

'Bloody hell, what a mess,' she mumbled, wrinkling up her nose at the stench. She and Paul had been the first ones to enter the boarded-up house, her sense of smell leading them to the discovery far quicker than any sixth sense. 'That's someone's son.' Her mind flew to the snarling, screaming face of the woman who'd stabbed Naz a few days previously. 'In fact, that's Constance's son – and he's only eighteen. Or was.' She imagined in that moment how his mother's surly expression would be exchanged for one of grief. 'Whatever people might think about Constance Olawi, or the gangs, I wouldn't wish this on anyone.'

'Me neither.' Paul shone his torch about the blood-spattered room, bringing it to rest on the large zombie knife still embedded in the dead boy's chest. 'Looks like the Dons have avenged Boy Blue. It's the same knife as on their tattoos.'

'Yep. But why cut him to pieces?' she asked, her arm passing through the air over Kelvin Olawi's dead body in incredulity. His clothing was ripped to pieces and slash marks disfigured almost every inch of his visible skin.

'The zombie knife *must* have been the cause of death, judging by its position – straight through his heart – so why all the other injuries. He must have dozens of slash marks, Paul.' She took a step backwards. 'I can't understand the need for this much violence.'

'Nor me, Charlie, but it certainly rams home their message.'

'What? That the Dons are brutal? As if we didn't know that. But the circumstances also show up their stupidity.' Charlie exhaled loudly. 'They might like to think they're clever, tailing their victim here, but Franco Nannini is clearly not as smart as his phone.'

It was what had led them there. At 23.23, Franco Nannini's mobile was located close to Southfields Recreation ground, and it had stayed in situ until approximately 00.20 early on Saturday morning – two minutes after Kelvin Olawi's mobile had been switched off in the very same park. Nannini's phone had then been tracked around several streets, finishing up opposite where they were now standing, in Chester Avenue. Franco Nannini had been caught red-handed, deep in the Soldiers' territory and there could be only one reason for that... Revenge.

In addition to the phone tracking, the record showed he'd also made a call to 3D's phone from Chester Avenue at 00.29, nine minutes after he'd left the rec. The call lasted for two minutes, enough time to give a quick rundown of Kelvin Olawi's movements and supply details of his current location. Five minutes later he'd moved off.

Paul's brow was furrowed in concentration. 'So, we can put him nearby, but we can't actually prove he was inside here as yet. And I doubt in the short amount of time before his phone leaves the area, he'd have had time to do all this.'

'I agree.' Charlie swung her torch around the room focussing this time on the boarding and open door. 'It's much more likely that Nannini was the scout, sent out to locate their target. Once done, he phones it in and legs it home where his phone—'

'And 3D's.' Paul interrupted.

'Yep, and 3D's, are shown safely tucked up for the night. As usual they're happy to have their phones for the preliminaries but when the murderer, most probably Nannini and/or 3D came back it was without their phone – and at least a few hours later.'

'How'd you work that one out?'

'Because Olawi is lying on the settee and was almost certainly fast asleep when his attacker entered – so it won't have happened within five minutes of his arrival. No, I reckon he's been taken completely by surprise, with no time to react, probably because he thought he was safe here. He hasn't even had time to get to his feet, otherwise he'd be on the floor somewhere else.'

'And...' Paul aimed his torch beam along the edge of the settee and around the floor at its base. '...there's no sign of his phone or weapon, unless they've been stolen?'

'They won't have been stolen. I'd say the attack was so quick and unexpected, I doubt he even had time to reach for his phone, never mind switch it back on or call for help. I bet when he's searched, we'll find it tucked in his pocket, along with some type of blade. There's no way he'd have been unarmed.'

They stood for a few moments in silence, mulling over the young man's murder.

'He was a sitting duck. The person, or persons, who did this, must have thought it was their lucky day tracking him down so easily. Boxer has been executed where he lay. He wouldn't have stood a chance.'

'KO'd in the first round,' Paul agreed.

'Yep,' Charlie turned and headed towards the door, flashing her torchlight against the frame, and out towards the roadway outside. 'But who is responsible? Could be any one of the Dons, or another rival with a grudge. We've certainly got our work cut out mate.'

❋ ❋ ❋

It took no time at all for Charlie to get the crime scene arrangements underway. Chester Road was in a residential area, so apart from a few of the residents coming out to express shock, a large section of the road was swiftly cordoned off, with uniform officers posted to strategic points. As well as sealing off the derelict house they also had to locate any possible reconnaissance sites for Franco Nannini. Mobile phone positioning data was good, but it wasn't pinpoint perfect – and there was always the possibility it hadn't been Nannini himself in possession of the phone. So, any help with fingerprints, DNA or CCTV would be very welcome. Charlie hated smoking and litter but she always cheered when a fast food container, fag end, or discarded cigarette packet was found.

The force medical examiner arrived first, his stethoscope soon confirming what they already knew. Kelvin Olawi had been dead for some time and with rigor mortis beginning to subside, it was thought likely he had been silenced within hours of his phone.

The photographer came next, with spotlights, flashlights and high spec camera, illuminating the squalor of the room, the violence of the murder and the pathos of Olawi's broken body from every distance and every angle.

'Another boy,' Charlie commented, as the photographer was replaced by the SOCO, complete with his team of highly specialised forensic investigators.

'They all are,' the SOCO replied, bending down to examine the handle of the embedded knife. 'It looks like a zombie knife to me, but I don't believe it's the knife that has made the majority of the wounds,' he said, shining a torch at the slashes on the boy's legs and arms. 'Or that they were all made while the boy was still alive. Some wounds have a lot of blood around them signifying that his heart was still pumping when they were inflicted, but others have none, suggesting they were exacted after death. And they're too clean. The edges are sharp. If they'd been made with a serrated blade, like zombie knives have, the edges would be rougher. It's like the difference between a saw and a filleting knife, but the coroner will be able to give a more conclusive report.'

Charlie bent over, concentrating on one particular slash mark which ran across the top of Olawi's leg. 'I did wonder about that, but I presumed the killer had just used the one knife, and returned it to the boy's chest when he left.'

'Or when *they* left.'

Charlie's mind rewound to the phone call logged between Nannini and 3D. 'So we could be looking for two suspects?'

'Yes, you could. Two suspects with a knife each, or one suspect with two knives. Whichever it is, we're missing one of the murder weapons.'

With that in mind, Charlie called on the assistance of several dog handlers and a specialist team to search for the knife. It would be laborious work with every inch of the house and garden needing to be dissected and inspected. If the knife was there, it was her job to find it.

She was just finishing their briefing, a few yards from the house, when she looked up to see Ross McBride and his team pulling up. Ross was young, ambitious – and single, a fact that Paul had taken great pleasure in emphasising to her.

'We're here to conduct your house-to-house enquiries,' Ross smiled. 'After the warrant, we all wanted to make amends for not having prevented your officer being injured. We're here to help in any way we can with this investigation.'

'It wasn't your fault. It was mine.' It also hadn't escaped Charlie that if Kelvin Olawi had been prevented from leaving his flat during the course of the warrant, he wouldn't now be lying dead in a filthy, derelict house. Playing politics would never happen again on her watch, but with the imminent visit of Superintendent Woodall, the senior investigating officer on this case, it would remain to be seen whether he would take all, or even part of the blame. 'But thank you,' she said, knowing the answer already.

'We're all in this together,' Ross winked. 'If one officer gets injured, we all hurt. Now what can we do?'

'Find me a witness!' she smiled gratefully. Ross was a nice bloke and a good skipper, and it pleased her more than she'd expected, to know he was on her side. She turned to his team.

'You know what to do, but to be clear, I need you to speak to every person in each house, not only the one who opens the door, and make a note of which houses you get no reply at. We can try those again later. If anyone heard or saw anything – and I mean, anything – get their details. We need to know what they saw or heard and at what time. Franco Nannini is very distinctive, what with his size and tattoos. He's not called The General for nothing, and he's not someone you'd forget – so if it was him lurking about outside at any point, with or without 3D, then I want to know straight away.'

She shoved the thought of Supt Woodall to the back of her mind. The blame game could come later. For now, she had two murders to solve, including that of a suspected murderer, and it was her duty to explore every option, treating everyone as a possible suspect until proved otherwise.

'Oh, and check out if anyone has any private CCTV, a video doorbell or vehicle dash cams in operation. We're presuming 3D or Nannini are involved, but it could be any of the other Dons. Or someone we haven't thought of at all.'

Chapter 17

'Mum, pick up if you're there.'

It was her fifth time of trying and rather than wait for another set of unanswered ringtones, Charlie shouted out a message, threw a bag in the car and set off to her family home in Lingfield. Things had gone quiet around her flat, which could mean her good-for-nothing father might have transferred his attentions back to her mum.

It was like a sick game of ping pong.

Forty minutes later she was pulling up outside the house that she had lived in and loved for most of her life. The curtains were drawn in every room, but the lights were all on, visible through the gaps in the material, but Meg never had the house fully illuminated, being conscious to not waste energy. Charlie pulled on the handbrake feeling suddenly nervous. This house, this building, had always felt safe – a brick-built fortress of calm in times of trauma – so the knowledge that it now did not, seeped into her bones and filled her with dread.

Only in her first few years had she lived anywhere else and she remembered little of life before London. In a rare unburdening of their joint past, Meg had spoken of Charlie's birth in a slum tenement in Glasgow and how, over the first three years of Charlie's life, she'd lived in fear of her father. After the birth of her younger brother, Jamie, things had become impossible, so one night under cover of darkness, Meg had scooped up her two young children, with what meagre belongings she could carry, and headed south. A few torrid years followed, keeping their heads down in an equally ugly block of student housing in London, while her mother trained to be a nurse.

It was only with news of Frazer's incarceration could Meg finally relax and start to live. A whole new world opened up to the family with the addition of a step-father to Charlie and Jamie, and later, two half-sisters, and the move to Lingfield. The new house was large and airy, safe and secure. There'd been tragedy along the way, with the loss of Jamie in a seaside drowning accident, but it was still home.

She was thinking about Jamie as she climbed out of the car and gathered up her stuff. What would he have looked like had he still been alive? Would he have been tall and as ruggedly good-looking as Ben, or as camp as Paul? Or more disturbingly, would he have looked and behaved like Iain Frazer?

The sound of the TV blaring out through the closed windows brought an end to her musings. No wonder her mother had not heard her phone. Pulling out her keys she stomped across the gravel to the porch. 'Mum,' she shouted, opening the door wide.

Casper, their old black Labrador, padded across the hallway towards her, whipping his tail from side to side. 'You're not much of a guard dog are you, boy,' she said bending down to hug him fondly. 'But then I'm surprised you even heard me at all with this row going on. Mum, where are you?' she called again, standing up and looking around when there was no reply.

The lounge door was open and it was from this room that the majority of the noise was coming. The TV had to be on almost top volume.

'Bloody hell, Mum,' she shouted over the racket, glancing around the room to locate the remote control. 'What's going on?'

'Charlie?' Her mother's voice seemed to be coming from somewhere behind a large mountain of cushions.

'Are you all right Mum?' She rushed over to where her mother sat, curled up in the corner of the sofa, directly opposite the TV with her back to the door. Her legs were drawn up to her chest with only her face peeping out from the top of a maroon and cream chequered pad. In one hand she held the remote control, and in the other was a photo of her three daughters. Charlie prised the remote control gently from her hand and turned the volume down.

'What's happened?' she asked, taking her mother's free hand in hers.

'I can't bear it any more.'

'What's he done now?'

'That's the problem, Charlie. As usual he hasn't actually done much but he's here, all the time, goading me. I can't see him, but I can hear him, moving things around, little inconspicuous things that nobody else would notice. But I notice, Charlie.'

'Such as?' Such as what he'd done at her flat, the subtle touches that could only be him. She understood exactly what her mother meant without her saying a word.

'Well, yesterday I saw that one of my planters had been moved. Not by much, just enough to prompt me to go outside to push it back into position. When I looked at it, I was horrified. He'd dug out several of my bedding plants and replaced them with thistles, you know like he did in the beginning.'

She nodded. How could she forget her first introduction to the man who was her father, standing on the doorstep of her flat, unannounced, with a bunch of flowers, in the centre of which was a large thistle; the Scottish national emblem.

'And this evening, as it got dark, I heard the sound of bagpipes by the back door. I couldn't see anyone, but it was obviously him with a recording. I didn't go out. I didn't dare. I just made sure all the doors were locked.'

'Then switched on all the lights and turned the volume up on the TV.'

'Sound and light.' Meg unclasped her hand and put the photograph down, covering her ears up instead. She squeezed her eyes shut. 'It's always been my way of shutting out the world.'

'What you can't see or hear can't hurt you?' Charlie took her mother's hands from her ears, holding them both within hers.

Meg nodded miserably. 'I just want things over.' She picked up the photo frame of Charlie with her two half-sisters and walked across to the sideboard, placing it in its usual position. 'Lucy and Beth are due home from uni in a few weeks' time. I can't have him frightening them too, or worse...'

'Worse?'

Her mother frowned, before giving an almost imperceptible shake of her head. 'It's me that he wants – and he won't stop until he gets me. So, whatever he has in store for me, I want it done now.'

'Mum. Stop it.' Her mother was frightening her now. 'We'll go back to the local police and update them with his latest antics.'

'And tell them what?' Meg snorted. 'That there were thistles in my planter – and bagpipes playing outside my door? If they haven't already got me down as some sort of crazy woman they certainly would then.'

'I wish the Met covered this area. We'd get this place hooked up to all sorts of cameras and surveillance devices. Catch him in the act.' She shrugged hopelessly. The words were easy to say, but the reality wasn't correct. She'd discussed the possibility of doing just that at her own flat but, much as her father's campaign of harassment was unpleasant, it was insufficient to justify authorising surveillance. They were on their own.

'I really must try not to let him get to me, Charlie.' Her mother looked her straight in the eye, a thin smile signifying that she understood the truth. 'But he messes with my head.'

'I know he does.' She drew her mother into an embrace, at once shocked at how fragile she felt. Meg's shoulders drooped and her body was limp. Gone was the strong, fearless posture of old; the woman who had brought up her three daughters almost single-handedly, even when swamped with grief at the loss of a son.

She took a step backwards, her hands gripping her mum by the shoulders, willing her to stand tall, a thousand thoughts now bombarding her brain. What would Jamie have made of his father, or the situation? A vision swirled into her mind of him swimming upwards, straining for air, fighting until there was no breath left in his body and he could fight no more.

'You go and make a cup of tea, and I'll pop outside and check that he's not still around.'

Her mother started. 'No Charlie, you can't go out. You don't know what he's capable of.'

'No, I don't know what he's capable of...' The statement came out brusquer then she meant. 'But I do know, Mum, that he's not going to break us.'

❖ ❖ ❖

Charlie's heart was beating at breakneck speed as she stepped outside with Casper. The words so defiantly spoken a few minutes earlier were now lodged squarely at the back of her throat making it almost impossible to breathe. She still had no idea *exactly* what her father was capable of, and the lack of this knowledge was exasperating.

The sky was clear and the moon was a thin crescent as she moved around the perimeter of the house. Shadows leapt out at her, then retreated again as the light from her torch stabbed into every corner and crevice of the outbuildings. Until now, she hadn't realised there were so many dark places in which to hide and the large, heavy stick she gripped in her other hand did little to dilute her fear.

'I know you're out here, Iain Frazer,' she shouted, stopping to listen for an answer. Silence. 'Come out and show yourself if you dare.' The phrase made her suddenly grin. It was like the corniest comment, from the worst horror movie in the world, and one that she'd be raging against if she were the viewer. *What the hell do you think you're playing at? Don't go outside, you bloody idiot...*

A twig snapped somewhere at the end of the garden. Casper gave a low growl. She flicked her torch in the direction of the sound, the grin wiped instantaneously from her face. The beam of light spread out across the bushes, too weak and weedy to penetrate even the outermost foliage.

She heard a click, then the eerie squeal of bagpipes started up; the initial discordant wail gradually becoming melodic as a Highland lament threaded itself out across the lawn. The music wasn't loud, but it was there. Just as he was.

'What do you want from us?' The blood was pumping so loud in her ears she could barely hear her own voice. 'Either come out and tell me, or leave us alone.'

The ballad continued, but from one side of the garden came a rustling of leaves, the sound of footsteps coming closer, a low chuckle.

Her shadow tensed as the light from the kitchen window silhouetted her figure, two-dimensionally across the grass. She lifted a matchstick arm, shining the torch into the blackness. Sweat moistened her grip on the stick. 'This isn't a game, you bastard.'

'Isn't it?' His accent was strong. 'Who says it's nae a game?'

'I say it's not.'

'Well it's nae yer decision, missy. It's mine – and I say it is.' The footsteps retreated along the edge of the fence. The recording switched off and the garden became still. 'So ye'd best be prepared. Ye have nae idea what's coming to ye next.'

Chapter 18

Franco Nannini stood flexing his biceps in a tight-fitting black T-Shirt. The neckline was low, allowing the zombie knife tattoo to protrude from the fabric straight up the side of his neck. Ross McBride and his team had brought him in earlier, on suspicion of murder, and he'd barely said a word. Beside him at the custody desk was his brief; half his size but with twice the influence. Charlie watched from one side, eying their suspect up and down. It was the first time she'd seen The General in the flesh and he certainly was huge. Up until his solicitor's arrival, he'd refused to sign a thing – but that was his prerogative and there was no skin off her nose.

'Sign here, here and here.' The custody officer pointed to three separate sections on the monitor screen; rights, medical, and property. His brief gave a nod and Nannini stretched out, scribbling his name on the electronic pad. Three signatures. Three illegible squiggles, but was she imagining it, or had his hand shaken as he'd made them?

Charlie perked up. Last night's confrontation had not only stopped her sleeping, it had filled every waking moment with worry. Should she return to the family home temporarily and endure the extra journey, or transfer Meg up to her small but secure flat and sleep on the couch, or move her to a completely different location? Whichever path she chose would bring less sleep and more hardship, even taking into account the distinct possibility that her mother would refuse to leave her home unoccupied. Somehow, though Charlie had to shield her mother.

'Come this way, Franco.' She tucked the decision away at the back of her mind and ushered him towards an interview room. There would be time for discussion later. Right now, she had to focus. She winked at Paul as they settled in and went through the preliminaries. She had a good feeling about this. Nannini was nervous. He was fidgeting in his chair, rubbing his hands together, unable to settle. If she could only take advantage of his unease and goad him into talking then they might actually get somewhere.

'No comment' the usual stock reply to her first line of questions dampened her spirits.

No comment, no comment, no comment. The answers came in quick succession and her initial enthusiasm drained away, but she had to persevere. The allegations had to be set out in interview, and whether she liked it or not he could choose how he wished to reply.

'Franco,' she took a deep breath. They were coming to the end of her interview notes. 'You do realise this is your opportunity to give us your side of the story. Now, before I conclude this session is there anything you want to say. You don't have to follow the advice of your solicitor.'

Nannini blinked, and looked questioningly towards his brief. He shifted in his seat, his huge frame straining against the arms of his chair.

'Can I?' His voice was a low growl, but his eyes were wide, like a schoolboy searching out his teacher for permission to speak.

The solicitor shook his head 'I'd advise you not to say anything.'

'You might not get another chance,' she threw the comment in, like a small incendiary device.

He wiped his hands on his knees, and his lips twitched slightly.

'Franco, we know you were there.' She piled on the pressure. 'We have your phone records. We know that you followed Boxer.' A thin film of sweat was prickling on his forehead. He reached up and wiped it away on the back of his hand. 'And we know that you phoned 3D from right outside where Boxer was murdered.'

He was like an animal caught in the headlights. 'But it weren't me that killed him,' he suddenly blurted out.

'So who was it then Franco?' She leant forward; her expression daring him to explain. 'It was a Zombie knife that was stuck right through his heart, wasn't it? Just like the one drawn on your neck.'

His hand flew to the tattoo, his fingers rubbing against the skin, stretching out his palm to cover the ink.

'Was it your knife, Franco?'

'No it weren't mine, I swear.'

'So there'll be none of your prints or DNA found on it?'

Nannini's brow creased in a frown. His eyes widened further, panic-stricken. 'I said it weren't mine.'

'So it must be 3D's. You phoned him up, and you told him where to find Boxer.'

He was shaking his head vehemently now.

'Or perhaps you both came back together to make sure you did the job properly? Poor Boy Blue, felled by the mighty Soldiers. You had to avenge him, didn't you? You even said so in the note you Dons left outside his door. What was it you said?' She read from her notes. 'Ah yes, here it is. *You will not be forgotten. Revenge will be ours.* You believed it was Boxer that took out your boy, didn't you?'

'Only 'cause *you* did.' Nannini stretched out one arm, pointing at Charlie. 'You thought it was 'im too, otherwise you wouldn't've gone to his house.'

'So was it you and 3D, Franco?' She had him cornered and she wasn't going to let him slip away by deflecting the blame onto them. 'That's what the word on the street out there says.' She picked up an intelligence report and read from it. 'Nickname 3D and nickname The General killed nickname Boxer in revenge for the killing of nickname Boy Blue. The Dons are boasting that they cannot be beaten.'

'3D might be boasting, 'cause that's what 3D does. He's always tryin' to big up the reputation of the Dons but it weren't us – an' it definitely weren't me. I swear on my mother's life.' He dipped his head and gave the sign of the cross. 'I might 'ave followed Boxer to that house, an' I might 'ave phoned 3D but I never went back. We was as surprised as anyone when we heard he was dead.'

Chapter 19

'What do you reckon then Paul?' Charlie leant back in her chair.

'He was lying because he knew he'd been caught out.' The pair of them had returned to the office, where Bet was making them all a brew. 'If it wasn't him then it must have been 3D, or someone sent by him. And if that's the case then he's still guilty of conspiracy to murder. Who else would have known Olawi's location unless they'd been told by Nannini? Even the Soldiers didn't know where he was, or else they'd have produced him.' Paul threw his bag down on his desk and rummaged inside for some gum, offering a piece to Charlie first then throwing two in his mouth. 'Nah. Nannini's well in it. He's guilty as hell.'

'I'm not so sure, Paul.' She popped the gum into her mouth and started to chew. 'It's rare that we get any conversation out of the gangs, never mind one of the top boys admitting that he'd tracked our victim down. He didn't have to say that. He could have claimed someone else had his phone and that it wasn't him. As yet we've got no one who can actually identify him.'

'He still informed 3D though. That must be conspiracy.'

'But there weren't any calls between them after that – until mid-morning. Nor were there any calls onwards from 3D's phone.'

'Well not on that phone maybe, but it doesn't mean he doesn't have another mobile, or several come to think of it.

You're not telling me that after identifying that their enemy was lodged in a derelict house all alone, that they both then went to bed?'

Charlie frowned. 'I don't know Paul. Perhaps they thought it would be too obvious if he was killed straight away, especially knowing, only too well, that the first thing we'd check would be their phones.' She paused, pushing the gum to the side of her mouth. 'Maybe having housed him, they'd decided to put it off for a day or so. I think there's something weird going on.'

Paul spat his gum out in a tissue, as Bet approached with a tray full of teas. He selected a mug and piled two spoonfuls of sugar into it, grinning weakly as he did so. 'Sorry, I need the extra energy, and it looks as if you do too, Sarge.' He smiled as he handed one to Charlie. 'Either that or you must be going soft. Stop worrying. Nannini's bang to rights.'

But he wasn't bang to rights, and Charlie knew it.

Slumping down into her chair in Hunter's office she mulled over what they had. A bit of preliminary evidence. A partial admission. One murder weapon. And a lot of loose talk. There was fuck all else.

They were waiting for everything – and anything. Forensics, phone data, cameras.

Worse than that. With nothing more concrete to keep Nannini locked up, in the next half an hour they'd be releasing their main murder suspect back onto the streets. God knows what would happen then. After Kelvin Olawi's early death, she was dubious whether he'd even survive the night.

If the threats circulating were to be believed, it was only a matter of time before full scale war broke out on the streets of SW19 and they were powerless to stop it happening.

She leaned back, yawning and rubbing her eyes, her thoughts returning to Iain Frazer. From experience, the problem with her father would only get worse. The question was, how much worse?

Picking up the phone she dialled Anna Christophe, her counsellor. Perhaps her psychologist could shed some light on the behaviour of stalkers. She'd come highly recommended to Charlie by Caz, a local prostitute they'd both known in their professional capacity. Anna had counselled the young woman, and helped Ben with his PTSD, as well as giving her a few psychological pointers in several challenging cases. Charlie considered her as much a friend as a professional ear.

'Hello, Anna Christophe speaking. How can I help?'

'Hi Anna, it's Charlie Stafford here. Long time, no speak.'

'Charlie. It's lovely to hear from you.' Her tone was warm and it was immediately clear that she meant what she'd said. 'How are you?'

'I'm fine, Anna. How are you?'

'Busy, busy, busy. I've got more clients than I can handle and kids that scream for my attention every spare minute when I'm home.'

'Have you heard from Ben?' She couldn't resist the temptation. Ever since her ex-boyfriend had disappeared to 'clear his head' she'd been desperate to phone Anna to ask if she knew where he was. With Anna being his emotional crutch, there was every chance they were still in contact.

'Come on Charlie. You know I can't answer that. It's confidential.'

'Well say hello when he calls.' She grinned to herself. She could well imagine the look on the psychologist's face.

'What are you like!' Anna's voice rose an octave. 'You don't change. So how are you really?'

'I'm honestly fine, thank you Anna. Just working on an interesting case. I was wondering if I could pick your brains.'

'Ah. I didn't think it would be social.'

Charlie laughed. 'You know me too well.' Anna had spent much of their previous encounters trying to persuade her to talk through the death of her brother, but Charlie was as stubborn as her mother. Some things were better left buried.

'So what do you need to know?'

'Is a domestic stalker likely to go on to kill?'

'Wow. That's like asking me how long is a piece of string. It depends on so many variables. Without naming names, give me a potted history.'

'Okay, well, our suspect is a male, in his late fifties, Glaswegian, with a history of violence. I don't know too much about his formative years but when he was twenty-three, he had a relationship with a girl of sixteen. The relationship was abusive. He was coercive, controlling and violent. They stayed together for about five years and had two children, but in the end the woman escaped, taking their children with her, and fled to London.

'A short time afterwards, the male was involved in a pub brawl and stabbed another man to death. He was sentenced to life and has been in prison ever since. He's served pretty much all the recommended thirty years due to violent attacks on prison staff and other inmates but was released on licence a few months ago.

'Since then, he's tracked down his ex-partner and daughter and has been stalking them both.'

'And his other child?'

'Unfortunately, dead.'

'So...' Anna paused, obviously taking in the rather blunt reply. 'What sort of behaviour has he been exhibiting recently?'

'Well, he started off with flowers and apologies, trying to persuade his ex-partner and daughter that he was sorry for everything and they should take him back – but when they refused, he changed. His pleas for forgiveness have turned to abuse and he's alternating between stalking each of them. So far, he's done relatively innocuous things, moving stuff about, playing music, messing with their heads but last night he was outside the mother's house, making threats.

'So it's gradually escalating.'

'Yes, it seems that way.'

'And what are the police doing?'

She paused. What were they doing? 'Not a lot,' she admitted. 'So far, apart from a minor breach of his licence for not staying at his registered address, he's only really done trivial stuff. He keeps himself hidden, and moves around mainly at night, so we can't properly identify him, and the offender rehabilitation unit in Glasgow don't want to know re the breach of licence because he's not in their jurisdiction any more. So this guy can do what he wants. And now he seems to want more. How far do you think he's likely to go?'

The line went quiet. Charlie pushed the phone to her ear, desperately running through their previous conversations. Had she spoken of her childhood to Anna? Could Anna have worked out the identity of the mystery man? She didn't really want to risk any awkward questions.

'He could go all the way.' Anna's tone was serious. 'Stalking a former spouse or partner is the most prevalent – and it's also the most dangerous. Ex-intimates are at the greatest risk of all stalking victims.

'Précising what we know, there are seven types of stalker, and I would say that your man fits into at least three of the categories. *Domestic*, i.e. he's terrorising a former partner; *Lust*, he's moving from one victim to the next, possibly with a sexual motive, and *Love-scorned*, i.e. he desires an intimate relationship with at least one of his victims but he's rebuffed. He might even be suffering from erotomania, which is a delusional disorder where the stalker believes his victims are actually in love with him.'

'Well, that last one's certainly not the case.'

'But.' Anna ignored her rather flippant remark and went on. 'It's important to remember that only about a third of stalking allegations actually result in physical assaults and only a tiny percentage of those result in murder. I'm giving you the worst-case scenario here. In most cases the offender will gradually lose interest, or move on, especially if there's intervention by members of the judicial system or mental health specialists.

'As a matter of interest, was your man a substance abuser, do you know?'

'I'm not sure I'm afraid,' Charlie mulled over what to say about her mother's refusal to speak in detail about him. 'The woman is a bit reticent to say exactly what he did, or didn't do, when they were together, but you know, as well as I do, that drugs are widely available in prisons so I wouldn't be surprised if he took some to get by, especially given his violence. I'll try to find out. Why?'

'Because there's evidence to suggest that stalkers with prior criminal convictions and/or a history of substance abuse are more likely to go on to commit more serious offences. 'But...' Anna paused. 'Remember Charlie, the majority of stalking goes on over the internet these days, and like I say, two thirds of cases *don't* involve violence.'

'What about stalkers who have had thirty years planning what to do? You know, the ones who've sat brooding in their cells deciding that they can't live without their families – and their families won't be allowed to live without them?'

'Well, I certainly wouldn't dismiss the possibility that your man could turn killer.' Their conversation was interrupted by a knock on the door. Paul was peering through the glass panel at her. 'But odds on he won't.'

Chapter 20

'Relax, babe.' The woman stayed her partner from raging at the receptionist for a third time, her hand hot against his thigh. Their appointment time was long since gone, the half-hour wait to see her social worker having doubled in length since they'd first taken their seats.

The waiting room was like a fridge, the air conditioning unit in the corner of the room churning out wave after wave of cold, clammy air, in a futile attempt to dampen the tempers of those sat fretting.

'For fuck's sake,' his usual low growl was tinged with menace. 'They're taking the piss.' She felt his muscles tighten, saw the set of his jaw, the vein bulging in his forehead. 'And no one takes the piss out of me.'

He yanked her hand from his leg and shot to his feet, his fists flexing and balling.

'We're ready for you now.' A large man appeared at the door to a dingy-looking room off the main lobby. 'I'm Larry. We're sorry to have kept you waiting. Won't you please come through.'

'About time too.' He exhaled noisily; his brows still creased with rage but his hands relaxed. She rose to her feet, taking one of his huge palms in hers. His fingers folded around hers, squeezing them hard. 'This had better be worth my while,' he whispered in her ear.

The room was bare, with dirty cream walls. Graffiti had been scratched into the plaster and then painted over in a vain attempt to hide the words. *Social workers are scum!* The etching was reduced but still legible under the mismatched pale colour. His eyes ranged over the comment and he snorted. 'Too fucking true.'

Marion, her usual case worker was sat at her desk, a thick file on the grubby surface in front of her. Larry positioned himself at her side, clearly there to act as her minder, in case of trouble.

She recognised Marion, screwed up her eyes, tried to smile an apology. 'Sorry,' she said, putting a finger to her lips to quieten his rage. 'We're not used to all this.' She saw his frown deepen, felt him tighten the grip on her hand. This was not going well. She winced as her fingers mashed together. 'We just want our daughter back.'

'Please sit down.' Marion spoke politely. 'It's good to see you looking so well.'

'I've been trying, real hard.' she said. 'You should see my place now. All cleaned up and nice like.' She straightened her shirt. 'And I'm clean now too. Got off the gear all by myself after you lot came.'

'That's good to hear.' Marion smiled, but her eyes remained cool.

'This is Mia's dad.' She gave a nod towards her partner, smiling gratefully as he let go of her hand to extend his own. For once he'd done as she'd begged.

'I know.' Marion dipped her head towards him but kept her arms by her side. He held his hand outstretched for a few seconds longer, before dropping it on to the table with a thud, grinning when the social worker flinched.

Larry shifted in his seat.

'He's been away for a while but he's back now and he wants to get to know his little girl, don't you babe?' She took his hand in hers, patting it gently, frantic to steady the increasingly fractious meeting. Marion was sparring with him, and it was having an effect. He was becoming increasingly enraged, like a bull cornered in a stadium. One more red rag and he was likely to tear the matador apart.

'Yes, I understand he was released from prison on Monday.' This time the social worker's eyes lit up. She sat up straight and smiled triumphantly at them both. 'You must be very relieved to have avoided a trial. Insufficient evidence so I hear. I gather the prosecution were loathed to drop the case but they had no choice.'

'They had no choice, because they had no fucking evidence,' he growled.

Larry tensed. He tensed. For a second, both women held their breath.

'It's amazing where alibis suddenly pop up from, isn't it?' Marion switched the focus to her; the tone only slightly less provocative. The atmosphere in the room was becoming ugly. It was clearly time to reduce the testosterone levels.

'We was hoping that you might have some news about Mia.' She ignored the dig, grasping the opportunity to change the conversation. 'How is she?'

'She's doing very well.' Marion turned her attention to her file, flipping open the front cover and pulling off a photograph that was clipped to the first page. 'Here's an up-to-date picture.'

She reached forward in a breath, took the colour image from Marion's hand and stared down at Mia, dressed in a pink baby grow with a tiny white pelican embroidered on the front. She was surrounded by a mound of colourful soft toys.

'Look babe. It's Mia.' She held the photo out, at once ecstatic to see her baby girl after so long, while at the same time distraught not to have her there in her arms. Tears ran down her cheeks as her body reacted, her breasts aching at the memory of her baby's sweet pink lips latched on to a nipple and the soft suckling sound she would make. 'Ain't she beautiful?'

She watched as her partner took the photo, his gaze focussing on the shiny print. His brows furrowed as he concentrated on his little daughter. Was she mistaken, or were his eyes misting over? Could they really be glistening slightly in the stark fluorescent light? She couldn't be sure.

'When can we have her back?' It was clear what this was leading to. Surely if they were being offered a photo, they would be offered their child.

'I'm sorry but that's not possible yet.'

She heard the words but she didn't understand. What was the social worker saying? *That's not possible?* What did she mean? *It wasn't possible for her to have Mia back.* But then she'd said *yet.*

'*Yet?*' She latched on to the three-letter word. Yet, yes, now. Please God, now.

'Well actually it might not be possible at all. Not now your circumstances have changed.'

'What do you mean?'

Marion coughed nervously and raised her hand to her mouth. Her face twitched and for a second or two, her mouth opened and shut as if uncertain whether to continue, and unsure as to what she should say.

'Well... with your partner being here.'

'But he's Mia's father. Can't you see what she means to him?' Her voice was rising. This could not be happening. 'He's part of her family.'

'He might be her family,' Marion glanced across at Larry. 'But he's also got a long history of domestic violence. If he's violent to you, and others for that matter, we can't take the risk that he might also be violent to Mia.'

'But he won't hurt Mia, will you babe?' She pulled at his arm once, twice, but he didn't move. He was sitting motionless, his gaze still fixed on the photo, the scar on his cheek changing shape as he ground his teeth together. 'An' it was always my fault if we rowed. I provoked 'im, deliberately like. It was me what made 'im lash out – an' anyway he never really hurt me, did you babe?'

'He's put you in hospital a few times. We can't allow him to do the same to Mia.'

She was sobbing now, her tears flowing thick and fast, washing away all her dreams. 'But he won't hurt Mia. She's his kid. You can see how much he loves her just by looking at him.'

She wiped her face, rubbing a dark smudge of mascara across the soft skin on the back of her hand. The dirty stain mixed with mucus from her nose.

'Look at him,' she pleaded, crying out in pain as his hand gripped her viciously around the arm, dragging her to her feet.

'Stop crying. You look a fucking state.' She felt herself yanked towards the door, his rebuke ringing in her ears. Larry shot to his feet. 'And you can fucking stay where you are.' He shoved the minder back down on his seat, snorting with laughter as Marion whimpered and shrunk away from him.

Turning towards the two officials, he spat across the desk, before nodding his head in the direction of the graffiti. 'Whoever wrote that is right. Social workers *are* scum. You're all scum.'

'Come on.' He pushed her roughly through the door, his voice still thunderous. 'I don't know why we wasted our time.'

She grabbed hold of his arm, struggling to stay upright, as they then lurched through the main door, nearly bowling into a woman with a pushchair. The woman jumped to one side, her hand reaching automatically to stroke her little girl's blonde hair, to comfort the child.

The sight stopped her dead in her tracks, transporting her instantly to a vision of her childhood doll, before its long golden hair had been cut off. The doll packed with memories of two people who had once stood in her way. The doll she still loved. Goldilocks.

It was then that she noticed the photo of Mia still clutched in his hand; Mia's olive skin and cheeky smile, her soft downy hair. And as she gazed into her child's eyes, she knew, without doubt, that nothing and nobody would ever stand in her way again. She wouldn't allow it.

'Don't worry, babe.' She reached up, her finger tracing the scar on his cheek, at once feeling fear and pleasure, pleasure and pain. She felt him relax, respond. It was how it had always been.

'It ain't been a waste of time.' She smiled and grasped him by the hand, lifting the photo of their baby girl up to eye level, so they could both see. 'We'll get her back. And I promise we'll get her back soon.' A vision of her friend's child playing innocently on a roundabout swam into her mind. 'But from now on, babe, we won't try and play it the way that they want. We'll do it my way.'

Chapter 21

The GSM Club was situated in the centre of Wimbledon, in a private square at the rear of the railway station. It was the main club in Wimbledon and the one which Maria Fontana had almost certainly alluded to as having links with the drugs industry. Intelligence suggested the employees in the establishment provided as much cocaine to its clients, as music. Its front door was a plain wooden affair, with the name of the club carved on a separate oak plaque set neatly above its frame. It was barely visible and that was how its clientele preferred. Game, Set and Match boasted exclusivity and privacy on its outside, while no expense was spared on its interior.

According to descriptions on its website, its front lobby sported sparkling white floor tiles, glass chandeliers and a wide assortment of black and white photos showing well-known tennis stars and the odd TV or music celebrity gracing its dance floors. Jamie Smythe-Hamilton, the day-to-day manager and son of the owner, liked to claim privately that GSM *catered for the affluent, not the effluent* in society.

Charlie, however, knew differently.

As far as she was concerned all drug dealers were effluent; whether delivering pure cocaine to the rich, or doling out crack cocaine to the poor. It mattered not a jot if they plied their trade on a freezing street corner or from the exclusive lounge of an upmarket club. A dealer was a dealer wherever, or whoever, they were – and she had no time for any of them.

So, with Maria Fontana's words running through her mind, she was in no mood to take any shit. Franco Nannini was definitely up to something and if, as intelligence suggested, the GSM club was one of the establishments that Maria had alluded to then she wanted to know more. She owed it to Rocco Fontana.

She stood back, peering at the spyhole, as Paul rapped hard on the door. The merest hint of a movement would give the game away should no one choose to answer. And if no one chose to answer… then she'd be applying for a warrant. With Maria's new claims of drug dealing and the mound of historic evidence that they'd unearthed, there was plenty of information to satisfy a magistrate, irrespective of GSM's self-proclaimed pedigree.

After ten seconds Paul banged on the door again.

'Who is it?' A window opened next to the door and a man's face appeared. He had dark hair and an ordinary face, with unappealing, lacklustre eyes and a nose that looked to have been broken several times.

Charlie and Paul held up their warrant cards.

'What do you want?' The man narrowed his eyes and stayed at the window.

'I'm Detective Sergeant Stafford and I want to speak to Jamie Smythe-Hamilton. I presume he's your boss.' By the look of the man, he was plainly the hired helper.

'Hold on.' He shut the window and they heard him shout out to someone in the background. Another minute went past, then the catch slid across and the door was pulled open.

'Come in.' The same man beckoned them through. 'Jamie will see you now.'

'Why thank you,' she replied, unable to hide her sarcasm. Jamie Smythe-Hamilton obviously had ideas above his station.

The interior of the club didn't disappoint. They were ushered straight through the swanky main lobby, up a set of stairs and into a large, well decorated room, divided unevenly in two. In one corner was a small computer desk with a swivel chair and a large coat stand, from which several Barbour jackets and an assortment of caps hung. In the main part of the room stood a much larger desk, on which were several TV monitors. There was also a sofa, enabling a comfortable view through a one-way mirror to the chequered dance floor below. The room, like most of the club, was monotone, black desks and sofa, white walls and flooring and an assortment of greys in between, with only the occasional spot of colour dotted about.

As they entered, a man stood to greet them. He had a good head of matt black hair, a tidy black beard and moustache and was wearing a black suit, white shirt and a shiny grey tie.

'Jamie Smythe-Hamilton,' he purred, holding out his hand. 'And you are?'

'DS Charlotte Stafford, and DC Paul Parker,' Charlie replied, gripping his hand firmly. 'I hardly saw you there, you were so well camouflaged.' She smiled sweetly and released his hand, glancing round the room and making a point of noting the two-way mirror. 'Nice,' she said with a nod. 'So, you like to blend into the background and keep an eye on things then?'

'I like to keep control of what's going on, yes officer. It's my job.' He indicated for them to sit down as two chairs were placed opposite his at the larger desk, then nodded to the man who'd obliged. 'Take a seat Wayne.' He paused for a moment. 'Let me introduce you all. This is Wayne.

He's my security supervisor. I'd like him to be present – even up the numbers and all that.'

Wayne took a seat at the desk in the corner and Jamie Smythe-Hamilton sunk down on to his own executive chair. He leant back and folded his arms. 'Now, what can I do for you both?' His manner was polite but there was no mistaking he'd picked up on her coolness.

Charlie folded her arms too. He was right. She'd taken a distinct dislike to this suave, supercilious spiv.

'I'll get straight to the point, Mr Smythe-Hamilton,' she said, her voice steely, but professional. 'We've had information that you, or the management of your club, may be in liaison with the leaders of some of the local gangs in order to set up new lines of drug dealing.'

'I am the management, officer.'

'Well then you will know exactly what I'm talking about.' She wasn't going to let him get the upper hand. 'And if you don't, then I suggest you should. In the last few days, we've had two young boys horrifically murdered on the streets of Wimbledon and the talk is that it's all connected to drugs.'

'You shouldn't listen to talk.' He tutted and waved a finger in the air.

'Well, maybe you should come and listen to the family of one of the young victims talk then. Maybe you should see the sixteen-year-old, whose body was ripped apart.' She breathed in deeply, steadying her anger, her hands itching to clap a set of handcuffs on his wrists and drag his arrogant arse to the station.

He lowered his finger, rubbing his beard instead, but his eyes remained hard.

She continued. 'Because the word out there is that it's connected to you. So, I'm here to serve notice on you that we'll be investigating every detail of these allegations and putting a stop to any further illegal activities. You might think that because you're upmarket, the law can't touch you, but I assure you it can – and it will, if I have anything to do with it.'

She stood up to leave, indicating for Paul to do the same.

'Yes, that's right, you'd better leave.' Jamie Smythe-Hamilton climbed to his feet. 'I'll be contacting my solicitor about this.'

'You do that, because I'll be contacting the licensing officer – and when we establish the connection between GSM and the gangs, the local magistrates will be the first to know. They'll have your licence off you in the blink of an eye. You'll never open your elite black and white dance floor to the public again.'

'Don't you mean if?'

'No, I don't mean *if*. I mean *when*. So be warned, and don't underestimate me.' She strode across the room, before turning one last time. 'Now kindly ask your doorman to show us the way out.'

❊ ❊ ❊

'That bastard is up to something and I'm going to find out what it is.' Charlie could barely control herself as they walked back across the square towards the police station.

All around them the retail outlets were beginning to close, and the restaurants were starting to open. Very soon the eateries would be heaving with diners; the numbers swollen by those eager to see the latest Wimbledon Theatre production, offering an early dose of summer. Mamma Mia was doing the rounds.

'How long did it take them to open the doors!'

'Those sorts of places always do,' Paul agreed, side-stepping a couple dressed in vividly coloured ABBA costumes. 'Making sure that there's nothing dodgy left out on display.'

'His hired thug made sure we didn't have a chance to see anything, never mind have a little sniff around.' She paused as they crossed the road. 'It's a shame we can't watch what they're doing from up there.' She pointed to the upper floors of Wimbledon Police Station. It was so close, that the windows on the fourth floor would have looked directly down on the club, if it weren't for the railway station multi-storey car park blocking the view. 'And that man! Jamie fucking Smythe-Hamilton. What an arrogant bastard.'

'Funnily enough I thought you felt that way.'

'Oh dear, was I that obvious?'

'Just a bit.' Paul grinned. 'But you were far more professional than I would have been – and anyway I agree. He was acting like some big-time gangster in one of the old black and white movies. I'd love to bring him down a peg or two.'

'Me too, and as far as I'm concerned, *the management* is going to wish he hadn't rubbed the foot soldiers up the wrong way.' She paused, looking up towards the multi-storey car park. 'Let's see if we can't get some surveillance authorised to keep tabs on the premises. Perhaps we can get some hidden cameras rigged up, looking down on the square – see who's frequenting the club and what deliveries are going in… and out.'

They bounced up the steps of Wimbledon Police Station, and pushed through the door; a new sense of purpose driving them up the two flights of stairs and into the office.

'Paul, can you start getting the paperwork together for a warrant, and I'll get authority for surveillance,' she called, as they split on arrival at Paul's desk. 'Let's see if we can't get Superintendent Woodall to locate his balls this time.'

'Funny you should mention Superintendent Woodall's name.' Bet spun round towards her, with a frown. 'He's just phoned, wanting to speak to you, Charlie. He said he'd had a call from some pretty heavy-duty solicitors threatening us with litigation. You're to leave Jamie Smythe-Hamilton and the GSM club alone.'

Chapter 22

'All quiet last night, Mum?'

'Yes Charlie, all quiet.'

'Excellent.' Charlie breathed a sigh of relief and rubbed her pounding temples. After the Superintendent's unwelcome order the previous evening, she and Paul had drowned their sorrows with several pints. It had been a good chance to update him on her errant father, but they'd stayed far too long. In the end they'd both crashed out at her flat. She checked her watch. A few minutes past seven and Paul was still fast asleep on her sofa. 'All quiet at mine too.' She reached down and shook Paul's shoulder, at the same time unsure whether to be pleased at the news, or concerned. If her father wasn't at either of their homes, then where was he?

With any luck, back in Glasgow, but then she was a realist. If she'd inherited anything from Iain Frazer it was his persistence. She'd never give up and neither would he. The game had only recently started and it was anyone's guess what the outcome would be. She just hoped it wouldn't be as Anna suggested.

She pressed the phone to her ear.

'Are you sure you won't change your mind?' It was a pointless question and she didn't wait for the inevitable answer. Her mother had adamantly refused to take Casper and leave the family home. Seemingly the welfare of the house was more important than the welfare of its occupants, but it was as she'd expected. 'I've arranged for a locksmith to upgrade all your locks, and the Crime Prevention Officer to do a complete security assessment. They'll be round mid-morning. If you're keeping us out in the wilds of Lingfield we need to be prepared.'

'Thank you, Charlie.' Her mother ignored the dig. 'I've woken with a fresh dose of positivity. I'm sure we'll be okay.'

'Well, we're going to have to be.' She wished she had the same confidence. 'Right, I've got to go, Mum. I'll see you later.'

Paul was stirring. His eyes were still tightly shut, but he was moaning and yawning. She gave him another shake and he squinted up at her. 'Why do we always do this?' It was a common consequence of spats with the management.

'Because we can and because you're my best mate. It's just a shame you prefer boys.' She looked down at him fondly. 'Anyway, I never hear you complaining when I cook you our hangover remedy.'

Ten minutes later they were tucking into hot sweet coffee and bacon butties.

'I've had an idea how to get around sod all Woodall,' she said, chewing on a particularly rubbery piece of bacon.

'Oh yeah.' Paul looked up, grinning.

She swallowed down the dregs of her coffee, pulled a face and then grinned back.

'Well, I thought, while we're up in this neck of the woods...'

❈ ❈ ❈

Three hours later they were turning into the yard at Wimbledon Police Station with the authority to apply for a warrant and an application for directed surveillance all signed up and ready to go courtesy of their previous boss in Lambeth.

'Glad I stayed in touch,' Charlie chuckled, patting the file of papers on her lap and glancing up at the senior officer's floor. 'It doesn't say anywhere it has to be the Superintendent for *your* borough that signs the paperwork. I'd love to see the look on Woodall's face when he finds out what we've been up to.'

'He'll be shocked,' laughed Paul.

'But not as shocked as Jamie Smythe-Hamilton will be when we shut down his precious club and take away his license.'

They were still smiling as they pushed open the door to the office. Their usual numbers had been swelled by Ross McBride and his team.

'Ah so you've obviously heard the good news?' Bet said, looking at their blank faces before continuing. 'Naz will be back with us tomorrow. She called in earlier to say that, aside from a bandage, she's raring to go.'

'That's great news, though she'll have to take it easy for a bit.'

'You've got to be joking, Charlie,' Sabira snorted. 'Naz, take it easy… no chance.'

Charlie tilted her head to one side. 'Hmm, Sab, you could be right. I'll have to select the quieter jobs for her to do, like kicking down doors.' She laughed. 'Okay, talking about jobs, bring me up to speed on our two murders. Bet, you've been collating stuff on Rocco Fontana, and Sabira, you have the details on Kelvin Olawi?'

Bet nodded and stood up first, walking across to the board containing photos of their victims and pointing to Rocco Fontana laid out on a mortuary slab. 'Cause of death is the stab wound to his chest, which pierced his heart, with severe blood loss a consequential factor. He had thirty-eight separate slash wounds to his body, from the same knife, all of which were inflicted before the knife was then plunged into his heart killing him.'

'Unlike Kelvin Olawi, where the forty-three slashes he sustained were carried out after his death,' Sabira chipped in. 'And with a separate knife. Dr Crane, the pathologist thinks the suspect, or suspects, for Olawi's murder wanted to copycat the killing of Rocco Fontana by leaving the knife sticking out of his chest. The visual's even more shocking.'

There was silence for a moment as the group considered the photos of the two bloodied bodies and the murder weapons used against them.

'Anything more on the kitchen knife that was used in Rocco's murder?' Charlie looked towards Bet.

'Apart from it being from the set we seized at the Olawi's flat, forensics have found traces of soil and a tiny sample of DNA which has now been matched to Kelvin Olawi.'

'Excellent.' Charlie clapped her hands together. 'Confirming the partial fingerprint.'

'Yep. We can be a hundred per cent certain that Kelvin Olawi has had that knife in his possession at some point.' Bet paused. 'And I doubt it was to help with the cooking. But interestingly a soil sample has been found on the knife used to kill Olawi too, although I don't think they match.'

Sabira nodded. 'The zombie knife was clean. No fingerprints or DNA, just minute traces of dirt. The Dons were happy enough to use their signature knife but didn't want us naming any of them as suspects.'

'Which leads us nicely on to our suspect, Franco Nannini, who very kindly corroborated the phone data and admitted to tracking Olawi to opposite the crime scene.' Charlie turned towards Ross McBride. 'Any luck with the house-to-house, Ross?'

'Nothing seen and nothing heard. We've covered every house with no joy. Our best hope is with the house immediately adjacent to the derelict house. It has a camera facing down the driveway and across the road to where Nannini admitted hiding, but the occupier is away on business and nobody has his contact number. We won't know until he returns if the camera has caught anything – or if it was even working. I've left a note for him to phone me on his arrival home, but so far, nothing.' He shrugged, and held her gaze. 'Obviously, I'll personally let you know the minute we get anything.'

'Thank you, Ross. I'm sure you will.' She sat down on a table, feeling a warm rush of blood rising up her neck – and cursing how bloody unprofessional it would look. Pulling her shirt collar up further, she concentrated on the Dons pyramid, grateful when the heat receded.

'It would be nice to actually see Franco Nannini there, but I gather we have some forensics now that back up his story, Sab?'

'Yes, we have one half-smoked Rothman's cigarette, with traces of Nannini's DNA on it, picked up from a driveway almost opposite the crime scene, next to a parked up Range Rover. But, and here's the clincher, SOCO also found a partially smoked Rothman's fag end in the derelict house. It's the same brand of cigarette and it also has his DNA on it.'

'Yes!' Paul was next to clap his hands. 'That's brilliant, Sab. So he did return. I knew it. The lying shit.'

'Well, I'm still not so sure.' Charlie frowned. For the second time in two days, the hairs were prickling on the back of her neck.

'Something's not right.' She shook her head unhappily, thinking back over Nannini's interesting outburst during his interview. 'We're being asked to believe that Franco Nannini thoroughly wiped down the handle of the zombie knife, having meticulously tracked his victim – but then chucked away not one, but two, incriminating cigarette butts for us to find?'

Chapter 23

Before Charlie could make a decision, a loud, panicky voice across the radio interrupted the moment. 'I need more units to Wimbledon Common urgently.'

'Grab your stuff and let's go,' Charlie pushed her worries to the back of her mind, zipped up her stab vest and clipped on her radio. 'It's all kicking off.'

'DS Stafford on way,' she radioed in, as they hurtled down the stairs. All around were officers running, doors slamming, the sound of engines revving, cars screeching out on to the roadway.

She jumped into the front passenger seat as Paul buckled up. Sabira threw herself across the rear seat, and they headed off, Paul navigating the well-worn route up towards the common.

'Bloody hell,' Sabira gasped, holding on to the front seat as they flew around a corner. 'I didn't think it would actually happen.'

'I did, unfortunately.' Charlie pulled a police cap on over her hair. 'The drums have been beating all morning. It was only a matter of time.'

Report after report had been flowing in from informants giving times, locations, protagonists. All the gangs were involved – and they'd all be tooled up. The fight had been planned for around 4 p.m. just as the schools kicked out, to cause maximum confusion. Of course, the Met had responded with carriers of TSG patrolling the outskirts of the common, waiting in side streets; a vast uniformed army ready for action – but Charlie knew they'd still be outnumbered. They always were. Outnumbered and outplayed. Wimbledon Common was huge. It totalled well over a thousand acres of heathland, with thick wooded areas to mask any skirmishes, and lakes and ponds for disposal of knives.

'We've got dozens of officers up there, but we're too thinly spread. And we're no match against the speed and versatility of the gangs.'

She'd seen it too many times before. The gangs used social media. It was their weapon, their conduit; a latter-day Morse code that flashed message after message across the airwaves faster than any could be written down. So, at the last minute the location had changed. They'd been wrong-footed again, leaving the majority of the police troops positioned on one side of the common while the fight raged on the other.

As they neared the location, they were forced to slow. Throngs of school children were running towards them, darting across the road, pushing past groups of bewildered shoppers in their haste to get away. Paul switched off the sirens, conscious not to cause any extra panic.

'Bloody hell,' he swore, slamming the brakes on hard. 'It's like a scene from a disaster movie.'

As they rounded the bend at the top of the hill, the scene opened up. A full-scale battle was raging between groups of hooded-up teenagers, their faces covered with thick scarves and bandanas, some still waving knives or sticks in outstretched arms. Many more were cowering in fear, their heads and bodies covered in blood.

'Shit.' Charlie had rarely seen anything like this. 'You're not wrong. Quick, put your sirens back on.'

Paul did as she said, the sudden noise galvanising the groups into action. Some dropped their weapons, others turned tail, darting and weaving in an attempt to avoid capture, or the clouds of CS spray and tasers from eager teams of arriving officers.

For several minutes there was chaos; the kids doing battle with the cops, the sound of sirens wailing, more police vehicles skidding to a halt. The three of them jumped out to join the fracas, not quite knowing where best to start. Paul had switched off the two-tones again and the noise became human; shouted orders, screams of pain, a thousand footsteps clomping along moorland tracks.

Charlie scanned the mayhem. Most of the youths were dispersing, those able to run heading off, those unable lying prone on grassy verges, or leaning against tree trunks, clutching bloody limbs. Some of the youths she saw escaping were so well covered, even their skin tone was indistinguishable. There would be little or no chance of identifying which gangs were there, let alone the members of each gang.

'Help.' She heard a shout, and saw a young girl, not much older than fourteen, dressed in a bottle-green school uniform waving her arms frantically from the edge of a small copse. 'Please, someone help me.' From where she stood, Charlie could see the panic in her eyes, her open mouth, a river of tears streaming down her cheeks. At her feet lay another girl, also in a bottle-green school uniform, but not moving.

She started to run towards them, her heart thudding with alarm. As she neared, the crying girl dropped to her knees, shaking her friend by the arm, sobbing hard, her voice squeaky and desperate. 'Rochelle, talk to me. Rochelle.'

'Rochelle,' Charlie repeated, as her eyes ranged across the girl's unconscious body. There were no obvious injuries. 'Rochelle,' she said again, this time bending forward and placing her ear above the girl's mouth. No response. Not even the feel of breath on her skin. She looked down the length of her body. The girl's chest was static.

She took a deep breath. She needed to stay calm, think. Adrenalin was surging through her body. Sabira was standing nearby, speaking on her radio. 'Sabira,' she shouted, watching for her friend to react. 'Call for an ambulance. Fourteen-year-old female. Unresponsive. Not breathing. Then come and help.'

Sabira nodded and ran across.

'What's your name young lady?' Charlie asked the first girl, while checking Rochelle's airway and quickly ripping the casualty's shirt open, scanning her chest and abdomen, for injuries. Nothing.

'It's Saskia,' the girl said, sniffing and wiping her face.

Charlie checked Rochelle's mouth for obstructions, then turned her on to her side, conscious that she was still not breathing. She had to act fast. Somewhere in the hubbub she could hear Sabira updating control.

'Saskia, do you know what happened?'

'We were on our way home from school,' she replied. 'A boy ran up behind us.'

Charlie didn't need to hear any more. The back of Rochelle's bottle-green jacket was heavy with blood, the material now a dirty brown.

'Probable stab wound to the back,' she murmured to Sabira, lowering the girl's inert body back down. Getting her breathing was the priority now she knew what was wrong. Checking the severity of the injury would come later. If they had a later.

'We need to start CPR.' She leant across, placing her hands on Rochelle's chest, and started to pump.

Sabira put the radio to her ear. 'They're sending the air ambulance,' she said, putting an arm around Saskia and moving her to one side.

Charlie nodded and exhaled, concentrating now solely on getting a steady rhythm. 'Come on Rochelle,' she implored with every lunge. 'Come on, Rochelle, you can't die. You're too young to die.'

Raising her eyes to the sky, she scanned the horizon, watching for the tiny speck of yellow, which would signal the arrival of the helicopter. Everything went quiet. Even the branches of the trees stilled. Her ears tuned in to the silence, desperate to register the drone of its engines, the distant throbbing of its mechanical heart.

She continued to pump.

Only when its rotors stopped turning would she know if she'd done enough to make Rochelle's heart beat again.

Chapter 24

She hadn't.

'She's gone I'm afraid.' The words of the air ambulance paramedic sent an overwhelming wave of grief crashing over Charlie. 'There was nothing more you could have done.'

His follow-on did nothing to stay the tide. She was exhausted. Stepping away, she slumped down on to a fallen tree trunk and put her head in her hands. Sabira dropped down beside her, and put an arm around her shoulder.

'She was only fourteen,' Charlie said, wiping at her eyes. 'Why couldn't we have saved her?'

'You did all that you could,' the paramedic was speaking again. 'We all did. Few, if anyone comes back from a knife wound to the heart.'

It made not a bit of difference to her sense of failure. After battling to perform CPR for over twenty minutes, the helicopter had arrived, bringing with it noise, movement and hope. Tree boughs had swung crazily and the longer fronds of grass bowed over to allow the flying doctors access. The wind from its rotor blades had literally blown new life into their tired bodies; Charlie's compressions performed with renewed vigour and Sabira's breaths strong and direct.

For a few minutes they had hoped it might work, that they might have done enough to stop Rochelle's organs from failing and keep her alive, but the expressions on the faces of the crew quickly told them otherwise. The doctor tried. The crew tried, as hard as they could for almost an hour, opening the young girl's chest in the heat of the late afternoon sun, massaging her heart, until their foreheads could crease no further and their flight suits became sodden with blood and sweat. In the end they could do no more. No one could.

Some of the helicopter crew members were leaning back on their heels, looking physically and mentally shattered. Some were starting to clear medical equipment away.

Other casualties had already been stretchered off in the back of ambulances.

Charlie watched as the doctor walked towards a small huddle of civilians and officers, leaning in to speak to a smartly dressed black woman with the wide, wild eyes of a mother facing her worst nightmare. She saw his hand gently take her arm, watched as the woman sunk to the ground, listened to the howl of anguish.

Again and again, the noise surged and with every fresh note Charlie froze, her sense of failure quadrupling. It was a sound she'd heard many times before, and it was one that she never forgot – the hollow sound of loss.

When the wail faded to a whimper, Charlie stood and walked slowly across to where Rochelle's mother now sat. In the midst of the carnage, Dawn Edwards had run panic-stricken to their sides, no doubt in response to a phone call from her daughter's school friend. She had cried out in horror from a distance, held back by the strong arms of an officer, as Charlie and Sabira fought to save her child. She had been shielded from the worst, as the paramedics did their bloody work, but she had been present for something that no mother should have had to witness.

'I'm so very sorry for your loss.' Charlie dipped her head as she reached Dawn Edwards. It was the same futile sentiment that she'd offered to Maria Fontana. 'We did everything we could to save Rochelle.'

'I could see you did.' Dawn Edwards held her gaze, clearly accepting the truth of her words. The woman looked totally bereft, her eye make-up smeared across her face and her voice husky from crying. Her previously stylish appearance was gone, replaced instead by an air of wild desolation. She reached out grabbing Charlie's hand tightly, her grip firmer than Charlie expected. 'Thank you for trying,' she sobbed, her voice breaking with each word. She let go of Charlie's hand and threw her hands to her face. 'I know you all tried your best.'

❋ ❋ ❋

It was with a heavy heart but a renewed sense of determination that Charlie, Paul and Sabira finally returned to their vehicle. A clutch of uniformed senior officers was taking control of the scene – and the press briefings – with Charlie and the team sent away to get cleaned up and make a start on the requisite statements. A positive spin would be a necessity to allay the distress of local residents, so any battered or bloodied officers were being swiftly shipped out.

As she climbed into the car, Charlie took a final look across the heath. It wore all the detritus of a battlefield, bloody dressings, ripped packaging, discarded clothing. The total numbers of casualties read like the body count of a military skirmish, one dead, four hospitalised and at least another six walking-wounded.

'Bloody hell,' she shook her head at the sight. 'All this because a tiny minority of teenagers want to wage war on each other. And as ever, it's the law-abiding majority that get caught up in it all.' She stared out of the window; her thoughts returning to Rochelle. 'Let's have a drive around first, shall we Paul, before heading in.' She wasn't yet ready to fully retreat. 'See if we can spot any gang members still hanging about.'

'I doubt there'll be too many around, after that but we'll give it a go.' Paul swung the car into a side road and engaged a low gear. 'It always amazes me how many murderers return to the scene of their crimes.'

They cruised the small residential streets, their eyes peeled for the tell-tale uniforms of the gangs, Charlie indicating at intervals which way they should go. Gradually, like a moth drawn to the light, she found herself pointing towards the rear of the railway station.

'Paul, stop here,' she instructed, as they neared the multi-storey car park. 'Let me check something out.'

'By something, you mean the GSM club.'

'Maybe,' she grinned, getting out as Paul stopped the car and slipping along the alleyway that led to the square. A man dressed in workman's overalls was repairing a gutter at the rear of the car park. She recognised the man. Very soon there would be a tiny portable camera surreptitiously fixed to the downpipe, its lens capturing the comings and goings at the club.

As she neared the end of the alleyway, Charlie heard voices. She stopped, peering cautiously round the corner of the wall. Jamie Smythe-Hamilton stood in the doorway to the club facing outwards, with the shadowy figure of his security officer at his side. He was talking to two hooded-up figures standing with their backs to her. One was of average build, lean and athletic with a dark tracksuit and flashy trainers. The other was twice his size, the elastic material of his top straining to contain his huge shoulders and biceps.

Silently she pressed herself against the wall, willing the two youths to turn round, but they remained stationary, deep in discussion with the club manager. It wasn't hard to work out who they might be, but she couldn't be sure. She strained to recognise the voices or the subject of the conversation but they were too far away. All she could hear was the indistinct hum of debate, punctuated with the odd murmur of assent.

After a few minutes the voices faded. Jamie Smythe-Hamilton stepped back into the club before emerging a few seconds later with a small package. He handed it to the leaner youth, who stuffed it down the front of his tracksuit bottoms. A shake of hands and the youths headed off along the opposite alleyway, towards the square, their faces still obscured. At the same time the door to the club slammed shut. Business was complete.

For a second, Charlie was tempted to chase after the youths but a scraping from above changed her mind. The workman was heading off. She stared after the retreating figures and made up her mind. Why fritter away the chance of obtaining proper footage by bowling in now? Suppose they saw her coming? They'd be gone in an instant, vanishing into the crowds of commuters, the package discarded or hidden. And what then? Their interest would be noted and any further liaisons between the two parties would become more guarded.

No, she would wait – for the surveillance footage, for the CPS decision on charging Nannini, and for the evidence to put a stop to the war. She turned and headed back to the car, directing Paul to return to the police station.

'I can't help feeling a tiny bit sorry for Jamie Smythe-Hamilton, now he's on your radar,' Paul joked.

'Well don't,' she answered a little too stridently. '3D and Nannini might think they're the big shots, but I've a feeling it's Jamie who's pulling their strings.'

Chapter 25

The woman had often wondered whether they would die together.

Somehow it had always seemed a romantic notion, particularly when he was beating the crap out of her. The idea of going out in a blaze of glory, like Bonnie and Clyde or Romeo and Juliet, was one that appealed to her sense of drama. Perhaps it had always been her destiny; the two of them taking on the world, taking on the establishment.

She'd never wanted to die alone.

Now, as she watched him expertly breaking into a car, the thought popped into her head, and gained traction. It was all or nothing this time. If they didn't get Mia back, then life wouldn't be worth living, for her, or for him.

'Come on then babe, get in.' His voice was rough, gravelly, serious – it demanded obedience. He leant over and threw the door open. She walked across, opened a rear door and placed a holdall into the footwell and some clothing onto the rear seat. She then closed the door, and climbed in to the front. No rush. Nobody would dare interfere if they caught a glimpse of his bulk. A Mike Tyson lookalike. He would bite your ear off rather than be told what to do.

Marion and Larry had been lucky.

The car he was stealing was almost certainly owned by an old soldier; having bright red poppy field car stickers on both rear side windows and a British Legion car sticker on the boot. Its exterior was well cared for and its interior was clean and tidy. Several crocheted cushions adorned the rear seat, and the whole car smelt of roses. A frog-shaped air freshener hung from the rearview mirror, swinging where he'd nudged it with his head. The frog had a wide mouth. It was smiling and dancing as it bobbed about. Her eyes focussed on its movements. Mia would have laughed at its antics.

Mia.

Her attention returned to her partner; to the hammering of a screwdriver, metal against metal as he ripped out the car's ignition switch. He didn't do the new-fangled keyless ones. He thumped it again, cracking the facia, yanking it away from its position under the steering wheel. And then it was done. The dashboard lights came on. The radio came on. The engine spluttered into life. They were on their way.

He manoeuvred out from the car park at the rear of the red-bricked block of flats across the road from her bedsit and headed away from town.

'You know where you're going?' she asked.

'I know some of the way.'

She pulled out a map from her pocket and opened it up, resting it on her lap and searching out their location. Very soon, when they'd left the city, their mobiles would be switched off so she'd have no access to sat nav. She peered at the map. The destination was marked with a cross; her ideas discussed and agreed on the way home from the social services office. For once in their lives he had listened, allowing her to make suggestions, even embracing her plan.

There was no time to waste if they weren't to lose Mia forever. Plan B was being instituted, and it helped that he hated her friend.

'Stay on this road,' she instructed, her finger tracing the biro marks already scored on to the map. 'Remember the camera I mentioned that we need to avoid but otherwise this route takes us straight out of London and into the countryside.'

He grunted his understanding, his eyes flicking towards the rearview mirror.

She twisted round checking on all sides. There were no flashing blue lights, no sirens wailing. 'No sign of Old Bill,' she laughed. 'Relax, babe, we'll be well away before the old codgers who own this motor even realise it's gone.'

Her eyes strayed down across his chest.

'Here, give us that babe.' She pointed to the screwdriver on his lap, noting the slight hesitation of his fingers on the handle. He hadn't yet fully forgiven her. She reached across, gently levering the tool from his grip. Softly, softly. Better that it was out of sight and out of mind.

'Turn this shit off,' he growled.

Smooth Radio was playing 'Band On The Run'. She put the screwdriver into her door pocket then reached forward and turned it off. Nothing had changed, unless he'd somehow become more perceptive to the subtlety of her actions.

'Thank fuck for that.' He pulled a pack of cigarettes from his pocket, flicked it open and tipped one into his mouth. 'Give me a light.'

She smiled to herself. No nothing had changed. He was still the same ill-tempered, domineering bastard that he'd always been. Reaching down she lifted the holdall from the footwell, and pulled a lighter from a side pocket, striking up a flame and holding it out.

He sucked on it greedily, opening the window wide and expelling the smoke from the corner of his mouth. A raft of warm, smoky air wafted into the car, prompting her to check on the weather. The forecast was fair at least for the next few days. Then rain.

Not so good. They would have to try to find a more sheltered spot.

'Pass me your mobile.' She switched her own phone off and removed the battery, then held out her hand.

He hesitated again. 'Are you sure?'

'Babe, we discussed this last night.' She was treading a thin line. 'If we're gonna do this, then we have to do it right, or the feds will be all over us. You know what they're like.'

They both knew from experience the powers police had; the tracking, the monitoring, the cameras. They couldn't avoid all the CCTV, but they did know the positions of the ANPR cameras on the main roads, the certainty that their phones would be traced, that any digital transaction left an indelible footprint.

'We can't take no risks when we get out of town. If they find out where we're heading, the whole thing's fucked.' She held her breath and wiggled her fingers. 'Come on, babe.'

'Fuck it! Okay.' He passed her his mobile, glancing across as she unzipped the holdall. They'd prepared well. People left all kinds of things in their sheds these days and what hadn't been scavenged the previous night, had been easily nicked from the local stores.

'What 'ave you got that fucking scruffy old thing for?' He nodded towards the bag.

On the top was Goldilocks, her plump little body folded and squashed in a corner. She reached in and gently retrieved her doll. 'You know she comes wiv me wherever I go.'

'I don't know why.' He lunged towards the doll with his left arm but she easily nudged him away. 'She's ugly and old. She needs to be binned.'

'You know why I bring 'er. She holds memories for me. Of me mum an' a few others.' She stroked the ragdoll's short blonde hair, and put her safely to one side. 'I've 'ad 'er all my life. An' anyway, Mia loves 'er too. Almost as much as she loved 'er Dilly.'

She lifted out the little stuffed dinosaur with its long floppy neck. 'That's for when we get 'er back.'

'You're sure they're gonna give 'er back?'

'They'll 'ave to.' She rummaged around in the holdall and pulled out a thick plastic carrier bag, unfolding it from around its contents and placing the screwdriver inside. 'A bag for life,' she laughed. 'How appropriate.'

Silently she stared down into the top of the bag, ticking off each item in her head; the rope, the duct tape, the half dozen burner phones, the pair of scissors, the knives, the length of electrical cord, the cable ties, the blindfold. 'Or should I say, a bag for a life.'

❂ ❂ ❂

An hour later they arrived. The North Downs stretched out on either side as they followed a long, narrow road across the top of Box Hill and snaked down several hairpin bends on its rump. The river was shown meandering along at its base, a thin blue line that entered on one side of the map and vanished at the other. According to her friend it deepened at narrow stretches and widened at others to form shallow waters in which the children played.

Somewhere along the shallower stretch were the stepping stones and somewhere along the deeper, less accessible parts was where they would set up camp.

'We're here babe.' She flung her head from side to side, taking in the vivid scenery, her eyes widening with excitement. Every minute of the journey had been agonising, her anticipation ratcheted up at every intersection until she was fit to burst. Now they were there, she could contain it no longer. 'Pull into the car park and we'll explore.'

'Remember what we've come for.' His voice threw a bucket of cold water on her delight.

'Yes of course, babe,' she frowned with frustration. 'But let's have a quick look round first.' Nothing could dampen down her momentary delight. Here, was the picture on her wall, the beautiful scene where a little girl's memories were formed – a place so tranquil and serene that no one could ever imagine it otherwise.

There were only two other vehicles in the car park, so he headed to a secluded spot, stopping under the shade of some trees. She threw open the door impatiently, breathing in the scent of freshly cut grass in a meadow nearby. A public footpath ran from the car park along the edge of the field to the river. As she slammed the car door, a dappled grey horse started, breaking off from chewing the longer grass at the base of a hedge, to instead stare at her.

'Come on, babe. Let's just take a look.' She ran to the riverbank, counting the stones across its breadth, as she stepped out across them. One, two, three.

'What the fuck are you doing?' He stood watching her, a spade in one hand, a pickaxe and machete in the other. 'Work before play.' The phrase sounded strange coming from the lips of a man who'd never done an honest day's work, but she buttoned her lip. His choice of business had paid for her lodgings, it had provided her gear. It had put people in hospital. It could yet put her in the same place.

She turned around and jumped back across the stones. Who was she to argue with him now when he was doing what she wanted?

'Isn't it beautiful,' she smiled, reaching out to take his arm. They began to walk, away from the shallows, away from the public picnic area, along a well-trodden footpath, until the banks of the river became more and more overgrown and impassable and the path veered away across the nearby fields. They continued to track the river as its flow quickened, surging relentlessly along the base of a high chalk escarpment. He forged ahead, while she followed wordlessly, their feet splashing at times through shallow pools. On one side rose the Downs, too steep to climb, and to the other was thick woodland, with tall trees whose gnarled roots grew out across the water in a bid to escape the dense strangulating undergrowth. At times they were forced to divert away, but with perseverance and the aid of the machete they were able to proceed, slowly, patiently along the water's edge.

'What do you think of this?' He stopped all of a sudden, standing on a thin verge of mossy soil, his head tilted slightly upwards following the path of the river, his eyes wide.

Catching up with him, she followed the direction of his hand as he pointed towards a dark recess in a nearby rocky outcrop. It was set back from the water, raised up by several feet, and partially concealed behind the drooping branches of a willow. He pulled the leaves to one side and they peered into a perfectly hollowed out cave, left high and dry in years gone by, by the changing course of the river.

'Bloody hell, babe,' she gasped, clapping her hands and stepping into the space. The ground was soft underfoot, still damp from the proximity of the water, but dry enough to stay quite comfortably for as long as it took. In the next few days, they could come and go, away from the hustle and bustle of the city, away from the tower blocks and estates of London, unnoticed and unknown. And if, in the event that they happened to be spotted by a group of nosey ramblers, or any other curious onlooker, well they would simply be another young couple out walking in the beautiful Surrey countryside.

'It's so fucking perfect.' She pulled him to the ground, laughing as she straddled him, and unbuttoned her shirt. 'It's just what we need, babe. A place out of the way.' She leant forward and whispered in his ear. 'A place to die for.'

Chapter 26

Superintendent Richie Woodall threw the newspaper down on the desk in front of Charlie and slammed the door.

'Take a look at this,' he shouted.

Splashed across the front page was the headline: *SLAUGHTER OF THE INNOCENT,* with a subheading: *Gang warfare breaks out on the streets of SW19.* Underneath was an almost full-page photograph of Rochelle Edwards in school uniform.

'What the hell have you been doing?'

Charlie kept her mouth shut. What was the point of spelling out to this raging man, that she, Sabira and a team of paramedics had spent almost an hour and a half the previous afternoon, trying to save the young girl's life – or that her mother's howl of anguish was still ringing in her ears. He clearly had his own agenda.

'I always had my reservations about leaving you too much responsibility,' continued Richie Woodall. 'After all, you are Inspector Hunter's protégée – and he had a reputation for being somewhat of a renegade.' He slammed a fist down on the newspaper and glared at her. 'I hope you're not following in his footsteps, or you can kiss goodbye to any further promotion.'

She bit her lip and stayed silent. As soon as she'd finished having her bottom metaphorically smacked, she'd be straight out doing exactly what Hunter would do.

'They're straightforward tit-for-tat gang killings, Sergeant. Rocco Fontana was killed by Kelvin Olawi, and Franco Nannini then killed him in retaliation, and well, Rochelle Edwards was unfortunately in the wrong place at the wrong time. Collateral damage, as it were.'

Rochelle Edwards' face smiled out from the front page of the paper. 'Collateral damage, sir?' She shook her head disbelievingly. 'This girl *was* slaughtered.'

He ignored her. 'DS Stafford, you have Franco Nannini by the balls, and yet you're wasting your time trying to dig up some dirt on one of Wimbledon's most law-abiding and, I might add, generous members of the community.'

'Sir, we were waiting for a CPS decision.' She couldn't let him get away with that.

'And while you were sitting on your arses, you let this happen.' He picked up the newspaper, screwing his eyes up and read aloud, '"In the last week there have been three teenagers murdered on the leafy streets of Wimbledon. Residents are frightened. They claim the police have lost control." Lost control?!' He threw the paper towards the bin, cursing further as it hit the rim and dropped onto the floor. 'For fuck's sake Sergeant, if you'd been out there doing your job then this would never have happened. I want Nannini brought in and charged immediately. I need results, figures. Give me some good news to feed to the vultures.'

❀ ❀ ❀

Charlie was fuming as she headed downstairs.

As she approached the main office, her mood was further worsened by the general hubbub of raised voices and laughter. It was buzzing. Ross McBride and most of his unit had joined Bet, Paul and Sabira; all being well and truly entertained by a jubilant Naz.

'Great to see you back, Naz.' She grinned, genuinely delighted to see her friend looking so well. 'But... we've work to be done. Superintendent Woodall wants Franco Nannini brought in and charged. Or he'll be kissing goodbye to his next promotion – and we can't let that happen now, can we?' Her voice was heavy with sarcasm.

Paul caught her as she headed for the privacy of her own small office.

'You okay?'

She nodded 'Just the usual arse-covering crap.'

'Oh, no surprise there then. Had any more trouble with your dad recently?'

'No, all quiet again, thanks. I actually prefer it when he's up to something. At least you know what he's doing and where he is. When he's silent it's worse.' She pursed her lips and frowned. 'Could you and Ross get things ramped up to bring Nannini in for me please, I'm going to go through things. See if there's anything we've missed.'

Paul nodded. 'I don't know what Woodall said, Charlie, but I've every faith in you.'

'Blimey Paul.' She raised her eyebrows and gave him a smile. 'What have I done to deserve that?'

'Nothing, Sarge,' he winked. 'Just saying.'

※ ※ ※

It seemed like no time at all before Ross poked his head round the door. 'Nannini's binned up downstairs, waiting to see you. He can't wait to talk apparently.'

Ross walked in, twisted a chair round to face him and straddled the seat with both legs, then peered over the back of it at the pile of paperwork on her desk. 'Looks like you've got your work cut out. If there's anything I can do...'

'You'll be the first to know,' she smiled, the blush warming her cheeks. 'It's mad really, but I have a feeling there's something not quite right going on.'

'I gathered that.'

'What do *you* think?'

'I don't rightly know, but I've dealt with a lot of the gangs, and I have to admit, Nannini's nervous.'

'In what way?'

He shrugged. 'Well... he's not accepting it. If they're guilty, they might not like getting sent down, but most sort of accept it. Like it comes with the territory. But Nannini... he seems worried. Let me know what he says.'

He got up to leave.

'I will, and seriously Ross, thanks for your help.'

'No problem.' He turned, scratching his nails across his scalp. 'Bloody TSG helmets,' he said. 'They're hot as hell, and itch to buggery. Oh, and before I forget. The occupant of the house next to the Olawi crime scene has just returned. As far as he knows his camera was working. I'll whip down there as soon as he bells me and download any footage.'

'That would be good.'

'See if we can't get an image of Nannini returning later. That'll put an end to his denials and back up the evidence of the fag end found at the scene.' He winked and swivelled on his heel. 'Would also put your mind at rest, one way or another.'

Chapter 27

Franco Nannini was sitting forward in his chair in the interview room when Charlie and Paul walked in. Next to him was the same solicitor as before.

'Good afternoon, Franco.' She settled herself, going through his rights and entitlements slowly, pedantically, taking time to move things about, reposition her pen, her paper, noticing how with every small adjustment, he became more agitated.

'Why 'ave you brought me in early?' he demanded. 'I'm not due back on bail for another week, innit.'

'Something's come up and I need to ask you some questions.'

'Oh yeah. Well, I ain't got nothin' more to say.' He folded his arms tightly, and sat back in his seat, a thin smile playing on his lips, but he didn't fool Charlie. One correctly worded question and he would snap.

'You might want to answer me when you hear the question.'

'I've advised you of your right to remain silent,' the solicitor chipped in.

He frowned at his solicitor, one knee starting to twitch, his foot tapping against the desk leg. She paused, deliberately elongating the moment before she asked him the question. The tension in the room was palpable.

'A cigarette end with your DNA on it was found in a driveway opposite the murder scene, next to a Range Rover.'

'For fuck's sake. Is that the best you can do?' He glanced across victoriously towards his brief; the pressure, like a tyre blowout, gone in an instant. 'I've already said I watched Boxer from there. Now you mention it, the car was a Range Rover. Remember thinking it was a nice-looking motor, if you know what I mean.'

She smiled her understanding. 'So, you smoke Rothman's?'

'Yeah.'

'And you had some with you that night?'

'Yeah, probably.'

'So why was another Rothman's cigarette butt with your DNA on it, found inside the murder scene?'

'What?' He jumped to his feet but she pressed on.

'Yes Franco. Right on the floor next to Boxer. It's even got some of his blood on it too. So that's your DNA and the murder victim's DNA both found, not only in the same room, but on the same cigarette...'

'You're lying!' he roared.

The solicitor put a hand on his arm. 'Franco. My advice is to make no further comment. Do you understand?'

'Yeah I understand.' He yanked his arm from the solicitor's grasp and smashed both hands down on the desk, every tendon in his neck stretched tight as his jaw clenched. 'But it ain't true. They're fitting me up!'

She pressed the alarm and pulled Paul to one side as Nannini reared up, screaming out in anger. The door opened and three burly coppers charged in, restraining him against the wall. The solicitor shrunk away as his client fought, lashing out with his arms and legs, using every huge muscle in his tightly-honed body to do battle. Only when the handcuffs were clamped around his wrists did he calm, the fight gone in the instant his fists were stayed. 'I ain't done nothin' wrong!' he moaned, twisting round, his eyes coming to rest on the face of his solicitor, still squeezed tightly in a corner. 'Honest, I ain't. The feds are fitting me up.'

※ ※ ※

'Franco Nannini, you're charged that on Saturday 1st June 2019, you did murder Kelvin Olawi. That is contrary to Common Law.'

Charlie and Paul listened as the custody officer read out the words of the charge and cautioned him through the small wicket opening in the heavy metal cell door. They were taking no further chances.

There was no need to worry. Nannini said nothing, did nothing. He was beaten and he knew it. He could provide no legitimate reason for his DNA being at the murder scene so the CPS instruction was clear. Charge him. It didn't matter what the neighbour's CCTV may or may not show. The prosecution had all they required. They had a clear unassailable motive, a murder weapon, mobile phone data, a partial admission and indisputable forensics proving his involvement in the run-up to the murder and now, damningly, at the scene. Whether on his own or not, he was fucked.

'One down,' Paul leaned across and whispered to her, listening as bail was refused.

Nannini stared through the aperture. His expression was blank. He nodded to the custody officer then turned his eyes to Charlie and Paul.

'This won't stop now though, bruv. There's something happenin' on the streets out there. Everyone's all stirred up. It's not just the Dons and the Soldiers. No one knows what the fuck's going on and this shit is just the start.'

Chapter 28

Saturday morning dawned clear and bright; Charlie was up and out early. The streets were quiet and the shutters still down on the majority of shops as she entered the police station.

To her surprise the rest of the team were already in, calmly and efficiently completing the paperwork on Franco Nannini that had taken up much of the previous day.

'All quiet last night?' Paul gave her a thumbs up.

'Don't say the Q-word!' Charlie crossed the fingers of both hands. There had been no sign of her father on the home front, and seemingly no trouble from the gangs overnight either, but Nannini's warning had unnerved the whole station. 'Rumour has it they frightened themselves on Wednesday killing Rochelle Edwards. Innocent young girl and all that. Apparently, they're all lying low because of the increased police presence and the interest from the media.'

'Unlike Richie Woodall, who kept appearing yesterday, like a bad smell.'

'Yep. He's watching my every move.'

Paul put on a pompous voice, to mimic him, 'Well, the Wimbledon tennis tournament will be starting soon, don't you know? And I want everything done and dusted by then.'

'Which is why I've come in today. With him off for the weekend I want to go through everything we have.' As

Friday had worn on, she'd become increasingly convinced they'd missed something. 'And if I get a chance, I'd also like to view some of the surveillance footage from the GSM club.'

'You go for it, Charlie – while you can.' Paul grinned.

She was about to get started when the door opened and Ross McBride came in. He was holding a small clear plastic property bag inside which was a memory stick.

'Got the recordings from the house next door to the crime scene,' he shouted, ducking towards Paul and giving him the bag. 'Come on, let's take a look.'

They all gathered round as Paul fired up the media player on one of the computers. 'Wouldn't it be the dog's bollocks if we saw Nannini return,' chirped Naz, squatting down to get a better view. It was good to have her back.

'I haven't had a chance to look yet, so don't get too excited…' Ross glanced at the small crowd, suddenly defensive.

'Don't worry,' Charlie gave him a nod. 'Hopefully it'll show what we want.'

'Here we go,' Paul clicked the play icon and the screen came to life. The footage was great in the daytime, but dull and speckled at night. In the main, it showed the owner's drive but it was set at enough of an angle to take in some coverage of the road – and more importantly the driveway of the house opposite the crime scene.

'There's the Range Rover that Nannini hid behind,' Charlie pointed to the vehicle. It was still light and the registration number was clear. 'Wind forward to around quarter past midnight on Saturday 1st June, Paul. Let's see if we can spot him.'

They watched as Paul started to fast forward through several days' worth of recording.

'The occupant of the house was away on business from the previous Sunday,' Ross explained, turning directly to Charlie. 'He always leaves the camera on when his house is unoccupied. Says he's had his car broken into several times and his front door attempted once. He blames the derelict house for most of the problems – said it attracted squatters initially but it's been better since being boarded up.'

'Until now. I wonder if it was Kelvin Olawi who broke in, or whether he found it already open.'

'I'll go through the recording and check if we can see him coming and going in the previous few days,' Bet chipped in. 'See whether he's being followed or watched by anyone else before he was killed.'

'Thanks Bet.' She silenced, as Paul stopped the recording. As he started it playing again, half a dozen pairs of eyes switched to the base of the screen where the time was now showing 00.15. The footage was grainy, the street being in shadow, but to their delight a nearby street lamp cast a thin light across the frontage of the driveway in which the Range Rover was parked. They watched silently as the time ticked by one minute at a time until 00.18.

'Right this is the time when Olawi's phone is switched off, and he leaves the rec.' Paul commented. 'Two minutes later Nannini's phone is on the move. We know from phone tracking and from Nannini's admission that he was following Boxer, and that they went along a few side streets until they got to Chester Avenue.'

Charlie concentrated on the footage.

At 00.24 a young couple walked across the screen from right to left on the opposite pavement. 'Possible witnesses,' she commented, making a note of the time.

At 00.25 a lone male jogger came past. 'And another,' she added.

At 00.26 a male walked from left to right on the pavement closest to the camera. He was dressed in a dark tracksuit with the hood up and he wasn't hanging about.

'Here we go. That looks like Olawi,' Paul leant forward. 'Though it's difficult to tell in the second or so he appears on the screen.'

'Right sort of height and build, and same type of clothing,' Charlie nodded, thinking back to his attire at the crime scene. 'I would say so.'

They peered towards the screen as a minute later, the shape of a man appeared on the opposite side of the road. The man was tall and of a large build, wearing a t-shirt and jeans. For a second, he paused, then he tucked himself into the driveway opposite, crouching down behind the Range Rover and staring out across the road.

'Zoom in on him,' Charlie said, straining forward as Paul focussed on the figure. Although hazy, the light from the street lamp cast a slight glow on the man's skin, illuminating the dark shape of a tattoo on his neck.

'Franco Nannini.' Paul clapped his hands. 'We've got you, you bastard. Smile for the camera.'

They watched as two minutes later a small light appeared on the screen. '00.29. Bingo. That'll be his phone, at exactly the time he made the call to 3D, giving the location of Olawi.'

Another two minutes ticked by, and the light went out. Five minutes after that, he stood and checked both directions before heading back in the direction from which he had come.

'Excellent,' Paul shot a glance at Charlie. 'At least we have the proof, not just his say so. All the evidence corroborates his story so Nannini can't change it now.'

'Yep, perfect.' Charlie shrugged. 'But it's only what he's already admitted.' In the back of her mind something about what they'd just viewed was niggling her. Something was missing – again – but she couldn't quite put a finger on what it could be. 'What I'm interested in is the next few hours, whether it captures him returning, either on his own, or with 3D.'

Paul clicked the fast forward icon and they watched the footage speed up until it was running at twice its usual speed. Naz and Sabira drifted away to get on with their work, leaving Charlie, Paul, Bet and Ross scrutinising the film. They watched as the minutes rolled by, pausing to check any further passing pedestrians, with Charlie noting down times and descriptions. Any one of them could prove to be a crucial witness, if identified.

At 02.03 a person came into view, slowing to a stop on the opposite kerb. Even speeded up, the figure looked suspicious. 'Stop the video,' she yelled excitedly. 'This must be our man.' Naz and Sab looked up from their desks, and then ran across to view what she'd seen.

Paul rewound the clip and they watched the figure at normal speed. It was a man, of average build and height, dressed in a tight-fitting tracksuit, gloves and baseball cap, the peak of which was pulled low over his forehead. He glanced around and then moved into the driveway of the house opposite, squatting next to the Range Rover, head down. After a few seconds, he backed out, twisted round on the spot and set off diagonally across the road, towards the derelict house.

'Zoom in on him,' she said again, waiting as Paul did as she asked. 'He's way too small for Nannini, so who the hell is it?'

'3D?' Paul asked.

The close-up view didn't really assist. The man was of a similar height and build to 3D but the peak of his cap obscured his face, the light from the street lamp casting a shadow across his facial features. Even his skin tone was impossible to work out.

'Shit,' Paul leant back, pushing the computer mouse out across the desk. 'If it is 3D we'll never prove it.'

'Hang on,' Charlie was standing, staring at the screen. 'Wasn't he there earlier? One minute before Nannini came into view, there was a jogger. It was 00.25. I noted it down.'

Paul took a screenshot of the image and saved it to the computer, then rewound the footage to 00.25. As the jogger came into view, he paused the recording, zoomed in on the man, and then opened up the saved image. There, on either side of the screen, was the same man.

'Bloody hell, Charlie. You're right,' Paul enthused. 'Or at least his height, build and clothing are right. Shame we can't see his face.'

As well as wearing a peaked cap, the shot of the man jogging showed that he also had the hood of his sweatshirt up, concealing his face still further.

'That's strange!' She leant forward concentrating on the two images. 'Why cover your head and face so much when you're jogging, then leave your hood down when you're walking. If anything, you'd do it the other way round.'

'Unless it's 3D and he didn't want Olawi to recognise him,' Bet chipped in. 'Maybe they were both watching him. 3D goes on ahead while Nannini follows Boxer, then when Nannini sees him go into the derelict house he makes a quick phone call to 3D to tell him about his hiding place. They agree a plan of action, then 3D comes back later.'

'Except that 3D's phone was home all the time.' Charlie shook her head.

'And it was Nannini's fag end found at the scene.' Paul added.

They all lapsed into silence. It didn't make sense. If anything, the footage was casting further doubt on their charging decision and giving more credence to Nannini's denials, but there was something about the two images that was ringing alarm bells.

'I can get the footage sent off to be enhanced. I've a contact who works at the lab and he's on call this weekend for urgent exhibits,' said Ross, picking up his phone and keying in a number. Charlie waited while he explained what they had, her adrenalin running riot. What if they had got this wrong? Or more precisely, what if *she* had got it wrong? Much as she'd had her doubts, she'd still rather them be disproved.

'If I get the memory stick to him now,' Ross was saying. 'He'll have it ready in twenty-four hours.'

She nodded.

Twenty-four hours until they found out whether they had potentially charged the wrong man. Twenty-four hours to find out whether her first solo murder investigation had hit the skids.

Chapter 29

It was done.

The perfect hideaway – the perfect prison.

For hours they'd slaved to create their hide, a flawlessly camouflaged cave; its ceiling held up by the roots of the forest and its floor, a soft carpet of fallen leaves. A piece of old curtain had been tied to the entrance, to act as a door, hanging behind a further wall of leafy branches and twigs constructed to mask its existence.

Standing silent and still on the riverbank, she inspected their toils, trying to make out its position against the wooded backdrop of trees and foliage in the forest. It was difficult to spot, though she was under no illusion that their footfall would be heavy and their passage to and fro would be difficult to hide.

'It's bloody brilliant,' she enthused. 'The bastards will never find us here.'

'They'd better not.' His voice was muffled, barely audible from within the hide. She climbed the few feet to its entrance, carefully pulling the foliage back and peering in. He was lying on one of the blankets they'd brought to fend off the chill, his huge chest rising and falling as he breathed in the earthy atmosphere. It was dark and gloomy inside, only the light from a single torch lighting the space.

'Open the door,' he instructed. 'Let's not waste the batteries.'

She did what he asked, rolling the curtaining up and pushing it to one side. The sun slanted inwards, casting a greenish-brown hue on all that it touched. She crawled inside, further admiring their handiwork. Several old cushions taken from a skip were laid directly over the leaf-strewn floor, along with several grubby-looking sleeping bags to provide further warmth. Even with the milder daily temperatures, it still got cold at night. Two buckets stood near the entrance, one for use as a toilet, and the other to be filled with water directly from the river, for drinking and washing.

She glanced down one side of the cave to where three large boxes were stacked, containing food and drink for the first few days – along with their tools of persuasion; knives, duct tape, spare gags. They could top up provisions as they went along. After all, they'd still have to travel into town to send instructions and ransom messages, to ensure compliance with their demands. But for now, they had everything.

She laid down beside him, listening to the sound of the river, water rushing over stones, the clunk of a floating log as it hit a branch extending over the surface. It wouldn't be easy. The space was small and cramped. It would be cold, dark and smelly, but it would all be worth it to get their daughter back.

Tomorrow they would return to London for a day making final preparations; double-checking her friend's address and family, the daughter's school – ready for Monday.

Monday was when her plan would be put into action. Monday afternoon – straight after school.

With the weekend over, there would be fewer families out on the Downs, more opportunity to come and go unseen during the day. And during the night – more time to steal another car.

'I can't wait until Monday,' she murmured into his shoulder, laughter bubbling up her throat.

She flipped on to her back and lay staring into the depths of the cave. Her eyes alighted on a thick root sticking out from the compacted soil and rock above, and marvelled at the way the solid woody structure thrust out into the air before vanishing back into the rocky ceiling. The rope that hung from it was still now, coiled up in readiness for the moment it would be tied around the young girl's wrists, ankles, neck.

She felt the familiar surge of excitement shudder up her spine. It had been a while since she'd last experienced it, but it was there, the growing anticipation of taking control.

The power to give life – or take it away.

Chapter 30

The house looked like a fortress as Charlie crunched across the gravel. In normal times, on a warm June evening like this, her mother would have thrown open at least some of the windows, but tonight they were all pulled shut, with curtains drawn, making their usually happy family home seem gloomy and depressed.

She opened the front door and dropped her bag in the hallway, expecting to find her mother curled up on the sofa, in hiding again, but the house was cool, and empty.

'Mum,' she called, striding anxiously into the kitchen. 'Where are you?'

'I'm out here, love.'

The back door was open. Much to her surprise, her mother was sitting out on the rear patio with a large glass of gin and tonic and a box of Milk Tray. Casper lay on his side in a warm spot next to the table. 'While you've been at work, I've been busy. I've dusted down the patio set and dug out the umbrella from the shed, and planted a few pots.'

'You're brave,' Charlie said, peering out across the lawn to where she'd last heard her father's voice, and then bending down to pat Casper.

'Well, it's too nice to be stuck inside, and as it's been quiet for a couple of days, I thought I'd take the risk.' Her mother looked up from the book she was reading and smiled. 'I've decided I can't let him stop me from living.'

'That's very topical.' Charlie pointed to the book. '*How to Survive a Stalker*. Any tips?'

'Anna Christophe recommended it. I took you up on your suggestion and gave her a ring. It's actually been very useful so far.'

'Ah Anna? Did you chat?'

'Yes, she's a very nice lady.' Her mother ignored the question. 'I mentioned your name – and Ben's. Said what a shame it was that the pair of you split.'

'Mum!'

'Don't worry, Charlie. I didn't say anything else,' she grinned. 'Apart from saying how nice it would be to have a man around the house at the moment, and if she ever heard from him, to say he'd be most welcome to visit.'

'Mum! You simply can't be trusted.' But it was no more than she'd already intimated to Anna herself. She sat down on the chair next to Meg's and rubbed her temples, for a moment smoothing away the day's difficulties. 'So... what did Anna say?'

'Nothing, of course. She's far too professional – but I think she might. Especially after I'd laid it on thick about what your father's up to.'

She raised her eyebrows. 'Have I missed something?'

'No darling. Nothing today, but according to Anna, oh, and page sixty-one – an obsessive ex-partner will use all types of behaviours in order to win. Sometimes they'll attack, and sometimes they'll retreat. It's all part of the ploy to unsettle their victim. Hence the patio furniture. After chatting to Anna, I've decided I'm not hiding away, scaring myself half to death. I know exactly what he's capable of and I'm ready.'

She watched as her mother opened the lid of the Milk Tray box. Inside, instead of chocolates, there was a syringe containing a clear liquid, prepped and ready.

'Ketamine,' Meg said, with a smile.

'Horse tranquiliser?'

'No, it's used perfectly legitimately as an anaesthetic at the hospital. I got it from work.'

'But it's still a controlled drug.'

'It's only Class B. No worse than a little bit of weed – and anyway I don't have it in my possession for my own use. Or at least, not to be injected into me. You won't dob me in, Charlie?'

She frowned. 'No, but I don't like it Mum.'

'Well, I don't like it either but I know what Iain's like, and he won't give up. This really is the calm before the storm, so I'm getting prepared.' Meg reached over and clasped Charlie's hand. 'And the chances are I'll be on my own.'

'You won't be, Mum.'

'I think I will. You work long hours Charlie as you have to. So, when the storm hits, as I know it will, I have to be ready.' She picked up the book and read from it. 'An obsessed stalker is unlikely to stop, unless they're physically prevented from doing so.'

'That's cheery.'

Her mother laughed. 'It is what it is. Your father might have to be physically stopped, and it's no use me grabbing a stick, or a knife, because I know I wouldn't use it.' She flipped the lid down on the chocolate box. 'But I would use this. I'm trained and I know what I'm doing. One jab and he'll be out cold. If I'm on my own and he comes through my window when it's dark one night, it'll be him, not me, being surprised by the contents of my box of Milk Tray.'

Chapter 31

The woman couldn't believe their luck.

Two minutes after they had parked up in the shadow of a large tree outside the adjoining property, the front door had opened.

There on the steps of the big, beautiful house was her ex-best friend, the woman who had betrayed her, dressed flawlessly as usual, her short dark hair blow-dried and sprayed into place, and a subtle covering of make-up seamlessly applied. She wore a perfectly co-ordinated outfit; pale blue linen slacks, a cream camisole top and a thin summer cardigan. She held her arm around the shoulders of a young girl. It was Gemma, grown taller, slimmer and older, but still the innocent child imprinted in her memory, with hair that shone like the sun, and cascaded halfway down her back; a waterfall of beautifully flowing tresses. A shudder of delight ran through the woman's body. Subconsciously she reached out, her hand hovering in the warm air outside the car's open window. She couldn't wait to touch it.

A car had pulled on to the front driveway, clean and tidy with an extra aerial and a sat nav attached to the windscreen. *Airport Cars* was the sticker on the rear screen. The driver got out, as a man appeared from within the darkened interior of the house carrying a suitcase and a carefully folded suit bag. A young boy was in tow, scampering round in his shadow.

Her ex-friend reached out towards the boy, taking him by the arm gently.

'Say goodbye to Daddy,' she said.

'Aw, Daddy, do you have to go?' came the plaintive cry of the boy, Brett, she seemed to remember.

'I'll be home before you know it.' The man reached over tousling the blond hair on the boy's head, then leant down to kiss the girl on the forehead. 'Be good, you two, and do everything you're told.'

'As always, Dad.' Gemma shook her head and rolled her eyes.

She recognised the action, the tone of the girl's voice. Young enough to need telling, but old enough to believe she didn't. Challenging! The next few days might get tricky, but would definitely be fun.

The cab driver lifted the man's suitcase into the boot of the car, and opened the passenger door.

'Right, I'd better go, darling. I don't want to get caught in traffic,' the husband said with a grimace, stepping towards her ex-friend and kissing her on the cheek. She saw the way their hands brushed each other's, the look that passed between them, the lingering smile to the kids. They were the perfect couple, the perfect family.

They continued to watch, as the man turned on his heel, took his seat, and waved goodbye to his family. Any second now the door would be shut and the two children would be left with just their mother, the traitor.

But it was one less adult to stand in their way.

She stared wordlessly as the woman gathered her children round, all waving as the car reversed out of the drive and accelerated away. They then stepped back into the house; the big, beautiful, perfect house with two gardens, floral blinds and a wind chime tinkling from a perfectly pruned magnolia tree.

As the door closed, she struggled to contain the jealous, pitiful rage that had always directed her life. Her friend had everything; every thing.

The perfect fucking life.

And she had nothing! She motioned to her partner to drive – away from this unattainable perfection, and back to reality. All she'd ever wanted was a chance, just a tiny chunk of the same happiness that others had. She closed her eyes, smiling now at the ingenuity of their plan. In the next few days, if it wasn't forthcoming then she would take exactly what she was owed.

Chapter 32

It was almost twenty-four hours to the minute when Ross burst through the doors.

Charlie jumped to her feet, the now familiar lump in her stomach rising up her throat as she watched him throw the file of photos down on the desk and open it up. The tension of the last few days, both at home and at work was getting to her and nausea seemed to be a constant feature.

She waited while he pulled out several photos, laying them flat across the desk, as the others came over in a repeat of the previous day. There were six images in total; two that clearly showed Franco Nannini, two of the jogger, and two of the man who had returned a couple of hours later.

'Well, that confirms Franco's partial admission,' she said, staring at the first two. 'There's absolutely no doubt that's Franco Nannini. Size, tattoo, everything. But who the hell is this?' She glanced from one to the other. 'It doesn't look like 3D now we can see his face and clothing better. There's no knife tattoo, but, hang on!' She lifted up one of the later photos, holding it up to the light, her eyes not quite believing what she was seeing. 'Look! Look at the peaked cap. I know you can't see the colours but see the pattern? It's a Union flag.' She peered across to the photo of the jogger. 'And if we weren't a hundred percent sure facially that it's the same man, look at the two peaks, the same lighter coloured lines.'

Her mind rewound to a bright flash of colour in a monochrome office. A Union flag cap hanging on a coat stand. The sight of a man, standing in the shadowy recesses of a doorway - and as her eyes flicked from one image to the other, she recognised the face; the same blank eyes, the splayed out nose.

'Bloody hell,' she shouted. 'I think I know who it is.'

❁ ❁ ❁

Five minutes later, she was sure. Wayne Hurley stared out from the GSM club. The surveillance camera set on the wall of the car park had captured him perfectly, providing a clear image of the man standing at the door, wearing the same style of Union flag peaked cap.

Just looking at the photo made her squirm. He wasn't as large as a typical security guard, but there was something about the way he and his boss acted together that disturbed her. Jamie Smythe-Hamilton was the mouthpiece. He was smug and self-assured and she'd taken an instant dislike to him, but there was something about Wayne Hurley that had also hit a nerve; taking his time to answer the door, slinking around on the coat-tails of his boss. Always there. There was something sleazy about the man and she meant to find out what.

'It's got to be him.' She watched as Paul pulled up a custody image of Hurley, from one of his previous arrests. He looked like a thug; his broken nose squashed almost flat in profile, his dead, emotionless eyes – but was he a murderer?

'Right.' She clapped her hands. 'Wayne Hurley, date of birth 3/12/1976, previous convictions for assault, criminal damage, class A drug possession and a range of public order offences. He acts like your stereotypical thug in public, but he's not. He's smart, or he likes to think he is. So, we now know that he was in the vicinity of the derelict house on the night of Kelvin Olawi's murder.'

'Well, we can't prove for definite it was him,' Paul interrupted. 'Sorry, but the images in the Chester Avenue recordings are too fuzzy to stand up in court as positive identifications. All we have is the Union flag cap – and who knows how many thousand similar caps there are in circulation.'

'Okay,' she paused. 'Well let's presume it is then. Yesterday when we thought it might be 3D, we decided that the reason he had his hood up was so Olawi wouldn't recognise him. But if it was Hurley, I think it's fair to assume he was actually hiding away from Franco Nannini. Nannini would know him. I've seen them both talking together.'

'It's an awfully big risk.'

'It depends on how high the stakes are – and whether Jamie Smythe-Hamilton is involved. Hurley's in the thick of it at the club and I'm willing to bet this is all about drugs. So that night he was doing a bit of homework on the gangs for his boss. Everyone knows where the gangs hang out. He sees Olawi leave the rec, then he sees Nannini so he keeps an eye on them both, staying one step ahead so he's able to watch Olawi go into the derelict house, but also to see Nannini slip in beside the Range Rover.'

'So far so good.' Paul agreed. 'But why come back? We know Nannini's in the frame for Olawi's murder because we have the fag end with his DNA on it at the crime scene, and—'

'Wait,' she interrupted. 'Paul, put the neighbour's footage back on. There was something missing when we watched it yesterday and I think I know what it was.' She took the controls, fast-forwarding it to the point where the jogger, potentially Hurley, ran past, and then, to two minutes later, when Nannini is seen crouching down by the side of the Range Rover, then using his phone, before getting up and leaving.

'That's it. Look.' She rewound the scene, grinning broadly. 'Here comes Nannini, and it's all dark. We can barely make out the knife tattoo, but then, see how easy it is to see the mobile phone light.'

'So?' Paul looked bemused.

'So, where's the cigarette? A cigarette butt with his DNA on it was found next to the Range Rover – so he'd be smoking, but he's not – otherwise we'd see it glowing. That's why Hurley stops there later. We know Nannini and 3D go round to the GSM club regularly. How easy would it be to pick up a few of Franco's old Rothman's dog-ends and plant them there?'

Chapter 33

'Nice theory, sergeant, but it simply isn't credible.'

Charlie stood in front of Superintendent Woodall, feeling like a twelve-year-old school girl receiving a dressing down from her headmaster. Having listened to her in stony silence, he was delivering his verdict, and from the set of his jaw, it didn't bode well.

'But—'

He cut her off, his voice cold and controlled. 'But... we have a suspect for Rocco Fontana's murder and that suspect is now dead. Kelvin Olawi's fingerprints were found on the murder weapon, and he's not here now to explain them away.'

He breathed in deeply, and tapped his pen on the desk. 'And you're trying to tell me that an employee of a reputable club that caters for the celebrity clientele of the tennis world is somehow guilty – of what, Sergeant Stafford? Murder? Correct me if I'm wrong but I think you need evidence.'

He opened the file, flipping the pages open until he came to the enhanced stills from the Chester Avenue recording.

'So, what can you tell me about the murder of our murderer? That someone wearing a Union flag cap, who you say is Wayne Hurley, has planted two cigarette ends belonging to Franco Nannini at the murder scene, while you ignore the fact that the Dons have had one of their own taken out, and, in the eyes of their peers, are perfectly justified in taking revenge. For what reason? It doesn't make sense.'

He slammed the file shut.

'DS Stafford, you can't make out anything about this man, apart from the cap. Do you know how many Union flag caps are sold in the two weeks of the Wimbledon Tennis Championships every year? Hundreds, if not thousands. There's probably one in every household in SW19.

'And that's without the fact that we have a gang nominal, whose DNA has been found at the murder scene, charged with the murder. Franco Nannini has been remanded in custody and is now awaiting trial, on the advice of the CPS – advice I'd urge you to take on board.'

'But...'

'But what Sergeant? Do I have to spell it out for you? We have clear-ups for the first two murders. They're sorted, so forget about them. The media are far more interested in Rochelle Edwards, a young innocent child brutally cut down as she walked home from school. So, I don't want to hear another word about the deaths of Rocco Fontana and Kelvin Olawi. There's a young girl's family out there who require justice, and I've promised the papers they'll have it.'

❀ ❀ ❀

'Woodall's such a bastard.' Charlie slammed the door to the main office and threw the file down on the first table she came to.

'What did he say then?' Paul and the others in the team came closer.

She picked up the file again and indicated her office. There were a few secondments to her usual team and she didn't know as yet if they could be trusted. 'You can come too,' she said, beckoning for Ross McBride to join them. 'You know all the grisly details.'

Shutting the door behind Bet, she slumped down on her chair and spread her hands. 'Well, it was a carbon copy of what you said, Paul. He thinks what we have is not credible; in fact, he went as far as saying it's totally unbelievable. I thought he was going to take me off the case – and that's without him knowing about our secret surveillance at the GSM club.'

She leant forward; her voice conspiratorial. 'So from now on we'll work smartly – and quietly. I don't want a whisper of what we're doing getting back to him, and I certainly don't want Hurley or Smythe-Hamilton spooked. We need every bit of dirt we can dig up on them, so I'll go elsewhere again if I need any more authorisations, and I'll see if I can't get a small surveillance team working on them. And don't forget we still have the warrant in our back pocket. We have so much, but at the same time, there are a lot of gaps that need to be filled. Is Wayne Hurley our actual killer? Is he working on his own, or in league with Jamie Smythe-Hamilton? We all know there's something much bigger going on.

'But it's so bloody risky.' She stood up, frowning. 'How long before another murder happens? The gangs won't stay scared off forever and if it is Hurley and Smythe-Hamilton stirring things up, they'll be up to it again very soon. For the next few days, we'll have to watch their every move.

'I've seen too many young people stabbed to death or severely wounded. I can't risk seeing another.'

※ ※ ※

Naz hung back, gazing out of the window silently as the others filed into the main office. Charlie went across and stood next to her, noticing immediately that her friend was subconsciously rubbing her injured arm.

'You okay?'

'Could be better,' Naz tipped one hand from side to side. 'I've just been told that Constance Olawi has been let out on bail on compassionate grounds. It's a bit of a kick in the teeth, Charlie, but I suppose, with Kelvin now being a victim, as well as a suspect, it's understandable. Do *you* think Kelvin killed Rocco?'

'Who knows? As far as Woodall is concerned, he did, but I'm not sure. Everything is up in the air at the moment.'

'What if he didn't, and we went looking for the wrong boy? I know we were perfectly justified with his fingerprints being found on the murder weapon and all that, but what if we got it wrong. Constance was simply trying to protect her son. She is his mother after all.'

'Just as Dawn Edwards is Rochelle's mum, and Maria Fontana, Rocco's sister. I'm sure those families have issues too, but neither of them go around stabbing police officers. In fact, anything but.'

'Well, everyone to their own, I suppose. My two boys might act like little shits some days but I'd defend them until my dying breath. I suppose that's what mother's do.'

Charlie smiled at her friend, thinking back to Meg and her box of Milk Tray. 'You know,' she agreed, throwing an arm around Naz's shoulder and giving her a squeeze. 'I think you might be right.'

Chapter 34

It had been one of those days.

One of those good days, when the sky above the common opposite Anna Christophe's office was a bright azure and the solar energy from the sun's rays heated the windows, radiating life into the whole room. Even the dark oak panels, so often guilty of incarcerating the office in a rather sombre, humourless atmosphere had taken on a lighter sheen; the shadows of leaves from the trees outside dancing and swaying against the wood, giving the walls the appearance of a living, breathing forest.

The day had been busy, and the positivity of the weather seemed to have rubbed off on each of her earlier clients, injecting them all with joie de vivre; something not usually on display.

Anna checked her watch. It was nearly 4.54 p.m. Only two more clients to go – both of whom were coming to the end of their individual courses of counselling – and she'd be on her way home. The weight of their worries had been lifted from their shoulders, and their perseverance was all that was required to keep them contented.

She ambled across to the new coffee machine she'd recently installed on a table by the window, just as the sun was momentarily eclipsed behind a single grey cloud. Shrugging off a split second of unease, she selected a capsule of cappuccino and slotted it into its holder, stretching her spine out vertebra by vertebra from her coccyx to her shoulder blades as she waited. Her Pilates teacher had been exhorting the practice on her weekend course. Flexible minds required flexible bodies, or so her instructor insisted.

The machine was gently hissing and gurgling to completion, with a stream of frothy milk spilling over the surface of the coffee. Anna waited for the last bubble of milk to drip from the nozzle before picking it up and holding it to her nose. The aroma of the coffee filled her nostrils, giving her mind an imaginary boost of caffeine. She felt alive and the stresses and strains of the last few months were at last beginning to seep away.

Her mobile phone vibrated from where she kept it hidden from clients, in the drawer of her desk. Not all her visitors were as trustworthy as she would have liked.

She walked across and opened the drawer, and saw that a text message had pinged in with her daughter's name filling the screen. Her eyes flicked automatically towards the photos on her desk, as she smiled at her children's images grinning out from the frames. How quickly time had flown. Gemma had started high school the previous September and it was unbelievable now that she'd soon be in year eight. She caught the bus home by herself these days, not wanting to be collected by Isobel, their childminder, who still waited at the gates of the junior school for her younger brother, Brett.

Anna keyed in her pass code whilst guessing at the content. Gemma would no doubt be wanting to know what time she'd be home. What was for dinner that night, or whether she could increase her hard fought for hour's worth of social media. She attempted that one every day. To Anna, their daily spat was well worth the momentary irritation. She considered herself lucky with Gemma.

They had always maintained good lines of communication, and she was, on the whole, well-balanced and for a near teenager, reasonably manageable.

Anna read the message, but it made absolutely no sense.

She read the words again, as an icy chill permeated every square inch of the room. The mug of boiling coffee slipped from her hand, its contents splattering against the wooden floorboards, but she was oblivious to the scalding liquid splashing up her leg.

Pls help me, Mummy, I'm scared. They told me to tell u they're going to kill me if they don't get what they want.

Her hands began shaking violently as a further message hit the screen. She stared at it blankly. It was from a different phone with a number she didn't recognise.

DO NOT CONTACT THE FEDS! We will contact you again soon. If you do what we say Gemma will not be hurt. But if you betray us... she will die!

Chapter 35

'Pick up,' Anna screamed at the phone. 'Please, whoever you are...'

She dialled both the numbers again and again; each desperate stab at the buttons becoming less controlled, her hands still shaking and her fingers sausage-like and almost inoperable.

'For Christ's sake, pick up.'

She pressed the phone hard against her ear, panic bubbling up her throat.

'Talk to me!'

The metallic click of the mobile dropped her to her knees, as she realised both phones were switched off. Tears streamed down her cheeks. The spilt coffee swilled around the floor, wetting the hem of her dress. An ugly brown stain soaked the material. She stared as the liquid spread out across the fabric; thinking, thinking.

What the hell should she do? Her husband, Scott, was over three thousand miles away in New York on business. She checked her watch. They were five hours behind. He'd be at work now, more than likely in a meeting. She dialled his number, and listened as his strong, calm, voice came on the answerphone...

'Leave me a message and I'll get back to you as soon as I can.'

'Scott,' she said his name, trying to keep the sense of panic from her voice. 'Gemma's in trouble. Call me back as soon as you get this. It's urgent.'

Done. At least she'd done something, but it wasn't enough. How long might it take for a response? Minutes? Hours? It could be dark here by the time he'd finished work, and even then, what could he do?

She got to her feet, her wet dress slapping against her legs. She couldn't just wait and do nothing. Too soon it would be dark and Gemma hated the dark. She was already scared. She'd said as much, but she'd be so frightened. She'd be frightened to death. *Death*. She shuddered at the mere thought of the word.

Bending down, she retrieved the mug from the floor, trying to slow her mind. She had to think, reason, work out what she could. Shakily, she dried her eyes with the heel of her hand and scrolled back to the messages, concentrating on her own advice. Breathe. Breathe.

Pls help me, Mummy. I'm scared. They told me to tell u they're going to kill me if they don't get what they want. Anna read the messages again, scrutinising each word.

Just the use of the word *Mummy* took her breath away. It was a term that Gemma hadn't used since starting at high school. *Too babyish*, she'd said. Anna closed her eyes, swallowed. Opened them again. Gemma had used the term *they*.

And *they* had also used the term *we*. So there was more than one. There were at least two, three, four? How many were there?

DO NOT CONTACT THE FEDS! We will contact you again soon. If you do what we say Gemma will not be hurt. But if you betray us... she will die!

She focussed on the second message. The word *feds* was one that she'd heard many times before – on the streets of Lambeth, on the lips of clients, even from a few friends. It was a slang term for a federal government officer, adopted from the USA. From New York.

For a moment she stopped. Could it somehow be connected to Scott's work? But she doubted it. The term was too common. It was everywhere in London.

She recalibrated, picking out the most important words from the message. *Contact. Gemma. Betray.*

But when would they contact her? Soon, but how soon? In an hour, a day, a week? Please God not a week.

And they'd used Gemma's name. Not *your daughter*, or *your child*, but her name. Its use was more personal, less official. As if they knew her.

Then *betray* – a peculiar choice – and one that did not sit right within the context of the demand. It spoke of disloyalty, treachery, dangerous revelations. It was a word she'd heard often in the course of her counselling. People spoke of betrayal by parents, family, partners, friends. Not by a stranger. It was more intimate than that. It triggered a response.

She was thinking about this when her phone rang.

'Anna, it's me. What's happened to Gemma?'

'Oh my God, Scott.' She was crying again now. 'She's been kidnapped.'

'Kidnapped?' His tone was incredulous.

'Yes. They've sent a message telling us they'll kill her if we don't do what they say.'

'Slow down, Anna. Who has?'

'I don't know, I don't know who *they* are. But Gemma said the same. That they'd kill her if we don't do what they ask.' She was babbling.

'You've spoken to Gemma?' Scott's tone was as desperate as hers.

'No, not spoken. She sent me a text. Hang on.' She scrolled to the message relieved that he'd not questioned her any further. Quickly she read the text out. 'Oh Scott, she called me Mummy.'

'So she's alright. She's got to be alright if she sent you a text.' She heard him sigh

'But that was twenty minutes ago. Goodness knows where she is now, or what they've done to her.'

'What do the police say?'

'I haven't called them yet. The message says not to contact the police. Listen, this is what they've written.' She read out the full text, her voice catching as she did so. 'Scott, I don't know what to do. I can't call the police. I don't know how many there are of them. They could be out there watching my office, or the house. Oh my God, I haven't warned Isobel and Brett.'

She could feel the panic filling her lungs, rising up her gullet, a solid mass that squeezed the oxygen from her body. She swallowed it back, choking and gasping with the effort of taking a breath.

'Hold on Anna.' Scott's voice was strong. 'I'll call Isobel now, ask her something innocuous, to make sure they're safely home. I don't want to frighten her until we work out what to do.'

'Okay.' She waited while he called, her insides settling slightly. She needed to stay calm. They both did. She ran back over the message, checking the time. The school would have made contact if Gemma had failed to turn up to her lessons. 4.58 p.m. – so it had to be after school was out. It had to be recent.

'Brett and Isobel are fine.' Scott's voice came back on to the line. 'I told her that Gemma was going to tea with a friend – and that we'd just had a warning from our neighbourhood watch group that dodgy door-to-door sellers are in the area. I've told her to make sure the house is secure and not to answer the door. It's no more than we've had on quite a few occasions. She's fine with it all.'

'Thank goodness.'

'I'm going to get a flight home straight away.'

Anna breathed a sigh of relief. Two minds would be far better than one, and anyway, she needed him home. 'What should I do in the meantime? I think Gem's been snatched after leaving school. Should I contact the school? Maybe they've seen something, or know something.'

'I think we should contact the police, Anna. We can't do this on our own. And why on earth have we been targeted? What could they possibly want from us?'

'I don't know Scott. Let me think.' *She will die.* She couldn't get the final words out of her mind. *If we betray them – Gemma will die.* Could she risk phoning the police - having a squad car turn up at her office, or home, all guns blazing. She closed her eyes to think, dismissing her worry almost immediately. Of course the police wouldn't turn up like that. Fear was playing games with her mind. But what if they did?

She will die.

When she opened her eyes again, she found them drawn to her diary lying open on her desk at that week's page. Across one of the days was written *Call Meg Stafford back.*

'Charlie. What about Charlie Stafford?!' she blurted down the phone, her professional ethics irrationally kicking in even as she expressed the thought. She bit on her lip. Could she really call Charlie? After all, she was a client – or was she? They'd spoken before, recently even, but more as friends, or colleagues working on a case.

It was Ben, Charlie's ex, and her mother, Meg who were her clients, not Charlie. 'Do you remember her?' He'd met her on several occasions. 'I'm sure she would help.'

'Charlie's good.' Scott sounded positive.

She rang off, and immediately clicked onto her contacts. Half an hour had now passed since she'd received the text messages. Quickly she dialled the number, her foot tapping impatiently in time with the ringtone. A few seconds later her friend answered.

'Charlie! It's Anna,' she almost cried with relief. 'I need your help.'

Chapter 36

Charlie listened as Anna poured out her story.

It was shocking. Anna, and her family were some of the nicest people anyone could hope to meet. 'Who could have done this?'

'I have no idea,' Anna stifled a sob. 'I've been wracking my brains.'

'Keep thinking then. I'll make some phone calls.'

'But…'

'I can't keep this to myself, Anna. It's too big for me, but don't worry, the unit I'll call is specialist. They have the skills and equipment to deal with this type of thing – they do it all the time. Stay put, and start writing the names of anyone who might have a grudge. We'll have Gemma back before you know it.'

She ended the conversation and immediately made the promised call. One of her former colleagues worked for the unit – it had been he who had dealt with the gang kidnappings.

'Paul,' she shouted into the main office. 'I need you and Ross to take charge of the gang stuff for a short while. Something urgent has come up.'

He came to the doorway of her office, looking slightly bemused.

'Sorry mate, the less people who know the better.' She passed him a file, before taking off her ID lanyard and placing it in her bag. On no account could she show out as a police officer. 'That's the surveillance authorities. We've got a surveillance team jacked up for Hurley and Smythe-Hamilton. I'll tell them to liaise with you. Meet them away from this area and brief them on what's required. You know the case as well as I do, Paul. I don't want to waste our warrant – or let those bastards know we're on to them but we need something substantive to get them both nicked and kept in custody.'

Five minutes later she was weaving through the traffic in an unmarked police car.

'Anna. Come to the cafe by Tooting Bec Tube Station and I'll pick you up there,' she instructed, through the hand's free set. 'My colleague will meet us nearby.'

'Okay Charlie. I'm on way.' There was a pause, then, 'You will be quiet, won't you?'

'I'm coming from Wimbledon.' She frowned at the question. 'But of course, I will.'

❀ ❀ ❀

Anna was already in the cafe when Charlie arrived. She looked ashen. Charlie greeted her as she would a friend, walking across and hugging her close.

'It'll be all right,' she whispered. 'Pretend we're old friends.'

A half-smile flickered on Anna's face. 'Well, we are really, aren't we?'

The cafe was almost empty; one table occupied by a couple of older women, and one by a workman in a hi-vis jacket. The manager was clearing up. Charlie bought them each a take away coffee, her eyes scanning the occupants, and out to the street beyond. There was nothing unusual.

'Come with me,' she said, as she checked the contents of a few texts.

She led Anna out, and around the corner, sauntering unhurriedly along several small side streets, all the time watching for anyone following. When she was sure it was safe, she took Anna to her car. 'Can't be too careful,' she said, looking around once more.

The journey was short but she drove in the same manner as she'd walked, taking in various streets and doglegs, all the time watching for any vehicle that might be following them. Confident it was all clear, she pulled into a car park at the rear of some flats, edging up alongside another vehicle. The passenger window of the other car slid open and the driver leaned across. 'Hi Charlie,' he said. 'Bring Anna over.'

Once they were settled into the rear, she introduced Anna to the man smiling across from the driver's seat. 'This is Tony Ludlow. He's a detective sergeant from SCD7, the specialist kidnap unit – and Tony's the best. I've worked with him before and you won't get a better, more experienced officer than him.'

It was important that Anna warmed to the detective. Tony was toned and muscular, a bear of a man; and his smile and gravelly voice reminded Charlie of Idris Elba. Depending on what side you were on, he could either scare the hell out of you, or hold you safe in strong, accommodating arms.

He held out his hand. 'That's some recommendation,' he said, gripping Anna's hand in his. Anna smiled back, but her eyes flicked nervously towards Charlie. 'And Charlie will be working with us too. I understand she knows you and your family quite well.'

Charlie listened as Tony took the cue. He was, perhaps, the best person she knew for reading body language.

His training and wealth of experience meant he could quickly put a person perfectly at ease and establish the trust required in delicate negotiations.

Anna nodded. Her shoulders slumped and a modicum of colour returned to her cheeks. They were on their way.

'Right, let's get down to business.' He slotted a DVD into a laptop and passed it to Charlie and Anna to view. 'I popped into Gemma's school on the way here and pretended I was researching whether a local sex offender had been breaching his conditions by hanging about local schools. They've allowed me the CCTV footage from the school entrances and exits.' He tilted his head. 'At this stage the fewer people who know what's going on, the better. Right, this is the main entrance of the school. Tell me when you see Gemma.'

The time on the base of the footage was 15.15.

'She won't be out yet,' Anna said. 'It's far too early. She usually does netball after school on a Monday.'

'I was hoping you wouldn't say that.' Tony was frowning. 'I checked what afterschool clubs were scheduled for today, just in case – and the netball was cancelled. Their teacher was off sick and all the others were already taking clubs.'

'Shouldn't the school have made the kids stay?' Charlie chipped in, the realisation dawning on her, in an instant, that they might now be well and truly playing catch-up.

'I asked that. Apparently, the girls only have to stay if there are arrangements in existence to be picked up from school. Afterschool clubs are not compulsory, obviously. So, if they live nearby and want to leave, they're free to go home.'

Anna clapped her hand over her mouth. 'So Gemma could have left school at 3.15, instead of 4.45 like I thought? That's an extra hour and a half they have on us straight away.'

'Let's not jump to conclusions,' Charlie said, trying to sound more confident than she felt. 'We don't know what time she left yet.'

They watched in silence, as the trickle of children became a flow; a tide of navy blazers and trousers, white shirts with turquoise and sky blue striped ties, most of which were loosened and flapping, now school was out for the day. Anna leant forward, her eyes never leaving the screen, clearly understanding the importance of pinpointing the exact time when Gemma had left.

'There she is.' Anna almost jumped in her seat, pointing towards one of the shorter girls, with long blonde hair in a French plait, and a red ribbon tied to her large blue school rucksack.

'She put the ribbon on it, so her bag would stand out when they have to leave them in a pile,' Anna explained.

'That's handy for us.' Charlie concentrated on the girl. Gemma Christophe had grown up so much since the last time they'd met. Then, she had still been at junior school, a bubbly kid, with her long locks tied in two pigtails that swung wildly as she ran. Now, with her hair tamed, she looked every bit the young adolescent.

She was about to comment to that effect when she heard Anna sob. She glanced round, watching helplessly as her friend cupped her face in her hands. There could be no doubt what thoughts were filling Anna's head as she watched her eldest child walk through the school gate and head off out of view.

Charlie had exactly the same fears running through hers.

Chapter 37

The house was quiet when Anna pushed open her front door. A quick call to Isobel had ensured that for tonight at least Brett would know nothing of his sister's disappearance. He'd had his dinner and had been *encouraged* to do his homework. In addition, Isobel had readily agreed to take control of the domestic arrangements for as long as it took.

'Thank you so much,' Anna whispered to a pale-faced Isobel as she ushered the two police officers into the lounge. Brett, for now, was holed up in his bedroom, concentrating to the exclusion of everything else, on one last go of the Play Station before bed.

Charlie looked around the room. It was similar to her family home; filled with sunken soft furnishings, small piles of clutter and a dozen family montages splashed about the walls. She watched as her friend squared her shoulders, summoning the courage to say goodnight to her son whilst trying to pretend that everything was normal. She waited for her to leave the room, before then checking around the photos. She spotted one tucked behind the clock on the mantelpiece, still waiting to be framed. It showed Gemma proudly wearing her new school uniform and had obviously been taken in the previous few months. She picked it up, making a mental note to ask Anna if it could be used, if required. They would need a good colour image of Gemma to provide to the press, if things didn't go to plan.

Until then they would be doing everything possible to get Gemma back, without alerting her kidnappers to their involvement. To that end, both Charlie and Tony would be staying with Anna through what was looking to be the longest night of her life. Tony had the tech required there to mobilise his troops, record any further phone contacts, and advise on negotiations. So far there had been no further contact, and with every passing minute the tension was increasing.

It was now nearly 9 p.m. – four hours after the first text. Sixteen minutes before sunset.

Tony was finishing a phone call when Anna returned. She walked straight to the window. 'So far, so good,' she said, staring out. 'Thank goodness for video games. He barely noticed I was there, never mind that I was talking to him. Isobel's going to help me out, and I'll keep him off school in the morning.'

Charlie moved across to where she stood, and guided her instead to the table, where Tony was sitting with his laptop.

'Right,' he said, marshalling their attention. 'So we've seen Gemma leave school and turn right, in her usual direction.' Charlie and Anna followed his gaze as he stared at the map on the screen. 'We know she would've headed towards the shops at the end of the road, where the bus stop is situated.

'But we also know that she didn't arrive, because I've just had a call from one of my team. He's obtained some CCTV from the newsagent's shop near to her bus stop and gone through it from 15.22 when we know Gemma left school, right up until when you got her text at 16.58 – and there's no sign of her.'

'Is there anywhere else at all Gemma might have gone?' Charlie ran her finger across the screen, and then zoomed in on the names of several side streets that joined the main road from both sides. They'd already asked Anna several times but it didn't hurt to try again. 'Any reason you can think of why Gemma might have gone into any of these streets?'

Anna shook her head. 'No, she knows not to hang around. And, like I said, her best friend lives near here. They would usually meet up and come home on the bus together, but her friend prefers hockey – and obviously because of the cancelled club...' She paused, shaking her head. 'Why couldn't Gem have given Isobel a ring? The junior school is nearby. They could have come home together.'

'Because she's all grown up.' Charlie put a hand on Anna's arm. 'And once she's been given these first few freedoms, she won't want to relinquish them.'

'So...' Tony's voice broke into their conversation. 'We have the team looking for CCTV in any of the adjoining roads which might flag up a vehicle or person acting suspiciously. And we're doing a lot of work on the phones. The last time they were used was on the outskirts of London...'

'So practically speaking we're doing everything we can.' Charlie was desperate to inject some positivity. Time was ticking by. 'Keep trying to think of anyone who might have done this.'

Anna nodded, drawing them both back to the window. 'I am,' she said hoarsely, staring out into the gathering gloom. 'But there's no one I can think of.'

'We need a phone call, or text,' Charlie voiced what they were all thinking.'

'Yes, something that can be traced and tracked,' Tony added.

'Something to tell me that Gem is alive. That she's okay.'

Charlie swallowed. It was hard listening to her friend's anguish – especially as she felt it too. They all did. Tony rose from his chair and moved across to join them, placing a strong arm around Anna's shoulder in support. Then they all watched in silence, as the sun slipped down behind the neighbouring rooftops and took with it the last of the light.

Chapter 38

The woman leant back against a leafy mound, her head trained up to the sky. She had rarely seen so many stars before. In fact, she had rarely seen any at all. Her whole life had been spent in the bright lights of London, ferreting about for food, for drugs, for love. There had been no time for nature.

She watched the boughs of the trees moving gently in the breeze. The moon was thin, but becoming brighter each minute. It had been a warm evening, was even now a warm night but nonetheless she shivered. She pulled the blanket tighter round her shoulders, listening, wondering. Was it the chill rising up from the cold water of the river, or the threat of the forest that made her tremble? Or could it be the thrill of the chase.

She twisted round at the sound of crying, angry in an instant at being disturbed. Moving the old curtain to one side, she stared into the gloomy recesses of their hide.

Her torch picked out the young girl's frightened eyes, the shiny surface of the duct tape stuck across her mouth, her long blonde hair so perfectly plaited down her back. The woman loved hair – the way every style was so unique – thick, thin, wavy, curly, black, blonde, red. And Gemma's hair was beautiful. She shone the light around their lair, further spotlighting the shape of the girl crouched on their makeshift flooring, her hands held together with a set of handcuffs, her legs tethered with electrical cord. She tilted the beam upwards, her lips curling at the sight of the rope tied tightly around the root of the tree then looping down towards the girl, once, twice around her neck, then fastened with a knot.

'You okay?' she called out, her irritation diminishing as she shone the torch directly into Gemma's face. 'I'm sure your mummy will do everything we ask.'

For a moment she wanted to laugh. If you didn't ask, you sure as hell wouldn't get. She knew it was cruel, but then, so was life. She'd been betrayed again and again by her parents, her partner, her friends. There was no honour amongst any of them.

The girl was crying louder now.

'You wanna come out?' she called again, Gemma's baby sobs pricking her conscience. It wasn't the child's fault. It hadn't been Mia's either.

The girl nodded, her eyes widening.

The woman got to her feet, stretching out in the moonlight, then bent inside the entrance to the cave, and made her way across the leaves and cushioning.

'One noise and it's back on, you understand,' she said, ripping the sticky tape from her mouth, and pulling a knife from her pocket.

'Yes Miss,' the girl sobbed.

She smiled at her new title. It was the same term as prison inmates called their warders. Apt, under the circumstances.

Untying the rope, she helped the girl to her feet, her fingers straying to the elastic band holding Gemma's hair in place. She slipped it off, unwinding the French plait and running her fingers through the mass of golden curls. The texture of the hair evoked a thousand memories of people from her past, gone now but never forgotten. Good memories. Bad memories. She let her mind wander, thinking back to the girl's capture that afternoon, the delicious moment when she'd spotted Anna's daughter walking along the street. My, how she'd grown.

Only once when they'd first called her over, had she allowed the girl to address her by name. 'Hello Gemma,' she'd smiled from the rear seat of the stolen car. 'Your mother sent me to find you.'

'Oh, really?' Gemma had looked surprised, but had then confirmed her vague recognition of her by saying the woman's name. It had taken her aback, considering the few times they'd met and the length of time since their last meeting. Several months, maybe even a year. Children have fertile memories.

But then, so did she.

'Jump in,' she'd leant across and patted the seat, deciding then, it would be the last time Gemma called her by name. It was too personal, too friendly. The child had to understand that, for the next few days at least, she wasn't a friend. She was anything but. In fact she could be cruel, if provoked. 'She's organised a surprise picnic, seein' as the weather's so nice. She's gone ahead with Brett to get your sandwiches ready, in your favourite picnicking spot.'

'But she hasn't told me.'

'Because it's a surprise.'

For a moment the girl had been unsure, frowning and toying with her phone, her eyes flicking anxiously across to the driver.

She'd understood Gemma's reticence. Stranger, danger, and all that.

'Don't be worried,' she'd hastened to calm the girl's apprehension, nodding in the direction of her partner. 'This is my boyfriend, CJ. He might be big, but you've no need to be scared. Your mum invited him too.' She smiled again, patting the seat one more time, for a few seconds wondering whether they'd have to resort to more physical means. 'Come on Gemma. Get in. They'll be waiting for us.'

The girl had paused – but then she'd climbed in, sitting wide-mouthed with alarm as the door locks had clunked into place and a set of handcuffs was slapped onto her wrists. The knife was the clincher though; its presence, like glue, sealing her lips and making her incapable of speech. So, she'd stayed silent, her eyes wide with terror as her mobile phone was prised from her hand, switched off and the battery removed.

Even as they'd parked up in the glorious North Downs, Gemma had remained mute. She'd maintained her silence, wedged between the two of them, as they'd walked along the river's edge; to all intents and purposes, a young girl in full school uniform out for a walk with her parents.

And she'd never said a word.

Until now.

'Thank you, Miss.' The girl's plaintive tone brought her back to the present. Gemma had clearly rediscovered her voice. 'I'm frightened of the dark.'

'Well, you'd better get used to it.'

She held the child steady, as Gemma shuffled across the flooring, her legs bound tightly at the knees. The girl clung to her arm as they ducked under the old curtain, squatting down obediently where she pointed.

'This place is nice, isn't it?' she said, pulling out a brush and running it over Gemma's head, again and again until her blonde hair shone in the moonlight. 'Your mum's got good taste.'

Gemma nodded, glancing up and down along the river. 'Where's CJ?'

She shrugged, wondering for a second who the girl meant, then remembered how she'd introduced him.

A sudden thought; perhaps the girl was looking for a chance to escape now they'd been left on their own.

''e's out sending messages to your mum, like 'e did earlier. Telling 'er what she's gotta do. Why?'

'What did you say earlier on the text to my mum?' Gemma's bottom lip was trembling. 'I saw you writing it on my phone.'

'Only what I thought you might say', then, mimicking a child's voice, 'Mummy, I'm scared. Mummy, please help me.' She laughed nastily, flicking the blade of the knife open. 'That sort of thing.' The blade shot out, its sharpened metal edge, glinting darkly in the beam of the torch. 'Oh... and that we would kill you if she doesn't do what we ask.'

Gemma gasped, throwing her two hands up to her mouth, the handcuffs clanking together as she did so.

'What is it you want?'

'Well, your mother broke her promises. She betrayed me.' She leant back against the same leafy mound and relaxed. The girl was tied securely, with no possible way of escape. 'She snitched on me to the feds and the social services busybodies. They came and took my baby away – pulled 'er right out of me arms while I held 'er. And they won't give 'er back.

'So, your mum is going to speak to the authorities an' help me get my baby back – or else.'

She twisted the blade of the knife in the moonlight. 'But CJ... now 'e's a different story.' She stared up into the starry sky recalling her age when she'd first met him, how he'd drugged her, raped her and ridden roughshod over her cries. ''e might want to get his baby back too, but you'd better watch out if 'e gets you on his own because... well, I've no idea what else 'e might want'.

Chapter 39

'Quick, there's a text message just in from Gemma's number,' Anna shouted, pointing down at the phone.

'What does it say?' Charlie motioned to Tony who was already barking orders down his mobile.

She watched, her heart in her mouth as Anna picked it up and read out the words. 'Mummy, it's me. DO NOT CONTACT THE FEDS. I'm OK at the moment. I've been given food, and I'm safe but things WILL change if you don't do what they want.'

'Quick, text her back,' Charlie repeated their previous instructions. They'd already briefed Anna on what she should do. 'Ask if you can speak to her. Keep them in conversation for as long as you can.'

Anna nodded, then tapped out a reply and sent it.

If that's you Gemma, please phone. I need to speak to you, so I can be sure you're alright xx

'Please call. Please call.' Anna's expression became more haunted with every second that passed.

Another text pinged in from a different number.

I will phone you tomorrow. But if we find out you've gone behind our backs, then Gemma will die.

Charlie grabbed the phone, checking the call details and relaying them to Tony. It was from the same unregistered number as before. He nodded, passing them on down his phone.

Please let my daughter go.

Charlie punched in the message and pressed the send key.

'Shit, they've gone. They've switched off.' Tony sat back in his chair grimacing. 'But we did manage to trace the location the texts were sent from. I've got two of my units heading there now.'

He stood up, pacing across the floor, then put his phone to his mouth. 'I don't need to remind you to be discreet. They cannot know that we're involved. One unit only down the road they were last located.'

'That's brilliant, now we're getting somewhere' Charlie enthused. 'Where were they traced to?'

'Mitcham. Not far from here, as you know, but also not far from the borders with Surrey and Kent.'

'In a house?'

'No, in a public car park near to the common, but I doubt it's where Gemma's being held.'

'And,' Charlie paused. 'Just because it was her phone, it doesn't mean it was her.'

'Oh my God, so we don't know for definite it was her the first time? I hadn't thought of that.' Anna closed her eyes. 'Or if she's even still alive...'

'Unfortunately, texts don't talk, that's why we want to make voice contact.' Charlie walked across to where Anna sat. 'But before you panic even more, it's highly unlikely that they would have done anything to Gemma. She's their bargaining tool. They'll need her alive and well and talking to get whatever it is that they want.'

Anna nodded, stood up and walked shakily to the mantelpiece. She picked up the photo of her daughter in her new school uniform. 'Here, take this,' she said quietly, holding the photo out towards Charlie. 'You might need a photo if we don't get her back straight away.'

'Damn it! There's no one there this time.' Tony slapped his phone down on the table and shook his head. 'They've gone. I'm so sorry.'

Charlie turned back towards Anna. 'Thank you. I saw it earlier and was going to ask if we could use it for our briefings but we won't make it public yet,' she replied, reaching out to take the photo. She gazed down at the young girl's expression, her fledgling confidence, her timid smile. *Where are you, Gemma?*

The photo reminded her of Rochelle Edwards; a similar age, adorned in her bottle green school uniform. A young girl whose life she'd been unable to save. Another child lost.

It couldn't be happening again.

Chapter 40

The man chuckled to himself as he settled into a new motor. It was slightly more roomy; an old, red Vauxhall Astra with low profile tyres and a swanky built-in sound system.

Ten minutes' drive from where he'd switched off the phones was enough to throw any feds off his scent. Anna *fucking* Christophe couldn't be trusted. He'd always known she was a bitch – and he was sure the hatred was mutual. For years the snivelling shrink had taken his partner's side over his, actively encouraging her to leave him and snitching on him to the feds.

So, this little plan suited him down to the ground. It would teach the bitch a lesson while at the same time providing him with a tantalisingly innocent, new, young plaything.

He would enjoy every second of Anna's – and her daughter's – torture. And if, by chance, they got Mia back – well, so much the better. It would keep his partner happy and stop her from pestering him.

So, he'd listened to her instructions and today they'd been put into action.

He'd stayed quiet when he'd had to; sent the texts that she'd told him to – and his next task had been to steal another motor. He'd parked the first stolen car round the corner, parallel to the kerb in an unrestricted road, far enough away from where he'd used the phones to be hard for the feds to find, and unobtrusive enough that the residents wouldn't take notice. He wasn't stupid. It had served its purpose well but it had to go, having been used to move to and from the hideout, and more crucially when they'd picked up the girl. They might have been careful in using the side streets and avoiding the main ANPR cameras but they couldn't push their luck.

The thought prompted him to look up, and around. There were far too many fucking cameras around these days, but he'd chosen well. This street was quiet and residential. There was no obvious CCTV and the house, in whose driveway he now sat, was in darkness, with its curtains half-drawn.

He ripped the ignition switch away from the facia, rammed the screwdriver into the lock and smiled as the dashboard lights came on. Bingo! With any luck the occupants would be away and the car wouldn't be reported as stolen for a while.

Winding down the window, he switched on the engine and slowly edged forward, checking along the roadway. It was clear. Slotting the car into gear, he pulled out onto the road as quietly as possible, and drove to a spot two streets away. Time to relax before he headed back to the hills. He took a snap-bag of weed and a packet of Rizlas from his jeans pocket and rolled himself a joint. His partner would be waiting, with no phone, and no way of contact. She would probably be worrying, but then, why should he care.

He flicked a match, inhaling the sweet pungent skunk and taking a moment to lean back and dream. All he could think of was Gemma.

He took another deep breath, blowing the smoke out of the window and watching lazily as it curled up to join the thin layer of cloud now forming in the sky. It swirled and rotated, hazy and unclear, as indistinct as their next few days. The plan might be hers – but it was fluid – and it could be tweaked to cater more for his needs.

If it worked, then she would get Mia back.

And if it didn't, as he doubted it would, they'd both be thrown into prison.

No matter. Whichever way it ended, made no difference to him. He'd spent half his life inside and these days it held no fears.

He took another lungful of cannabis and smiled to himself. He'd just have to make sure he had his fun first.

Chapter 41

'What the fuck did you let her out for?' the man growled.

Gemma Christophe shrank further into the rear wall of the cave. As they'd heard his steady progress up the riverbank in the silence, so he must have heard their chatter and movements.

'She was frightened,' the woman explained. 'And anyway, she's well tied up again now, an' I fixed the rope back up round her neck. There's no way she'll be getting away.'

Gemma didn't understand what was going on. She'd known the woman from a while back; she wouldn't have got into her car otherwise. She'd been nice then. Friendly. Her mum had helped the woman move into a flat. In fact, they'd all helped her to make the place look nice. Gemma had done some drawings and they'd had a collection among all their friends for furniture and knick-knacks. The flat had looked lovely.

But then they'd all got busy. Her mum had been working hard. Her daddy was often away – and she'd started at her new school. But she did remember her. She remembered her name, although she wasn't allowed to say it.

She started to cry. Everything hurt. Her knees ached from the electrical cord binding and her wrists were sore from the constant chafing of the handcuffs; large wheals opening up on the bony points where the metal gripped too tightly. The woman had stuck tape across her mouth again, even though she'd pleaded to have her mouth left free. It made her feel panicky, having to try to breathe all the time through her nose.

The darkness panicked her too. It had been dark sitting on the river bank but at least there had been stars and the moon, and the woman's torchlight. It was so inky black inside the cave that she couldn't see her fingers in front of her face, or make out shapes or textures or even be sure her eyes were open or closed.

She could hear CJ talking again, though the woman had called him several times by a different name. CJ sounded angry, the volume of his voice rising and falling as he spoke.

'While I'm off risking my neck, you're sitting 'ere chatting,' she heard him say. 'Well, I'd better go an' check 'er then.'

She squeezed her eyes shut and drew her legs up tightly to her chest, remembering the woman's words. What had the woman meant, about what he might want? Her heart was beating so fast that she could hardly breathe. She reached up with her hands, her fingernails scraping at the tape, trying to peel it away from her mouth. What *did* he want? There was a scrabbling from outside and she opened her eyes as the man pulled open the curtain, the beam of his torchlight flickering around to partially illuminate him. He was so big that he filled the whole space, shutting out the sight of the sky. Just his sheer size frightened her.

'Where are you, you little bitch?' he snarled, flashing the beam of light about the shelter before bringing it to rest on her face. It was as intense as a laser, the ray so brilliantly white in the blackness that it dazzled her. She couldn't see him – but she could hear him, shuffling closer, his breath rasping from the effort of the short climb to the cave from the riverbank. And she could smell him. His clothes smelt strange, pungent; unlike anything she'd smelt before.

'What have you been doing?' He stopped in front of her, still aiming the torch in her face. Laughed. 'Well, take a look at this, babe,' he called out, waiting for the woman to come in and join them. 'The little bitch has only been trying to escape.'

She squeezed herself further into the wall, her spine scraping painfully against a solid root. The rope tightened around her neck. He leaned in towards her, his stench growing stronger, his fingers rough against her cheek as he pushed the tape back into place.

Please don't. I can't breathe, she wanted to cry.

'Perhaps we should have put the handcuffs on around her back.' The woman's voice was cold, icy, any earlier notes of sympathy gone. She felt herself hauled to her feet, the torchlight flashing about crazily as they grabbed her by the arms. It made her dizzy and uncoordinated. She tried to keep her arms in front of her body, shielding herself, as one wrist was released, but the man was too strong. He was panting with exertion, excitement, his huge hands running over her body, gripping her arms, forcing the cuffs on around her back.

'You're just like your mother,' he hissed, swinging the torch over her body and unbuttoning the front of her school blazer. 'But unlike her, you're going to learn to do what I say.'

She dropped to the floor and curled up into a ball, understanding now what the woman had meant. CJ was forceful. He was brutal and powerful, and his intentions were becoming clear. She would do best to obey him.

But it was the woman who frightened her most. The woman who she'd thought was her friend. One minute warm, the next minute cold. Callous.

'Leave her alone, babe,' the woman said. 'For now.'

She watched as CJ moved with the torchlight to the entrance of the cave, then out into the night, listening as he struck a match, and dragged on a cigarette. The same sweet, pungent smell drifted into the cave, into her nostrils.

But as the darkness wrapped itself around her, it was the woman's voice she heard whispering through the silence, so close that she could feel her breath against her ear.

'Or maybe we should do the same as your mother did to me – maybe we should just abandon you too...'

Chapter 42

It was gone 6 a.m. when Charlie woke to the feel of a hand on her shoulder. She jumped to her feet, her heart pounding.

'Woah there. It's only me.' Tony stretched out both hands in an effort to placate her. 'What's got you all hyped up?'

She blinked, her pulse still racing, and tried to focus on the blurry giant directly in her sights. 'Sorry, Tony.' His face became clear. 'Got a few things going on at the moment.'

'Care to expand?'

'No, not really.' She turned around, plumping up the cushions on the sofa. It was bad enough that Anna would have heard from her mother about their problems with Iain Frazer, without her personal life being turned into another real-life drama. 'Once this is over, maybe.' She smiled back at Tony. 'Sorry, you made me jump.' He was one of the good guys, totally trustworthy, and wholly discreet. Perhaps he would come in handy if needed. 'What have you got?'

'Their car, or at least some CCTV of their car.'

'Excellent. Let's see.' She popped a mint into her mouth, sucking hard on it as she waited for Tony to explain. 'Nothing worse than bed breath,' she commented, rubbing her eyes blearily. 'Not that I've had much sleep, and I doubt Anna has either.' After waiting up until midnight, Anna had disappeared upstairs to call and update Scott, and try to sleep. He was due back later in the day but in the meantime, she'd need all the strength she could muster to get her through the next few hours – they all would.

'Right, here we go.' He clicked play and she watched as the screen came alive. It was timed at 21.32, shortly after the sun had set, but before its residual light was completely lost, keeping the footage predominantly clear. This time the camera was focussed on the front of a pub with an entrance and exit out on to the main road. A pub sign, showing a large yellow sun on a bright blue background was positioned dead centre. 'We couldn't find any CCTV for the car park on Mitcham Common where both the texts were sent from, but one of my officers did a scout of the area and found this pub, The Rising Sun. It's on the junction that leads up to the common, and its cameras show the main road, and just enough of the junction to identify any cars coming from the common.

'At this time of night there are still a few vehicles using Commonside East, the road from the car park, but it's not a main road, and there are not so many vehicles that we can't check out each one.' He pointed to the right-hand corner of the screen as a small silver car pulled out and turned right, across the junction. It straightened up, driving slowly past the pub and continuing along the road until it was out of sight.

'We think it's a Volkswagen Polo,' he said.

'Well,' Charlie was disappointed. 'Is that it? It doesn't show the driver, and we can't see the registration number.'

'Little steps,' Tony replied, winding back the recording. He stopped it as the car was directly in front of the camera and zoomed in on the nearside windows. The front passenger window was open.

'Well, I can just about make out a black hand on the wheel,' she said. 'So the driver is black. But I can't see any more of their body or face. I couldn't even say if it was a man or a woman.'

'I wasn't looking at the driver,' Tony pointed towards the rear side window. 'Or at least I was, but I was looking more at the sticker that runs across the base of that window.'

'Poppies?'

'Yes, poppies. Now look at this.' He minimised the screen and brought up another, centring a small silver car in their eyeline. 'It's got to be the same silver Volkswagen Polo, caught on a camera not far from Gemma's school, but it was on a main road, so, initially, there were too many vehicles to check every single one individually. It was only when my officer was going through the last piece of footage, she suddenly remembered the poppies. Look.'

Charlie leant forward towards the screen, concentrating as Tony focussed on the rear side window of the car. There on display was the same sticker, a field of red poppies, on green stalks that gave the impression of the wild blooms growing upwards from the base of the window.

'It's the same sticker on the same car, and look, there's Gemma.' The girl was facing directly ahead, her blonde hair just above the poppies, giving the impression she was lying in a field, peeping over the flowers. Nobody was sitting in the seat in front of her, the driver being diagonally across, and they couldn't see if anyone was sitting next to her. Both front windows were open, and she could again see one of the driver's hands on the wheel and the other slung up out of the car, its fingers drumming on the roof.

'Looks like a bloke, if you ask me,' Tony said, zooming in as close as possible on the hand. 'Too big for a woman.'

Charlie squinted at the screen, frowning. 'And it looks like he's wearing a large gold ring on his right hand.'

'What's that you've got?' The door to the lounge opened and a tired-looking Anna walked in. 'Thought I heard voices.'

'Sorry if we disturbed you,' Tony returned the image to the one of the side of the car.

'You didn't. I couldn't sleep.' Anna stared down at the screen, starting a yawn, but then stopped midway as if she'd seen a ghost. 'Is that Gemma?'

Charlie nodded. 'Yes, it is. It's from near to the school.' She turned to Tony, who was shaking his head, looking suddenly crestfallen. 'So, what's the registration number?'

'We don't know it yet.'

'But we must have it?'

'Both cameras were facing directly out and so both times the shot of the car coming and going is at too much of an angle to see the plate properly. We only found this one a couple of hours ago and I've got every spare member of the team seeing if we can catch it on camera further down the road.'

'But the poppies must help?'

Tony shrugged. 'Only in identifying that it's the same car in the two different places. It won't give us a registered owner, which is what we need.'

'Hang on, I've got an idea.' Charlie checked her watch and picked up her phone. 'One of my colleagues, Bet, is a senior analyst, with excellent knowledge of the search facilities on our computer systems – and she'll be in now. If that car has ever come to notice, for whatever reason, and the poppies have been mentioned, then she'll find it.'

She waited until Bet answered the phone, and quickly explained what they needed. It might take her colleague hours to diligently work through every system, but she knew Bet wouldn't rest until she'd scrutinised every possibility.

'Is Paul in yet?' she asked, before ringing off.

'It's a bit too early for him.'

'I thought so, but could you ask him to give me a shout with any updates on Hurley and Smythe-Hamilton. I want to keep up to speed with that too. Thanks, Bet.' She finished and rang off, her head spinning. It felt like she was trying to keep three plates revolving at the same time; the gang case, her troublesome father and now this. And not one of them could be allowed to slow down or drop. Lives might depend on it.

'How're things at home?' Anna, as usual, seemed to be able to read her mind.

'Quiet, thank goodness.' She checked on her phone. 'Or rather, hopefully. I haven't yet had my morning text.'

Tony pricked up his ears.

'Anna knows my mother,' she said in explanation, thinking that at some point she really would tell him. With Paul working on a separate job, she might need a new sounding board to prevent her from going insane. 'Just some trouble with an ex.'

Tony raised his eyebrows. 'Ah, I know what that's like.'

They lapsed into silence. 'I'll go and make coffee,' Anna said after a minute or two. 'And I'll also make a start on cancelling today's appointments.'

'And Brett? School or no school?' They'd discussed the pros and cons of him carrying on as usual; whether to make up a story to explain Gemma's absence, or tell him what little they knew. At nine, he was old enough to sense something strange might be happening – but was he too young to fully appreciate the need for secrecy.

'He'll be staying at home.' Anna was firm. 'Scott and I spoke. We can't take the risk of him being snatched too. Not until we know what this is about.'

Charlie nodded. Anna was also mentally spinning plates.

Chapter 43

'I've got the car.'

'Bloody hell, Bet, that's quick.' Less than half an hour had elapsed since Charlie had put Bet on the case. In that time, she'd received a text from her mum saying all had been quiet, and a phone call from Paul, informing her that the surveillance on Hurley and Smythe-Hamilton had, as yet, been uneventful. Smythe-Hamilton had left the club at around midnight and Hurley had left half an hour later. They had however established a vehicle for Hurley and confirmed the address of where he was living. So far, so good.

'Tell us more, then.' She put her mobile on to speakerphone, and turned up the volume as Anna came back through the door.

'Well, I checked on CAD first to see if there was any mention of poppies on any vehicle involved in an accident or in crime, but there was nothing really of note. And nothing at all linking poppies to a small silver car.'

'That's the *Computer Aided Despatch* computer,' she whispered loudly to Anna. 'Every call that comes in to the police via 999 or 101 goes on that system.'

'Then I searched on CRIMINT, the criminal intelligence system,' Bet explained, having gauged that somebody non-police was listening in. 'But there were hundreds of reports which included poppies; from descriptions of people wearing them, to several poppy sellers being robbed – so then I thought I'd try CRIS.'

'The system for reporting crimes,' Charlie whispered again.

'And voilà! It's a silver Volkswagen Polo.' Bet continued, reeling off a registration number. 'And it's shown as stolen, since last Thursday. We were lucky. It's only because its owners obviously love it that they'd phoned up early to give a full description for our records, including the poppy stickers down both rear side windows. They sound quite unique. It had to be your car.'

'That's brilliant,' Charlie had jotted down the index, before turning to Anna. 'Police have to submit a form to the stolen vehicle database seventy-two hours after a vehicle is stolen. In case it's found with the plates taken off and its ID removed.'

She switched back to Bet. 'Who's the registered owner – and where's it stolen from.'

'Shown as a Mr Arthur Tonstall, of London Road, Norbury. It was stolen on Thursday 6th June from the rear of their block of flats, which is Hillview Manor.'

'I know that block,' Anna piped up, turning to Charlie. 'It's the big Tudor style one, by the junction with Green Lanes, just opposite where Caz lives.'

'Shit.' Charlie felt the colour drain from her face. 'Caz.'

'What's the matter with Caz?' Anna asked, before sitting down suddenly. 'Oh my God, Charlie. That first message. They used the words *feds*, and *betray*. I thought it sounded weird. But they're the sort of words that Caz would use. She was always talking about being betrayed.'

'And it would explain why Gemma might have got into the car so readily, as she seems to have done. There were no calls to a fight, or a female being bundled into a car or anything similar. Gemma would know her. I thought when we saw her position in the rear of the car that there was probably someone else sitting next to her, even though we couldn't see them.'

'It has to be her. But why?' Anna looked confused.

'And they used the term *we* – so who was the driver?' Charlie's stomach was sinking with every question.

Tony was staring at them as if they were both mad. 'Caz? Who's Caz?'

'Charlene Zara Philips, but she calls herself Caz.' Charlie explained. 'She helped me out with a bit of info on a murder case in Lambeth that I dealt with. She was a prostitute, with quite a chequered past, but she knew everyone.' Charlie gave a nod towards Anna. 'In fact, it was Caz who introduced me to Anna.'

'I've been working with her for years.' Anna took over. 'I haven't seen her for a while, but in the last year or so she's been making great progress. She's got herself clean from drugs and has been living in a lovely little bedsit my friend on the council had managed to find. She's even had a baby, Mia, who she's looking after now.' She paused, creasing her eyebrows together. 'But, a chequered past is a bit of an understatement. I can't say too much because of client confidentiality, but she was certainly a troubled soul. She believed she'd been betrayed by her father, and mother – and more latterly her partner.'

'Clinton James Roberts, AKA, Razor,' said Charlie. Even his name sent a chill down her spine. 'So called because he liked to use a razor on his victims. He was her pimp. But he's in prison at the moment on remand for the murder of a girl called Redz, another prostitute he ran, and the attempted murder of Caz. His trial is due any time now.' She stopped talking, her mind running over and over the scene she'd just watched. The large black hands. The gold ring. The stolen car. The fact that she'd been given an early court warning for the fortnight that had just finished, but she'd heard nothing else. No actual date. No overnight warning.

She shook her head. 'No, it can't be him.' But her gut told her it was. It had to be.

'But why would Caz want Gemma?' Anna frowned. 'After everything I've done to help her.'

Charlie turned back to Tony, who was listening intently. 'Anna provided a witness statement about eighteen months ago, describing how she'd had a call for help from Caz. Caz was claiming to be hiding from Razor after he'd threatened to kill her. Anna drove out and rescued her in the middle of the night, putting herself in great danger. She took her to her office, but he found them. He smashed down the door and assaulted Caz, then dragged her off – in a stolen car.

'He liked stealing cars. And he always wore a large, gold, signet ring.' She paused, watching Tony as he processed what she'd said, before going on. 'Anyway, despite having been assaulted by him, Caz gave an alibi statement for Razor, in the murder case of another prostitute, but she later withdrew it. It was one of the small pieces of evidence that helped to swing the decision for him to be charged. In the end, a bag containing the murder weapon and some of the victim's hair was found in a utility cupboard connected to his flat. His DNA was found on items in the bag – although he always denied knowing anything about it. But it was the final piece of a very circumstantial jigsaw. The CPS agreed to all the charges; murder, assault, kidnap and theft. He's been on remand ever since. He should've been up in court for his trial during the last couple of weeks.'

'Could he have been released?' Tony cocked his head to one side.

'I would hope not, especially as we haven't been consulted. He's a violent predator who preys on women and young girls. If I had my way, he wouldn't be allowed out on the streets. Ever.' She picked up her mobile and pressed Bet's number again. 'But there's only one way to find out.'

❊ ❊ ❊

'Why the hell didn't you speak to me first?' Charlie paced around the room. She pressed the mobile to her ear, and took a deep breath, staring up at the ceiling in disbelief. 'How could you have let him out?!'

One quick name check by Bet had revealed her worst fears. Clinton James 'Razor' Roberts had been released from prison the previous week – and nobody had thought to let her know. Or to ask their advice. Now after watching her explosive reaction to the news, Tony was busily phoning his team members, while Anna had made herself scarce.

'Well, I did email the OIC several times to ask for his input.' PC Brownlow wasn't going to go down without a fight. 'And he didn't get back to me. So, what was I supposed to do? I had the GBH victim turning up with her solicitor to make withdrawal and alibi statements, and the CPS forced to change their decision.

'And...' he persisted. 'You try arguing with the sanctimonious Ms Patricia Goodfellow.'

Charlie groaned. She'd locked horns with the solicitor before and they disliked each other intensely. 'So, who precisely did you email?' She closed her eyes and ran a hand through her hair, knowing exactly who he'd say. The detective had used the masculine gender.

'DI Geoffrey Hunter, of course. He's shown as the officer in the case.'

'Shit!' she said, slumping down on the sofa and feeling suddenly deflated. 'Shit, shit, shit! Hunter's on leave at the moment.' She still couldn't bring herself to admit he was suspended. 'Okay, I apologise. You had no way of knowing. It's just galling after all the effort it took to get that maniac charged. Razor is one of the most violent men I know out there. It took ages to get him put away, yet it seems like a few wordy submissions in a judge's ear has made the whole case unravel. He's already out doing his worst.'

'I'm sorry too,' PC Brownlow replied, clearly recognising her anguish.

The war of attrition was over. They both knew it was the public who'd lost.

Chapter 44

They were on their way to the bedsit in Norbury, in Tony's sleek, black, unmarked BMW.

'No sign of movement,' came a voice over his squad radio. 'All received,' he replied. 'Keep watching the flat. I have a locksmith arranged to meet us there.'

Charlie stared out from the tinted rear window, watching as the houses and streets flashed past. A blanket of grey clouds threatened rain, sinking low over the rooftops, further darkening her mood. Now they suspected Razor was involved, Gemma's situation had become a damn sight more perilous. They couldn't risk the young girl being under his control a second longer than necessary.

Razor liked young girls. He drugged young girls. He raped young girls. And he hated Anna.

Charlie knew it – but worse than that, Anna knew it too.

'So, we know who our suspects are, and what car they're in.' Charlie was trying to remain positive. 'And Caz's flat might give us some clues as to what's been happening and where they might be.'

'Gemma might even be there?' Anna whispered, almost inaudibly.

'Let's hope so,' Charlie smiled and gave Anna's fingers a squeeze. They both knew that probably wouldn't be the case, but Charlie still had to check. The possibility, however remote had to be ruled out. 'But we still have no idea why?' She changed the subject.

'It can't just be because Razor hates Anna, can it?' Tony asked.

Charlie shook her head. 'No, it's coming from Caz. She's the one who's made all the moves to get Razor released – and it does sound as if she's been having problems more recently.'

After first checking with Tony, Charlie had briefed Bet on the situation, with a view to her speaking to the team. Paul, Naz and Sabira all knew Razor well. They had first-hand knowledge of the ways he worked. And they could be trusted. This time they were being trusted with Gemma's life.

'I don't know why Caz didn't call me and leave a message,' Anna murmured, frowning. 'Although perhaps she did. I've seen a few missed calls from her but I've been pretty busy and haven't returned her calls. I feel awful now.'

'It's not your fault, Anna. And anyway, it's still no reason for her to do this to you. You've done so much for her in the past.'

Bet was in the process of putting a timeline on Caz's problems. Over the last six months there had clearly been issues, with several reports of her having been spotted in her old haunts; the shadowy streets of Brixton synonymous with the sale of hard drugs. More recently still, there had been numerous calls from neighbours about hearing the baby cry, with suggestions that the bedsit was dirty and perhaps Mia wasn't receiving sufficient care. Police had attended. Social services had been informed. The situation was ongoing and the reporting sporadic. Bet was doing her best to piece everything together but the latest intelligence was far from being up-to-date.

And all the probing still had to be done in secret.

So, the spontaneous surveillance on the flat was covert, any intelligence gathering discreet and their entry to Caz's bedsit in a few minutes' time would need to be cautious. They couldn't risk Gemma's kidnappers knowing that police were involved.

The locksmith arrived at the same time as they did, pulling up at the given location, two streets away from the flat, as Tony slid the car into place. 'Any sign of movement,' he asked across the radio. 'No, no sign of life' came back the reply.

The choice of wording made Charlie squirm. Not only would they be looking for Gemma, but, with the delicate nature of the ongoing situation they still had to locate the baby. There had been no sign or sight of her in the silver VW.

'Stay here,' she instructed Anna. 'I'll come and get you as soon as we're in.' *When we know there're no nasty surprises.*

The door to the bedsit was closed. Putting an ear to it, Charlie could hear nothing. She stepped back and exhaled. Silent places always made her nervous.

'It's been forced open quite recently.' The locksmith pointed to a crack in the frame, close to the lock. 'Should make it a bit easier to get in and out without leaving a mark.'

Two minutes later, the lock was sprung. She pushed at the door gingerly, stepping inside and scanning the remnants of Caz's life. It looked a mess. Not filthy dirty, but untidy – as if the occupants simply couldn't be bothered. The bed was unmade, the kitchenette cluttered with unwashed dishes left piled in the sink. The cushions on the sofa were stacked haphazardly on top of each other and piled at one end. Only the cot in the corner of the room was clean and well-made but... unoccupied.

On first glance, the whole flat appeared unoccupied.

Wordlessly, she and Tony searched around the room, under the bed, behind the sofa, inside the wardrobe, even opening the kitchen cupboards. Gemma obviously wasn't there – but the baby? Nothing could be left to chance.

Her phone rang, making her jump. It was Bet.

'Mia Philips was taken into care approximately six weeks ago, after numerous calls from a concerned neighbour. I've just spoken to her social worker Marion Bishop; I made up an excuse about needing to update our records. She apologised for not having sent their report on sooner. And if you're still wondering about Razor – he and Caz are definitely together. They turned up playing happy families at her office last week, asking for Mia. Razor caused a bit of a ruckus when they were told it wasn't going to happen.'

'Precisely *because* he was there, I should think.'

'I thought the same, but Caz was apparently distraught. As if she'd really believed having the pair of them together would be enough to get their daughter back.'

Charlie shrugged. 'That's sad. I don't think she's ever really had a family of her own. Maybe she believed that this time she could. Hang on…'

They were disturbed by the sound of footsteps, as Anna came hurtling through the door.

'It's them,' she called out, shoving her phone towards Charlie. 'They're asking if I've called police.'

'Keep them engaged but whatever you do, don't let them know that you've told us.' Tony said, as he got straight on the phone to his team.

Charlie nodded, and read the text.

Have you contacted the feds?

Charlie texted back.

No, I haven't, but pls let me talk to Gemma. I really need to know she's OK

The answer came back straight away.

She's safe

She waited a few seconds, trying to elongate the conversation.

When can I see her, or talk to her?

When we say so.

A few seconds later, Charlie texted.

Who are you?

Don't you know, Anna?

Desperately, she typed, determined to keep the dialogue going.

What do you want?

We want OUR daughter back and you're going to get her for us. Or else you won't see YOUR daughter again.

Tell me what I have to do?

Be ready at 4

'Shit. They've switched off again.' Tony pressed the phone to his ear. 'But we've got a location.'

Charlie held her breath. If they could only get an idea of where the kidnappers might be, or a proper hook on the silver VW, Tony had an experienced surveillance team ready and able to follow them.

'Unfortunately, it's a busy high street,' he said with a grimace. 'We're checking CCTV as we speak but so far there's no sign of the VW.'

She closed her eyes. 'Come on, come on. It's got to come past.' After all their hard work they couldn't let it slip through their fingers.

'Still no trace.' Tony glanced down at his watch. 'And with the volume of traffic going backwards and forwards between the two phone masts we're going to have dozens, if not hundreds of vehicles to check.' He strode across to the window, staring down at the line of traffic snaking past the bedsit, nose to tail on the main road. 'That's if we can even see the index numbers when they're so close together.'

Charlie turned away despondently, her eyes falling instead on Anna. The woman was bent over a pile of correspondence at the side of the bed, with her hand over her mouth.

'Oh my God Charlie! Caz thinks it was me who got Mia taken into care. Look!' Anna straightened and held out a small diary, covered with a floral design, and pointed to an entry on the last day of April. Scrawled across a double page was a mass of untidy lettering, starting with the words, *Anna Christophe is a BITCH!!!* The writing was hard to decipher but with a little patience she read out the message aloud. '*She's abandoned me, and she's betrayed me!!! She hates me coz I'm not good enough for her, or her cosy fucking family. She never phones or comes round – and she don't answer any of my calls.*

'*All I needed was a bit of help!! But instead she's gone behind my back, and snitched to the council. She's just like the others!! No – she's WORSE!! She made me believe I could be worth something – but I'm not. I'm just a fucking loser. And now it's too late.*

Mia's gone – and it's all Anna's fault!!!'

❖ ❖ ❖

Clinton James 'Razor' Roberts peered out of the driver's window, and up towards the flat.

The man standing at the window of the flat was definitely a cop. He was tall, black, stocky, shaven headed, not unlike himself, but there was something about the way that he stood, upright and arrogant – as if he owned the fucking place – that made his blood boil. He wanted to rip the prick's head off his shoulders, then mark him with his razor blade; deep, hard, unforgettably scoring his signature 'R' in his flesh. It was his way. The way of the streets. The only way he knew.

A woman came into view, coming up close, holding something out towards him. It was Anna. He'd recognise her prim, pained expression anywhere. The cop leant down towards her, their heads so close that he could almost imagine their whispered words of conspiracy.

The lying, conniving bitch!! He'd known all along that she wouldn't keep her mouth shut. She couldn't be trusted. She'd snitched to the social. Now she'd snitched to the feds.

Well, this time he'd show her.

This time he would teach the bitch a lesson. Or at least he'd teach her daughter a lesson. A lesson Gemma wouldn't forget – for however long she lived.

In a couple of miles, he would be back on his streets – the streets that he knew and loved. He would seek out a friendly dealer, buy some crack cocaine, and return to send Caz on an errand.

He grinned at the thought.

Anna's precious little girl wouldn't know what had hit her.

Chapter 45

So now they knew who, how and why – but they still didn't know where.

Charlie stared around the tiny bedsit, desperately searching for a clue to their whereabouts, but there was nothing standing out in anything she'd read, or anything she'd seen.

'Do you think they'll come back here?' Charlie asked, fingering the diary. 'I don't really want to leave this.' It provided all the motive they'd require in any future criminal trials. Page after page, it gave a heartbreaking insight into Caz's frame of mind; her gradual decline as her cries for help went unanswered, her efforts to get clean after Mia was taken from her, her desperation to provide the family that she'd never had. And in her broken logic, it was Anna, or the lack of Anna, who should shoulder the blame. *Abandoned and betrayed. Abandoned and betrayed.* The same two words featured in her scribblings time and time again.

Regardless of the offers of support from Marion, from housing officials, from medical practitioners, in her mind it was all down to Anna. A stack of letters bore witness to their offers of help, from rescheduled appointments, advice on rent arrears, letters gently urging compliance with postnatal health checks, suggestions of new ways to cope.

All had gone unanswered until the fateful day that Mia had been taken into care.

That had provided the impetus for revenge. As she'd read through each painful entry, Charlie had noticed the switch. Caz's mindset had altered; from victim to avenger. A new aspiration. A tit for tat swap. A child for a child. Simple. Chilling. Cruel.

'It's all my fault. I should have returned her calls. I should have come round. I could have stopped this from happening.' Anna was sitting stiffly on the bed, the find of the diary having halted her in her tracks. It was as if she'd been struck down by lightning, the flash of awareness kicking her legs from underneath her and sending her mind spinning off at a tangent. All she could do was sit grimly and sob, repeating over and over that she was indeed to blame.

'Is there anything else you can see that might give us a clue to where they might be?' Charlie said, as she went across to her friend, gently urging her to her feet. There was no use keep telling Anna it wasn't her fault. She needed motivation to start afresh, refocus.

Moving with her around the room she watched as Anna searched, her brows knitted together in concentration as her eyes flitted from wall, to floor, to furnishings.

'Nothing I can see.' Anna shook her head miserably.

Anything that's changed from when you were last here?' She had to keep the momentum up. 'Anything that's usually here, that's missing now. Anything they might come back for?' She was still debating whether to take or leave the diary. If they were likely to return then every little thing had to be replaced in its previous position.

For a few minutes she waited as her friend continued to stare around the room until finally looking towards the cot.

'They've taken Mia's favourite soft toy. Dilly the dinosaur I think she called it. It belonged to Gemma as a child but she'd donated it to Mia in the months before starting high school. Too babyish apparently. Hang on.' She paused, moving around the bed, checking under the pillows and inside the bedside cabinet. 'Goldilocks is gone too.'

'Goldilocks?'

'Caz's childhood doll. She treasured it more than anything in the world – except for Mia. It was a gift from her mother; a beautiful ragdoll with long golden hair, until her father cut it off. Even so Caz still loved it. She used to take it with her everywhere, but since moving here and becoming more settled she'd occasionally leave it behind. She'd had it restuffed and it always took pride of place in the centre of her bed.'

She turned to face Charlie who was still holding the diary in her hands.

'If Goldilocks is gone, I doubt Caz will be back.'

Chapter 46

'How's it going?'

It was gone midday, four hours before the kidnappers were due to call back and, while Anna and Tony were both busy, Charlie was taking the opportunity to meet up with her team.

To that end they had arranged to meet in a cafe midway between Wimbledon Police Station and Anna's house in Balham; near enough for Charlie to return easily when required, while at the same time being well away from the sharp-eyed Superintendent Woodall.

It had started to rain again, but this time, instead of the previously light showers, the clouds were heavy and sodden, slinging water relentlessly onto the sun-baked earth. Large puddles were forming in every dip or hollow and small tributaries merged together sending rivers of rainwater flooding down the gutters. Charlie and her team settled themselves at a table in the corner, peeling off their wet jackets and shaking out their hair.

After fending off their rage at Razor's early release and filling them in on her progress, Charlie was impatient to hear an update on the Rochelle Edwards' murder.

'Well, the jungle drums are pretty quiet, even after almost a week.' Naz started them off. 'It's more than likely the media presence. There're still a fair few journalists hanging around the nick and out towards the common.'

'Excellent! Let's hope it stays quiet for a lot longer then – or puts a stop to the madness altogether. But keep me posted ASAP if it looks like it's changing.' She turned to Sabira. 'Any developments in identifying Rochelle Edwards' killer?'

Sabira had been tasked with trying to link the description of Rochelle's murderer with any likely looking youths caught on CCTV around local shops, and in many of the usual gang haunts. If a suspect could be spotted making their way home, or hanging around in a recreation ground or park, then the hope was, another camera might provide a useable facial image.

'I've got two possible facials on a suspect who fits the bill. He looks like a youngster, quite small-framed, and wearing a dark tracksuit with a small gold lion motif on the left breast pocket. He was wearing a scarf up over his face on the common but he's taken it off in our shots. Not much to go on I know but he's been caught twice on separate cameras and he looks frightened; stopping to check all around him, and ducking down behind cars. The close-ups aren't great, but I'm hoping the lab can sharpen up the images so I can put them out to our informants and officers.'

'We're cautiously optimistic,' Naz chipped in. 'He looks vaguely familiar and I've got a good feeling about this one but we need a better quality photo or else we'll run into the same problems as we have with the image of Wayne Hurley. Oh, and then, we'll need Rochelle's friend to pick him out in an ID parade.'

'Good work.' Charlie was impressed. Scanning through hours of footage could be mind-numbingly boring, but it could also bring moments of pure, solid gold-plated elation. There was nothing like identifying a killer through sheer bloody hard work. 'No pressure then – but let me know when you've named him.'

She turned to Paul who was reading a text.

'Right, Paul. Give me some good news on Smythe-Hamilton and Hurley.' She sat forward in her chair, sipping on a much-needed double espresso. 'What are they up to?'

'Well they're up to something. Or at least Wayne Hurley is.' Paul said, scrolling down through various messages. 'He's back at the club now with Smythe-Hamilton but he's been really active this morning. The surveillance team have tailed him from his home address, to the vicinity of the Soldiers' recreation ground.

'That's weird. Why would he be there?'

'No idea. The team couldn't get too close without showing out, so we don't know exactly what he was doing, but he was carrying a blue rucksack and spent a good fifteen minutes in the area. After that he drove past Wimbledon Park, opposite the All England Tennis Club, until he came to some allotments. They watched him leave his car and walk through the gates of the allotments carrying the same blue rucksack, then head along parallel to the hedgerow towards several potting sheds. He unlocked three padlocks on the first one that he came to – it has a faded green painted door – and disappeared inside. He stayed in the shed for approximately ten minutes.'

'I can't see him as a gardener.'

'Me neither, and they have no idea what he was doing, but when he went in, he was carrying the rucksack, and when he came out, he wasn't.'

Chapter 47

Four o'clock came and went. Then 4.15 and 4.30.

With every minute, the speed of Charlie's pacing grew faster, round and round the sofa trampling a thin path into the carpet, her feet thudding in time with the rhythmic drumming of Tony's fingers on the table. Only Anna stayed still, staring statuesquely out of the window, as if any slight movement while they waited might provide the motivation for killing her daughter.

So, at 4.31 they all jumped when her phone started to ring.

Tony glanced down at the phone. 'Shit, if it's them. They've changed their number.' He nodded to Anna. 'We'll need extra time to get this one tracked so keep them talking for as long as you can.'

'Anna?' The voice coming through the speaker was muffled, but it was definitely a man. 'Have you contacted the feds?'

Tony shook his head and made a zipping motion across his mouth.

'No, no. I've done exactly what you said.'

'You're a liar!' This time the voice was clear, loud, angry. 'I saw those bastards earlier – right after I told you not to speak to them.' There was a pause. 'So what do you think I should do now? Your choice.'

'Please, please don't hurt Gemma. Please let me speak to her.' Anna's eyes were wide with fear. She sat down heavily on the sofa. 'I promise to do everything that you ask of me now.'

'Now?!' The man laughed. 'What makes you think that you're not already too late? I did warn you.'

'No-o-o,' Anna howled. 'Please tell me Gemma's alive. Please.'

'Put one of those bastards on the phone. I know there'll be one with you, recording every word that I say.'

Charlie looked across at Tony who was shaking his head again. 'No,' he mouthed, going on in a low whisper. 'This could be a trap. It's only his word that he saw us. Tell him that you can't.'

'I can't,' Anna repeated, clearly terrified. 'I swear they don't know.'

'So, you're not just a lying bitch, you're also a fool. Well, since you think you know us – get us custody of our daughter. You have twenty-four hours.' The man laughed again. 'Or else I won't be responsible for what happens to Gemma.'

'Oh my God,' Anna threw her hands to her face as the phone line went dead. 'They know about you.'

'We don't know that for certain.' Tony frowned. 'It could still be a ploy to find out if you've told us.'

Anna shook her head. 'They know. There was no hesitation. The second I said no, he was straight back at me.'

'But when could they have seen us?'

'Coming in and out of Anna's house?' Charlie thought back over the last few hours. 'Or they might have seen one of your guys or girls, tracking the location of the last texts. Or us at Caz's flat? They could be watching us watching out for them, and however careful we all are, they've only got to spot one of us for the game to be up.'

'And we're sure it is Razor?' Tony asked.

'It's him,' she replied. 'I interviewed him for hours, and I'd recognise that voice anywhere.'

Anna nodded. 'It's definitely him – and Caz.'

'So now we know it's Caz and Razor for certain, we've got to presume that they know we're involved.' Charlie ran her hands through her hair.

'In which case I've placed Gemma in even more danger. And there's no way the social services will return Mia to these two. They might have possibly over time, had Caz stayed on her own and with me vouching for her - but not now she's got Razor – and not a chance after this.'

Charlie nodded. She didn't even want to consider the fact they had nothing to offer in return for their hostage. 'Any luck on the new number, Tony?'

'Nothing at all. By the time my guys got the number logged into the system it was all over – they'd switched off. We will get a location, but they'll be long gone by the time we get anyone there. That's if they're all still together anyway.'

'So Gemma could be on her own?'

Charlie cocked her head to one side wishing Tony hadn't put the idea into Anna's head. They'd discussed earlier the nightmare possibility of there being three separate locations to find. 'More likely that Caz will be staying with Gemma, while Razor makes the calls. And I presume the phone is unregistered?'

Anna looked visibly relieved. 'Caz might be messed up, but at least she's unlikely to be violent.'

'Yep.' Tony grimaced. 'But this guy is living up to his nickname. He's pretty sharp. He's had a lifetime as a drug dealer trying to evade us. He knows all about what we can and can't do – so he's got spare burner phones, he speaks and moves on, and keeps the mobiles switched off. But he can't do much to avoid all the cameras - so if we can't use the phones we'll concentrate on his transport.'

'Which is why we really need to find the stolen VW Polo.'

Chapter 48

The rain hadn't eased for hours and Caz was pissed off.

Everything, including her, was fucking soaked.

Not only was the river becoming a torrent, but its width had swelled considerably filling the whole riverbed and starting to rise up the banks. In addition to the river, the surrounding trees were proving hostile, the leaves storing up miniature puddles of rainwater which cascaded down cracks in the roof of the cave. Water dripped in everywhere, wetting the dirty cushions and making everything smell damp and putrid.

And she was bored. Razor had been gone hours. She had no phone to play with and Gemma was too young to provide any proper company. In fact, the little brat was hard work. Every couple of hours she asked to be allowed to use the toilet, or wash, or eat. The girl was always hungry or thirsty or uncomfortable or sore.

She glanced across towards the girl, checking her bindings. Before Razor had left this morning, they'd moved her arms to her front and pulled the duct tape to one side. It was easier that way for Gemma to eat, to move, to position herself over the bucket for a shit or a piss – but it was also now possible for her to try to untie the rope around her neck, or loosen her leg straps. Or call for help. Not that she'd tried doing any of that. After the previous night's incident with the tape, Gemma was less testing, more compliant. She smiled to herself, swearing silently as the girl caught her eye. *Compliant* had always been one of her favourite words. It was what the feds used to describe their non-aggressive prisoners. Apt again. She was enjoying this.

'Miss.' The girl might be compliant – but she was trying her patience. She was too fucking needy.

'What now?'

'Can I use the toilet again?'

'I'm going to stop fucking feeding you if you keep needing to piss.'

'Please Miss. I'm bursting.'

She nodded and got to her feet. At least it was still relatively dry where they both sat in the rear of the cave.

'Bloody rain,' she mumbled, loosening the rope around Gemma's neck and allowing her to move to the bucket at the front of the cave. 'Be quick.'

The girl shuffled forward, struggling with her trousers and underwear, head down, her eyes flicking from the back to the front of the cave.

'Throw it out when you're done.' She didn't want the girl's stinking piss inside their hide. 'And don't try anything.' She got up and moved forward herself, shadowing her. Rain or no rain it wouldn't do to be sloppy. If Razor was doing his bit, then so should she. He was out passing on their demands this afternoon, and stealing a new car. A different day; a different phone and a different car. It was the only way to stay ahead should Anna have gone behind their backs.

'Miss, why have you brought these toys here?' Gemma moved past her, bending to pick up the dinosaur. 'Dilly was one of my favourites as a child. I loved her long neck. I'm glad Mia liked her. Where's Mia now?'

Caz said nothing – and in that instant she thought she might cry. Where was her daughter? Where was Mia? She had no idea when, or even if, she would see her again.

'What happened to the doll?' Gemma was lifting Goldilocks, holding her precious memento of her mother in her piss-stained hands. 'It's a shame her hair is cut short. Did you cut it, Miss?'

'Let her go.' The noise coming from her mouth sounded unearthly, unrecognisable as her own. It shrieked about inside her brain. 'Give her to me.' She launched herself at Gemma, snatching the doll from her hands and shoving her backwards into the wall of the cave. How dare she touch Goldilocks.

The girl gave a yelp, then slumped down in a heap, her hands clutching the top of her head. A trickle of red, slipped through Gemma's fingers and ran slowly across the shiny silver metal of the handcuffs and on down her arm.

She stood for a moment shocked at the sight of the blood, then slowly, carefully wound the rope around the girl's neck and fastened it tight.

Chapter 49

At a few minutes past eight the front door was flung open and Scott walked in.

'Anna, I'm home.'

Charlie stood up as Anna crumpled, crying, into the arms of her six-foot tall, athletically built husband, with blond curly hair and piercing blue eyes. He wore a pair of silver framed glasses, which he pulled off immediately and threw on the sofa.

'It's all right,' he soothed, pulling his wife into his body and stroking her hair. 'We'll get Gemma back, I promise.'

Charlie waited until Anna's sobs settled into a rhythm, wishing she felt as confident as he, then she held out her hand.

'So, what's happening now?' His hand skimmed hers.

'We're doing everything we can. This is DS Tony Ludlow,' she said. 'He's from the specialist kidnapping unit, coordinating the case. He'll brief you on everything so far that we know. I'm here as a back-up and to provide support for Anna.'

'Well, I can do that now.' His tone was not as harsh as his words seemed. 'Sorry, no offence, but if you need to get on with other things.'

She smiled. 'No offence taken, but I might take you up on your offer, at least for a short while.' Paul had been in contact in the last few hours and it seemed that the

SARAH FLINT

surveillance team were being kept busy. 'Things seem to be moving on another case I'm dealing with.'

She gave a nod to Tony. 'Right, as we discussed, I've set up a street search for the VW Polo and left messages for both Surrey and Kent police. If anyone sees it they're not to approach any occupants or go near the vehicle. They're to phone you or me straight away.' She picked up her bag and headed towards the door, turning a last time towards Scott and Anna. 'If it's out there we'll find it. Until then it's a waiting game.'

⊠ ⊠ ⊠

The rain was still lashing down as Charlie made her way back to Wimbledon. She peered out, as it battered the windscreen and ricocheted off the bonnet. *I hope you're inside somewhere safe Gemma,* she thought, *and that you stay safe until we find you.*

They had less than twenty hours before Razor was told that Mia would not be returning. No number of safeguards could be placed on the little girl to keep her from danger. Drugs, pimps and babies just didn't mix.

'So, Paul, what have we got?' Paul was waiting at the back gates to the yard when she pulled up. He jumped into the passenger seat as she pulled to a halt.

'Something's going down, Charlie, and whatever it is I think it's going to happen tonight if the cameras opposite GSM are anything to go by. 3D has visited the club at least three times on his own; twice when he was met and taken inside by Smythe-Hamilton, and once when he was met on the steps by Hurley. Interestingly Hurley stopped him going in. It looked as if they were making arrangements. They both checked their watches together, like they were synchronising times.'

'What times were the visits?'

'The two to Smythe-Hamilton were early afternoon and lasted about half an hour before he headed off with a big grin on his face, like the cat that got the cream. And the one when he was met by Hurley a few hours later.'

'So what are you thinking?'

'Drugs. It's got to be. Maybe 3D has now proved himself enough to be doing business with Smythe-Hamilton, who we know has connections with some pretty heavy-duty importers. I've no idea what they were discussing but I would say that Hurley is the go-between – and he's just gone out on the move again.'

'In this?' she stared up at the sky. The rain had eased slightly but a light drizzle was still falling steadily from a mass of heavy grey clouds. What last remaining light from the sun had been snuffed out completely and the sky was almost as dark as at midnight.

'Well, it's perfect if you want camouflage.'

'And even better if you want to cover your tracks.'

'I hope you don't mind.' Paul squirmed uncomfortably. 'But, in your absence I thought it might be good to get 3D's phone cell-sited since he still has it. See if he and Hurley might be heading in the same direction.'

'That's brilliant Paul. Of course I don't mind. Where is he now?'

'Still at home.' He checked his phone again. 'But Hurley is out and about with his Union Flag cap on, carrying a light grey holdall with a fluorescent Nike tick. The surveillance team are on him now, but he's leading them a merry dance, going round all the backstreets and continually stopping. Might be trying to work out if he's being followed – or simply biding his time.'

'Or both.' She checked the time on her watch, and picked up her phone. 'Half past nine. So do I ramp up some back up or send people home?'

Chapter 50

Razor wiped his arm along his brow and swore.

He was trying to force the ignition switch on another car, but the engine stubbornly refused to start. Now every inch of the interior was covered in condensation and he was soaking wet and dripping with sweat.

Angrily he lashed out with a foot, his heavy boot smashing the plastic facia surrounding the steering wheel. What the fuck was going on? He was losing his touch. He got out, slamming the door, and walked sullenly back to the red Astra. It would have to do, and with any luck it hadn't been reported stolen as yet. If the rain would just fucking stop, then tomorrow he'd try again.

It took him less than half an hour to reach the outskirts of London. As the bright lights of the city started to fade, so he became accustomed to the dark, unlit streets of Surrey. Water ran in streams down the edges of the carriageways and the cats-eyes down the centre of the roads winked intermittently from underneath fallen twigs and branches.

There were far fewer cars on the road tonight, the weather driving almost anyone with a bit of sense inside. The forecast was for more rain with the chance of flash floods in some areas. The street traders in Brixton had been moaning that it drove down their business. The drug dealers moaned too, though their gripes were only about how to keep dry. The business of drugs barely altered whatever the weather. So he'd easily tracked down a mate and caught up with the gossip, before setting off on the drive to the North Downs with a dozen rocks of crack and some weed tucked down the front of his pants.

He was navigating through a small country village when he glanced in the mirror. A cop car was tailing him. Automatically he reached down to his crotch, checking his packet of gear was still in place. It was, but so were the cops, hanging back slightly, a fair distance behind, but there still, stalking him.

Immediately a huge wave of adrenalin surged through his body, making his heart pound and his palms sticky with sweat. He wiped his hands on his knees, and grinned to himself. He loved this reaction; the thrill of the chase, the exquisite moment when he would win, or lose. It mattered not whether he was the hunter, or the hunted, even what the end result might be. What mattered was the process.

At this moment they would be checking on the car, ascertaining if it had been reported stolen, to whom it belonged, and whether it was road legal. Any second now flashing blue lights would show him whether its owner had returned, and whether or not they had tax and insurance. He slowed, indicating left, and pulled off the main road, keeping his speed down, watching and waiting.

The cop car turned too.

His foot twitched over the accelerator as he waited for the night sky to be filled with light and noise, but nothing was happening. The road was narrow, no more than a small country lane. He slowed still further, scanning the hedgerows and driveways, searching for the right one. It was a ploy that he'd used on several occasions. *Just visiting friends, officer.*

The cop car was closer. He could almost feel their eyes burning into his skull but here it was; a drive in the shape of a horseshoe. One way in, an escape route out. He couldn't afford to get trapped. Throwing on the indicator he slowed even further, edging over the tarmac, watching for their headlights to follow him in. He braked to a stop, swivelling his head and peering out through the window as a squall of rain battered the glass.

He could just make out the outline of their car stopped at the entrance to the driveway, the flashes of fluorescent down each side shining yellow in the reflected glow from the house. He turned off his headlights, waited, poised to put his foot down if required. For a moment, everything remained still, the silence broken only by the hammering of the rain, and his heart. Then, slowly, smoothly, the cop car moved off.

'Too fucking wet out there is it, you bastards?' he roared into the silence, banging his hands down on the wheel in triumph. The Astra obviously hadn't been reported stolen as yet. And now, he had the whole night ahead to do as he wished. Inching forward to the end of the drive, he pulled to a halt and climbed out, checking that the coast really was clear.

Rain splashed down on his shaven head, soaking him in a warm, victory shower. He didn't care. Raising his head to the sky, he opened his mouth, letting the clear fresh rainwater splash onto his tongue. There was no sign of the cops.

'You prize fucking wankers!' he shouted, in the direction they'd gone. 'If only you knew.'

❖ ❖ ❖

Ten minutes later Razor pulled into the car park, stopping in the furthest corner under a huge old oak. He switched off the lights, plunging himself into deep, murky darkness. Neither the moon nor the stars were visible through the thick blanket of clouds.

Turning the engine off, he got out, at the same time as a strong gust of wind blew a bucketful of water down off the tree, soaking him through to the skin.

He laughed, wiping his hands over his head and flicking off the excess water. It was still warm, and nothing could dampen his mood.

The cops were all fucking clueless. So, Anna Christophe could do her worst. She could snitch all she wanted 'cause the feds wouldn't catch them. He was too fucking good.

Tonight, with or without the rain, he was going to take what he was owed.

He turned on his torch, swinging the beam across the watery terrain. The river, so placid on their arrival, had risen so much that the stepping stones were hidden under the surface and water swirled in fast-moving eddies over the rocks by the banks. Gingerly he started the trek up the river, kicking back the scrub where the river forced him further up the banks. A few times he tripped on a root, cursing as his foot slipped into the fast moving water. The rain had stopped, but the trees were still sending intermittent showers down, swelling the stream.

Slowly, steadily, he moved upwards, until he could make out the entrance to their shelter. A tiny light glinted out from within, but the sight didn't bother him tonight. No one in their right minds would be out in the woods.

Only them and their captive! And tonight, they'd all be out of their minds on gear.

❈ ❈ ❈

Gemma heard him before she could see him, the sound of twigs snapping underfoot as he approached, the noise of his disgusting grunting.

She squirmed further into the corner, under the root. Perhaps if she couldn't be seen, he might forget she was there?

She wished more than anything that she wasn't.

Her hair was thick and matted with dried blood and her head still throbbed painfully from the blow to her skull. *Miss* had said nothing, done nothing to help, even as the blood had flowed down her cheeks and she'd sat half concussed sobbing silently to herself. She still felt light-headed now; though more from the thought of what had occurred, and what there was still to come.

The grunting was rising to a crescendo now, as the curtain was pulled back. CJ knelt, peering in, a grin spread over the whole of his face. In the light of the torch he looked manic; terrifying, with mad wild eyes flitting from side to side before fixing squarely on her. Water dripped down his forehead and cheeks. He licked his lips.

'Ah there you are, you little bitch. Don't think you can hide from me.' He took a step towards her, laughing nastily.

She started to cry. Not that she wanted to. *Miss* didn't like it when she cried, but she couldn't help it. She wanted her mummy, and daddy. She wanted to be home, tucked up in bed. Not here. Anywhere but here.

'And guess what?' CJ turned towards the woman, shuffling forward into the shelter and pulling the curtain back into place. 'The feds know – because your best fucking friend told them. Then she tried to say she hadn't. But I saw them, as plain as day, in your gaff – wiv 'er there, standing next to one of 'em.'

Miss looked shocked; moving towards him and taking him by the arm. 'What did you say to Anna, babe?'

'Just that I'd seen 'er, wiv 'em. And that she had twenty-four hours to get us back Mia or else…' He sliced his hand across his throat. 'Gemma gets it. Talking about Gemma…'

She shrunk even further against the wall at the mention of her name, watching horrified as he shoved his hands down his pants and pulled out several packages. 'I've brought her a present.' He jiggled them about in the air and came up close.

'What've you done to 'er?' He swung the torch in her face, blinding her, then reached down and yanked her to her feet.

'I ain't done nothin' to 'er,' the woman said. 'She fell.'

Gemma screwed up her eyes, her head spinning at the sudden movement. The same sweet pungent smell as she'd smelt on him earlier, wafted up her nostrils, making her even more heady. She guessed it was drugs, but what sort? She had no idea, even less what he would do with them.

Her legs felt shaky and weak, and she could barely stand with the throbbing in her temples. His hands were all over her, touching her face, her body.

She wanted to scream, but her mouth wouldn't work.

She wanted to lash out, to push him away but her arms were leaden, dangling limply at her sides.

She opened her eyes as the light moved away, blinking into the gloom. She could just make out the shape of the woman standing to one side, unmoving, her expression blank. Why wouldn't she help?

Her vision was blurring; what little she could see becoming fuzzy and indistinct. Nothing made sense any more.

His hands were gripping her shoulders now, hurting her. She stared towards the woman again, silently pleading for her help, but her pleas went unanswered, and as everything turned black, she felt herself falling, straight into his arms.

Chapter 51

By 21.45 Charlie had everything organised.

A phone call to Ross McBride had ensured his team would be staying on to assist them, if necessary, with Bet monitoring both the camera on GSM and the cell-site on 3D, and Naz and Sabira paired up together to shadow his movements. All they were waiting for now was a spare radio of the type used by the surveillance team and they'd be good to go. She just hoped she'd made the right decision to keep everyone on.

She sent a text message while she waited.

Sorry Mum, I'll be stuck at work late tonight. Ring me straight away if you have any problems.

Will do darling xx

She was still staring guiltily at the message when Paul came running in, throwing the spare surveillance radio towards her.

'Quick, Hurley's on the move,' he panted.

They listened as a voice trilled over the radio. 'Off, off, off, north along Durnsford Road.'

They sprinted to their car and Paul jumped into the driver's seat and strapped himself in, while she updated

Ross. He and his team would be moving in parallel, providing the muscle behind any confrontation.

'Now turning left, left, left, into Revelstoke Road.'

Charlie pulled up a map of the area, following the route with her finger. They were travelling along the back streets of Southfields towards Wimbledon Park.

'He's heading in the direction of the allotments,' she said excitedly.

A few more junctions and they were there.

'Subject One slowing down, outside the main gate to the allotments,' the surveillance officer continued. 'Brake lights on. Stopping outside the main gates. Someone else take the eye.'

'Bloody hell!' She passed on the information to Ross, before turning to Paul. 'What on earth is he doing there at this time of the evening, and on a night like tonight? It must be important.'

'He's out of his vehicle, hood up, carrying a light grey holdall with a fluorescent Nike tick.' A woman's voice came on to the radio.

'That's the same one I saw him with at the club earlier,' Paul whispered.

The commentary continued. 'He appears to have a set of keys in his hand, and a torch. He's opening a padlock on a pedestrian gate to the left of the main vehicular access, and is now heading along the hedgerow towards the same row of sheds as earlier. Subject only partially in view but the torchlight is now stationary outside the first shed. Door opening and he's in, in, in.'

She checked her watch. 'Five to ten. What's he doing in there?' Every minute seemed to last forever.

'Standby, standby. Door opening and he's out, out, and stationary.'

'Probably putting the padlocks back on. He must have something pretty important to keep it so well secured.' She checked her watch again. It was exactly ten o'clock.

'Subject on the move again back towards the car. Locking up the gate. All units he no longer has the holdall. He is now carrying the same blue rucksack as earlier.'

'He's done a bag swap.' Charlie commented.

'Yes! And it's got to be drugs,' Paul swivelled round in his seat, gripping the wheel tightly. 'Come on Wayne. My guess is he took it there ready for the deal tonight. Much safer in this out-of-the-way spot, than coming direct from the GSM club in the centre of town.'

'Subject back in his car. Lights on, and off, off, off.'

'Where next?' Charlie stared at the map. 'And who's he going to meet?'

'All units, 3D has just left his house.' Bet's voice piped up. 'Moving slowly through the Roehampton Estate towards Putney Common and Wimbledon.'

'Shit Paul, I spoke too soon. It's happening.' She picked up the radio,' Naz get yourself down there. As and when the phone leaves the estate, do a drive past. See if you can confirm 3D is the one carrying it. We can't risk the phone being put out with a decoy.'

'Will do,' called Naz.

'Still on the move,' Bet confirmed.

Charlie listened to Bet as the cell-sited phone moved closer to the roadway.'

'It's out on to Roehampton Lane.'

'Positive ID on 3D,' Naz called a few minutes later. 'He's out on foot, dressed in his usual dark tracksuit. He was talking on his mobile and I could clearly see the knife tattoo across his cheek in the light from the phone.'

'Subject passing Roehampton cemetery and left, left, left, into Stag Lane. Now left, left, into Central Drive. Vehicle slowing down – and stopping, just past the junction with Stag Lane.'

They listened as the lights went off and Hurley got out of his car. He pulled the rucksack over one shoulder, locked his vehicle and headed off into the trees that surrounded the playing fields, directly opposite where his vehicle was parked.

'So 3D is a little way off, but heading on foot in the direction of the Evans Memorial Playing Fields at the edge of Wimbledon Common, and Hurley's already there.' Paul summed up, as Charlie checked her watch again.

'22.17. So, I'd guess their meeting will be 22.30.' She looked out through the windscreen at the heavy grey clouds. It had stopped raining for now, but more rain looked likely. 'If I was him, I'd stay in my car for as long as I could. He's a little bit early to be out already on foot.'

Chapter 52

3D was almost there.

Charlie and Paul were plotted up around the corner, with the others all nearby.

She could feel the hairs on the back of her neck prickling as Bet updated them all on his progress.

'Let's go,' she said to Paul, climbing out from their car and heading towards the field. She ducked into a garden as they neared the junction, squinting along the road as a figure turned the corner. 'It's 3D,' she mouthed to Paul. 'All units.' She whispered down the radio. '3D is approaching the suspected rendezvous point. From now on maintain radio silence, until I shout.'

She zipped up her stab vest and pulled out her CS spray canister, taking a few deep breaths to calm her nerves.

This was exactly what she'd joined for, but drugs and gangs equalled danger – and seeing Naz stabbed so recently had made her feel vulnerable.

Paul slipped in beside her, his expression as grim as hers. They peeped around the fence, watching as 3D crossed over, looking around. He put one hand in his pocket, held it there, eyes about, then he ducked into the bushes, directly opposite the junction following the same path as Hurley had trodden.

She nodded to Paul and held up her watch, counting the seconds before their plan would be set in motion. If things worked out well, 3D and Hurley would be ambushed mid-transaction. Too soon and they'd risk only Hurley being in possession of drugs. Too late and it'd be 3D. Charlie wanted them both, as implicated as each other.

Twenty seconds crawled by, then thirty. Charlie gave Paul a nudge and dipped her head. They were off. Quickly and quietly they skirted the garden, crossed the road and slipped in behind a couple of trees, listening for any sound of movement. For a few seconds she could hear only water; dripping and trickling off the sodden trees, branches creaking with moisture, but then above the movement of the woods she heard voices, raised voices.

'Move up quietly,' she whispered into the mouthpiece of her radio. Something was wrong. Drug deals usually went down swiftly, silently, the negotiations made long before the meet. This sounded fractious, bad-tempered.

The talking stopped. Then silence. Then a long, agonised scream. More shouting. The snapping and rustling of twigs in the undergrowth. More shrieks.

'Go, go, go! Charlie quietly but firmly commanded over the radio, whilst sprinting forward towards the noise. She followed the shouting, switching on her torch and kicking her way along an overgrown footpath, before bursting through a clump of wet undergrowth and into a clearing where she could just make out the shape of two darkly-clothed figures wrestling on the muddy ground. 3D was pinned to the forest floor, his cheeks and neck wet with blood, his face screwed up tight as he sought to hold on to the arm of Wayne Hurley. By the light of the torch, she could see the outline of a knife in Hurley's hand.

'Get back!' she shouted. 'Get off him, and get back!'

Hurley's head spun round towards her, his eyes wide with confusion, then he jumped to his feet, the knife still gripped in his hand, poised to attack.

'Drop it!' she screamed, aiming the canister of CS directly in his face. 'I said, drop it!'

For a split second he held on, his eyes narrowing as he stared at the canister. Then he threw the knife to the ground, and shrugged.

'Thank goodness you're here, officer. Nice to see you again,' he said, taking a step backwards and holding out his hands as Paul ran forward and slapped some handcuffs round his wrists.

'You're nicked for attempted murder, for starters,' Paul panted. 'You don't have to say anything but it may harm your defence, if you fail to mention something you later rely on in court. Anything you do say may be given in evidence.'

'This man attacked me.' He pointed to 3D who was lying on the ground, clutching his neck. 'I thought I was going to die.'

He glanced across, a thin smile playing on his lips as Naz and Sabira came bursting into the clearing, closely followed by Ross and his team. 'Well, well, the cavalry have arrived – and not a second too late.'

Paul yanked him to one side, as Charlie dropped to her knees next to 3D. Blood was streaming through his fingers, a dark tide of crimson, staining his chin and his hands. It almost looked in the torchlight like it was dripping from the blade of the knife tattoo on his cheek.

'Call an ambulance,' she shouted, pulling on some gloves and staring down as yet another teenager fought for their life. It was like watching Rochelle Edwards all over again, except that this time the victim, 3D, wasn't an innocent.

'We'll take over,' Sabira said, as if reading her mind. She bent down beside her and moved 3D's hand to one side, exposing a deep gash across the front of his neck. 'Leave him to Naz and I. You deal with Hurley.'

'Thanks, Sab.' She backed away, grateful for the opportunity to get back to their suspect. Ross was calling an ambulance and already had most things under control. His team were spreading out, checking for any possible witnesses and cordoning off the crime scene. At this point in time, 3D's injury could go either way.

Charlie shone her torch around the area, her eyes scanning the glade, searching for the package full of drugs that they hoped for. The knife Hurley had dropped was lying in the wet grass. It was a red-handled kitchen knife, not unlike the one used to kill Rocco Fontana, with its blade still smeared with 3D's blood.

'That's what he used when he jumped me.' Hurley was watching her closely. 'I wanted a small bag of weed to help me to sleep after late nights at the club, but then the filthy scum tried to rob me. I managed to wrestle his knife off him, and fight for my life.'

'Did you now?' She didn't believe him but then she didn't know what had started the fight either.

'Wearing gloves?' She pointed to his hands covered in a thin pair of latex gloves. She'd noticed them as he held his hands out to Paul.

'Weed stinks.'

'So, why meet him here?'

'I bumped into him in Wimbledon Town Centre. It was his suggestion to come here and I went along with it. Wouldn't do to get caught with some weed near the club, would it? But now I know why. The lying bastard obviously had this planned all along.'

She said nothing in return. Paul had observed their earlier conversation, but without audio how were they to know whose suggestion it had been? Everything in her head was screaming it was him but that wasn't enough. She turned away, aiming her torch at the ground, searching for any packages, or his bag. Where was his bag? Spreading out a little further she noticed a strap sticking out from behind a tree.

It was the blue rucksack. Donning a new pair of gloves, she walked towards it and picked it up, her heart pounding. If only... The bag felt light. Nervously she unzipped it and aimed the torch into the main compartment. Nothing, or at least not what she wanted. It was dirty, with a thin layer of dust on its base. Inside she could see an empty bottle of water, a pair of plastic gloves and a scrunched-up Benson and Hedges fag packet – but no packets of white powder, or pills. She tried the smaller compartments but again, nothing.

'Has he been searched, Paul?' There had to be something.

'Not yet.'

'Well search him now, please.'

'I assure you, officer you won't find anything untoward.'

She watched as he squared his shoulders and spread his legs, unrequested, standing with an expression of amusement as Paul frisked his pockets, checked in the palms of his hands, his socks.

'Nothing,' Paul shrugged when he'd finished. 'Except two sets of keys and a hankie... so far.' It remained to be seen if there might be something secreted under his clothing.

'There's nothing.' Hurley confirmed, smirking. She turned away, desperate to find something to wipe the smile from his arrogant face.

3D was still lying flat-out on the ground, but he was conscious, and appeared stable. Naz and Sabira were doing a good job in stemming the flow of blood from his neck. He wouldn't be able to speak for some time but could she search him? An image popped into her mind, of Richie Woodall's face on hearing the news that she'd gone through the pockets of a victim of crime while he lay half-dead on the ground — but then there was also a fleeting memory of 3D touching his pocket as he entered the woodland.

Could it be that he was checking the cannabis Hurley was claiming to want? Or might it be something else. Either way she had to find out.

She knelt down, speaking quietly in 3D's ear. 'I'm searching you for drugs, and because I need to make sure you have nothing that could do harm to my officers, or the medical staff,' she said to the youth. His eyes widened, his gaze flicking about the tops of the trees. She patted him down, her hands moving immediately to the pocket she'd seen him check. If Hurley's allegation was true, there would be a large bag of weed, soft and spongy, but instead her hands came to rest on a hard metal object.

It was a knife and as she pulled it carefully from his pocket, she knew, without doubt it was Hurley who'd lied.

'Come on, Paul. Let's get him into the car. Ross you come too. There's a section 32 search to be done.'

Within minutes they were belted into their cars and on way, with Ross following on behind.

Hurley sat smugly strapped in the rear, next to Paul, with Charlie driving. Every few seconds, she checked in the mirror. Down past the common she drove, then towards Wimbledon Park. Hurley stayed smirking. As she turned into the road where the allotments were situated, the smile began to look strained. He started to fidget. She slowed down further, watching him squirm; leaning forward to gaze out of the windows, then at each of them in turn, and down at his feet.

'What's the matter Wayne?' she asked, slowing to a stop outside the gates to the allotments. 'Cat got your tongue? Paul, give me his keys and get him out. Let's go for a walk.'

She waited as he clambered out of the car, his hands still held in cuffs to the rear.

'I found those earlier, on the ground in Wimbledon Village.' He nodded towards one of the sets of keys. It had four keys on a ring with a green fob. 'Was going to hand them in at the nick later.'

'And you didn't think to mention that to us earlier when we found them?'

'Didn't see the need.' He was starting to sweat. 'Anyway, you may as well keep them.'

'Thank you, we will.' She lifted up the bunch with the green fob, pushing each key individually into the padlock on the pedestrian gate. 'Ah here we go.' The catch sprung open and she opened the gate, recalling the route described by the surveillance team. They headed along the hedgerow towards the area of the potting sheds, stopping at the first one with the faded green door. It was lined up next to three others, all about ten feet by six feet in size, but it was the only one of the four that was so well secured. 'Let's try this one shall we Wayne?'

Hurley tried to shrug nonchalantly, but the action looked stiff.

'You can do what you like,' he said, a little too gruffly. 'Like I said, I know nothing about those keys, or where they're for.'

'No worries,' she smiled, trying to keep her hands from shaking as she opened each lock. One, two, three. Open Sesame!'

The shed was pitch black, and smelt dank. She stepped inside, swinging her torch around the walls, gaping in disgust at the posters lined up side by side, overlapping each other, the handwritten slogans.

'So this isn't your cap?' In the corner was a coat stand, much like the one in Jamie Smythe-Hamilton's office at the club, and there hanging on one of the pegs was the Union Flag cap.

'No, it isn't my fucking cap.' Hurley squinted towards her, his eyes hard.

'So we won't find your DNA all over it when we check it for hairs? Come on now Wayne. Don't lie. It was your knife, not 3D's, wasn't it? He had his own knife, still in his pocket; a miniature zombie knife, in its own leather sheath. So, why would he use a bog-standard kitchen knife? He's a Don, after all, as if you don't know. In fact, he's their leader.

'And as for the drugs. It wasn't 3D who was supposed to be bringing them, was it?' She swung the torch round the shed, its beam coming to rest on the fluorescent tick on a grey holdall. She bent down carefully unzipping its top, then pulled back the edges. Inside were six perfectly wrapped parcels. 'It was you. You left it here earlier when you came from the club, along with your cap. You swapped it for the bag containing the knife.'

Hurley was frowning.

'How do you think we know all about this, eh, Wayne? Think about it.' She pointed the torch down into the bag then back in his face, reading the exact moment when the pieces of the puzzle fell into place.

'You've been watching me, you bitch.' He reared up, jerking his handcuffs from Paul's grip and launching himself forward, his head aimed at her face. Before she could respond, Ross reacted, throwing himself at the man, knocking him to the floor of the shed. He jumped astride him keeping him restrained, as Hurley tried impotently to buck and spit.

'You won't get away with this. You've got nothing on me.'

'I think you'll find we have, Wayne – and by the looks of it you've given us plenty more to look through.' She turned away from him, concentrating again on the posters pinned to the wall. An image of Adolf Hitler stared out from one. Another had soldiers posing with Nazi salutes alongside photos of the German war machine and National Front posters. Two hand-scrawled notices read:

No space for our race!

Asylum seekers – go home!

She flicked the torch around the walls, spotlighting an assortment of knives lined up along a back shelf. 'Yes, there's plenty enough. Now take him away.'

He was hauled to his feet, Paul at one arm, Ross at the other. As they marched him away towards the car, they paused at the gate and Charlie turned round to take a satisfied look at their suspect. Hurley twisted round, his face contorted with hate, as if sensing her watching.

'My boss has connections,' he screamed. 'You wait, DS Stafford. You wait.'

Chapter 53

The GSM club appeared locked and secure. One small light shone out from behind the closed shutters of a room at the rear. A couple of others were dotted around inside.

'Are you sure that he's in there, Bet?' Charlie asked over her phone, licking her lips nervously. Arresting the rather downmarket doorman of a celebrity night club was one thing. Taking out the likes of Jamie Smythe-Hamilton was something else completely, but there was no time to waste. Suppose his boss had been awaiting confirmation from Hurley that the deal had gone down. In the time elapsed at the allotment, he could be cleaning up any trace of their illicit drug dealing and disposing of evidence.

'Yes Charlie, I'm positive. I've checked back on the cameras – and he definitely hasn't come out.'

They'd already discussed what they knew of the layout. The rear of the club consisted of a number of rooms, on three levels; the one with the light being in the basement, backing on to a quaint cobbled yard. A ramshackle outhouse filled most of the space, with the yard itself boxed in on all sides by the high walls of adjoining properties, with no exits into the streets at the rear. The club's single, inconspicuous, entrance, along with two equally unobtrusive fire escapes emptied out on to the front square – exactly where the camera was pointed.

'It's not open to guests on a Tuesday night,' Bet added. 'But both of them were here earlier. After Hurley left, Smythe-Hamilton stayed on. He switched most of the lights off about half an hour ago, but there're a few random ones dotted about the building, and one in a room at the rear. I've taken a quick walk across to the multi-storey and his Porsche is still parked in its usual spot.'

'Well, we'd better see what he's up to then. Thanks, Bet.' She ended the call and confirmed the warrant was safely in her pocket, and then she picked up the second set of keys found in Wayne Hurley's possession. The warrant might give them the power of entry to the club but the keys would give them the means to take their target by surprise.

It was perfect.

And if he complained– well they were just saving him the cost of a new door.

'Right, let's go,' she nodded to Ross. With Paul booking Hurley into custody, and Naz and Sabira guarding 3D at the hospital, none of her usual team was left. So Ross and his squad had stepped in and, having shadowed them through the whole investigation, they were raring to complete the task.

On Charlie's signal they lined up in pairs behind her along the side of the club while she tried the key in the door. The lock clicked aside, and she nudged open the door. It was just as she remembered it and as she stepped forward into the black and white foyer, she felt more like an actress in an old movie than a cop stepping into the unknown. With no detailed floor plans available and Hurley's reluctance to let them wander around on their previous visit, they were going in blind.

She indicated a camera blinking in a corner, remembering Smythe-Hamilton's office and the CCTV of the dance floor. Perhaps he had cameras situated right through the club and was watching them right now. Ross reached up and stuck a piece of paper over the camera. Better their man had a blank screen, than track their progress towards him.

They moved on, one pair remaining at the front door, another two pairs covering the fire exits. Charlie held a torch in one hand, and her CS in the other. Ross gripped his taser. Instinct led them gradually towards the rear of the premises, with various pairs branching off to check every other lit room. On they went down a short flight of stairs until there was only the two of them left, creeping silently along a darkened corridor. They turned a corner, and stood still, staring towards a thin chink of light squeezing out around the frame of a door on the right.

'That's got to be him', she whispered, giving Ross a thumbs up. They edged forward, listening for the tiniest noise. A camera at the far end of the passageway winked, and seconds later came a scuffling, scraping sound.

'Shit, he must have seen us.' Charlie took off, sprinting along the corridor until she came to the room that was lit. She grabbed the door handle, turning it hard up and down, but the door wouldn't budge.

Ross pulled out the taser, aiming it direct at the door. 'Ready,' he shouted.

She stepped back, took a deep breath then kicked at the door, sending the lock flying across the floor of the room with a loud crack. The door flew open, its handle crashing back against the wall.

As the light hit her retinas, she threw her hand up to her eyes, blinking momentarily. Two long tables were positioned against either side of the room. One was covered with a mountain of cardboard boxes, their outer packaging stamped with the Golden Wonder motif. Some had been ripped apart with unopened packets of crisps scattered about. On the other table, and the one to which her eyes were drawn, was a pile of empty crisp wrappers, their contents tipped into a box on the floor. Cellophane packages sliced carefully apart, scales, silver foil and white powder covered a chopping board – shitloads of the stuff.

But there was no Jamie Smythe-Hamilton.

Ross ran forward into the room, taser poised to aim, closely followed by Charlie. A door on the opposite side was swinging open. She heard footsteps, another door slam. She ran on, through the room and out into the rear courtyard. The security lamp was on, its light bouncing off the wet cobbles. She twisted round trying to see in which direction their quarry had run, nodding towards an old, wooden outhouse. He had to be there.

Together they crept across the yard, with Charlie calling for backup as they neared the door. She pushed it with her foot and it sprung open. A set of wet footprints led away from the threshold across the wooden floorboards and down the side of the building. She pointed towards them, and Ross nodded. 'Stay here,' he murmured directly into her ear. 'In case he tries to double-back and leg it.'

She dipped her head in return and then felt about by the frame for a light. Her fingers located one and she flicked the switch, but the building remained in darkness. Indicating her torch instead, she whispered 'I'll light up your path.'

She watched as Ross crept forward, the red dot of his taser going before him.

'Come out, Jamie,' he instructed, his voice booming loud and authoritative in the gloom. 'We know you're in here.'

Nothing.

He crept forward again with Charlie pointing the beam of her torch from behind him, barely able to make him out through the clutter. Boxes were stacked haphazardly on either side of the walkway, overflowing with paint pots and brushes. Brooms, lighting poles and speakers slanted out across the passage.

She heard him call out again. 'Come on now Jamie. Give up and make it easy on yourself.'

Before the words had left his mouth, a set of bolt croppers thudded down against his skull, dropping Ross to the floor and sending his taser clattering to the ground. Instinctively she ran towards him, just as Jamie Smythe-Hamilton leapt out from behind a stack of boxes.

'Get back,' she swung her CS canister towards him, trying to locate his figure in the beam of her torch. He ducked out of the light, and as she squeezed the spray impotently into the vacant air a tiny red laser light lit a spot on her chest.

Before she had time to cry out or move, the sting of two taser lugs pierced her shoulder and her abdomen, and she heard the crackle of electricity as 50,000 volts hit her square on. Her legs buckled beneath her, and her arms dropped to her side as she fell flat on the filthy floor boards, the current ripping through every cell of her body.

'Me, give up,' she heard him say. He took a step towards her and grinned, releasing his grip on the trigger and allowing the taser to drop to the ground. 'Oh and thanks for lighting up your mate's path, by the way.' He laughed. 'Your Superintendent warned me you were good – but I didn't think you'd be this good.'

'You shouldn't listen to talk.' She grabbed his leg as he stepped over her, gripping on to the fabric of his trousers. With the shock gradually fading, sensation was returning to her arms and legs. Instead she felt drunk, her head fuzzy and her limbs uncoordinated, but her mind was now working fast. 'That's what you said to me once.'

She hung on grimly as he raised his leg over her head.

In the distance she could hear shouting, the trample of boots on the cobbles.

'In here,' she screamed, concentrating on keeping hold of his leg. His head shot up, his expression changing from triumph to resignation in a breath, as four of Ross's team came sprinting towards them.

He glanced down at Ross's bloodied body next to her on the floor then held his hands up in submission. 'Now, now officers,' he said, as they thundered towards him, lifting him bodily into the air. 'There's no need for violence.'

Chapter 54

Wayne Hurley leant back in his chair in the interview room. His knees were splayed outwards, his arms folded and his eyes cold and composed.

Charlie settled herself into the chair next to Paul, watching him closely.

Gone was his earlier sneering self-confidence, replaced instead by calm satisfaction. She'd kept him waiting in the custody office long enough for him to spot his boss's name on the whiteboard. Cell 5 – Smythe-Hamilton – PWITS, class A. She noticed how his eyes stayed fixed to the board, thinking, planning. He'd know exactly what PWITS meant; possession with intent to supply, class A drugs. He'd know that the game was up. So now he was a man on a mission – alone, unrepresented, refusing all offers of legal advice.

And he wanted to talk.

In fact, as Paul pressed 'record' and Charlie went through his rights, twice, it was clear that he was enjoying every minute. He leant forward smiling, and rotated his hand impatiently.

'Come on DS Stafford, let's get on with this.'

She sat back, slowly turning to her notes, pulling out a biro. This interview would be conducted at her pace, not his. She wasn't going to give him, or any representing barrister the chance to allege malpractice. 'Okay, Wayne,' she said unhurriedly. 'Talk to me. We know what you've done but I want to know why.'

'Why? Why not?! Because I could. And because they deserved it.'

'Rochelle Edwards deserved it?'

'She was black.'

Charlie sat up straight. 'And so, she deserved it?!' She couldn't believe what he'd just said.

'Well put it this way,' he grinned. 'That one was unplanned – but not unwelcome.'

'Not unwelcome?' She couldn't ignore it, but he didn't respond. She paused, open mouthed, before rallying. She had to stay on track. 'So the others were planned?'

'Well-planned and well-executed. In fact, very well executed.' He leant back, his eyes gleaming.

'And you want to tell me *all* about it?' She could see he was itching to boast, but she knew also that the racist language he'd likely be spouting, would sicken her to the core. 'So start with Rocco Fontana. Why him?'

'He was one of 3D's boys. Simple as that. And he was easy. 3D, The General, and some of their cronies had been visiting the club. He was with them one day, acting as 3D's messenger boy, doing his dirty work for him.'

'But I thought you got on with 3D? He was working with you?'

'Not me.'

'Well Jamie then?'

He paused, fixing her with a hard stare, as if waiting for the one word that would give him permission to speak.

'We did a warrant.' She looked him square in the face. 'On GSM. That's why he's in custody.'

He smiled, and nodded imperceptibly. It was all he required. 'I told Jamie not to involve them. We had a perfectly good business. We didn't need scum like that. Dirty filthy immigrants who thought they owned the streets. But Jamie got greedy. Kept telling me if we passed some of our gear on down, we'd make thousands. I had to stop him somehow.

'I knew if I killed one of 3D's own, that he'd have to retaliate. I thought it might take his eye of the ball, and show Jamie his mistake. I'd just have to light the touch paper and boom! So one day when I saw the boy out on the streets I stopped him and arranged for him to meet me on the common to sell me some weed.

'But I weren't there to buy weed, was I, just like I weren't with 3D neither. You might like to tell his big sister that he cried like a baby.' Hurley leant forward and stretched out his neck so that his face was directly in front of hers. 'Called her by name, he did. *"Oh Maria, I'm so sorry."* Very moving, it was too.'

Charlie swallowed hard, her mind recalling the spotlessly clean flat, the dignified young woman, the regrets. Even with his juvenile dealing, she and her brother were as different to this disgusting racist as was possible.

'And the knife that you used?' She couldn't let him see he was getting to her.

'Found it.' He threw himself against the back of his chair. 'It's not hard. Just go to their hideouts and you'll find 'em. Hidden behind bushes. Stuck in the soil. The fucking pricks don't care where they put them, and they don't even make sure they're wiped clean. I got them all like that too.'

It was all falling into place. The soil samples found on the blades. The surveillance team spotting him go to the rec. The selection of knives in the potting shed. Forensics would no doubt match the samples to the rucksack and locations.

'So why carry on?' she asked, changing the subject. 'If, like you said, you'd lit the touch paper with Rocco, why go on and kill Kelvin Olawi yourself?'

'Hmmn now that's a good question.' He tilted his head to one side and pursed his lips. 'Perhaps, like Jamie, I got greedy. It was exciting and I liked what I'd done. In fact I enjoyed it so much that I wanted to do it again – and again. What's wrong with getting rid of a few more bloody foreigners?

'And wouldn't it just look like revenge? The mighty Dons avenging their boy. And of course you lot helped. 3D told me everything. *"The word on the street, bruv."* He loved spouting off how you'd got a warrant, how you'd gone into Boxer's flat. How his bitch mother had kicked off and stabbed one of your woman officers. Shame about that, by the way, but then I heard she was black too, so... ' He shrugged and winked at her. 'Pretty much an own goal, wouldn't you say?'

'So, was Rochelle Edwards an own goal?' She could barely look at the man. He was sickening.

'Well sort of, but I prefer to think of her as collateral damage. I'd killed Boxer, purely for the thrill of it, framed The General for his murder and pretty successfully started the war. In fact, I was sitting back enjoying it. Just remind me, how many of those little bastards got mown down on the common?'

'Rochelle Edwards was an innocent girl on her way home from school. She wasn't even in a gang.'

'I heard that. But who really knows, eh? If it weren't for her though, it would really have kicked off. Shame really. They all got scared, the pussies. But it gave me the excuse to get things started again.

'3D?'

'Yep, 3D. Not that I minded. By then Jamie was pushing to do the big deal. To see how much gear 3D and his gang could put out on the streets of South London. He wanted a bigger slice for himself, and if 3D was willing, then so was he.

'So you decided to stop him?'

'Yeah and have a bit of fun for myself. In fact, lots of fucking fun. It was priceless. 3D thought he was about to get the biggest pay packet of his life. You should have seen his fucking face when, instead of drugs—'

'You pulled out the knife.'

'Yeah, I was just getting to the best bit. The knife through the heart – until you lot put paid to that. A minute later and I'd have had my way.'

'Instead, you jumped at the chance to claim self-defence. Pretty clever, until you take into account we'd been watching your movements.'

'Well it was worth a try.' He winked at her again. '3D would never have said a word, for fear of what I might have said, or done – and he sure as hell would have given us a wide berth in future. Alive, or dead he'd have been removed from the picture, I could have returned the drugs to the club and Jamie would have settled back into what we'd worked so hard for.'

'Dealing cocaine to all your celebrity clients?'

'Yep.'

'And paying off the local Superintendent?' She hadn't forgotten Jamie's reference to her boss, but Hurley looked confused. 'Jamie intimated that he'd had words with Richie Woodall. I got the impression he had him in his pocket.'

'Nah. Superintendent Woodall might be stupid and naive, and he might open his gob far too much, but he ain't bent.'

Charlie leant back in her chair, as a great wave of relief and fatigue washed over her. At least they wouldn't be facing an allegation of corruption.

'So would you have carried on killing?' she asked.

Hurley leant back, mirroring her movement, for a moment deep in thought. 'Without doubt,' he said with a tilt of the head. 'Hitler, and that Norwegian fella, Anders Breivik, had the right idea by wanting to keep their countries pure and uncorrupted for the superior race, and get rid of all the foreigners who were ruining them.'

'And that includes the Jews, and homosexuals?'

'Perhaps.' He looked pointedly at Paul.

Charlie shook her head in disgust. 'They were kids, Wayne. Rocco Fontana was barely sixteen. Kelvin Olawi was eighteen. Rochelle Edwards, fourteen. Even 3D was barely an adult. What sort of a man kills children?'

Paul got to his feet, staring back hard at Hurley. 'One who's going to prison for the rest of his life.'

Chapter 55

It was late when Razor roused. His body ached from the position in which he'd slept and he was cold. Too cold, and too wet! Only the relaxing effect of the weed had stopped him from leaving the cave last night. That and Caz, who'd stepped in to fuck him when the girl had fallen limply into his arms. Caz's actions had put the idea firmly out of his mind, just as her words had prevented him having his way with the little bitch. But God, how he'd been tempted. Gemma's pert young breasts and silky white skin had sent his pulse racing; but not quite enough to ignore the blood on her face and the inertness of her limbs. He preferred more of a fight.

'For fuck's sake!' he snarled.

His stomach growled back at him with hunger. He propped himself up on one arm, staring angrily at what was left of their hideout.

Everything in the shelter was sodden. The majority of the branches and leaves they'd so carefully stacked around the entrance had fallen under the weight of the rain and been swept away by the rising current. The river was lapping over the threshold of the cave. Even the curtain that had served as their front door was lying crumpled on the muddy ground, one end caught on a branch, the other end flailing in the water as the river attempted to drag it downstream.

He kicked off the wet blanket that was over his legs and drew them up in front of him, feeling cold water sloshing round inside his boots.

'What's there to eat?' Twisting round to check on the others, he frowned as he saw Caz and the girl squashed up together in the relative dry at the rear of the cave.

'We've got some more sandwiches.' Caz leant forward holding two pre-packed choices towards him. He took them both, swearing loudly as the soggy cardboard backing fell apart.

'These are both fucking wet.' He balled them up in his hands and launched them out into the river, watching as they tumbled and bobbed in the turbulent flow before sinking out of sight.

'What else have you got?'

Caz threw him a few packs of crisps and some chocolate. 'That's all we've got left.'

He took them anyway, wedging himself against the tree roots out of the rain and ripping into them greedily. As he chewed each mouthful he stared at the girl. She didn't really look like her bitch of a mother. Anna Christophe was petite, with short brown hair and brown eyes, whereas Gemma, well, she was tall for her age, slim, with long blonde hair that fell in curls now it had been released from its plait. She must take after her father.

'Can you bring us some more food when you come back later? We're bleedin' hungry too.' Caz was watching him closely, complaining. She was always complaining.

'Who says I'm coming back?' he smirked. 'Why the fuck would I want to spend another night out in this shithole?' He stretched out his hand, letting the rain drip on to his palms then slapped them together, making her jump. 'An' anyway. What the fuck am *I* supposed to get out of this? A woman that does shit-all but whine. A kid I never asked for or wanted?'

'But Mia's your baby too.' Caz was whinging again. 'If we get her back we might be a proper family, like what I've always wanted.'

'Maybe if you hadn't gone back on the gear you'd still have 'er.' He pulled out the rocks of crack cocaine from his pocket and tossed them at her, grinning as she scrabbled to catch them. 'Here you go Caz. This is all that *you've* ever wanted.

'An' as for Anna. If your precious mate doesn't help us get Mia then why the fuck should we care about her daughter?'

He turned round, and traced a finger across Gemma's ankle, letting it slide up along her calf to her knee. The girl stiffened. 'Please don't touch me', she whimpered.

He laughed nastily. 'Perhaps, I will come back after all.'

Chapter 56

'Charlie. Good news! We've found the VW Polo.'

'Anyone in it?' Her emotions soared. A quick phone call to Tony earlier had yielded no further useful updates, but could this at last be the lead they were hoping for?

'No, it's abandoned.' She stopped where she was, half way up the stairs to the office, staring out of a window into the grey morning. Rain had begun to fall again, slapping down her moment of hope.

'Shit! That's a shame, Tony. If only Gemma had been in it. How and where?'

'Found by uniform officers carrying out the street search you suggested; parked up all legally in a quiet side road on the outskirts of Mitcham, not too far from where the last call on Monday was made. I've instructed them to stay back and watch it from a distance until my own surveillance team can take over. You never know – our man might come back to it.'

'Hm.' She wasn't convinced. 'Does it look like it's been parked recently?'

'I don't know as yet. When my guys get there, I'll see if one can stroll past it and take a better look. Good shout though, the street search.'

'Only if it leads to something.' She carried on climbing the stairs. 'How's Anna?'

'How do you think? Pretty stressed. I've spoken to Caz's social worker, Marion Bishop, about Mia and, without giving too much away, have established that the best they could offer would be short supervised visits for Caz. Possibly with the pair of them in due course, but there's no way she'd hand Mia over, not unless she wanted to commit career suicide.'

'Nice turn of phrase, but I'd expected no less.' If they didn't get to Gemma before Razor, they might be facing the same. She checked on her watch and yawned as she reached the top of the stairs. 'Eleven a.m. – that's five hours and counting until we find out if they'll buy it. Give me a few minutes to top and tail my other job and I'll be right back with you.'

'I haven't spoken with Anna or Scott about this yet, but you know Caz and Razor well. So do *you* think it'll be enough to appease them?'

A vision of two women's bodies filtered into her memory; Redz – battered and bleeding, her hair cut off by Razor, and Dutch, who had committed suicide after being prostituted and regularly thrashed by him became too much. He'd been awaiting trial for the murder of Redz. Then there was Caz herself, beaten to within an inch of her death by him. She thought for a moment, allowing what she knew about Razor to run through her mind.

'No. Personally,' she replied with a shake of her head. 'I think we absolutely need to find them.'

🏵 🏵 🏵

Bet, Naz and Sabira were standing, silently huddled, around Paul's desk as Charlie walked in.

'What absolute scum.' Naz spun round as Charlie headed towards them. A photograph of the posters found on the wall of the potting shed was displayed on Paul's screen. 'Proper disgusting Nazi scum! So Hurley murdered Rocco Fontana and Kelvin Olawi in cold blood to start up a race war. Kelvin Olawi wasn't even our killer. He *was* a victim.' Naz rubbed her arm subconsciously. 'We needn't even have gone to his address!'

The sentiment behind her anger was easy to see. Naz wouldn't have been stabbed. She wouldn't have spent hours having blood transfused into her body. Her family wouldn't have been traumatised. She wouldn't have been traumatised.

And all because Wayne Hurley was an out and out racist, with an axe to grind against anyone who wasn't a white, Anglo-Saxon Englishman. Never mind the fact that he was quite happy to take money off celebrities or club goers of any ethnicity. He wanted the dirty, but very lucrative, business of drug dealing kept to the milky white likes of him and Jamie Smythe-Hamilton.

'Well, I took an instant dislike to him from the moment we met, but I didn't think he was capable of this... ' Charlie admitted. She was well aware it would hit her team particularly hard, being one of the most diverse teams at the nick. 'But hearing him boasting about what he'd done... ' She looked across at Paul, Naz and Sabira. 'And what he'd like to do. Well it made me feel sick to my stomach, not to mention ashamed.'

'You suspected he was involved though,' said Paul. 'Thank God you went behind Superintendent Woodall's back and kept on.'

'Well, now I need you all to finish it. I've got to get back to Anna and there's Hurley to be charged and Smythe-Hamilton to be interviewed, though I'm assured by his brief he'll be making no comment. I need Bet for a few minutes but I'm trusting you others to do everything required to get this evil pair put away for life.'

🔳 🔳 🔳

'Right Bet, can you get the found report of the stolen VW Polo that Razor was driving back up on the screen, please?'

While she'd been speaking, an idea had come to her. She waited while Bet did a check and then read out the wording of the report herself. 'Found abandoned, Sherwood Park Road, SW16. Right! Now do a search of the surrounding area. Give it a mile radius say. We're looking for any reports of thefts of any types of transport, be it cars, vans, even motor cycles. He's been careful with his phones so he'll be careful with his vehicles. And if he's dumped this one, as I reckon he has, then he's probably nicked another.'

While Bet worked on the computer, Charlie ran to the bathroom, splashing water onto her tired eyes. She'd managed to grab a couple of hours' sleep between the end of the allotment search and Hurley's interview but her body was tired and her face looked wan and grey. There'd be no chance of getting her head down for many hours yet. She stared critically in the mirror, running her fingers through her lank hair and damping down a rebellious tuft. Her eyes were even greener than usual, like cat's eyes, steely and determined, like her mother's.

She picked up her phone and dialled her mum's number. The answer phone clicked in. 'Hi Mum,' she said. 'Just checking in for a chat. Sorry I didn't make it home last night. Pressures of work again! I'm thinking of getting some cameras installed so I can keep an eye on you from my phone. Let me know what you think.'

She ended the call and frowned guiltily at her reflection.

They'd checked in as usual by text earlier and Meg had confirmed she was fine, but were they both becoming complacent? Perhaps with Iain Frazer's continued absence, they were allowing a tiny seed of hope to take root and germinate. Perhaps? Bending forward Charlie rubbed a last handful of cold water on to her cheeks. What was she thinking? He was her father. He would never give up.

A wave of unease rolled through her. It was Wednesday, and Wednesday's always made her feel nervous. Wednesday was the day on which her brother had died. It was the day, until recently, she'd paid silent tribute at his grave every week. Wednesday was a day to be *got through*; and one where almost everything went wrong.

'Charlie.' Bet was at the door, puffing with exertion and rubbing her back. 'I think I've found something.'

Shrugging away her nerves, she straightened her shirt and made for the door, following Bet at a pace to the office.

'I couldn't find any vehicles particularly nearby on the books as stolen. There's a van in the town centre, and a couple of motor bikes a bit further afield, but then I checked the calls yet to be assigned.' Bet crossed her fingers. 'And look what's just come in.'

Charlie peered down at the screen, her stomach churning as she read the text of the recent message. The phone call had come in barely quarter of an hour previously from a man who had returned from holiday to find his car was missing. The report hadn't even been officially filed yet. She read on, her heart rate increasing with every detail. The vehicle was a red Vauxhall Astra, but the clincher was the driveway it had been stolen from was in the very next road to where the VW Polo had been dumped.

'This must be it.' On a whim, Charlie threw her arms around Bet and hugged her. 'You're brilliant,' she shouted, breaking off as quickly to jot down the index.

Bet laughed. 'You ain't seen nothing yet.'

She tapped a button on the keyboard and sat down to read. 'I also found a report from yesterday evening that was logged at 21.33. There's no registration number shown but it relates to a red Vauxhall Astra. The occupiers of a house in Lambeth heard some noises outside and looked out to see a stockily built black man, walking away from their driveway.'

'Razor!'

'Yep sounds like it. Anyway he got into a red Vauxhall Astra parked a bit further down their road and then drove off. When they came out to check, they found their vehicle had been broken into and there was damage to the ignition barrel.'

'So he was trying to exchange cars again, but this time he failed.' She paused, thinking back to the previous evening. 'It was pissing down with rain on and off. Given the weather, I wonder if he bothered trying again?'

'I would say not, Charlie, look!' Bet scrolled to a different screen and pointed her finger to an entry at the top. 'About forty minutes after that call, a Surrey unit did a check on our red Vauxhall Astra. They didn't stop it, presumably because it hadn't been reported stolen yet and they'd not have had access to the previous Met message.'

'Where was the check done, Bet? You said somewhere in Surrey?'

Bet nodded and squinted towards the screen. 'In a place called Walton-on-the-Hill.'

Charlie frowned and pulled out her phone, searching the internet for the location. She peered down at the screen, reading out the description. 'Walton-on-the-Hill is a small village midway between the market towns of Reigate and Epsom, one of a dispersed cluster on the North Downs.' She scrolled down further. 'It has an ancient church, a pharmacy, a selection of old buildings and new housing, and a golf course.

'So what the hell is Razor doing there?'

Chapter 57

It took no time at all to check for the red Astra on the CCTV recordings.

As Charlie headed back to Anna's she received constant updates from Tony.

Already it had been confirmed as one of the vehicles passing slowly in traffic through Mitcham town centre the previous day after the 4.30 p.m. call reporting it stolen.

It had also been tracked on different stretches along the A217, the main road from London to Walton-on-the-Hill, heading out from the city – and back. In fact, if they'd seen it once they'd now seen it almost a dozen times.

Tony was waiting for Charlie as she pulled up outside the house.

'We fucked up.' Tony grimaced. 'I've had my team check on the Croydon council CCTV, which covers Norbury. The Astra passed Caz's flat while we were searching it. I've got absolutely no doubt that Razor must have seen us and that he was telling the truth when he claimed to know we'd been told.

'Damn it.' A knot tightened in Charlie's stomach. Despite all their precautions, they'd allowed themselves to be spotted, and so placed Gemma in even more danger. Who knew whether they'd be punished for their sloppiness – or whether they already had. 'Does Anna know?' she said, ducking under Tony's umbrella and shielding herself against the newest onslaught of rain.

'Not yet – and I don't want her to be panicked. She needs to keep an absolutely clear head if we're to get Gemma back safe and sound.

'If?'

'Well we still don't have any idea where she is.' He shook out his brolly as they got to the front door. 'Let's hope she's not out somewhere in this.'

❁ ❁ ❁

'Does Walton-on-the-Hill ring any bells with you Anna? Or Epsom, or Reigate?' With the exception of the last piece of information, Charlie was running through what they knew with Anna and Scott. 'Did Caz ever mention that area to you in her counselling sessions?'

Scott gripped Anna's hand. 'Think darling.'

'No, nothing. As far as I'm aware she's hardly ever left South London. She lived in Croydon with her parents before they both died, then she was taken into care in various homes in the borough.' Anna shook her head. 'And then she met Razor.'

'And game over!' Charlie rubbed her mouth thoughtfully. 'And as far as I know Razor was born and bred in Lambeth and apart from serving time in most of the prisons around London has pretty much stayed in the same area all his life too. Keep thinking then. There must be a link.'

While they waited on Tony to tell them his plans, she picked up her phone. 'Bet can you dig out Caz's diary? And can you go through every page from the beginning. I did look through it a bit when we kept it but I was concentrating more on her motives for taking Gemma.

If there are any places out of London mentioned by name, then give me a shout straight away – especially if they're in Surrey. Thanks, Bet.' She looked up as Tony came back through, and ended the call.

'Right, I've got units spaced out all along the A217, with ANPR cameras ready. When Razor comes through to hear whether we've got Mia back, we'll shadow him and wait for his call. Depending on what's said I'll make a decision then on how to proceed. Razor poses the greatest risk to Gemma. If we take him out, I might need Charlie or Anna to help talk to Caz.' He nodded to Scott. 'If I leave one of my team with you, are you happy to stay here?'

This time it was Anna's turn to squeeze her husband's hand. 'It'll be okay. Look after Brett while I'm gone.' Scott got to his feet silently and walked to the window, staring out at the driving rain.

'I know mate. I'd want to be coming too,' said Tony, pacing across to join him. 'Me and my guys can deal with Razor, but Caz... well we don't know what might be going through her mind.'

Chapter 58

The road from London to Walton-on-the-Hill was clear so they made steady progress. A stiff breeze was now pushing the rain in squalls at the car, battering the windscreen in short bursts, like rapid machine gun fire.

Tony drove, while Charlie and Anna sat huddled together in the rear, both deep in thought. Although it was still only early afternoon, the sky was dark, with densely packed storm clouds making the atmosphere heavy and oppressive. Charlie stared out as they passed each area a call had been made from, her sense of failure increasing. This time they really couldn't risk losing Razor.

She looked up as they started to slow, squinting out through the veil of water on the window glass and identifying a road name. They were in a side road, off the A217 in the borough of Sutton, half way between the grey streets of Lambeth and the leafy surroundings of Walton-on-the-Hill; the same sort of distance from the Met that Razor had previously activated his phones.

'Any joy with his mobiles?' she asked, knowing the answer but aware too, that both were being monitored.

'No, nothing as yet.'

It was what she'd expected. She glanced down at her watch. Just gone two. Less than a couple of hours before the call that would decide the course of the operation. For the next one hundred and twenty minutes every moment would drag.

'I'll stop here.' Tony's voice was strong and decisive, as they drew to a halt. Now they were physically out on the streets, he was more upbeat – and this, in turn lifted her spirits. He pulled on the handbrake, turned towards them and smiled.

'We've checked all the cameras and there's no trace of the Astra this morning, so it's fair to assume it hasn't yet gone by. But as soon as it passes, as I know that it will, my team will follow it covertly.

'And when Razor stops to make his 4 p.m. call, we'll be parked up close by.'

❈ ❈ ❈

Caz eyed Razor as he stood up and prepared to leave. 'Please come back after you've spoken to Anna,' she said. 'I have to know what she says, and whether there's even the tiniest chance we might get Mia back.'

She was still holding on to the possibility of holding Mia again, of getting custody of her daughter, even if it took time – and until she heard otherwise, she wouldn't give up.

Razor pulled a hood up over his wet head and nodded. After his earlier moodiness he'd mellowed. Stoking his ego with a little more weed and a whole lot of praise worked every time. 'Take this, babe. It'll give you a few extra minutes before the bastards can trace you.' She pressed a third burner phone into his hand, grasping his fingers as she did so. 'When you get back we'll find somewhere better to hide.'

It would depend on the answer to their demand as to whether the *we* included Gemma – but they couldn't stay where they were for much longer. During the morning the river had risen still further and was now openly flowing through the base of their hideout. In a quiet moment, earlier, she'd properly examined the space into which they were squeezed, under the roots of the tree. It looked to have been hollowed out by the water, which meant with the continuing rain, their shelter would likely be completely submerged.

'All right,' he grunted. 'I'll be back.'

She watched as he stepped down into the fast-flowing water, treading carefully along the edge of the bank until he disappeared around a bend and then she settled herself into a relatively dry spot.

'I need the toilet,' Gemma whimpered.

She couldn't be bothered to loosen the rope round the girl's neck. It was too bleedin' wet, and if she moved again now, she'd risk sending another shower of water cascading off the foliage. Besides, with the height of the river, there was no place to go.

'You'll have to piss where you're sitting.'

'Please,' the girl whined. 'And I'm hungry.'

'I'm hungry too,' she snapped back. 'But we ain't got nothin' left. So you'll just 'ave to wait 'til he brings food back wiv 'im later.'

Gemma started to cry, her hand caressing the neck of her childhood toy dinosaur. Mia's toy, Dilly. 'Please let me go, Miss.'

Caz stared at the girl, mesmerised by the action. It was the same gentle stroking motion she used with Goldilocks whenever she wanted some comfort. She closed her eyes and put her hands over her ears. She didn't want to see the girl any more or hear her pleas. She wanted silence to think.

The sound of the water dulled into the background but she could still hear Gemma's irritating sobs. Her mind turned to the wrap of gear stowed in her pocket. A little bit of crack cocaine would soon shut her up.

Chapter 59

'Charlie is that you?'

'Yes, it is Mum.' Her mother's name had come up on the screen.

'Charlie? I can't hear you. I was phoning re your question about cameras.'

The phone line was awful. 'What do you think, Mum?'

'I can't hear you, darling. I'll text.' The phone line went dead. She waited for the text to ping on to her screen.

I'm fine, and there's no need for cameras. I'm perfectly safe. Take your time. When you come home, there's somebody here who can't wait to see you.

She was about to return the text and ask who the visitor was, when Tony threw an arm up.

'Right! They've got Razor in sight.' He spoke calmly, but there was no mistaking the excitement in his tone.

'And it's definitely him?' Charlie sat up straight, the text forgotten. It would probably be one of her sisters back from uni a week or so early. She leant forward, straining her ears to pick up Razor's direction of travel on the radio. Having their man in view was so much simpler than casting around for mobile phone signals.

'Yes, definitely him.'

'Just him?' Anna asked.

'Unfortunately,' Tony replied. 'But one will hopefully lead to another.'

She listened as Tony's team gave directions. He was on the main A217 as they'd hoped, heading towards London, towards them, and on time for the call.

Instructions were to tail him to a stationary location where they'd speak – then the outcome of the conversation would direct their next move.

The red Astra was getting closer. Ten miles, five miles, two, then one. He was passing them now. Every sinew in her body wanted to give chase, but not yet. Tony stayed put. She took a deep breath. The Astra was pulling into a side road. It was stopping. Anna's phone rang from another new number. She checked on her watch. It was four o'clock on the dot. Time to talk.

'Hello Anna.' Razor's voice came across the speaker. 'Have you done what we said?'

'Please give us more time,' Anna repeated what she'd been directed to say. 'We've spoken to Marion Bishop, Caz's social worker and she's seeing what she can do.'

'Marion Bishop's a bitch. I met her once an' she talked to me like I was shit. So *she's seeing what she can do*? Fuck all, I expect.'

'She says Caz may be allowed supervised visits. You maybe later on too. It's a start, and it's something to build on. It's the best we can do at the moment.'

'The best you can do? Caz *may* be allowed visits? If you want to see Gemma again, you'll have to do better than that.'

'Please Razor, give us more time.'

'Us? So you admit calling the feds in?'

'You know that I did. I'm sorry Razor. I didn't know what else to do.'

'Well you could have kept your mouth shut and done what we fuckin' told you for one thing. An' you could have made more of an effort to persuade that bitch Marion to hand Mia back to Caz straight away. Caz thought you were a friend.'

'I am.'

'Well show 'er then.'

'I'm trying, but we do need more time.'

'What to find me?'

'To get things arranged.'

'Well, you've had all the time we can give you.'

'Please Razor, please stay on the line and speak to one of the officers. There's one here called Tony. He's a good cop and he can help you.'

There was silence. Charlie rotated her hand impatiently. *Come on Razor, carry on talking,* she mouthed. The longer they could keep him in conversation, the better chance of building a rapport.

'There ain't no such thing as a good cop, an' I don't want no other man telling me what I should and shouldn't do.'

Silence again. Anna paled, twisting round towards Charlie, panic-stricken. The moment was slipping away.

'I've a woman here if you'd rather talk to a female cop?' Charlie shook her head.

'What's her name?'

No! She closed her eyes. Anna wasn't supposed to mention her. She and Razor had history. Her presence might antagonise him further, but then perhaps he might enjoy the chance to pit his wits against her. Gemma's life was in his hands after all. It could go either way.

'Charlie.'

'Charlie Stafford?

'Yes. You know DS Charlie Stafford.'

'Of course I know her.' Razor's voice dropped a pitch, went quiet. 'She and her bastard boss, Hunter, believed Caz over me every time, even though Caz has now admitted she lied. Charlie Stafford got me sent inside for a murder I never done. Yes, I know the bitch. I've spent the last eighteen months thinking of no one else.'

He stopped speaking, and in the silence she heard him breathing, loud and slow. Angry.

'Please Razor, say something. Talk to me,' Anna pleaded.

'I'm done talking, Anna.' His tone was icy. 'An' it seems to me like you've made your choice.'

Chapter 60

'It's gone on to answer phone.' Anna was dialling and redialling the number, tears streaming down her face. 'Pick up, you bloody bastard. Pick up.'

Charlie watched as her friend tried the number a third time with increasingly shaky fingers. She'd never heard Anna use language like this, and now she felt numb.

'The phone's been switched off.' Tony confirmed what they all knew. 'But don't worry. Just because the conversation didn't go as well as we hoped we can still put an end to this. My team's got him in their sights. If he heads back towards Walton-on-the-Hill, we'll follow him. Hopefully he'll take us to where he has Gemma.'

'But if he doesn't? Anna asked.

'Then I'll decide what to do.'

Charlie and Tony had already had this discussion. Could they take the risk of losing him in the busy rush hour traffic? Razor knew London like the back of his hand. He would know all the rat runs and short cuts. And he'd already tried swapping cars. If they lost him now, they'd risk losing him for good. A new car, a new phone. They'd be back to square one – or worse, seeing as it was now plain that he hated her as much as Anna.

'He's moving off,' came a tinny voice over the radio. The atmospherics were affecting the clarity of the signal on the radio, as well as on mobiles.

They waited as he headed towards the A217. Left would take him back out towards Walton-on-the-Hill. Right, would take him into London.

'Turning right, right, right.'

He'd made his decision. Now it was time for them to make theirs.

❂ ❂ ❂

Razor sucked angrily on a cigarette. Instead of calming him, the nicotine seemed to heighten his fury. He wound down the window, exhaled, and swore as a flurry of raindrops hit the side of his head.

Fucking Anna, and fucking Charlie Stafford. Two more women like Marion Bishop telling him what he should do.

Caz too. His mind flicked back to the morning. *Get me food. Come straight back. Do this. Do that.* Well, she could go to hell. They all could. Nobody told Razor what he should do.

Closing the window, he ran his hand across his scalp. It was rough, unshaven, as was his chin, his neck, his top lip. He scowled at his reflection in the mirror. He looked like a fucking hobo; one of the losers he'd regularly seen in doorways, lying, dribbling in their own piss. That wasn't him.

On a whim he'd decided to head into London. To his barbers, in Lambeth. He could have a shit and a shave, treat himself to a shower perhaps. And food. Proper food.

Caz could wait. They could all fucking wait.

If he was going down, as was likely with the feds now involved, well, he'd go down looking and feeling good. For the first time in days he would do what he wanted.

He checked again in his mirror. Nothing close, but a dark grey car in the distance, with the shape of two people in its front seats.

He indicated right and waited until they came up behind him. As expected, the grey car indicated left. But the shapes were both men, and the men looked like cops. They had the same surly appearance; stern-looking, short-haired white males. He could sniff the bastards out from a mile away. He moved off, frowning as the grey car turned left.

How had they found him? They wouldn't have had time to locate his new burner phone in the few minutes the conversation had lasted. So that left only the Astra. It must have been reported as stolen. Damn it. If the other car had started, the cops would still be casting about in the dark. They wouldn't have found him.

If, indeed, they had found him.

The junction now clear, he turned off the A217 into a side street, watching for any unusual movements, any police type of vehicles. A sleek silver BMW dropped in behind, a long way off, but still there. *For fuck's sake!* He did another right, then another, skirting the block, then turned left on to the main road again.

Switching on the rear wiper, he concentrated hard on the rearview mirror. There was the grey car again with the feds – tucked in behind a white van and a motorbike. But unmistakeably there. Unmistakeably them.

For a moment he was tempted to put his foot down. Anger surged. Then he calmed. He lit up another cigarette, inhaled, and thought about what he should do. There was no doubting the fact he'd be sent back to prison, but for how long? This time, it wasn't his fault. It wasn't even his idea. It was Caz's.

It had been she who had set the whole thing in motion. Right from the start it was Caz. Caz who'd got him released from prison; Caz who'd driven their actions, tempted the girl into the car and suggested the location. It was her, even now, who'd been issuing orders.

Caz had done this.

But not just Caz. He thought again of the others; Anna Christophe, Marion Bishop, Charlie Stafford, all bitches who'd helped fuck him over. Each of them deserved being taught a lesson. So, if and when he was caught, he would say nothing. Do nothing. He'd act dumb; pretend Caz and the girl had moved on without him. Let the feds do what they were paid for. Let them find Caz and Gemma. Why the fuck should he help?

That decided, he slowed, indicated again and pulled into a lay-by. He watched as the grey car came past him, the passenger's head twitching round in his direction. Too fucking bad he'd soon be putting an end to their little game.

But first there was Caz. He switched on his phone and keyed in her number. Her mobile was off as expected but the answer phone clicked in.

'*Please leave a message...*' the automated greeting said.

Well, he'd leave her a message all right. One that she'd never forget. Holding the handset close to his mouth, he spoke loudly and clearly.

Then he grinned out through the rain-swept windscreen of the Astra, and ended the call.

Chapter 61

The atmosphere in their vehicle was tense. Charlie stared out of the window, frustrated that it wasn't her making the decisions.

The Astra had stopped again. Razor's new phone had been switched on for over a minute and she was waiting for Tony to decide what they should do.

'What's he playing at?' As she said what was on all their minds, Anna's mobile started to ring.

'It's him,' Anna gasped.

'Answer it,' Tony said, nodding towards Anna, as she held the phone out in her palm.

'Let me speak to Tony, the bloke you said was a good cop.' Razor demanded.

She passed the phone over.

'Tony Ludlow here. You want to talk?'

'I want to hand myself in, but only to you. Are you the big black dude I saw standing at the window in Caz's place?'

So it had been Tony who Razor had seen. There wasn't anyone else that fitted that description.

'Yeah, I am.' Tony winced at the realisation, grimacing apologetically at Anna. Charlie winced too, knowing how bad he would be feeling right now, having so recently been the cause of more problems herself.

'Well, like I said, I'll hand myself in, but only to you. An' just so you know, I didn't ask for any of this and it weren't me who came up with the idea. An' I ain't sayin' nothin' more 'bout nothin'.'

Five minutes later they pulled up behind the red Astra, with Tony giving Razor instructions over the phone. Charlie watched as their suspect climbed out of the car, hands out in front of him. He was as huge and intimidating as she remembered, even more so now with the thick layer of stubble all over his head. His face was wet, the moisture glistening off his rough, pitted skin and trickling along the scar on his cheek.

She opened the window a fraction, to listen as Tony handcuffed his arms behind him, and watched Razor as he puffed out his chest, his eyes ranging towards their car, wild and challenging. Anna threw a hand over her mouth.

'Look at him Charlie. He looks mad.'

She was thinking exactly the same.

'Hey ladies,' the voice boomed across the space. 'I can see you.' He grinned, his gold teeth standing out through thin lips, his eyes narrowing.

Before Charlie could stop her, Anna had opened the door and was running towards him. 'Where's Gemma?' she screamed, pummelling him on his chest with her fists. 'Where's my daughter. What have you done to her?'

Charlie sprinted after her, grabbing her arms and pulling her away. Anna was crying uncontrollably now.

'That's for you to find out,' Razor laughed, straining at the handcuffs. 'Ooh, where's Gemma. Now where could she be?'

A police van was pulling up behind them. 'That's enough.' Tony yanked him away, pushing him across the lay-by towards the side entrance of the vehicle. 'We need to talk,' he said grimly.

'I've said all I'm goin' to say.' Razor whipped his head round, staring at Charlie as she comforted Anna in her arms. 'So you'd better do your job DS Stafford.' He turned his face upwards, scrunching his eyes against the rain. 'You'd better find Anna's little girl, before it's too late.'

❀ ❀ ❀

So, it was down to her.

As she stood, soaked by the rain, watching Razor climb up into the van, she understood the finality of his words. He *would* be making no further comment, with or without Tony's desperate negotiations, with or without a solicitor's advice.

Perhaps it *had* been Caz who'd come up with the plans, but she was as sure as she could be that it was Razor who'd presented the most danger – and he sure as hell could have ended their anguish.

Squeezing Anna's arm, she led her back to Tony's car. It would be theirs now for as long as Charlie needed it. She helped Anna into the passenger seat, and shut the door, tilting her head upwards much as Razor had done. The sky was still a dark slate grey with a mass of heavy black rain cloud blotting out any light from the sun. The intensity of the rain had lessened but each individual raindrop was heavy, pounding against her temples like a battering ram. She closed her eyes and tried to concentrate, running through her options.

She couldn't use dogs. With the volume of water falling from the skies, any scent trails would be washed away in an instant.

Using a helicopter might be a remote possibility, but given the weather, flying would be hazardous and visibility next to none. Plus she had to assume the girls would be undercover and its heat-seeking capabilities would be useless if blocked out under wood, slates or metal. Even the trees of a forest or dense foliage would make the task near impossible. And in any case, where would they start? They still had no idea where Razor had driven from, or where Gemma might be.

So, while Tony worked on Razor, the rest of them could do little except sit passively scratching their heads, and wracking their brains for a solution – and there was no way she could do that. She had to do something positive. Think!

Her mind returned to her internet result.

Walton-on-the-Hill had a golf course, most likely with numerous outbuildings. It had a church, old and new houses, with sheds and garages – and they had to start somewhere. She'd call in anyone and everyone, and mount an organised search, spreading out from the village; north, south, east and west.

With Razor now in custody they had two potential victims.

She ran round to the driver's side of the car, and climbed in, glancing up anxiously one last time at the sky. If the rain would just hold off... but there was still little time to mobilise a team. She picked up her phone and summoned Paul, Naz and Sabira, and anyone else who might be free, then she fired up the engine and started to drive. While she headed first to the golf course, her team would get Surrey Police on board to help, knocking on doors, sending out urgent appeals on social media.

The evening was fast approaching and as it got darker their chances of tracking down Gemma and Caz would decrease. In a few hours' time the light would be gone, along with any real possibility of finding the girls for another night.

Chapter 62

Caz was bored, listless and irritable. She was also wet, hungry, uncomfortable and anxious.

Every once in a while, she got to her feet and stepped out from the shelter to search the banks of the river for Razor. After each fruitless venture, she splashed back inside, wetter and angrier, with sodden shoes and another bucketful of rage thrown on to her inner fire.

It had been ages since Razor had left and, since then, she'd seen and heard nothing. Hours and hours had passed, with the sound of the rain pissing down against what was left of their shelter. If you could call it a shelter! Christ, half of their refuge floor was now submerged. To avoid slipping into the river, they'd been forced into the farthest corner, under the thickest roots, a few inches above the muddy swirling water. Fortunately, although it was wet, it was still moderately warm, though with the onset of evening, the temperature would soon dip.

There was no way she'd be staying here another night.

She pulled a damp blanket around her shoulders and stared out across the river at the steep escarpment opposite, focussing on a young sapling clinging on to the slope with the fast-flowing water now lapping at its lowest shoots. Soon the soil that anchored it to the slope would be washed away and it would be pulled, rootless and displaced, into the torrent and carried away.

The sight made her think of Razor.

Where was the bastard? Hadn't he promised to return straight away? Hadn't he sworn to let her know about Mia? Everything round her was crumbling.

She got up, shuffled out, then slunk inside, pulling the blanket back into place.

'Miss, tell me about Mia.'

'I can't talk about Mia,' she snapped. Gemma was too damned nosey. 'I can't talk about my baby because they took her away. I don't have her any more. And your mum didn't help me. Nobody helped me.'

And Razor hadn't come back. There was no sign of him. She reached out and lifted her doll from the top of a large root, and held her close.

'But Miss, *I* want to help you.'

'How can *you* help me?'

'I don't know.' Gemma started to cry. 'But I don't want to stay here any longer. CJ scares me and I want my mummy.'

'Shall I tell you 'bout mine?' Caz felt her guts tighten. Gemma had everything; everything that she'd ever wanted. The girl had had a childhood full of pleasure, with a mother, and father, who'd given her so much. And what had she got from her mother? A mutilated ragdoll. That was all. 'My dad raped me regularly, an' me mum, well, she let 'im do it.'

'I'm so sorry, Miss. Where's your mum now?'

She laughed at the girl's wide-open eyes and gaping mouth. No doubt Gemma wouldn't have heard of such things. Those kinds of things didn't happen to *her* or *her* friends. Her mother was posh. Anna was privileged. But she'd let her down, like everyone else had; her father, her mother, the system, even Razor.

'Probably in Hell, 'cause she's dead,' she spat. 'That's where she is. An' CJ's name is really Razor, 'cause that's what he likes to use on his victims. An' you can stop calling me Miss now, 'cause you know my real fucking name is Caz.'

'I know,' the girl whimpered. 'I remember coming to your flat. I remember giving you and Mia presents. I remember liking you...' She clutched Mia's little dinosaur to her mouth as if trying to stop Caz from hearing her final word, but having to say it anyway. '...then.'

Caz frowned. She stared at Gemma and saw herself as a young child.

So, Gemma didn't like her. But then nobody liked her. Even her own father didn't like her. He'd simply used her, and in that second she was hurtling back in time; lying mute while her father grunted and sweated on top of her, then staring in horror as he stood at the top of the stairs, twisting a pair of scissors in one hand, laughing and taunting her. And in his other hand was Goldilocks, with her beautiful long hair. And she tried to scream but nothing would come out. And all she could hear in her head was the snip, snip, snip of the scissors. And all she could see was Goldilocks' beautiful hair lying on the filthy carpet, and him flying through the air to his death as she launched him down the stairs.

She blinked. In the half light of the shelter, he was watching her. There in the shadows, laughing at what he had done. Goading her. *Like father, like daughter.* Violent, vengeful, damaged. And she, in turn, was damaged. She could never change.

She pulled the knife from her pocket and lurched forward, grabbing hold of the dinosaur, sawing and sawing at its neck. And as she did so, she started to scream. And this time the scream wasn't silent. It was shrill, and desolate, filling the wet space, bursting out through the gaps in the branches, and resonating through the dank air until it was consumed in the leaves and branches of the forest.

And when she'd finished, she sat down and cradled her doll. And she cried. She cried for what had happened to her as a child. And she cried for what she knew she would have to do to Gemma.

Chapter 63

The outbuildings and storage containers at Walton-on-the-Hill Golf Club were clear. As was the church and the rear of the shops, and the garages and sheds of the houses. There was no trace of Caz or Gemma.

Now, as Charlie stood on the village green thanking the local residents for their support, her mind went blank. In the next few minutes, the people would disappear into their homes to dry off and settle down in front of their TVs, satisfied that they'd fulfilled their civic duty. And they would be left; she and her team, Anna, and a ragtag collection of officers from Surrey Police.

With still no idea of where Gemma might be.

When she'd finished talking, she watched silently as the people drifted away. Soon what remained of the light would disappear too.

'Any more luck, Tony?' It was a stupidly hopeful phone call. She knew the answer before he replied but she still had to ask. Tick.

Razor had said nothing. Caz hadn't, so far, made a mistake. There had been no trace of any of the phone numbers the pair had used being switched back on.

'Bet,' she tried the office. 'Any possible locations in the diary we found at Caz's flat?'

'No names of anywhere, Charlie. I'm sorry. And I've gone through both Caz and Razor's antecedents and backgrounds. I can't find any place mentioned for either of them in that neck of the woods.'

Anna was standing nearby, listening. She shook her head, clearly anticipating being the next recipient of the question. 'Me neither. I've rerun every conversation I've ever had with Caz and I can't think of a single time when she spoke of anywhere out of London. She was never taken on days out to the countryside by her parents, nor to the seaside on holiday.

'She wrote about that in her diary,' Bet chipped in over the speaker. 'She said it wasn't fair that some kids have everything, while she had nothing. In fact, she mentions listening to a girl describing a day out. She doesn't name the girl, or say where they went, but she was clearly jealous of her. She goes on to say if she ever had children, she'd take them out for picnics; that they'd have a favourite place to visit, somewhere special.'

'Oh my God, Charlie.' Anna threw her hand to her mouth. 'Box Hill! It's not that far from here is it?'

'Go on. Why?'

'Because it used to be *our family* favourite spot. I've been so busy thinking of past connections for Caz and Razor... that I didn't consider Gemma or *us*. I've never spoken to Caz about the place, and Gemma had only met Caz a couple of times, but perhaps she's told her about it.'

Charlie ended the call, and clicked on the map icon. 'It's about five miles away,' she said, digesting this new piece of information. It was all making sense. 'So, if Gemma did tell Caz sometime in the past, the chances are, she was the girl Bet was describing. Caz and Razor have been far too well prepared. They've arranged spare phones, stolen cars, where to make calls - so they must have decided the location of their hideout before they abducted her.'

She stared down at the map showing the area of Box Hill, a little over four square miles of upland, river and forest, with the village of Box Hill tucked to the east; all of which, presented thousands of places to hide. 'But Box Hill is huge,' she said, frowning up at the cloud-covered sky. 'And it's almost dark. Even in the daylight it'd take hundreds of police and volunteers to search it thoroughly.'

'Charlie.' Anna was shaking her head again. 'It'll be near to the stepping stones. Gemma loved them. If she told Caz about our picnics, she would have described them. She painted them once.'

'The painting on the wall at Caz's?'

This time it was Anna's turn to look confused.

'There was a painting on the wall at her flat. I saw it. It had a river, with trees and a horse – and stepping stones.'

'Oh my God, Charlie. That'll be it. How could I have missed it the day we were there? Gemma liked Caz. She gave Caz her toy dinosaur for Mia. She must have given her the painting as well.'

Charlie was about to update Tony when her phone rang. It was him.

'We've just picked up a cell site from one of the phones Razor used. It's not too specific because of the weather and poor quality of transmissions in the area but it appears to be coming from the south side—'

'Of Box Hill.'

Chapter 64

Caz stared down in horror at the last burner phone Razor had used. Up until a minute ago she'd stuck to the rules, knowing police tactics only too well, but she could stand it no longer.

She had to know if their demands had been answered.

As the sky had darkened so too had her thoughts. Razor hadn't returned and she now understood that he wouldn't. There on the screen was a missed call. It had to be him confirming he was pissing off. It was nothing more than she'd expected. His taunts were still fresh in her mind. *Who says I'm coming back?* Calling their hideout a *shithole*. At the start, his willingness to take part in her scheme had taken her by surprise. In fact, it had delighted her. But she'd never really expected it to work. He'd probably had no intention of seeing this through to the end.

'Razor, you bastard. Don't leave me here,' she screamed, tearing away the last few branches at the front of their shelter and wading in the knee-deep water. It was cold. It was inky black, and fast-flowing… and it was still rising. In the last few hours, it had breached the last few inches of the shelf into the rear of the cave. So, Gemma was squashed up against the large root at the back, her spine bent against it, her feet and legs sloshing around in the shallows. There was no place to sit that wouldn't mean sitting in water.

Caz bent down and lifted a wet cushion, hurling it out into the air and cursing loudly as it hit an overhanging branch and sent a shower of water cascading down on to her head. She watched as it plummeted into the water and was taken by the current, out of her sight. Razor had left her. He'd reverted to character and abandoned her.

Nothing had changed.

The phone bleeped weakly. Its battery was low and she had no more charged ones. An answer phone message was waiting. Her spirits lifted slightly. Maybe he'd left her good news after all. She'd listen before trying to make one last call urging him to return.

The answer phone clicked in and she heard his voice. 'Caz, give up now. I'm about to be nicked by the feds. They won't give you Mia. They said you're too fucked up. Marion Bishop says you'll never see Mia again.'

She listened to the message a second time, then a third. *They won't give you Mia. You'll never see Mia again.* Her mind darkened further.

Although she'd never totally expected the plan to work, she'd dreamed of a time when she too could take her child on a picnic; give her the life she'd never had, a future. Now, listening for a fourth time, that minuscule chink of light was becoming dimmer. The phone bleeped again feebly and then died… along with her hopes.

She stared down at the dead phone, allowing its blank, black screen to engulf her. Her future had been yanked from her grasp. Mia was gone, Razor was gone, and this time she felt truly alone. She'd never see her daughter again.

Her life was over – yet here was the girl. This product of everything she'd dreamed of, everything that wasn't fair. She thought of the look on her father's face as he lay dead at the foot of the stairs, and her mother's red sticky blood on her hands as she'd watched her die – while pleading for her to live.

Like father, like daughter. The thought came back to haunt her. If she was damaged goods, then she must pass this damage on. If she'd been abandoned then so must Gemma. If she was fucked up, then so should Gemma be fucked up. It was only fair and right. And if they both died in the process, well, so be it.

She carefully picked her way over the submerged floor of the shelter, and from a protruding, eye-level root in the rear wall, unhooked her bag. She rummaged in it until she found her syringes, a small bottle of lemon juice, and a lighter. What was the point in staying clean? She was a user; always would be. Forever fucked up. Then from her pocket, she took the package that Razor had tossed to her, the small silver foil wrap containing three precious rocks. He understood what she was. He'd always understood. That's why he'd picked her out from the other girls at the children's home. That's why he'd groomed her and sent her out on the streets. Because he knew. Trash would always be trash. If you were born in the gutter, you stayed in the gutter.

Ducking in between the roots, she pushed herself as far against the wall of the cave as she could, her pulse beginning to race with adrenalin and her hands starting to shake. She switched on the torch, aiming its tired beam through her fingers and up at her face, making the space blush an eerie red and the tips of her fingers glow white. Her lips twitched into a grin.

'What are you doing?' Gemma was wide-eyed with fear, her voice high and squeaky.

She gazed at the girl. Somehow the sight of her mud-streaked cheeks and wet, dirty school uniform encouraged her further. She held the lighter under the foil waiting for the rocks to become molten.

'How old are you?'

'Twelve.'

'The same sort of age as I was when I had my first hit.'

'I don't want it.'

'You don't have a choice. I've spent my whole life being told what to do and if I refused, I'd be forced to do it anyway. Every single time a little bit of luck came my way, or a sliver of happiness, it got snatched right out of my hands. Now, I've lost everything.' She stopped talking, perfectly calm now, concentrating instead on the tiny yellow flame, the silver foil starting to blacken at the edges, the spire of smoke drifting upwards. The rocks were starting to melt and bubble. 'I didn't ask for much, and I got even less. Don't you think I had dreams, just like you Gemma? But life's shit, an' the sooner you learn that, the better. People let you down. Razor let me down. Your mother let me down.'

She drew the plunger on the syringe, sucking up the molten liquid.

'Half for me, half for you. Trust me you'll love it. It'll take you away from this shit, to the place of your dreams. And there you'll stay until they find you. *If* they find you.' She laughed bitterly, tears of rage, joy and sorrow mixing together to stream down her cheeks. The girl was crying too.

'Caz, please. I'm frightened. Why are you doing this?'

'Because I can.' Caz aimed the torch at the crook of Gemma's elbow. 'And because I want to. And because I've done it before.'

Gemma jumped slightly as the needle pricked her skin. It hurt. She tried to move but there was nowhere to go. The rope was still tied tight around her neck and although Caz had allowed her to keep her arms at the front, they were still handcuffed, and her legs tightly bound. Water was swilling about her feet, sloshing and gurgling as it entered each crack in the root system, eroding the soil into smooth muddy holes. She wiggled her toes, trying to get some sensation into her ankles and feet. She was cold, freezing cold. The liquid was travelling up her arm. It was warm, and it felt strangely soothing.

She watched Caz stick the needle in her own skin, close her eyes, sway slightly, then with a flick of her hand, the needle was thrown to one side. Her head started to spin. Caz glided around in front of her, lifting her bag, selecting items to be crammed inside. She frowned as Caz lifted the ragdoll up to her cheek, kissed it, then tucked it away inside her jacket. There was something macabre about Goldilocks, the way the doll held Caz in its thrall, almost supernatural, or evil. Like a clown in a horror movie. It had been held to her chest when she'd done that thing. That awful thing. To Dilly her dinosaur. She screwed up her eyes searching for the little toy's head, but it was gone, taken away by the river. All that was left of her childhood memento was its sad tatty body swinging from its severed neck, grasped now in her freezing cold fingers. She dared not release it; watch it drift away in the water. It was all she had left of her home, of her family, Mummy, Daddy, Brett.

The warm feeling was moving up into her head, dulling her fears. She jammed what was left of Dilly under her arm and settled back against the wall, her head wedged upright between two large, dirty roots. A small clod of damp soil fell into her hair and down across her face. It smelt earthy and for a moment she imagined lying in a field, while a large, chestnut horse chewed at the grass, and water tinkled round a set of stepping stones. And there were sandwiches and cake and singing and laughter.

It was getting darker now, warmer and darker, but she wasn't afraid. The warm feeling was filling her whole body, making her eyelids feel drowsy and her limbs heavy. She opened her eyes, blinking as Caz moved towards her, swaying slightly, with the knife held out in her hand – but she wasn't afraid. She could feel Caz pulling on clumps of her hair, sawing against it with the knife, as she'd sawn through Dilly's neck.

'I love your hair,' Caz was murmuring.

'What are you doing?' she asked, feeling her mouth move but not realising it was she who was asking.

'I want your hair. I want it to fill Goldilocks, like I did with the others. The feds never found out what I'd done.' Caz was smiling, her voice dreamy. 'Redz' hair was beautiful. It was long and auburn. You could wrap it round your hand, and Dutch's was strong. Strong and black. They never even realised I took it when I finished them off.'

It sounded funny, what Caz was saying. What was she saying?

'And now I have yours. Blonde hair, to go with the red and black. Perfect.' Several large locks of her hair were swinging from Caz's hand. She watched as Caz brushed them lightly against her cheek then carefully pushed them inside her jacket, next to the doll.

She was feeling so sleepy. Vaguely, she saw Caz move away from her, taking the torch as she did so – its thin beam like a firefly flitting about in the night sky. In the darkness, the sound of the water was louder, but more soporific. She watched as the figure of Caz disappeared from view, then she smiled, as the little light danced across her vision and was gone.

Chapter 65

A squall of rain slapped the windscreen of Charlie's car as she pulled into the 'Stepping Stones' car park, on Box Hill, at the side of the River Mole. She stopped with her vehicle facing the river, its headlights casting an eerie glow over the fast-flowing water.

Unbidden a shiver ran the length of her spine. The sight of water, any water, scared her far more than any challenge she'd faced in her job. Even the sight of a placid sky-blue lake in the summer was enough to trigger the same blinding panic as she'd experienced as a child, watching helplessly as her brother Jamie had drowned. The trauma had scarred her indelibly, and left a void that could never be filled.

She stared out of the window concentrating on the trees and the fields to calm her nerves. Whilst on the way she'd marshalled more foot soldiers and requested the helicopter to assist in the search. Now, looking across at the malevolent eddies and white frothing flood water, it was as much as she could do to stop herself from driving out of the car park as quickly as she'd arrived.

Mentally, she and Anna had swapped position. While Anna was completely calm and focussed, it was she who was stressed, having been forced to confront her worst fear.

'Are you okay?' This time it was Anna who was asking.

Charlie took a deep breath and nodded. As a friend and 'almost' counsellor, Anna knew some of her history – and the cause of her fear.

Three more police vehicles pulled into the car park, their headlights like huge birds of prey scanning the scene, highlighting the extent of the area to be searched; a vast area of dense woodland, steep cliffs, river and fields.

She climbed out of her vehicle, tied the cord of her jacket hood tightly round her chin and beckoned the arriving officers over.

To her surprise, Ross McBride was there, sporting a waterproof dressing on the top of his head. 'It's just a few stitches, before you tell me to go home.' He pulled the hood of his jacket over the bandage and winked. 'I've just been discharged, and one of the guys collecting me from hospital told me about your search. You'll need every available person if this kiddie's to be found, so no arguing. I'm here to help.'

She smiled back at him, knowing better than to remonstrate, and held her hands up in surrender. 'I won't say a word, but thanks Ross. I really appreciate it.'

Turning back round she cast her eyes over the dozen or so officers. Paul, Naz and Sabira had followed on from Walton-on-the-Hill, as had most of Tony's team, plus a few others, all of whom had been provided with images of both Caz and Gemma.

'We'll fan out from here, in pairs.' Charlie instructed. 'This is where the Christophe family come for picnics. It's one of Gemma's favourite places and it's also the area where one of Razor's phones has very recently been cell-sited. It's off again now but we've every reason to think it was used by Caz and that both she and Gemma are somewhere around here.'

Each couple of officers equipped themselves with a strong flashlight and blankets. The rain was thinning but a stiff breeze still swiped intermittently at their faces. If their victims were exposed, they were bound to be cold. Charlie checked on her map, sending each of the pairs out in different directions. She and Anna would await the arrival of the air support. While they waited, she walked across the field to check the state of the river. Better to look into its nightmarish depths now than be unprepared in the middle of the operation.

'I've never seen it so high.' Anna had followed her over. She pointed to a spot under a large tree where the river bank was lower. Water had spilled out, spreading across a large area of the field. 'That's where the stepping stones should be.'

Charlie stared in the direction Anna was indicating, but there were no visible stones, not even ripples on the surface showing where they should be. She shivered again, marshalling her thoughts. The searching officers' flashlight beams had spread out now, swinging and deflecting, as they moved away along hedgerows and under trees.

She heard the throb of the helicopter blades from somewhere in the distance. With the sky growing darker by the minute, she was pinning her hopes on its ability to seek out heat sources, with its infrared eyes.

'Here comes the helicopter,' Anna's face lit up, but Charlie knew that its presence was as much to show her friend they were trying, as to get a result. In these conditions its efficiency would be questionable at best. But as the noise from its engines grew stronger and louder, so too did the buzz in her head, telling her that what she was doing was right.

'India 99 from DS Stafford.' She shone a flashlight into the air directly above her and spoke over the radio. 'I've got units with torches searching the flat ground at the base of the hill. Can you follow the river and check out the slopes. Let me know if you see anything, or if there're any buildings that might need to be checked on foot.'

'All received.' Its searchlights lit up the ground where they stood, their faces and hair buffeted by the down draft of air from its rotor blades, and then its nose dipped and the chopper swung away. And the night suddenly became blacker.

She texted her mother in the few seconds it took for their eyes to acclimatise. In the darkness fear nipped at her sanity.

R U still OK?

She waited. Nothing, but it was late. And her mother would ring if there was a problem, wouldn't she?

She crossed her fingers by her sides, watching the progress of the helicopter along the side of the hill. It stopped, seemingly stationary, hovering over the same small area of hillside. Or was it her imagination.

'Control,' the voice of its operator came across the airwaves. 'Do you have any units out on their own?'

'Negative.'

A pause. 'We have a heat source in the shape of a person heading downstream towards you. On your side of the river.'

She felt Anna grip her arm. 'Just one?'

'Yes, just one, but they're definitely heading in your direction, maybe five hundred metres away.'

'Stay here,' Charlie instructed Anna, and started to run. Could it be Gemma, or Caz, or a dog walker out late at night – but in this? It had to be one of their targets. She glanced round as Anna jogged up to her side. There was no point in trying to send her back. If it was her child, she'd be doing exactly the same. She smiled grimly.

'Guide us in please,' she said instead over the radio.

'All received. Keep going in the same direction. You're getting closer. Four hundred metres...'

They continued to jog, slowing now as the path became steeper, wetter; their feet sliding on thick mud. In places the river flowed across the path, forcing them further up the banks into thick foliage. Charlie led the way, kicking a gap through thistles and nettles as they gouged holes in her thin summer slacks.

'Three hundred metres.'

She clung on to branches with one hand and her torch with the other, the strong shaft of light swinging frenziedly across the river as she slipped and slid along its banks.

'Two hundred metres. Standby, the other heat source has disappeared. They've probably stopped under cover.'

'Gemma,' Anna shouted. 'Gemma, is that you?' She stopped momentarily and waited, but the sound of the wind in the trees drowned out any reply to their call. They battled on in the darkness. One hundred metres. They crept forward, slowing further as their passage became more onerous. Branches of trees hung precariously, snapped in half by the weight of the water. Mounds of fallen leaves camouflaged where the banks had subsided, leaving them stepping into nothingness, their legs disappearing into the fast-flowing shallows.

'You're almost up to where we last saw the figure.'

'And it was definitely a person?'

'Yes, yes.'

Charlie swung the torch into the foliage. 'Gemma,' she called out. 'Gemma if that's you; you've no need to be frightened. It's me, Charlie Stafford. You know me. I'm a friend of your mum.'

She waited, listening for the sound of twigs snapping, footfall. 'Gemma, your mum's here too,' she ventured again. It couldn't be Gemma. She'd have answered them, surely.

'Caz, is that you?' The sound of gentle laughter. 'Caz? It's Charlie and Anna. We're here to help you.'

More laughter, this time harsher. 'You've come to help me? Why now?'

'Because it's safe for you now, Caz. Razor's in custody.' Charlie pulled a shrub out of the way and stepped forward. 'But first you have to tell us where Gemma is.'

'I'll tell you when I'm ready to tell you.'

'Is she safe?'

'She's alive, or at least she was when I last saw 'er.' Caz climbed out from under a bush and switched on a torch, aiming the thin reedy light at the river. 'But who knows if she still is?'

'Oh my God!' Anna gasped behind Charlie.

Charlie held out an arm to prevent her friend getting past. She knew Caz of old but she'd never heard her speak in such a weird, dispossessed way.

'Caz, has Razor given you something?' The woman looked manic, her eyes wide and staring. She was clearly high on something.

Caz laughed. 'He's given me more than either of you ever 'ave.'

'Whatever you've done, or been forced to do, doesn't matter.' Charlie tried a different tack. 'We're here to help you get things sorted.'

'Razor was the only person who really tried to help me get things sorted. He was wiv me every step of the way, until you bastards caught 'im. 'e might not be perfect, but at least he was on my side. What have you two done? Anna, you betrayed me. You snitched on me to the social. It was you who got Mia taken away.'

Anna shook her head vehemently. 'It wasn't me Caz, I promise.'

'Yes it was!' Caz screamed. 'You told 'em I weren't lookin' after 'er. It had to be you who told 'em. That's what you've done.'

Charlie put her hands up in front of her. 'It wasn't Anna. I know that for a fact Caz because we've spoken to Marion. It was an anonymous neighbour. They claimed to have heard Mia crying, and alleged you weren't looking after her.'

'Why should I believe that bitch?' Caz paused. 'She didn't 'elp me. Nobody 'elped me.'

'And for that I'm so sorry.' Anna was crying. 'I should have helped you more. I got caught up with work and my family. I should have answered your calls and visited you like I promised. I'm sorry.'

'But you didn't and now it's too late. They won't give Mia back. Razor told me. They won't even let me see 'er again. Ever.'

'That's not true,' shouted Charlie. 'Marion said you could see her if someone was with you, for supervised visits. And then gradually if you got drug free again and did what they asked, you could see her longer each time, with a view to her being returned. Caz you *could* get Mia back.'

'You're lying.' Caz frowned. 'Razor told me what Marion said.'

'It's not us who're lying, Caz. It's him.'

'I don't believe you,' spat Caz. 'You and Hunter never liked him. You was always picking on him, smashing his door down. Just 'cause he looked after me and a few girls.'

'He hardly looked after you, did he? He beat up Redz and left her to die in an alley with her skull split apart. Then there was Dutch who deliberately overdosed on crack cocaine to escape from him. That's not what I'd call taking care.'

'At least 'e tried.' Caz fixed her with a glare. 'What have you done for me, Charlie Stafford, apart from sending 'im to prison? An' you Anna. You might think you 'elped me by taking me out of that world, but it's the only world I ever knew. You threw me a lifeline but then you abandoned me. You both abandoned me.' She leant back against a tree, staring instead at the river. 'Everyone always abandons me. Why should I trust either of you?'

Charlie could feel things slipping away. If they were going to find Gemma, she'd need to earn Caz's trust, and fast. That's if it wasn't already too late. 'Because helping us find Gemma is the only way you'll get to see your baby again – and because we're telling you the truth about Mia. Caz, come with us now. We know your history. I promise you we'll help. We know what you've been through.'

'You don't know nothin' about me.'

Charlie watched in horror as Caz lurched away from the tree, her eyes glazing over, staggering closer and closer to the river.

'Come away from the water,' she screamed, running forward, and trying to grab hold of the woman.

'It's too late for me.' Caz was teetering on the edge, her arms held out to get her balance, her feet, scrabbling to gain purchase on the slippery bank.

'I ain't told you nothin'. Nothin' 'bout what I've done.'

'Tell me what you've done,' Charlie shouted, reaching out and grabbing Caz by the arm.

Then they fell.

Chapter 66

Caz felt the water close over her head.

Everything was pitch black. She was still falling, twisting and turning in the current, fighting for breath. Filthy sediment filled her mouth. Cold water stunned her heart, and her ribcage refused to budge. She kicked out, smashing her leg against something solid, a root, or a stone or a branch of a tree. Pain shot up her calf as the skin was ripped open. Now the cold water was inside her leg. It was dragging her down, down, down, her feet touching the silty bed of the river.

Everything was hazy, the drugs and the lack of oxygen combining to deaden the pain.

She knew she was in the river, and, as she sank further into its depths, she found the realisation almost satisfying. She'd been watching the river for days, living its every move. Maybe she'd been waiting for this moment.

Her contentment was halted by a hand grasping her shoulder and pulling her upwards. She uncoiled her legs, pushed out with her feet, the instinct to breathe now forcing her towards the surface. Somebody had hold of her arm, their grip pinching her skin. She blinked hard, her retinas swapping one scene of black for another. It was still dark, but the intensity was altered. There were patches of grey and black shapes moving and swaying, cream coloured froth swirling around her. Opening her mouth, she spat out a lungful of foul-tasting water, gulping in mouthfuls of fresh, clean air.

'Caz,' she heard a voice shouting her name. 'Caz.'

Her momentum was slowing, the grip on her arm getting tighter. Freezing cold water splashed against her face. 'Hold on to this,' the voice next to her instructed. She stretched out her neck, trying to focus. The shape of a branch came into view, along with the face of the person who was shouting.

It was Charlie Stafford, the cop. The cop who had been talking to her just now. The cop who had listened to her past lies, who had believed her, not Razor.

But Charlie was kind. She was unlike most of the hard-faced, hard-hitting cops on the streets. Their relationship had been friendly, symbiotic. They'd relied on each other; she with information about several crimes and manhunts, and Charlie with help to deal with a lifetime of drugs and abuse.

She reached out, her fingers grasping a sturdy branch extending out from the main bough. She wrapped her arm round it, hugging it tight, as her legs were dragged underneath by the strength of the current. The pain in her leg grew worse as the broken skin chaffed on the rough bark.

'Hold on tight,' Charlie shouted again, taking hold of the sleeve of her jacket. 'I'll send for help.'

She turned her head up to the bank, as the shape of Anna materialised. Even in the murky shadow, Anna's face appeared pale, almost ghostly. She watched as Anna grabbed hold of a tree, stretching out her other arm, her fingers straining to reach them. But she was too far away. She tried again as Charlie responded, each of them struggling to grasp hold of the other's fingers, but again they failed. Anna's attempt at help went some way, but not far enough. It never went far enough.

'Go and get help, Anna,' Charlie shouted. 'Quick!'

Anna nodded, then turned tail and was gone. Just like that, like she'd left her before.

'Caz, keep holding on. She'll be back in a few minutes.'

Caz grimly clung on to the branch. From memory, the part of the river they were in was the steepest, the fastest; winding round large boulders and tree trunks, before opening up, widening and deepening. If she let go now, she'd be swept along by the raging torrent, at the mercy of anything in its path.

But she was a survivor. She'd always been a survivor, hadn't she?

Her leg was still scraping against the branch. In her mind she could see the wound opening up, her life flowing into the stream. A river of blood. She closed her eyes to the vision as cold water numbed her fingers and toes. Her core was already chilled from the last few days in the shelter, but now she was freezing.

'I don't think I can hang on much longer,' she shouted, as her hands started to shake, and her body convulsed in the cold.

'Yes, you can.' Charlie's voice was strong, her grip on the sleeve of her jacket tight. 'Do it for Mia.'

'Mia's gone.'

'No, she hasn't. Mia's waiting for you.'

Caz stared at Charlie, and in that second, she understood the truth of the words. Charlie Stafford hadn't lied, nor had Anna. It had been Razor, and she who had lied. Mia was waiting – but she'd be waiting for years.

And it was all down to her.

Lies, deceit and betrayal were all that she'd known. From the moment she'd launched her father from the top of the stairs, to her mother's suicide, Razor's broken promises, his failure to love her. It had been she who had lied, changed her statements and withdrawn her allegations.

And now with the charges against Razor dropped, the murder of Redz would be reinvestigated. Old evidence would be probed. New evidence established. Suspects reinterviewed. The presence of the blood, the weapon, the hair reanalysed. They might even reexamine Dutch's overdose. And what if they found out the truth?

That it had been she who had murdered, not once, but three times – and it was she who had probably done so again. It had been her idea to hold Gemma to ransom and keep her handcuffed and tied to the root with a rope, she who had tortured the girl and even mutilated her childhood toy. Gemma would almost certainly be found dead, drowned and drugged, with her blonde locks cut off – and it would be she who'd rightly be held responsible.

She would be thrown into prison for life, leaving Mia alone and waiting – always waiting.

She loosened her grip on the tree, feeling a strange relief as the water buffeted her to one side. She was tired of being a survivor. She wanted more. She wanted Mia. But now as she started to relinquish her hold further, she knew that Mia would always be too good for her. Her perfect little baby girl deserved better. She deserved a *whole* childhood, not a broken life like hers.

'Hold on,' Charlie was screaming in her ear, scrabbling to get a better grip on her jacket. For a second she stared at the woman trying to save her.

Yes, Charlie Stafford was kind, but she was also a cop, and a good one. This time she'd be certain to find out the truth.

The zip of her jacket burst apart and she scrabbled to stop Goldilocks being dragged away from her. Gemma's beautiful long blonde hair escaped through her fingers and she caught sight of the cropped blonde hair of her doll as it floated free, before being whisked away in the current. Then she let go completely, allowing her body to be sucked into the water beneath the branch. Goldilocks was gone.

Charlie was shouting her name, thrashing about in the water. The cop's hands skimmed her head, her fingers flexing, trying to grip her chin, her ears, her hair, anything. Then nothing, but a distant scream, the roar of water in her ears, the dull thud as her skull hit a rock.

She tumbled on; her body thrown from one side of the river to the other as it surged along the edge of the embankment. Pain wracked her body as her limbs snagged on broken branches and tree trunks, felled in the wind, until finally she stopped.

She opened her eyes, tried to breathe, shut them again. All around was watery blackness. No air, no oxygen. Nothing. She was under water and she was trapped.

So, this was it. This was what death felt like. She'd often wondered whether the old adage that life flashed before you were true. Now she knew it was.

She saw her father as she'd launched him out over the stairs, Redz as she'd taken a hammer to her head, Dutch whom she'd injected. Gemma.

She saw rape, blood, sex, murder and death; done against her, done by her.

And for what?

For Mia.

Mia was crying now, reaching out towards her, her tiny fingers gripping her hand. She lifted her baby up into her arms, kissed her, held her tight.

All she'd ever wanted was to be loved.

All she'd ever wanted was to love...

Chapter 67

Charlie's own screams filled her head as she watched Caz disappear. 'No-o-o!'

For a split second she'd considered going after the girl but something had stopped her. Perhaps it was just self-preservation, the innate realisation that any attempt to save Caz would be futile. But perhaps it was more. In fact, as she stared into the maelstrom of water, she knew it was more. It was the expression on Caz's face; the calm, resigned look of defeat.

Where Jamie, her brother, had been desperate to live, Caz seemed happy to die.

Caz had deliberately let go. And with Caz's decision, came the order to leave well alone; to allow her to leave. To allow her to die.

She'd clung to the tree branch, willing them both to survive, while accepting the probability Caz wouldn't. And as she hung on desperately, her body got colder and her grip got weaker. She could feel her strength ebbing away. Then, over the roar of the water, she heard voices, distant voices, one male, one female, calling her name. 'Charlie, Charlie, where are you?'

The voices grew louder, and torchlights grew brighter, sweeping the banks of the river and glancing off the raging water.

'I'm here,' she called out.

Again. 'Charlie, Charlie, where are you?'

'Here,' she screamed with all the strength she could muster. 'I'm here.'

This time the light fell on her, blinding, perfect light. She screwed up her eyes, listening to the crashing of branches, the voice of the man getting closer. It was Tony. She recognised his strong, deep intonation.

'Hold on,' he instructed her calmly. 'I'm coming for you.'

She clung on with both of her hands, not daring to release either one. Then he was there, his hand gripping one wrist, pulling her across to the edge. She kicked out, her hands now reaching out for the foliage at the side of the river, grasping a handful of nettles. It didn't matter. He hoisted her up onto the bank, as if she weighed nothing. She was flying. Relief and gratitude rippled through her.

'Where's Caz?' Anna asked, as she wrapped a blanket around Charlie.

She came down with a bang as a sense of failure returned. 'She's gone.' She opened her mouth to explain, but Tony stopped her, shook his head and held her tightly in his arms.

'There's nothing to explain,' he said, pulling out his radio and issuing instructions. His troops were to start searching downstream for Caz.

She closed her eyes, sobbed with exhaustion. Thank God he was there. But even in those first few seconds, as her body began warming, her mind was refocussing. Anna was there, which meant they'd not yet found her daughter.

'But I still don't know where Gemma is,' she stared up at Tony, panic-stricken.

'But I do.'

She was confused. So why were they waiting?

'You stay here,' he was saying. 'I'll send one of my team up to collect you.'

'No way, Tony. Where is she?' She pushed him away, adrenalin now commanding her movements. 'Let's go.' She started to climb upwards, leading the way, her feet slipping and sliding on the muddy banks.

Every so often Tony called on her to wait, for Anna to catch up, or to look at the landmarks along the path.

'We must be nearby,' he shouted eventually. 'The river bears round to the left and on the inside of the bend is a big willow tree, with its roots sticking out into the river. Apparently, they were uncovered a few days ago, but with all the rain...'

He stopped but, in her head, she finished the sentence. *It's now under water.*

'Gemma,' she shouted at the top of her voice. 'Gemma, we're here. Hang on in there.' If there was any chance... But she had to try. Hadn't she hung on tighter when she'd heard their approach? Hadn't their shouts strengthened her resolve?

The others joined in, shouting out Gemma's name. Then they fell silent to listen. Nothing.

Her heart was hammering wildly as they approached the tree, with Tony at her side. He aimed his torch around its base, lighting up an opening in a rocky mound behind it, its height clearly reduced by the level of water. 'I'm told there'll still be some space up inside at the rear,' he said.

She hoped he was right. He had to be right. 'Gemma,' she shouted again. 'Hold on, we're coming.'

She threw the blanket towards Anna, and borrowed her torch, then stepped down into the river, clinging on to the top of a root. The water came up to her waist. This time it felt colder, blacker, more dangerous. Tony climbed down behind her, holding his torch high above the dark swirling water, and threw his weight up against her. He aimed his flashlight towards the opening. She took a deep breath, then, keeping her head and hands above the water, and ducking to avoid protruding rocks and roots, pushed forward into the opening. The current pushed and pulled at her, freezing, but less ferocious as she entered the sheltered nook. She stood up inside, grateful for the headspace. There was still air inside, though it smelt stale and damp. The only sound was the noise of the river sloshing against the earthy walls. She flicked the beam of her torch around the inside of the cave, as Tony sloshed in beside her.

The main compartment was half-filled with water, with a number of cushions and other detritus floating on its surface. But it was as she pointed the torch to the rear that she saw what she'd feared all along.

Gemma's figure was pressed up against the furthest wall, unmoving. Dark, dirty water covered her legs, and lapped against her abdomen. Her hands were half in, half out of the water, fastened together with some kind of restraint.

'Bloody hell.' She sloshed towards the girl as Tony concentrated the strong beam of light on her face. Gemma's mouth hung open and her eyes were shut.

'Is she there?' She could hear Anna calling. 'Is Gemma in there?'

'Yes, she's here.' She moved closer to the figure, her eyes now drawn with horror to the rope tied around the young girl's neck, and what was left of her beautiful blonde hair.

'Thank God,' Anna's voice was filled with relief. 'Is she all right?'

Charlie threw her hands to her mouth, dreading having to give an answer. As she leant towards the girl's comatose figure, she just didn't know.

Chapter 68

Charlie watched as the ambulance, with Gemma and Anna on board, pulled out of the car park, with Naz and Sabira following on in their car. Its blue lights flashed across the treetops in the darkness and lit up the low cloud. For the time being at least, it had stopped raining.

She was dressed in a pair of Paul's old overalls, the type that he'd used when engaged in public order events. They were designed to fit over his clothes so they were hugely baggy on her; the legs and the sleeves rolled up at the wrists and ankles, and the waist held in with a borrowed belt. But they were warm and dry.

Ross was in the front passenger seat, regaling her with his hospital woes.

'Looking good, Charlie,' Paul grinned as he climbed in next to where she was sitting, warming in the rear of Tony's car. His tone changed to serious. 'Do you think Gemma will recover?'

'She's young.' It was the best she could do. Gemma's pulse had been weak but it was there, and that was all that mattered. She'd been unconscious when they'd found her, and she'd stayed unconscious as she and Tony had untied the rope around her neck and he'd run with her in his arms all the way to the car park. By the time she and Anna had navigated the treacherous pathway and arrived there too, Gemma had been placed in the ambulance, wrapped in several blankets and had been stabilised by the paramedics. With drip lines up and a host of fluids now filtering into her body she'd rallied slightly, occasionally opening her eyes but, as yet, there'd been no spoken responses.

'Thank goodness she's alive,' Tony said, as he opened the driver's door of the car.

Charlie nodded grimly towards him. It was her sentiment too, though it was anyone's guess to what extent she'd be scarred. Only time would tell.

Tony had changed out of his wet clothes into overalls too, but unlike her borrowed ones, his were his own – and he filled every spare inch of material.

'You were incredible out there,' she said, watching as he folded himself into the driver's seat. Without his size and strength, she and Anna would have struggled to get Gemma out of the river and up on to the bank, let alone to the car park. 'Thank God you were there.'

'You did pretty well yourself.' He smiled back at her.

'I lost Caz.'

'By the sound of it she pretty much lost herself. She must've felt guilty for what they've done to that poor girl.'

She paused, thinking back to the scene she'd just witnessed. It was one that would stay with her for life.

'So how did you know exactly where Gemma was?' The question had been intriguing her.

'Razor.'

'Razor?' It had to have been him, but until Tony said the name, she couldn't quite believe it. 'Really?'

'Yes, really, but it was touch and go.'

'Go on.'

'Well to start with he refused to say a thing, clammed up completely except to tell us we were all wankers. It was bloody frustrating. I could hear you on the radio, searching Walton-on-the-Hill, then making your way here, calling for more troops but there was nothing I could do. I had to stay with him, rapport and all that. To start with I kept him in the van, so we could stay mobile should he talk, but after a while I realised it was a waste of time. He wasn't going to say anything. So, we made our way to the local nick and booked him in. I thought I'd be more use here, and maybe some time in the cells might prompt him to talk.'

'It never has done before.'

'Well luckily, we never got that far. It all changed when I took him for a strip search. He was cocky at first, but then when he took off his T-shirt, I saw he had a photo taped to his chest, right over his heart. It was a photo of Mia. He might have wanted us to think he was a hard man, but inside... well, who knows?'

'You wouldn't say that if you'd seen what he did to Redz and his girls.'

'*If,* he did what you say to Redz.'

She raised her eyebrows. 'Hm, we'll have to see when the case is reopened. To be fair, I always had a few reservations but when Redz's hair and the murder weapons were found in his lock-up, there was never really anyone else it could be. Anyway...' she paused as another explanation came into her head. 'What happened with the photo?'

'He started to crack when I tried to take it off him. Said he'd always wanted a kid of his own but that it had never happened before Mia came along. I could see that he meant it, so I jumped at the chance to get him talking, man to man, like. I told him about my little boy and how I loved to play footie with him in the park.'

'You don't have a little boy, do you?'

'I can dream.' Tony smiled sadly. 'Anyway, it seemed to strike a chord with him. He fell apart. Told me that he'd simply gone along with Caz. Said that he'd never really wanted to take Gemma, but he was angry at Anna, and Marion, and society in general. Reckoned that as a young black boy he'd always been judged, and that he'd grown up with a lifetime of prejudice and injustice. Losing Mia was the final straw.'

'I don't think he helped himself much at Marion's office.'

'I don't suppose he did, but perhaps, after trying to go through the proper channels, he saw the door slam in his face – again – and he flipped. There're only so many doors you can have slammed in your face. I have to admit I did have some sympathy for the guy.'

Charlie was seeing Razor in a whole new light. 'So, he told you where Gemma was?'

'Yep! He described the whole route, every bend in the river, every tree, every landmark. Said that she was just a young child, like Mia, and she didn't deserve what had happened. He said to hurry, that he didn't want to be responsible for her death.'

Charlie pursed her lips. 'Well, we don't know yet whether he still might be – he and Caz.'

'Talking about Caz… Is there still no trace of her?' Ross asked.

'No, but I've got some Marine Support Unit guys coming at first light. There's nothing we can do until then. Hopefully, if the rain holds off, the level of water might fall enough for an underwater search team to check the lower reaches of the river, but I've no doubt what the outcome will be.'

'You must have a guardian angel looking down on you, when it comes to water,' Paul said. 'You're lucky to be alive.'

She flinched at Paul's words, twisting away to stare out of the window. The tints on the glass made the night even darker. Unbidden, the faces of Caz and Jamie appeared, spinning around in a slowly diminishing circle, Jamie desperate to live, Caz willing to die.

Then, as the two faces vanished slowly from sight, she didn't feel lucky, or happy, or sad. She felt guilt, and a gradual realisation that she'd been spared for a reason – and that reason was Meg.

Her first escape had brought her mother solace, continuity, after losing her son, but what might it be this time? It couldn't solely have been Caz's expression, there had to be more. Something had kept her clinging on to the branch, and it had to be her mother and her own desire to protect her. Meg needed safeguarding, not only by upgrading security on her windows and doors. Not just by the fitting of cameras. By her.

Meg had never properly replied to her question about cameras. Or had she?

Their last conversation had been patchy, the signal intermittent. But what had her mum said. *I'm fine. There's no need for cameras. Take your time. When you come home, there's somebody here who can't wait to see you.*

'Oh my God! Mum.' She spun round towards Paul, her eyes wide.

'What about your mum?' Paul caught her panic.

'She said there was *no need for cameras*. And she said to *take my time*.'

'So why are you so worried?' Paul looked confused.

'Because I'm supposed to be looking after her. And because I told her to phone if she had any trouble but she couldn't, because my phone's dead, from the river. What if she tried?' She was babbling. It was almost four in the morning but the previous day's unease was back with a vengeance. Paul reached out, touched her arm, but the gesture did nothing to allay the icy grip of fear tightening around her throat.

'She said somebody was there, who *couldn't wait to see me* – but I don't know who that *somebody* was. I presumed it was Beth or Lucy home early from uni, but why should they be so eager to see me? We talk all the time on the phone. What if it isn't one of my sisters? Who else could it be?'

Paul pulled his phone out. 'Standby Charlie, I can phone her. I've got your home number.'

She watched as Paul keyed in her name, noticing how his fingers had started to shake. Paul knew the situation with her father, as well as she did. The line clicked in, and the phone started to ring. Paul passed her the phone. She pressed the headset to her ear and waited – and waited.

In the background she could hear Paul speaking to Tony and Ross; the engine revving. The car started to move fast towards the exit, its tyres throwing up a shower of grit.

It was late, but her mum kept the phone by the side of her bed, for just this kind of emergency; in case one of her daughters called needing help. She'd answer, surely – but as the phone rang out and Charlie redialled, an awful sensation of dread came to mind; one that she couldn't dislodge.

What if *the somebody* was Iain Frazer, her father? What if her mum had been pleading for help with the use of a code?

Chapter 69

Charlie's pulse was racing as Tony expertly navigated the slippery roads, listening as Paul brought him and Ross up to date with her story. Hearing Paul starkly set out her father's campaign week by week, month by month, added flesh to the growing reality that while she'd been occupied saving others, she'd neglected her own.

The house was in darkness as they turned into the driveway half an hour later. Tony pulled to a halt, and she, Ross and Paul jumped out, her instinct to tear down the door suppressed momentarily in her shock at the scene.

She threw out her arms, palms down, urging restraint. It was eerily quiet. The wind had dropped so the clouds were now motionless, lying low over the rooftops, thick and suffocating. There were no sounds, no movement. No sign of life. Everything was hushed. It was like the moment of still and calm before a storm; except the storm had obviously already broken. In fact, it looked like the worst of its rage had been spent. Two windows at the front of the house had been smashed but had been patched up with old boards, and the wooden front door was splintered and cracked. A dozen broken plant pots lay across the front garden, turned on their sides, with their contents spilt across the gravel.

'Shit!' Paul gasped, as Tony closed the car door quietly and crept up to join them.

'I need to find Mum.' Charlie could hardly speak with emotion. She started to run forward but Tony grabbed her arm.

'Wait, he could still be in there,' he whispered.

'But I need to find Mum,' she repeated. 'And Casper.' The old dog was nowhere to be seen. At this point there was no knowing what the hell had happened, or who might be in her family home. Could Iain Frazer be holed up inside, waiting? Might her mother be lying in there trapped, or wounded, or... worse?

Tony put a finger to his lips, then nodded towards Paul and Ross. Charlie paused as the years of training kicked in. Wordlessly, they split, Paul and Ross heading down the side of the house, Tony and her staying at the front.

When they'd given the others time to get to the rear, she moved forward, key in hand and with Tony at her side. The front door opened and she took a deep breath, reaching in with one hand and pressing the light switch, but there was nothing.

If Frazer was there, then he'd have the advantage.

'Damn it,' Tony whispered, clearly thinking the same. In the dark, it was like she'd returned to the outhouse at GSM all over again, except this time it wasn't Ross she was with. It was Tony.

They switched on their torches and advanced, checking each room quickly, silently, thoroughly. The lounge, the kitchen, the hallway. All clear.

Then on up the staircase. The doors to all the bedrooms were closed.

Heading straight to the master bedroom, she pressed her ear to the door. 'Mum's room,' she mouthed.

Tony nodded.

She could hear nothing, but the tiny metallic click of the second hand on the carriage clock in the hallway and what sounded like an animal whining. She put her finger to one ear, listening. Tony nodded again, then pointed to the handle of the door. 'Me first,' he whispered.

On any other occasion she'd have argued, but this time she wanted it over.

Pressing the handle of the door down, she pushed the door ajar, shining the beam from the torch into the room. In the light, she could see the shape of a body lying perfectly still under the duvet, and heard a yelp. She gasped. Tony's head jerked in the same direction and he stepped into the room.

'So you've come back for more?!' a voice roared as a figure leapt out from behind the door knocking Tony to the floor and pinning him down on the carpet. 'Quick!' the same voice shouted. 'Pass me the rope.'

Another figure jumped out from behind the bed, running towards them. The shape of a dog appeared at its side.

'Here it is, Ben.'

'Mum!' Charlie shouted from the doorway, immediately recognising her mother's voice. 'And Casper. Oh, thank God, Mum. It's me.' She swung her torch past her mother, and on to the muscular figure of the man straddling Tony, whose body and voice she only now recognised.

The light bounced off the two men as they wrestled on the floor.

'Ben! He's with me. Leave him alone.' Charlie pulled at Ben, then at Tony, until they stopped in their tracks.

'Ben, this is Tony,' she said breathlessly, as they both got to their feet. The thunder of boots on the stairs, and loud voices, made her whip her head round. She held up her hand to slow down their back-up as they came into view. 'And this is Ross. And you already know Paul.'

The boys stopped at the door and Meg came across to join them, all four men glancing curiously from one to the other.

Charlie stood back, smiling into the rugged features of Ben Jacobs.

'Let me introduce you to my ex-boyfriend, and our apparent hero. Guys, this is Ben.'

Chapter 70

It took only a few minutes before the electricity was switched on and the kettle was boiling. Meg was in her element, chivvying the four men into seats round the kitchen table.

'I love the pillows *under* the duvet idea,' Charlie commented. 'But don't do it again.' She walked across and gave her mother a hug. 'I thought you were dead.'

'You don't seriously think I would put your mum on offer?' Ben chose a seat and pulled a face of mock outrage. 'I'd never have heard the end of it if I'd let something bad happen to Meg Stafford.'

'Too right,' smiled Charlie, tightening her grip around her mother and acknowledging guiltily it had been she who had almost allowed that to happen.

'Like I said, darling. I'm fine. And I know how much you put into your job.' Meg leant back from Charlie and looked her in the eye. 'So, after that night when you found me crying on the sofa, I decided a bit of self-help was required. The Milk Tray box was going to be Plan A.'

'The Milk Tray box?' Ben looked puzzled.

'Don't ask!' Charlie shook her head. 'Thank God you ruled that little box of trouble out. So I guess Plan B was...'

'Ben! You'd already said that Anna was still in contact with him, and I know you'd dropped hints, so I gave her a ring.'

'And there was I thinking you were seeing Anna to sort out your demons.'

'I don't have demons,' Meg chided her playfully. 'Or at least not in the plural. So anyhow, I dropped a few hints myself, hoping Anna might mention them to Ben, and it seems that she did, because yesterday afternoon who did I find on my doorstep, but my very own dashing Milk Tray man!' She moved across to stand behind Ben, placing her hands on his shoulders and gave them an affectionate squeeze.

'And there was *I* thinking you were just missing me,' laughed Ben, reaching up and putting a hand over Meg's. 'Now I find out you're only after my body.'

'Like mother, like daughter,' said Meg with a grin, winking at Charlie.

'Mum!' She felt herself colour as four pairs of eyes turned towards her, her cheeks glowing as red as if she'd been caught behind the proverbial bike sheds. 'So, what happened last night?' It was time to change the subject.

'We banished my demon.' Meg walked across to the kettle and poured the boiling water into six separate mugs.

'At least for the time being,' Ben took up the thread. 'We were sitting watching TV late yesterday evening.'

'So, it was still Wednesday?'

'Yes, it was. It had to be really.' Ben looked across and smiled gently at Charlie.

'What's the fixation with Wednesday?' Ross asked.

'It was the day Charlie's brother drowned,' Ben explained. 'She thinks it's unlucky.'

'It is.'

'Well, maybe for some. In any case, your mum updated me on your recent problems with your father, and a little of their history – and his. Although she said it'd gone quiet for a while, she had a feeling something might happen, especially with it being Wednesday, so we got prepared. Your mum sorted me out a place to sleep and we were about to head up to bed, when we heard him. Quietly at first, rattling the windows, calling through the letter box.

'"Meg, are you ready?" he kept asking. "Are you ready to play?" Then we heard a loud bang at the front door, and the sound of the letterbox opening. Then, "Let the games commence."'

'Bloody hell. Like when he was in the garden that time, it's a game to him.' Charlie shivered at the recollection of his previous words, the strong Glaswegian drawl. She'd lain in bed night after night replaying that voice in her nightmares, imagining the thin smile on his lips as he'd said them, the cruel glint of pleasure in his eyes. There was something pure evil in Iain Frazer.

'He likes to play games. He always did,' added Meg.

'Anyway, I wasn't having any of that nonsense– scaring your mum, like he was some sort of sick character in a horror movie – so I hid next to the door. When he bent down to speak his shit through the letterbox again, I flung the door open. The stupid bastard fell straight onto the floor at my feet. He wasn't expecting that to happen.'

'Nor was I,' Tony chuckled. 'That must be your forte.'

Ben grinned and raised his palm, and they slapped hands together.

'So, what did you do then?' asked Charlie. She was anxious to know how he'd handled it, and that Ben hadn't left himself open to arrest.

'Don't worry,' Ben turned towards her and winked. He'd always been able to read her thoughts. 'I kept control – just. I yanked him up to his feet and gave him a good talking to. Told him he was a snivelling arsehole for bullying women, and that he should crawl back into his gutter. That sort of thing.'

The other men were nodding their approval. Charlie too was pleased. Ben had, with any luck, sent her father packing – and without any nasty repercussions coming back on him.'

'But I think he'll be back.' Ben's words put a sledgehammer to that hope. 'He did all the damage as he left, like a toddler having a tantrum, chucking stones and kicking the plant pots about, from a distance. He only finally left when I chased him away – with a kitchen knife.'

He stopped talking while they all mulled over the possible consequences of that information – but no harm had been done. Meg carried the mugs of hot chocolate across the kitchen, setting one down in front of each person.

'Then, in case he was stupid enough to come back, we got even better prepared,' she continued. 'We turned off the electric and found a couple of torches. Knowing the layout of the house gave us the advantage. Ben laid down on some cushions by the bedroom door and I hung on to Casper and tried to keep him quiet, but I don't think any of us slept, what with the windows being insecure. We both heard the gravel crunching at the same time and thought it was him.'

'Hence the pillows.'

'Yes, hence the pillows, and the rope, in case any of you think I usually keep rope in my bedroom.' There was a murmur of amusement as Meg pulled up a chair and sat down in between Ben and Charlie. 'And the rest is history.'

'Hm, I wish it was. I've a feeling we're going to be dealing with my father for a long time to come.' She lifted her mug towards her mother and Ben. 'But I have to say, you two make a hell of a team.'

'As do we.' She turned to her best friend Paul, then to Ross, then finally to Tony. 'I wouldn't have managed without you and your teams.'

All three squads had gelled well together, through the good and the bad, the mistakes and successes. And as she looked at Ross with his bandages, and she and Tony in their matching overalls, and Ben with his cheeky smile, for no particular reason it made her think of the marriage vows, in sickness and in health, for better or for worse.

In the next few days, they'd be dredging the river for a body, dealing with a young girl's trauma, and charging the man responsible for a host of evil – and it was purely a result of all their hard work, and that of their teams.

So, let's raise our mugs,' she said with a nod to her friends. 'Here's to us.'

Chapter 71

The sun was high in the sky by the time Charlie rose the next morning.

From downstairs came the sound of voices, the same ones conversed with only a few hours before; Ben, Paul, Ross and Tony. Each had been provided with a place to lay their heads, Meg brooking no argument. They were her guests, whether on or off duty – and they needed some sleep.

Showered, and feeling fresher than she'd felt for ages, Charlie walked into the kitchen to a bacon roll, a steaming hot drink and a farewell from her friends.

Tony was heading out to speak to Razor.

Ross, in a fresh bandage, was off to liaise with his team, and assist with the paperwork required regarding Smythe-Hamilton and Hurley.

And the best news of the day… Gemma was now fully conscious and making a good recovery in hospital, though opting to speak to a male, rather than a female officer. So, Paul was now heading to gently debrief Gemma about her ordeal, while Naz and Sabira returned to Wimbledon to complete their enquiries on Rochelle Edwards' murder.

Which just left Caz to be dealt with by Charlie.

As the room emptied, she turned round to see Ben wiping a dollop of ketchup from his lips. 'Here, take a seat.' He patted the chair next to him. 'It's good to be back.'

'*Are* you back?' She sat down where he'd indicated but held herself away to one side. 'Or are you going to disappear again for months and months, without leaving a message?'

'I'm sorry, Charlie.' His head dropped. 'I know I hurt you again but you could see what I was like – and I didn't want you to hate me.'

'We could have worked through it together.'

'No, that wouldn't have been right. Like your mum said earlier, you put a lot into your work. It wouldn't have been fair to heap even more on your shoulders.'

'But I thought *we* were a team. I wanted to help.'

'My shit is my shit,' he shook his head. 'And at the end of the day it's down to me to get my shit sorted. I think it is – at least for now – though I can't promise it'll never come back. PTSD has a habit of rearing its ugly head just when you think everything's hunky-dory.'

'I wouldn't call what happened last night hunky-dory and you coped very well. Thank God you were here.'

'And I'll be here for as long as you need me.'

'Thanks Ben.' She shuffled across closer, linking arms and resting her head on his shoulder. It was as solid and strong as she remembered, but could it ever be stable. She'd been through this several times before. Life with Ben was a yoyo, one day up, the next day down, not daring to say a word, and with nothing she could do to raise his spirits. Had his time in the military left him broken forever?

'But I'm not sure this time if we'd be better off as friends.' Ben was speaking again. 'It looks like you've a few admirers ready to jump in my shoes.'

She sat up straight. 'But Paul's gay.'

'I'm not talking about Paul. I'm talking about Ross, and Tony. I've seen how they both look at you.

'No.'

'Yes, Charlie. You're a strong, sexy woman. Why wouldn't they?' He paused, frowning. 'Perhaps that's why *we've* found it so tough. *I'm* the one who's supposed to be strong, but I'm weak.'

'Don't be silly,' she reached out and took hold of his hand. 'You've lived through a war.'

'So have you! In fact, you're living it every day. The guys told me what you've got to do when you leave. The difference is *you* can deal with it. *I* can't.'

She felt him pull his hand away from hers, his expression now sad. It was awful to witness. 'But times have changed,' she said, desperate to stop his mood from falling any lower. 'These days, grown men *are* allowed to cry.'

'Not in my world, Charlie. And I suspect not in yours.'

Chapter 72

Box Hill had totally changed in the light. With the sun shining from a vivid blue sky the area was returning to life. Steam rose from the tops of the trees as the excess water was lifted away in the heat. Puddles shrank. The forest seemed to have grown taller, greener, lusher even in the last few hours, as if the uppermost boughs had been released from the weight of the rain like coiled springs.

Even the river looked more agreeable.

As Charlie pulled into the car park however, the brightness was marred by an army of navy uniforms, blue and white flapping police tape and the sight of a cluster of wet suited divers staring down at a shape on the ground.

'You found her then.' It wasn't a question. She'd known all along Caz would be discovered, but in the back of her mind, tucked into the furthest recesses was the hope that somehow, against all the odds, she'd still be alive; trapped against a branch or an obstacle, freezing and exhausted, but still breathing.

'Yes, just now.' A sergeant from the Marine Support Unit nodded. She followed the sergeant as he led the way through the car park and along the edge of the field.

As they came to the side of the river he pointed to a spot on the far side. 'Her body was there, trapped behind the stepping stones.' She stared in the direction he was indicating, her eyes searching the river. The level had dropped since the previous night, and the stones were now visible, just under the surface of the water; a solid, static barrier preventing the body from drifting any further. 'The current obviously brought her downstream.'

'Can you say where she drowned?' For some reason it mattered that Caz hadn't died too close to where she'd been lost; that she hadn't missed a last opportunity to save her.

'No, I can't, and I doubt that we'll ever truly know.' The sergeant pursed his lips, and stared at her with pale grey, serious eyes. He was an older man, with wispy white hair and a kindly face, lined by dealing with tragedy. 'I hear you tried to save her – so in case you're wondering, there wouldn't have been anything more you could have done. It's far too dangerous, even now, for my guys with all their equipment to enter the water further up.'

She nodded, relieved, the sense that she'd done everything possible increasing with every step. The group of divers moved away. She stared down at the shape on the ground, at the pasty white face of the young woman she sadly but undoubtedly knew was Caz. The skin on her face was torn in places, and large purple bruises were visible on her limbs and body; evidence of the ferocity of the water and the obstacles beneath. Her clothes were in tatters, her jacket pulled from one arm, and twisted around the other. Part of her torso was naked.

The sergeant bent down and rolled out a large black body bag next to her, smoothing it out in preparation for its tragic cargo.

Charlie's phone rang. It was Paul.

'I hear they've found Caz,' he said. 'Do me a favour before she's shipped off to the mortuary and see if she's still got an old ragdoll tucked inside her jacket.'

'Goldilocks, do you mean?'

'Yes Goldilocks. I don't know what the hell's gone on, but Gemma's had a great chunk of her lovely blonde hair removed. She says it was Caz who cut it off with a knife, *to stuff in her doll's body*.'

'Bloody hell, Paul, that's sick!'

'I know, but it gets worse. Caz told Gemma she'd already stuffed the doll with hair from two other girls called Redz and Dutch, who she said she'd 'finished off'. She boasted to Gemma that she'd never been found out.'

'So why tell Gemma?'

'Probably because she then injected Gemma with a large dose of crack cocaine, tightened the rope around her neck and left her to die.'

'Shit! Do you think Gemma's telling the truth?'

'She's got no reason not to and her account is borne out by the fact blood tests have identified a high quantity of cocaine in her body. That's the reason for her being unconscious when she was found. Charlie, Gemma maintains it was Caz who frightened her the most.'

The warmth of the day was lost as a cold chill ran the length of her spine. She'd always liked Caz but could the girl have played them all for fools? In that moment, she remembered the way Caz had stubbornly refused to tell them Gemma's location; it had been Razor, not Caz, who had helped save Anna's child. Now, as she ran through Paul's words, Charlie understood the reason why Caz had let go of the log. There could be no going back. Even Caz knew that. If Gemma died, she'd be done for her murder, but if Gemma lived... well she'd tell them the truth, the whole truth.

She pulled a pair of gloves on and bent down, her mind now turning to the doll. Could Caz really have hidden the evidence of her crimes right under their noses? As well as being sick, it was incredibly risky. 'Hang on Paul, I'll take a look, but I don't think it'll be here. There's not much left of her jacket.'

Carefully she unwound one sleeve of the jacket and pulled it over. 'No doll, I'm afraid. But, bloody hell, Paul...'

Wrapped around the zip on the front of her jacket were several hairs, long blonde ones, the same length and colour as Gemma's.

Chapter 73

Superintendent Woodall was giving a press conference as Charlie climbed the stairs. She listened through an open window as he proudly proclaimed that Wayne Hurley had been charged with two racially motivated murders, an attempted murder and, jointly with another male, supplying Class A drugs.

At the end, he explained how his officer's work had been exemplary. He was proud of how they'd used every legal method and justification in the book to obtain justice.

Charlie smiled to herself. If only he knew the extent of the lengths that they'd gone to, mostly behind his back. But perhaps he did now. She'd seen their old boss from Lambeth hovering about the front office.

'Do you have anyone yet charged with the murder of Rochelle Edwards?' one of the journalists shouted. Rochelle, being an innocent victim, was still making headlines, the media obviously making the distinction between her, Rocco Fontana and Kelvin Olawi who had been almost forgotten.

She closed her ears to his answer, not wanting to hear any more. In a few minutes she was set to find out.

'Charlie!' Sabira called her name as she entered the office. Usually the calmest, most quietly efficient on the team, today her expression was unreadable. 'We've got the enhanced photos of our suspect back from the lab,' she said grimacing. 'I think you're going to recognise him straight away.'

She headed across towards Sabira's work station. Naz and Bet were already there, gathered round, staring down at the screen, but instead of the usual delight at naming a suspect for murder, both stood in quiet contemplation.

'They were lifted from CCTV at a local shop, soon after Rochelle's murder,' said Sabira. Staring out from the screen were the frightened eyes of a fifteen-year-old black boy, small-framed and dressed in a dark tracksuit. A scarf hung around his neck, leaving his whole face uncovered – and the face was one that she knew only too well.

'He's the boy from the common. Are you sure he's the one responsible?' she asked, turning to Sabira.

'As sure as we can be. Rochelle's friend gave a good description of the suspect, including a specific lion motif on the clothing of the lad who attacked Rochelle. Of course, it might be dependent on the result of an ID parade but even without it, look...'

Sabira pulled another image up on the screen. It was a custody shot of a youth arrested for public order offences a few days before the murder took place. It showed the same small-framed boy, his eyes angry and challenging, wearing a dark coloured tracksuit. While Charlie watched, Sabira zoomed in on a small yellow lion motif on the left breast pocket. 'He's got the same tracksuit top on as he had on the day of Rochelle's murder, look.' She pulled up the previous image and there on the left breast pocket was the identical motif.

'It's unbelievable, isn't it?' Naz sat down heavily, her eyes never leaving the screen.

'The two faces of a young boy caught up in a gang.' Charlie placed a hand on her shoulder. 'I guess we need to go and pay him a visit.'

She wasn't looking forward to their next knock on the door.

※ ※ ※

The door opened as Charlie and the team approached. Naz would be sitting this one out in the van, as would Ross and his squad. There was no point in any more provocation than was necessary. She just wanted to get the job done and over.

'You won't need all them lot.' Constance Olawi gave a nod to the half dozen officers in full public order kit lined up along the front wall of her flat. 'We've been waiting for you.'

Charlie paused, unsure whether to trust the woman. After Naz's brush with death, she was determined to ensure all her team would be safe this time round.

'Here,' Constance held her hands out in front of her. 'You can put handcuffs on me if you want.'

'I never *want* to,' Charlie replied. 'It's a case of protecting my officers, but...' Constance seemed altered from last time, subdued. 'If you stay calm then I'll leave them off for now, but if—'

'I won't,' Constance anticipated her warning.

'In that case, I'll ask some of my officers to remain outside.'

'They won't be needed. My boy's got somethin' to tell you. Come in.'

Charlie beckoned to Sabira and a couple of others, then followed Constance through to the lounge. The room was filled with photographs, flowers and written tributes to Kelvin Olawi, the young man better known to his friends as Boxer. Unlike Maria Fontana, Constance seemed happy to have her son known by his gang nickname. Sitting on the sofa with his head in his hands was her youngest son.

The boy continued to stare at the floor as they entered.

Sabira stepped forward. 'Wesley Olawi,' she said. 'I'm arresting you on suspicion of the murder of Rochelle Edwards.' Before she could finish the words of the caution Wesley clapped his hands to his face.

'I didn't mean to kill 'er, miss,' he said, putting the fingers of one hand to his mouth and biting on the only remaining nail not chewed down to the quick. 'Everyone was running about wiv knives an' I got carried away, like. An' after what happened to Kelvin, well I 'ad somethin' to prove. I had to show I was as good as the others, that the Dons couldn't push us Soldiers around.'

'You're not a Soldier,' Constance fired the comment at Wesley.

'You didn't notice her school uniform then?' Sabira asked.

'I didn't really think, like. She was there on the common so I thought she must be wiv one of the gangs.' He lowered his eyes to the floor. 'An' I didn't realise one shank would kill 'er. Lots of other kids get shanked lots of times and they don't die.'

'Anyone who sticks a knife into someone else takes that chance,' said Charlie, quietly. 'You risk ending up dead or in prison if you run with a knife.'

There was no need to lecture either of them further. Simply looking at Constance Olawi's expression was enough to see what damage knife crime had wreaked on her family. In contrast to her previous hostility, she now looked broken. Kelvin was dead and Wesley would soon be locked in a cell. Even Constance herself had the prospect of a long term in prison stretching out in front of her.

Charlie glanced around the room, her eyes coming to rest on a photo of Kelvin as a boy. He was wearing a helmet and a pair of boxing gloves, pretending to spar. His face was alive, his cheeks round and rosy, his expression animated. A young boy with his whole life to live.

'Constance, I know everything went wrong on our last visit but I want to say how personally sorry I am about what happened to Kelvin. We had no idea about the activities of Wayne Hurley. He's been charged with murdering Kelvin, and other offences.'

Constance nodded. 'I know. Superintendent Woodall phoned me yesterday to tell me. He explained how that man came to have the knife with Kelvin's fingerprints on the handle and why you had to get a warrant because of it. He was nice, and he said that he'd write a personal report to be sent to the judge when I'm up in court.'

Charlie thought back to her battle to stem the flow of Naz's blood. It was a bit rich assisting a woman who'd violently attacked one of their own but, given the circumstances, a bit of diplomacy wouldn't hurt. Perhaps that was what being a senior officer was all about.

Constance's eyes were misting over. She sniffed and pulled out a tissue, then moved across the room and sat down next to Wesley, placing a hand on his knee.

'If it means anything, I'm sorry too for what I done to your officer. I know now she was just tryin' to be friendly, an' do her job.' She paused, rubbing her eyes with the tissue. 'An' Wes here is sorry for what he done to that poor young girl, aren't you Wes?'

The boy hung his head again and grunted an apology.

'I've made him promise he'll fess up to where he chucked the knife an' his clothing. What's goin' to happen to him? In fact, what's goin' to happen to us?'

Sabira stepped forward. 'Wes will be coming with us. He'll be interviewed about his role and intentions then it'll be up to the CPS to decide on a charge. At the end of the day a young girl has lost her life and there're another set of parents grieving.'

'But I'd like you at least to be able to visit your son.' Naz was standing at the door. 'Apologies over. We all make mistakes.' She walked forward and stopped directly in front of the two on the sofa. 'We're both mothers of young black boys – and we both understand the lure of the gangs, whatever their postcode area or ethnicity. If you're willing to step up and do everything you can to speak out against knife crime then I'll think about dropping the charges against you. With your help I'd like to start a club for other young boys in the area, and their families, to stop them being sucked in before it's too late.'

'It's too late for my Wesley.'

Charlie watched mesmerised as Naz held out her hand towards Constance Olawi and she in turn reached out tentatively. Naz's face broke into a smile as the two women took hold of each other's hands to shake.

'It's never too late.'

Chapter 74

Charlie was at Caz's bedsit, supervising the council's removal of the last of the girl's belongings when there was a knock on the door. Forensics had been and gone, seizing any evidence relevant to the current kidnap case, as well as anything that would provide further evidence of Caz's previous crimes. She looked up to see Anna.

'Come in,' she said. 'We're almost finished here.'

She opened the door and ushered Anna through, watching as her eyes went straight to the empty spot on the wall where Gemma's painting of Box Hill had been.

'We've taken that, Anna, for evidence, but if you want it back you can have it, after Razor's court case is over.'

'You think Gemma or I would want that as a reminder?'

'No, but I thought I'd better give you the option. I hear Gemma's back home. How is she?'

'She's recovering well. The doctor's say there won't be any lasting physical damage from the hypothermia or drugs – but it was lucky we got her out when we did. Her body temperature was dangerously low from lying partially immersed in the cold water. They don't think she would have survived much longer.'

'And how's she coping mentally?'

'She's able to talk about what happened, which is a good thing, and Paul is fantastic. He's coaxing it all out of her gradually.'

'And she's got you.'

Anna shook her head. 'I don't think I'll be the crutch she'll rely on. For a start she doesn't trust women – and secondly, I'm her mum. She won't forgive me yet. Not only did I fail to protect her, but it was me who allowed Caz into our lives in the first place.'

'You can't go blaming yourself.'

'Ah, but I can, and I will for a long time to come. Guilt is a powerful emotion and mother/daughter relationships are tricky at best, but I don't need to tell you all this.'

Charlie nodded. Roles reversed, but wasn't she experiencing exactly the same guilt at failing to protect her mum? However, now wasn't the time, or the place to discuss. 'The room looks so bare,' she commented instead.

'It does,' replied Anna taking the hint. 'I still can't believe that Caz has gone.'

'Well, she definitely has, and knowing what we know now it's probably for the best.'

Anna made no reply, instead stepping further into the room and staring at the boxes of belongings. 'There was a lot of good in Caz, but there was also an awful lot broken. Knowing a little of her history, I can understand what drove her to do the things she did.' She leant forward and picked up one of Caz's jackets from the floor, folded it carefully and placed it on the top of an open box. 'Maybe in time I'll forgive her. No child is ever born bad.'

Charlie raised her eyebrows. 'Really? After all that she's done to your family.'

'Well, let's just say Caz was complex. I tried for years to unravel her mind but I think in the end Caz only ever told me what she wanted me to hear. I don't think we'll ever really know the true extent of the damage inflicted on her, or the full story surrounding the death of her father.'

'Or Redz, or Dutch, and the part that she played.'

'She came to me directly after each of their deaths, traumatised. If she was responsible, then maybe there was still a small part of her conscience left.' Anna moved across to the window and looked out. 'What'll happen to Razor?'

Charlie joined her friend, gazing down at the slow-moving traffic. 'I don't yet know. Hopefully, the reviews into Redz' murder and Dutch's death, will get to the bottom of what really happened. When I leave here, I'm hoping to be debriefed by the new officer in the case. And of course, Tony will be interviewing Razor about Gemma's kidnap while he's still in custody.'

'It seems strange that in the end it was Razor, not Caz, who saved Gemma's life,' Anna mused. 'I guess, if I've learnt anything from this, it's you can't judge a book by its cover.'

Charlie made no reply. She was thinking about Tony's description of Razor with Mia's photo stuck to his chest, and the little dinosaur found under a root in the shelter, wet and dirty, with its head hacked off. Then her mind turned to Goldilocks, the soft fluffy doll stuffed with the hair of human murder victims. Everything she'd believed to be true had been turned on its head.

'What do you want me to do with this?' the voice of the council workman broke into her thoughts. She looked to where he was pointing. Mia's cot with its pink and white bedding. Her toys.

'Pack it up.' It sounded harsh but Mia would be well looked after from now on. 'The baby's been taken into care, pending adoption. She won't need these now.' She took Anna's arm and led her towards the door, stopping to take one final look at the remnants of Caz's life. 'At least Mia's been given a second chance.'

Chapter 75

'What was that all about?' Tony cocked his head at Charlie as she left Superintendent Richie Woodall's office.

'An apology for his lack of support in the past, and a promise of help in the future. We'll see if it happens.' She still didn't have too much faith. 'But guess what?'

Tony held his hands out. 'What?'

'My old boss has been reinstated. They've agreed there's no case for him to answer.'

She pulled out her phone and was about to dial Paul, when his name came up on her screen. 'Hunter's back,' they both said in unison.

'Tell the troops,' she laughed. 'I'll be in a bit later.' She ended the call and turned to Tony. 'Can we go for a drive?'

'It'd be my pleasure. Where to?'

'To Lingfield.' They walked to the car park in silence, each caught up in their own thoughts. Tony had sat in on her meeting with DC Brownlow, the new officer in Redz' murder case, and while the discussion had been useful, it had thrown up almost as many questions as it had answered.

It was only when they were leaving the outskirts of London that she turned to Tony. 'So, what's your gut feeling, now you've spoken to Razor more?'

Tony pursed his lips, shook his head.

'I don't think it was him who killed Redz. I've got no doubt he had given her a good hiding, but would he have taken a hammer to her head. I don't think so. He was her pimp. He needed to keep her alive for the money she brought in. Why would he kill her?'

'Because he's a violent man who'd totally lost control?' She was playing devil's advocate.

'Possibly, but then there's the bag containing the hair and the hammer.'

'I know. Caz had as much access to where it was found as did Razor.' She paused, shivering at the memory of the blood-soaked hair and hammer. 'But everything's changed after what she's said and done to Gemma.'

'Inadmissible as far as court proceedings go.' Now it was Tony's turn to debate. 'Gemma's still a minor, and don't forget she was injected with drugs. Any defence barrister worth his salt would dismiss what Gemma claims Caz said as fantasy.'

'What about cutting off her hair?'

'Again, it's only her word it was Caz.'

'And the hair found attached to the zip of Caz's jacket?'

'Only a few strands. It could have come just from being in close proximity.'

They both knew that wasn't true.

'What about Caz admitting to killing Dutch?' Charlie persisted.

'Exactly the same. The post mortem at the time showed she died from an overdose and there's no evidence to prove who had injected the drugs.'

'Unless you look at the fact Caz did exactly the same to Gemma and believe Gemma's account?'

'Same again, as far as a jury would be concerned. A drugged-up minor, no sign of foul play, and as for Dutch's hair being cut off and stuffed in a doll? Is that really believable?'

'So, we're back to square one. Like with Razor, we have a whole lot of circumstantial evidence, and nothing substantive to prove it was Caz.' She stopped talking and looked out at a swathe of rushes at the side of a stream. 'Unless we find Goldilocks.'

❖ ❖ ❖

Charlie directed Tony to the graveyard of the old church in Lingfield where her brother was buried. She wanted to square a few things in her mind. As Tony pulled in through the gateway he stopped suddenly.

'You know I said I dreamed of having a son?' he said hoarsely. 'I wasn't quite telling you the truth.'

'Go on,' Charlie turned towards him, recognising the slight hesitation. He was staring straight ahead through the windscreen.

'I do have a son, or at least I had one.' His voice was as low and gravelly as she'd heard it. 'But I lost him a long time ago, when he was taken away from me. My ex-partner went to live in America. To start with I tried to get over to see him, but each time I went she threw up more and more obstacles. In the end it got too hard.'

'I'm sorry.' She reached across, and put her hand on his shoulder, but he didn't move a muscle, stayed staring ahead.

'I'm sorry too. I used to dream of a son to play footie with, or a little girl like Mia. Razor had the same dreams. I think that's why he trusted me enough to talk – 'cause even though our upbringings and lifestyles couldn't be more different, underneath it all we both want the same thing. A family. You don't realise how important a family is until you lose one of its members.'

'I know that only too well,' she murmured, swallowing hard. 'Give me a few minutes, Tony, will you?'

Tony nodded and settled back in his seat. 'Have as long as you need.'

She smiled back in return, climbing out of the car and setting off along the path to the area of the churchyard where her brother's grave was to be found.

Anna had started the conversation by mentioning her guilt, and Tony had just compounded it. She might not have imported Iain Frazer into their life, as Anna had with Caz, but she'd still left her mother to seek out her own protection, and if Ben hadn't been there...

A smattering of white daisies and bright yellow buttercups were growing in front of Jamie's grave stone. In the weeks since her last visit the grass too had become longer and beautifully wild.

She sat down at the base of the stone, leant back against it, as if it were Jamie providing the support. Immediately, she calmed; the intensity of her grief replaced by a great sense of release. It had been Jamie who'd summoned Ben to watch over their mother. Meg was strong, Iain Frazer was stronger, but Ben was the strongest, and perhaps being cast in the role of their saviour had bolstered his lack of self-confidence.

For a few minutes, she thought of the three men vying for her attention; Ben with his shy smiling eyes, Ross with his humour, Tony with his brute strength and gravitas.

She closed her eyes, as an image of a little boy growing up without his father came to mind, letting the faces of the children she'd dealt with roll past. Mia, Gemma, Rocco, Kelvin, Rochelle, Wesley, some gone forever, others floundering in their today. Then she concentrated again on the three men, Ben, Ross and Tony, all different, all special, all part of her team, her family.

And as she climbed to her feet and said goodbye to Jamie, the words Tony had said to her took root in her mind. Maybe, up until now she hadn't properly appreciated the importance of family or friends, until they were lost. Perhaps now was the time to reassess her priorities, make her choice. Work or love? Work or family?

Was it one or the other – or could she have both?

Chapter 76

Two weeks later

Wimbledon town centre was heaving with tourists. A throng of excited tennis fanatics was pouring off every incoming train, intent on taking their place at the All England Lawn Tennis Club, or joining the queue in the hope of an empty seat at Centre Court or Court One. The Wimbledon tennis Grand Slam tournament had started, and people from all countries waved brightly coloured flags.

Many of them sported caps, clothing or bags emblazoned with national flag designs, such as the Stars and Stripes, the Maple Leaf, the Union Flag, and the Blue Ensign, to name but a few.

As Charlie walked out from the police station with Ross, she glanced round at the sea of patriotic people, then across at the multi-storey car park. The covert camera had gone. With the GSM club locked up and empty there was no need for its eye.

Officers from the National Crime Agency had taken over the investigation. With Superintendent Woodall's consent, they were minutely dissecting the activities of Jamie Smythe-Hamilton. His contacts were being traced, further search warrants executed and, so far, twelve men and women had been arrested for a variety of drug offences; importation, cultivation, supply, possession.

3D was one. Having recovered from Wayne Hurley's murderous attack, Dante Dario Donati was now awaiting trial at His Majesty's pleasure. Franco Nannini too, the charge of murder now replaced instead with one of conspiracy to supply Class A drugs.

'I wonder if all this would have kicked off if Smythe-Hamilton and 3D hadn't got greedy?' she murmured to Ross.

'Who knows, but I doubt if Wayne Hurley would have been able to keep a lid on his hate for the rest of his life. Did you read some of the stuff that they found on the computer in his potting shed?'

'Yes, it was foul. Even more extreme than Adolf Hitler himself. Not only did he want the removal of all ethnic minorities from this country, he wanted them eradicated from the world.'

She watched, smiling now, as two teenage girls ran across in front of them; one wearing a Union Flag T-shirt and cap, the other wearing the French colours, both waving placards proclaiming the names of their national sporting icons. 'I love seeing patriotic youngsters supporting their players but there's no place for Hurley's racism, violence and bigotry in this world.'

'And to think of him bragging about how he'd killed Rocco and Kelvin. Disgusting.'

'And that he believed he could outsmart us.'

'No way!' Ross exclaimed seriously. 'Now that's going way too far.'

She quickly turned to see Ross grinning towards her. The bandages had gone but there was still a bald spot on the top of his head where his hair had been shaved. The scar that remained was visible but healing well.

'As if I'd dare to suggest that! Like you said, we're a good team.' He winked and held her eye for a few seconds longer than usual, then swiftly moved on. 'Right, hurry up, we'd better get going. Can't keep the girls waiting.'

❋ ❋ ❋

Naz and Sabira's car was parked in the spot they'd all agreed, on Wimbledon Common. As Charlie pulled up, she looked out to see her two colleagues standing under a tree in the shade.

She climbed out of her seat, squinting against the bright sunshine.

About a hundred yards from where they stood was the clearing where Rocco Fontana had been murdered. A small wooden cross bearing Rocco's name had been laid by Maria, along with a bunch of freshly cut flowers. In the last week she'd buried her little brother next to their mother in an intimate ceremony attended by a few close friends, and Charlie. No gang members were welcome, and none had come. Maria was determined to honour his life, not the circumstances surrounding his death.

Roughly two hundred yards further on was the place where Rochelle Edwards had died. As Charlie looked towards it now, she could almost replay the sound of the helicopter hovering over the trees, the downdraught from its rotors, and the desolate cry of Dawn Edwards as she watched her child die. Rochelle's funeral was due to be held in the next few weeks, a much larger affair, but conveying the same poignant message.

Too many young lives were being lost – destroyed with the blade of a knife.

Ross joined her, and together they walked across to meet Naz and Sabira.

In the heat, both girls were dressed casually, Naz wearing a vest top, with a shirt hooked over her arm, the scar on her upper arm exposed. Like Ross's, the physical marks of her attack were fading but it was anyone's guess how long the mental scars would remain.

They greeted each other and started to walk through the woodland; along the pathways, down past the ponds, towards the recreation ground on the other side of the common. As they walked, they chatted about their plans for the future, and the lessons they'd learned from their past.

It was nearly midday by the time they arrived at the venue. A small crowd was already gathered, chatting in quiet tones, at the side of a run-down sports pavilion. Naz slipped her shirt back on and headed towards a cluster of smartly dressed men and women in light summer suits.

They looked like politicians, or councillors, standing straight and formal, nervously licking their lips and stepping from one foot to the other. Superintendent Woodall was on the periphery, dressed in full uniform, chatting to other senior officers, alongside Bet and Paul.

Charlie peered across, spotting two of the three women she'd invited. They were deep in conversation to the rear of the group. She made her way over, holding her hand out to greet Maria Fontana and Dawn Edwards.

'I see you've already been introduced. Thank you for coming. Naz and my team have been working hard with Wimbledon Council to try to address the problem of gangs on the borough. They've agreed to put aside funds to restore the pavilion and get some sports activities up and running. It means a lot to me and my officers that you've agreed to be at the forefront of our campaign.'

She was interrupted, as attention turned to a sleek, unmarked, police car with tinted windows pulling into the car park. The women stopped talking, the atmosphere suddenly taut. Dawn Edwards took a deep breath, lifted her face to stare silently as the rear doors of the car swung open.

Naz approached the vehicle and leant down, whispering a few words to the passenger in the rear, and then she took a step back and held out a hand. As Constance Olawi climbed out of the car, Dawn Edwards started to pace straight towards her.

Naz stepped between them, her eyes flicking from one to the other. Both women had lost a child to the blade of a knife, Constance's son killed by a white racist thug, Dawn's daughter taken by Constance's youngest son.

For a few seconds Charlie watched as Naz remained static between them. Now there were three strong black women.

She felt Maria Fontana take hold of her hand and Sabira's, and together they walked forward to join the trio.

Then, as Naz took a step back, Dawn and Constance embraced.

Chapter 77

Five-year-old Sally Hedges skipped along at the edge of the river. School was closed and it was the start of the summer holidays.

She was happy. Her mummy had promised her and her brother a picnic.

She pulled the sunhat down over her eyes and squinted against the strength of the sun's afternoon rays. It was hot. It had been hot for some time now and the river had shrunk to its usual slow-moving stream.

'Can I go for a paddle,' she called out excitedly as they came to the bend in the river where they usually stopped. It was shallow here, the current from the flash floods in June having hollowed out a path along the opposite bank. That side was still fairly deep, but their side was perfect; a bed of smooth pebbles covered with a few inches of warm water. Perfect for exploring, for splashing, for pulling up stones and watching the creepy-crawlies squirm about underneath.

'Yes, you can, but go careful. Not too far out and keep your hat on. I don't want you getting sunburnt.'

'Yay,' she cheered gleefully, stripping off her shorts so that she could splash bare-legged in the water.

Her brother was climbing a fallen log and Mummy was setting out the picnic blanket as she tiptoed into the river. The water was warm at the edge but as she stepped further out towards the centre, it got cooler and moved a little faster. She bent down, lifting one of the larger stones, watching as a tiny fish flitted away from her. Out of the corner of her eye she saw a flash of yellow, a piece of material fanning out in the deeper part of the river.

What was it?

She lowered the stone and took a few steps towards it, scrunching her eyes up to see what it was. It was trapped against a large section of fallen tree trunk, part of it held underneath. She took a few steps further. The water was colder here, up to the top of her legs. She leant over, squinting at the colourful item, seeing now a smiley face, short blonde hair, the yellow material of clothes.

Her heart soared. It was a doll. A poor dolly trapped under the water. Just waiting to be rescued. By her.

She took a few more steps, bent down, stretching out her hand towards it. It looked so close, but it was further away than she thought. Her tummy was wet now, and her T-shirt. She reached out, just managing to grab the doll by its head, as water splashed her face.

'Sally!' She could hear her mummy screaming her name, but she wouldn't let go. Not now she was so close. She pulled at it one more time. The water was wetting her hair, stinging her eyes. 'Sally!'

She held on to the doll.

Then she felt hands, her mummy's hands, grabbing her round her waist, pulling her up. She clung on to the dolly, and as she was lifted out from the water, she felt the doll come away from where it was trapped. It was free.

'Sally, what were you thinking of?' Mummy was crying. 'Oh my God, what were you doing?'

'It's fine,' she said lifting the limp ragdoll into the air. 'Look what I found.' She plumped up its wet body and held it next to her cheek.

'She's perfect. Can I keep her forever?'

Acknowledgments

My thanks to all of you who have given me so much encouragement to continue to write in the face of my problems getting published.

It's been a long time since the last of Charlie's cases came out in print and in the interim she's been studying for her next rank and battling to learn the new laws around Covid 19. In this book, she's been promoted and is raring to go. I hope you will enjoy her latest challenges and stick with her while she navigates her personal problems.

Many thanks to Trish Bellamy, for all her hard work copy editing and proof reading my work. It might have taken a while but it was all worth it. I've loved working on each part of the process and seeing the finished product gradually taking shape.

Finally, my thanks go to Grosvenor House Publishing Ltd for helping to bring my book to life. I hope we can continue to work together in the years to come.

Most of all, I hope all my lovely readers will enjoy the story and share my work with your friends.

Many thanks
Sarah xx